Secret Place

Secret Place

Leslie J. Sherrod

www.urbanchristianonline.net

Urban Books, LLC
78 East Industry Court
Deer Park, NY 11729

ISBN 13: 978-1-60162-894-7
ISBN 10: 1-60162-894-3

First Printing March 2011
Printed in the United States of America

10 9 8 7 6 5 4 3 2 1

Distributed by Kensington Corp.
Submit Wholesale Orders to:
Kensington Publishing Corp.
C/O Penguin Group (USA) Inc.
Attention: Order Processing
405 Murray Hill Parkway
East Rutherford, NJ 07073-2316
Phone: 1-800-526-0275
Fax: 1-800-227-9604

SECRET PLACE

A Novel
by Leslie J. Sherrod

Dedication

In memory of my grandmothers:
Novella, who inspired me,
and Lucretia,
who always believed.

Acknowledgments

What a journey! There are many I must thank who have joined me on this ride. First, I give all thanks to Christ, who is the Author and Finisher of my faith! Thank you, Lord, for the opportunity to creatively write about and for you once again. My prayer, Father, as always, is that you get the glory out of all this, that whatever you have purposed will be perfected, and that this story will be authentically encouraging and inspiring to everyone who reads it.

To Urban Christian: Thank you for warmly welcoming me onboard. I sincerely appreciate your support of and commitment to this project. Thank you, Joylynn Jossel, and all of the editors and staff for your hard work and excellence. Wow!

To my family: My, how you have expanded! Including and extending beyond my relatives, I have found kinship and love from church members, book clubs, other writers, enthusiastic readers, close friends, and a whole bunch of other folk. I do not even know how to attempt to give specific thanks, but I'm going to give it a try:

There is no way that I could have even begun or finished this novel without the love and support of my husband, Brian Sherrod. You don't just speak it, you do it. Thanks for being patient, willing, honest, and there. My children, Neyla, Nate, and little NiNi, you are part of *my* story, my inspiration, my reason for being. I love my family! That includes my parents; my sister; my in-laws ("in-loves" is how we say it); my cousins, aunts, and uncles; nieces, nephews, godsons; okay, everybody in the Datcher, Cole, Sherrod, and Greene family trees please stand. You have shown me by your words and actions that your love and support are endless. Aunt Joanie, thank you for your legacy that beautifully showed the creative arts as worship. Nana, I miss, miss, miss you, but I feel your love and prayers surrounding me even now. Thank you.

My friends are my family too. I'm scared to start listing names, but I do have to give a special shout-out to Angela, who has stuck with me since sixth grade and is my official brownie supplier. (Do you really think I could have gotten this book done without chocolate?) And where would I be without Mata, MaRita, and Yolonda? I know where I would be: lonely, lost, and still stuck in the first chapter. Cheri, I know you've got my back and you know I've got yours. Lisa, I am so happy that you are back in Baltimore. Your genuineness is necessary and refreshing. Burnett, thank you; you called it, and here it is. Alexandria, every time you send a card, it is right on time. Seriously. Stacey, I'm going to get to you in a minute.

My church family at Mt. Pleasant Ministries is second to none. Bishop Clifford M. Johnson, Jr., thank you for your support and your spiritual leadership. Your influence is all through these pages.

I could not have completed this novel without the technical help and assistance from a few family friends and loved ones who offered their expertise. Specifically, thank you, Mr. James Graham and Daniel Hollins, for sharing with me your professional experiences in the criminal justice system. A huge, huge shout-out goes to Stacey Jones, LCSW-C, who willingly and enthusiastically offered her insight as well. Thank you, Angela Benson!

Also, I want to thank my professors and colleagues at the University of Maryland School of Social Work. You have equipped me with the clinical skills and knowledge necessary to merge my dreams of writing for a purpose and working for a cause. Thank you, Denise Stinson, for opening a door for me and for many. God bless you always!

Now, to my larger extended family—the readers and book clubs who have supported me, encouraged me, contacted me, and kept me going—thank you! I do not take for granted your support; I continue to thrive on your encouragement; I cannot wait to hear from you; and, yes, we are going to keep going forward together. For "*as it is written, eye hath not seen, nor ear heard, neither have entered into the heart of man, the things which God hath prepared for them that love him*" (1 Corinthians 2:9)!

Thanks,
Leslie
leslie@lesliejsherrod.com

There is a place in the heart of God
That is furnished just for me.
It is shaped to who I am
And it fits me comfortably,
For He knows me personally.

I can go there when I'm happy,
When I'm hurting—anytime.
He waits with tender longing,
It is here we wine and dine
And He whispers, "You are mine."

Oh the rapture of His passion!
Inside His presence I'm complete,
This hiding place, my resting place
This secret place we meet,
And His love is sure and sweet.

When I heed His gentle calling
To come back where I belong
I fall into His embrace,
I am weak, but He is strong,
And He says, "What took so long?"

PROLOGUE

Twenty-four hours ago she had been a virtual unknown, a radiologic technologist working the night shift at the local hospital, the Sunday school teacher for the nine-to eleven-year-old girls' class at Greater Glory Worship Center.

Today, cameras surrounded her house. News vans with mounted antennas, reporters holding microphones camped in her front lawn and along the narrow city street waiting to capture any words she said, any movements she made, ready to broadcast and translate her life to the entire world.

"When you open the door, don't hesitate. Walk straight to the car we have waiting for you. Don't worry, Mrs. Joel, we will handle all of your public statements right now." The man next to her patted her knee and offered a firm smile.

She hated what she saw in his eyes. Pity. She did not need that, not for herself, not today, and especially not for her little girl. Where was April anyway? Charisma Joel scanned the living room, sealed off from the rest of the world with the shades drawn tight and the television muted. She could not believe what kept running across the screen. That was her face in the pictures, her life in the headlines. She had to find April. As if reading her mind, another suited man shouted over the frenzy in her living room. Were all these people really necessary?

"April's okay. We sent her to your next-door neighbor's house."

Next door. Charisma did not know whether to sigh in relief or cringe in horror. But she had no time to do either. They were already walking her to the door. It was time to face the cameras.

"Remember, let us do the talking." The man smoothed down his suit jacket and cleared his throat.

That was fine with her. She had nothing else left to say. Not a statement, not a story, not a prayer.

PART 1:
SHADES OF BLUE

Job 10:1–My soul is weary of my life;
I will leave my complaint upon myself;
I will speak in the bitterness of my soul.

CHAPTER 1

"Have fun." Charisma pecked her daughter on the cheek as the eleven-year-old slipped out of the passenger's side. Charisma did not miss the rolling eyes. "At least try to have fun."

She watched April drag up the walkway to the waiting porch light before gearing her old Grand Am back in drive. Charisma was grateful for the sleepover, grateful that the mother of April's classmate insisted that all the girls in Homeroom 6-14 be invited, not just friends.

As she turned off the narrow street in the heart of East Baltimore, Charisma tried to remember the last time she'd had a Saturday night free.

Free.

He was waiting at home.

A CD played in the portable CD player she had hooked up to her car stereo. A wire was loose but with a quick tweak to the right and then a pull to the left, one of the speakers in the back of the car played loud enough for her to hear the compilation of Kirk Franklin, Yolanda Adams, Fred Hammond, and another gospel singer, a local girl. She couldn't remember the name.

Charisma stopped at a traffic light, looked to the right and down Marigold Street to house 319. The lights were off, the door was closed, and the shades were drawn shut.

Darkness in the middle of an otherwise busy inner city block.

Children played in the street—jump ropes, bicycles, laughing, yelling. Teenagers lined the red brick walls of the row homes' exteriors. Boys were trying to look like the men they knew, swagger and unease in their stances. Girls, both sheepish and loud, grinned around them, teasing and taunting one another, each a showcase of elaborate hair and brand-name clothes. The elders looked on from their front steps, watching, aware, joining in the pre-night rituals of inner city community life. Hustle, activity. Life. Everywhere. Even Madelyn Windemere next door was outside, busy sweeping down her front steps. Charisma looked back at the house, her own house, 319. The lights were off, the door closed, the shades drawn shut.

He was waiting at home.

The light turned green. Without a second thought, Charisma snapped off the CD and kept straight down Orleans Street. Her heart beat faster with each passing light. She knew where she was going but did not want to let her mind acknowledge it.

She held her breath and pulled into the parking lot off of a side alley. There was one space remaining right next to the door. She parked then cut off the motor. The one-story building did not look as fancy as she expected, especially at night. There was chipped paint at the foundation and holes in the awning that she'd never noticed the other nights she'd driven by. None of the fancy frilliness she'd expected based on the flyers she'd seen posted around her block.

I don't have to go in. Charisma kept both hands on the steering wheel, waiting for her heart to settle. She'd imagined this outing the moment she found out about April's sleepover. Exactly when the daydream had turned into a plan, she was not sure.

She looked down at her leather coat, a hand-me-down from a church sister. A shorter-than-her-usual-style black skirt revealed plump but perfectly proportioned legs. A fresh coat of spicy raisin polish covered her trimmed nails, a dark contrast against her medium-brown skin. Shimmering lip gloss waited in her purse, and sequined shoes peeked from where she'd placed them under the driver's seat. She'd bought the shoes on a whim three years earlier, spotting them on a bottom shelf at Nordstrom's Rack, but she'd never had the courage to wear them until now. Courage. Somehow that did not feel like what this was. She tried to make herself not care.

He did not even notice what she was wearing when she left home, or at least he did not say anything.

Charisma snatched up her purse and carefully applied the lip gloss. She smacked her lips and teased the ends of her shoulder-length hair.

"Look at you, good lookin'."

The voice came from a man passing by her window. He wore a denim jacket, jeans, and rugged boots and looked all of fifty-five years old.

Charisma flashed a quick smile, tried to figure out something cute to say back, but no words came. Just as well, she figured, seeing that the man was already halfway inside. Music, laughter, dancing, alcohol peeked through the closing metal door. Screaming, cheering women with dollar bills in their hands were circled near a corner stage. There were men in there, too. And a lot of them. All she had to do was find a table in the back, sit, watch, listen, smile. Pretend.

She was almost ready to put on her shoes, almost ready to go inside when a passing headlight illuminated the inside of her car, lighting up her foot, her right foot. The scar on top.

I just don't want both of us to get burned 'cause you don't want to wait on Jesus. Words from a lifetime ago, the scar a constant reminder.

Charisma slung the shoes to the backseat, pulled her leather oxfords back on, shoved the key into the ignition, and put the car in reverse. Within seconds, the sign for Chocolate Heaven grew smaller in her rearview mirror. "Ladies' Night With G" soon disappeared completely from view.

"What was I thinking?" Charisma wiped a bead of sweat from her forehead. "I've got Sunday school tomorrow."

But that was last night, and tomorrow was now here. Charisma parted another section of her hair and listened as the thick strands sizzled between the plates of her flat iron. She'd been doing hair all morning, it seemed. After picking up a sullen April from the sleepover, Charisma purposely took extra time while straightening the girl's hair for church. She wanted her daughter to talk, to tell her how the party went, to tell her if she'd made any new friends, had fun, something, anything. But April's only words to her were, "What did you do last night?"

The sign from Chocolate Heaven flashed in Charisma's mind, and neither she nor April said anything else while Charisma finished heating down April's bangs. Now her own hair sizzled under the heat of her iron. Wait. Had she already done this section? Charisma tried to get her head out of yesterday, focus on the task at hand, and get ready to teach the stories.

She told her students the stories the same way they were told to her. With pictures. Maybe a flannel board. Videos and DVDs were nice. The Sunday school stories, the safe stories, those were the ones she told.

Charisma unplugged the iron and fastened the last button on her lemon yellow suit. The skirt flared out slightly at her knees. Yeah, even with the slight stain at the hem, the size fourteen suit did fit better than the blue one from that bag of hand-me-downs Pepperdine Waters gave her. Yellow was a cheery color against Charisma's sparrow-brown skin. The suit almost looked new. She smiled. *Good, no runs in these stockings. Oops, missed that one.*

"April! Bring me up a pair of stockings from the line in the basement!" She should not have yelled so loudly. It was early Sunday morning and most of her neighbors were still asleep. Surely Mrs. Windemere would lecture her before the day was over about how loud it was "over there." She was probably out sweeping her front sidewalk now, waiting for them to come out so she could start her daily barrage of complaints.

Charisma pulled a cotton curtain to the side to get a quick peek of the quiet street. A hidden broom was busy whisking clean a sidewalk somewhere, Mrs. Windemere at work, of course. She let the curtain go just as Madelyn Windemere surfaced in front of her row home, broom, dustpan, and green lawn bag in hand. It had been too late, anyway. The woman had seen her, Charisma could tell from the way the corners of her mouth turned downward as she turned her back to the house.

"We're good neighbors," Charisma murmured to herself as she clipped a pearl earring to her ear. "Just not good enough for her." But even as she spoke, her eyes graced a frayed black notebook stuffed with mementos and old greeting cards. The letters and journal entries were in it too.

And the invitation.

She shook slightly at the sight and forced her attention back to the stained wood oval mirror on the back of the bedroom door. She swirled around, letting the lemon yellow chiffon overlay of the skirt dance around her knees. A slight smile.

"I'm done. No, wait." She went to the cedar wardrobe in her room and pulled out an old hat box. She rubbed the bumpy cardboard, living a million different memories before shaking off the lid.

"Finally, I have something to go with you," she beamed. "Momma would be so proud to see her old hat matched up with a real suit from Macy's." She pulled out the single content and unwrapped the delicate tissue paper like a porcelain doll was waiting inside. No, a hat, a soft yellow hat with a sprig of felt flowers tied to the side. She put it on top of her head, making sure her shoulder-length brown hair, smoothed down in a slightly curled bob, fit perfectly under the short brim.

"Perfect," she nodded, pleased with the image in the mirror. The image. She did not want to study her eyes. There were too many stories in them, stories passed down, handed to her, chained to her like the pearl choker on her neck from Momma's jewelry box. Momma. Momma and now Gideon. The stories never ended. Charisma squeezed her eyes shut and inhaled.

"I'll tell them the same stories they told me," she closed the clasp on her beaded bag and grabbed a book labeled "Teacher's Guide" from her nightstand. The cover was a vibrant illustration of a white man in a blue toga-looking garment standing in a boat with his hands outstretched in the air. A crowd of people stood nearby on a patch of land, listening, waiting, hoping. The words "Kingdom Kidz: Part I—The Miracles of Jesus" were inscribed on the top and sides. She looked at the man in the picture and the faces in the crowd before putting the book, several handouts, and a puppet into a large tote bag. She straightened the small collection of bottles and perfumes on her dresser. Dying flowers sat next to them. She tossed them in the trash. All was ready. Except for the stockings.

"Mommy, here." April came from nowhere and thrust a pair of taupe pantyhose in her hands.

"Perfect timing." Charisma winked at her eleven-soon-to-be-twelve-year-old, smoothing down the puffy hair that topped her pudgy brown face. The girl had been begging for a relaxer since second grade, but Charisma refused to give in. Not until thirteen, when she would officially be a teenager. Charisma pulled at the thick hair, which was already kinking back up after the hot comb run-through she'd given it earlier that morning. April's eyes pierced into her mother's as she stood stiff, just a few inches off from being eye level.

"What is it, baby?" Charisma asked, but she already knew the answer, already knew April would never say. "Him?" It was all Charisma could ask before the lump in her throat threatened to break. A single eye held back rivers. April nodded, an incomplete nod that looked somewhere between a shrug and a question.

"Baby, it's okay. It will be okay." Charisma bent down to her daughter and drew her close in her arms, quickly burying the girl's face in her shoulder before her own face gave another story.

Stories. She would tell them the same stories that were told to her, the safe stories. Just follow the lesson plan, ask the follow-up questions, and guide the children in the simple take-home craft. And when it was all over, she had the flyer from Chocolate Heaven to stir her imagination, and a couple of steamy novels to keep out the stories on which she did not want to dwell.

Charisma stood tall, straightened her hat, and put

on her best smile. "All right, baby girl, are you ready to go to Sunday School? I'd be honored to have you in my class." She made her voice sound cheerier than usual, sensing that he was somewhere nearby. She felt his presence in the shadows, in the corners of the room. She never could shake the feeling.

"Mommy, I *am* in your class." It was the same joke, same rolled eyes, same routine every Sunday morning.

"Was he still downstairs when you came up?" Charisma tried to make the question sound light and not loaded.

April gave a slow nod.

"Well, don't worry. We can go out the kitchen door." Charisma kept the smile on her face as she gripped her tote bag tighter in her hands.

"Mrs. Windemere's going to be waiting. I saw her already outside hosing down her backyard."

"Well, Mrs. Windemere can wait all she wants. She don't need to know all our business, and neither do all your little friends in Sunday School." Charisma started out, but April remained firmly planted on the blue carpet in the small bedroom.

"Mommy, I don't want to go. We go every Sunday. God ain't gonna be mad if we miss just one Sunday. Just tell Him it was a sick day, like you be tellin' your boss at work."

"Now April—"

"Mommy, let's just go somewhere else today. Why we gotta go there anyway?"

Charisma sucked in a deep sigh and kept the smile planted on her face. She knew the reason April did not want to go. Sometimes she didn't want to go herself. Too many people with too many questions. *How is your husband?* Where *is your husband?* Simple questions. Complicated answers.

"Now you know that we go to Sunday School to learn all the stories of Jesus."

"Why? For what? What's the point?"

Charisma studied her daughter, standing there in a green jumper and a white shirt with a Peter Pan collar. It was her school uniform, the one recently required by the Baltimore City public middle school she attended and the only church outfit available for April to wear this week. The hand-me-downs that came for April never quite fit right. They were always just a little too small. *Or was April just a little too big?* Charisma let go of the thought and stared at her daughter, remembering when she was the one standing in her mother's bedroom, asking why she had to learn all those Sunday School stories. Only back then, her mother never had to rummage through bags of old clothes collected by an old church mother. "You'll see why going to church is so important one day," had been her mother's constant reply.

"April, you'll see why going to Sunday School is so important one day," Charisma breathed out, a smile hiding all she wanted hidden. It had gotten easier over the years. Hiding.

"Now come on, girl. I hear him snoring on the sofa down there. Let's go before he wakes up."

Passing by him, who couldn't help but gag at the sight? A pile of skin, bones, ash, smell. Nothing she wanted to wrap her arms around. Nothing she wanted wrapped around her.

They walked to the car in silence, Charisma's secondhand high-heels clicking on the stone pathway as she and April cut through the arched brick gateway that separated their row home from the one next door. No sign of Mrs. Windemere, Charisma felt her muscles relax as she slammed the car door shut. The engine of the 1993 Pontiac Grand Am roared to life.

Stick to the stories, the safe ones, she reminded herself, looking back at her tote bag full of Sunday School supplies. She kept the invitation in there too, taking it out of her black composition notebook every time she left the house. She didn't want him to see it. It was addressed to both of them, but he would never know, as far as she was concerned. Dr. and Mrs. Gideon Joel. She kept the invitation with her at all times.

It was an elaborate piece of cardstock with fancy letters, ribbons, and engravings. Good money was spent on it obviously. Charisma swallowed hard, thinking of how she would turn them down. Politely? Sternly? With an explanation? A lie?

"Tell me your name again?"

His question—his intention—had been more in his eyes than in his smile when we first met, I remember. I answered him back, of course, wondering if my smile was giving away just as much personal information as his was. It was his first smile, that crooked one he had when he was feeling especially happy or excited or optimistic, that smile that sent my heart pounding. I remember seeing earnest hope, anticipation, and desperation all wrapped up into one big bundle that showed off white teeth, full lips, and a freshly trimmed, perfect moustache. The hair over his upper lip, the hair on his head looked so soft I remember wanting to touch it and praying that it would feel the way I imagined black feathers on a raven's chest would feel—smooth, warm.

"Charisma." He'd said my name the way it was meant to be said, each syllable alive on his tongue. He said my name the way my mother must have thought it should be said when she let the word fall from her lips to the official document that would record the title I would have the burden of carrying the rest of my life.

I remember looking at his jacket—starched, white with deep pockets—and seeing for the first time the name badge it showcased across a broad chest. A name with a comma, and plenty of letters and periods after it. A doctor. A name with status, a name with answers attached to it.

That's really what I had come looking for that day. Answers. My mother sat waiting, I remember, looking lonely, blank, closed, waiting silently in that green chair. Green. I could never forget the color. It was everywhere in that unit.

"Don't worry, we'll talk again soon. I'll make sure you get that interview." I remember thanking him with a shy grin as I turned to leave. I had come there for answers. Not a job. Not him. But it was all one and the same to me. Despite my vow never to find another reason to enter those doors or stand between those green walls again, I had accepted that maybe that was all there would be to my life: those doors, those green walls. I accepted that the day he accepted me.

"Please, Jesus," I remembered praying silently, "Let him be the answer." I was unprepared for the sudden longing I felt, unprepared despite the many times I had imagined a moment like this.

Momma was waiting. I could still feel the metal, cold on my hands as I shunned the orderly's help and grasped the wheelchair handles myself to roll Momma along. The quiet whir of the elevator that required a pass code, the locks that clinked open and closed behind me with a thud, the staff who silently studied us from behind a clear plastic encasement as we passed, the lounge area with other patients watching TV, knitting, staring blankly, moaning softly—all sights and sounds that left me feeling nauseated, trapped, ashamed, embarrassed. But that would become a tortuous routine only as my mother would become a regular on the unit.

My mother didn't belong here, I wanted to scream that first time, that first walk down the green hallway. This was my mother. My mother: one of the first women in our neighborhood to own her own business, a popular beauty salon on West North Avenue. She was a rarity, a jewel, a prize among many.

How I wanted to scream. I remember looking back to see if he was still there and he was, his jacket white and crisp, his name badge long in letters. It was quiet in that long hallway as I pushed the metal chair to the room that would become my mother's home for the next three weeks. Caroline Jackson, Momma, sat stoic in the bed as I trembled outside the closed door. The doctor, Gideon Joel, came to my rescue with a tissue and a chair. And then a slight embrace. He stood tall beside me, but his face hung low. I did not see the stories in his eyes. If I had, maybe I would not have been so eager to follow my longings—longings stemmed from daydreams of first loves and first kisses.

Another chapter was beginning.

CHAPTER 2

Madelyn Windemere shut the blinds on her window after watching the mother and daughter get into their car. Charisma Joel had on a new suit, she noted. A new suit for her and the girl was still wearing that old jumper. She shook her head and offered up a prayer. It wasn't right, the way that Joel woman always looked like she was sneaking in and out of her own house. And to think she didn't have the mind to wrap that little girl in a warmer jacket. It's the beginning of March, not the end, for goodness' sake.

Madelyn sat back down at her kitchen table with a heavy thud, her china plate and teacup rattling with the impact. She was nearly finished with her usual breakfast—sliced cantaloupe and toast, tea with honey and lemons—so that meant it was time to get ready for church. Her morning routine was nearly complete, including sweeping then washing the pavement around her house, replacing the kitchen and bathroom towels, and starting the day's dinner in the slow cooker. It was Sunday, the Lord's Day, so order and routine were especially important. That's how she'd done it all these years, how she'd maintained, kept house, and raised four children. Routine.

That Joel woman needed to take a lesson from her. Something weird and downright crazy was going on over there, Madelyn was sure of it. She'd tried to fish it out in the early days, when the family first moved into the small brick row home next door almost a year ago. But she knew from the first conversation, when Charisma Joel avoided disclosing where they came from or what she or her husband did for a living, that anything to be known about that family would come only from careful observation.

And the things Madelyn did see—the lawn that grew just a little too high in the summer, the snow that stayed unshoveled just a little too long in the winter, the closed window shades, the bags and cartons of carry-out junk food in their trash all the time—did little to improve her opinion of that woman and the way she ran her home. Young mothers these days. There was no routine over there, couldn't be. What kind of woman would serve mashed potatoes out of a box and gravy from a can?

It disgusted her, trying to figure out what was going on over there. In Madelyn's decades on Marigold Street, the neighborhood had attempted to keep its integrity despite the crumbling blocks surrounding it. The Joels had to come and stink it all up, with their dead garden, humble-looking child, and especially the music. The music to Madelyn was the worse. One day she was just going to go ahead and call the police. All times, all hours of the day and night, music would be blasting out of that small home. Gospel, jazz, rock, country, even polka. Mrs. Windemere was sure she heard it once.

"They are going to make me go deaf with all that noise."

Madelyn finished ironing a slip to put on under her new church dress, which was a tasteful pale green, without too much shimmer and shine. The green was a good contrast against her maple-brown skin. Flashiness was not appropriate for church. That went for both appearances and actions. As much as she paid for the ensemble, she could not imagine going to one of those churches where people got up and down, and up and down, and danced in the aisles until sweat threatened to mess up their hair-dos and stain their underarms. That's just nasty and unnecessary; Madelyn shook her head at the idea.

Charisma Joel went to one of those churches. Madelyn tried to talk her out of it, give the woman at least some hope of dignity. When Charisma insisted on joining Greater Glory Worship Center, Madelyn washed her hands clean. There was nothing else she could do for the woman. Her religion was as disorderly as her home. But what could one expect?

Madelyn had nothing against that type of congregation, if that's what they wanted to do. She just preferred a more orderly service and had taught her children the same. Even her late husband, Harold, agreed with her on that part. Worship was a private affair, a quiet affair. She knew Jesus and He knew her. No need to yell and scream to get His attention. Order. Routine.

It was almost 10:33 A.M. She would leave in six minutes to get to her favorite seat at the eleven o'clock service at Christ Cathedral on time. Six minutes and twenty-three seconds. That was enough time to re-polish her left shoe and clear out the voice messages.

As the black patent leather dried to a shiny gleam, Madelyn adjusted her reading glasses on the bridge of her nose and sat down at the old secretary's desk in the foyer. The black walnut desk was her favorite antique in the house, and she held her breath as she rolled up the delicate wood. Stationery, organized by theme and holiday, was revealed underneath, as well as small shelves filled with paper clips, rubber bands, postage stamps, and two phone books. A telephone and an outdated answering machine were tucked to one side of the writing surface.

Madelyn checked her watch before pressing play on the machine. There was only one message, a call from the day before. Obviously a telemarketer or another stranger, she reasoned before the message picked up. Anyone who knew her would know that she would not have been at home 3:17 P.M. yesterday. Saturday afternoon grocery shopping was a routine she'd only broken five times in forty-two years. The times she'd missed had been due to childbirth.

She arched a finger to press erase before the message came on, but it was too late. The familiar voice that pierced through the speaker froze Madelyn's finger in mid-air. A scowl wiped over her face, and she pulled the plug on the machine before a second word from the caller could come through. She slammed the top of the antique desk down before she could catch herself. It was not until after she'd pulled the belt of her overcoat too tight around her waist that she took two deep breaths and felt her heartbeat slow down to its normal pace.

"I will not let you get to me today." Madelyn spoke to the machine as if the caller who left the message could hear. She took another deep breath and checked her watch. "10:39 A.M. Time to go to church." Madelyn locked both locks on the front door and tucked her handbag under her arm. Her white Lincoln, parked exactly six inches from the curb, was waiting.

Order. Routine. It was necessary.

Pepperdine Waters grabbed the desk in front of her and eased back on her feet with a low grunt. She made the trip once more to the other side of the church office and pressed her ear hard against the wood door.

He was still out in the hallway. She could hear his whistles and the usual jingle of coins and keys in his pocket. Then silence. And then more jingles.

"What is he doing and why is he here?" Pepperdine mumbled under her breath as a quick well of annoyance bubbled up in her stomach. But as quickly as the irritation arose, shame shot through her and squelched the rising ripples. "Forgive me, Jesus," she chuckled to her longtime Friend. "I'm too old to be carrying on like this. Might as well get it over with." Pepperdine grunted back to the desk and picked up the stack of papers she had carried into the church a full hour earlier than the Sunday School teachers were expected. She was not one of the teachers, but as head of the women's ministry at Greater Glory Worship Center, she always found a way to help with anything woman- or child-related at the church. Today, she wanted to place copies of an inspirational poem she had found in a digest magazine the day before in each of the Sunday school teachers' folders.

"We can all use some encouragement sometimes." She hobbled to the door, feeling every ounce of her two hundred-pound frame on her arthritic ankles. She hesitated again, resisting the urge to press her ear against the thick wood once more to see if he was still on the other side. Finally, she shook her head and entered the bright hallway.

"Praise de Lawd, Sista Waters!" His voice boomed in her ear, spraying her with spittle as he spoke and stuffing the air with the scent of menthol lozenges.

"Good morning, Deacon Caddaway." Pepperdine flashed a quick smile, doing her best not to give more than a curt nod at the solemn brown face that stared back at her. He was a wide-bellied deacon who had eyes that seemed to be looking everywhere at once and at nothing in particular. He kept a gold crucifix around his collar and his lips in a permanent frown. His voice was scratchy from years of shouting in church services and yelling about hell flames to anybody who smoked, drank, or otherwise looked heathenish. Pepperdine waited for him to let her by, but he was not budging.

"What are you doing here so early, Earnest? I didn't hear you come in." Pepperdine checked her watch and wanted to kick herself. People would be starting to file in for Sunday School within the next twenty or thirty minutes, and she still wanted to get copies of the poem in the teachers' folders. Why had she asked him a question, opening a door that was near impossible to close?

"I got a word from de Lawd for you this morning, Pepper."

"Pepperdine. Not Pepper, please." She kept the smile on her face, and prayed silently that God would bless her dear brother in Christ. He did not pause at her words and had already rolled his eyes up to the ceiling. His body began to shake and his voice began to rattle and moan like a preacher on his third point at a Friday night revival service.

"Ah, I been sent to you this day. Amen"—he let out a deep groan—"to tell you that the days of your mourning are over."

"Thank you, Deacon Caddaway, but—"

"Weepin' may endure for a night, ah, but joy—it comes in the morning. Good God Almighty! Hallelujah. Amen!" He was getting louder with each word, the wind-and spit-storm intensifying. "The book of Isaiah says that God's got beauty for your ash!"

"Deacon Caddaway—"

"And some oil of joy for your mourning. Ah! Now—"

"Earnest—"

"—The time has come for you to take off your widowing rags, amen, and put on a garment of praise! Hey, ah! God sent me here to comfort you in your mourning."

"Deacon—"

"I know your pain, my dear Pepper, amen! You don't have to thank me or even try to explain. God will reward me for my obedience to Him! Now my Ethel died nine months ago, but you don't see me with no heavy heart no more. Hallelujah, amen!

"Deacon Caddaway, with all due respect, my husband's been dead over thirty years and—"

"Now don't interrupt when the Spirit is movin'! That's the difference between you and my Ethel, but I'm prayin' 'bout your rebellion! The Lord told me that all them loose and heathen Jezebels you oversee in that women's ministry are rubbin' off on you. You need to repent! But God is good! Amen! Hallelujah! He has something in store for you! A gift, amen! It's coming! The windows of heaven are open and your blessin' is here! Right here! Ah, amen! Pepper! Hey, Pepper?"

Pepperdine could take no more. Deacon Caddaway had been known for his "words from de Lawd" for years, but ever since Mother Ethel Caddaway passed away last June, Earnest's direct line to heaven had become a twenty-four-hour hotline for him to scribble down specific messages from the Most High for all of Greater Glory's single women over seventy.

"Forgive me, Lord." Pepperdine shook her head again as she finally stepped into the adjoining church hall and slipped the poem copies into each of the Sunday School teachers' mailboxes. "I ain't a perfect woman, but I trust you to guide my steps and my words to whoever needs to know you care today. Love you, Jesus." Her prayer faded into a whisper as young voices and giggles began to fill the bright blue and yellow hall. Mothers and fathers pecked their little ones' cheeks and metal chairs scraped on the tiled floor. Opening activities for Sunday School were soon to begin.

Pepperdine kept her eyes open.

CHAPTER 3

The committee usually did not meet on Sunday mornings, but this time was an exception. The Baltimore Metropolitan Hospital's one hundredth-year celebration and fundraising gala was a short five weeks away, and the event planners had to come to an agreement on key issues. This meeting included several of the hospital's world-renown doctors, surgeons, and department chairs, and this Sunday morning was the only time such a time-pressed crowd found sufficient overlapping space in their day planners and palm pilots to discuss their roles, input, and concerns for the premier money-making occasion.

In the midst of beeping pagers, a nonstop intercom system, mugs of coffee, and trays of powdered donuts, the exclusive attendees converged around a fifty-foot marble and oak oval table in the Pavilion Room on the East Wing of the main hospital building. A woman with short black hair and a Latin cadence in her speech stood at the helm.

"All right, we've just about finalized the speakers for both the morning telethon and the evening banquet. I just need one more person to be available to offer opening comments for the brunch in the atrium." The organizer's voice was one of many circulating in the ornate meeting room but the only one speaking directly about the function. "Excuse me." She was polite as she leaned forward on the table, competing with backslaps and rolls of laughter coming from the leather padded chairs filled mostly with men in white jackets and suits with stethoscopes, a few women.

"Dr. Glaskow can give another lecture on his cocaine-addicted rats," someone volunteered from the rear. More laughter.

"How about Dr. Winston? His research on baldness is sure to bring some 'hair-raising' results." This voice came through the speaker-phone set up on teleconference mode. Snorts and cackles rolled once again as a couple of doctors quietly ran fingers through sparse hairs on the tops of their heads.

"Well." The woman rocked on her toes, her lips a straight line as she studied the papers in her hand. "I was thinking, given the community we serve and the latest PR campaign initiated last Tuesday, we might want to consider having at least one face of color on the program. Uh, one of our preeminent doctors, professors, or researchers, with an ethnic background reflecting the diverse population we serve here in urban Baltimore, should have a public speaking role during the gala weekend's events." She paused, waiting and watching as all eyes turned to a doctor at the opposite end of the table.

"Can't do it." The doctor spoke with a thick Nigerian accent while checking his Smartphone. A bright red bowtie peeked through his lab coat, and he adjusted it and readjusted it before setting down his phone. "I have a conference that weekend in Wisconsin. Genetic mutation of the X-chromosome."

"I got it." Another doctor clapped his hands together loudly. "Dr. Miles Logan, the new chair of the psych ward. I heard he was quite the speaker at the psychopathology conference when he did his residency here a few years back. How did we ever let him get away to begin with?" Mumbles of praise and agreement buzzed as all eyes turned to the empty seat where the name card 'Miles K. Logan, M.D.' sat untouched.

The woman cleared her throat. "Or what about Dr. Logan's predecessor, what was his name? Dr. Gideon Joel? I couldn't make sense of these papers. He's still on staff, right? Or is he on some kind of sabbatical?"

She looked up from her notes to see thirty-seven pairs of eyes staring at her in wide-eyed silence. Complete silence. For the first time that morning she had a true audience.

"Um," she flipped loudly through her papers. "Dr. Joel, right? I'm not personally familiar with him, but from what I gathered from the files he came highly recommended from Johns Hopkins, and his research on diagnostic procedures for mood disorders was well-received by the APA." She looked up again. Chairs squeaked, a pager was silenced, and a pencil drummed loudly on a notepad somewhere. Otherwise, quiet.

"I, uh, already extended an invitation to him to participate. I mailed it a few weeks ago . . . Was that a bad idea?"

Someone coughed and a pen fell to the floor.

"Well, we can revisit this later. The last item for discussion is . . ."

The chatter, the laughter, and the joking resumed.

Finally, he had the house to himself. Gideon Joel sat up on the worn sofa and rubbed his eyes. His plan had worked. It worked every time. Charisma and April left quicker when they thought he was sleeping.

Darkness filled the small living room even though it was nearing late morning. Charisma knew better than to open the shades. She'd finally learned. He needed the darkness. He needed the darkness to think, to survive.

It had been daylight when it happened months ago. Bright daylight. He could still see the glass, the broken metal, the outstretched hand.

The blood.

He never told Charisma. He never told anyone. Light brought with it too many bad memories.

Gideon rose from his place and headed for the kitchen. He opened the refrigerator and scanned its few contents: an empty jug of milk, two Coke cans, a rotting roasted chicken carcass, moldy Swiss cheese. Maybe he should let Charisma bring home new groceries. The girl, his daughter, had to eat. April was eating somewhere—that was obvious from the slight fat that lined her face and body. But if Charisma came home with bags of groceries, it would only remind him of how she paid for it. With her money. From her job.

What kind of man could not provide for his own family?

The air was leaving him again. Gideon gasped for breath as he stumbled in the darkness, colliding into the kitchen sink. Fruit flies, crusted food, dirty dishes. The smell. He could not hold back the vomit. He put a quick hand over his mouth, but the effort was pointless, much like everything else he did. Pointless. Thankfully he had not eaten since yesterday morning, so there was not much for his stomach to empty. Even still, it meant more for him to clean, more for him to deal with.

He needed to wash the dishes. He told Charisma he would wash them, refused to let her do it, made it clear that she could not do it. He needed to wash them, and now, thanks to his reaction to the smell, he had more of a reason to clean out the kitchen sink.

Gideon stared at the faucet for several minutes. The dish detergent was next to the hot water spigot. "Joy," he read the bottle. He stared at the rusted steel pad and the stiff-dried plaid dishrag. The pots in the sink, the plates on the counter, the bowls and glasses on the table. The silverware. It was too much.

Too much. Gideon gasped for air again as he fell into a nearby wooden seat, his head hitting the stained-glass chandelier that swung over the crowded table as he collapsed.

Too much. Dishes all over the place. Where to begin. His head hurt. Pointless. Everything he did was pointless.

The pill bottle still sat on the edge of the kitchen table. Still sat there unopened. It was a sample given to him by a pharmaceutical representative for use in his practice; he'd kept it for himself. He could start taking them, the pills. Maybe he would even start to feel better if he took them.

But if he took the pills, he grimaced, what would that say about his faith?

"I claim healing in the name of Jesus." The words felt foreign, empty in his mouth as a low moan took the place of an amen.

The pill bottle sat unopened.

The question still blurred in his head.

There was the knife. Gideon looked through the near darkness at the long black handle sticking out of a wooden block. Even with the blade hidden, he could picture it, feel the weight of it. Its jagged teeth and sharp point would sparkle in the dimly lit kitchen like a multifaceted diamond. The knife was there all the time. He looked at it every day. Long looks. Long thoughts. An easy answer. This time a fool-proof plan.

One day . . .

Gideon squeezed his eyes shut and forced himself to stand. He followed his feet back into the living room and fell back onto the sofa. The radio. He reached for the dial and waited for the seek button to land on a station, any station. Reggae was the winner today. He turned the volume up. The bass beats sent vibrations up his arms, chills down his back. He imagined he had dreadlocks that flowed down his body, dark brown coils that wrapped around his lean, coffee brown torso and curled around his neck. The image calmed and frightened him all at once. He turned the volume up again, this time not stopping until the knob could turn no more.

Finally, the way he liked it. The only way to listen. He took off his T-shirt to use as a pillow and stretched out on his back. There was nothing else to do but listen.

CHAPTER 4

I laughed when he first showed me, a loud laugh that sent eyes all over the cafeteria staring at us.

"You don't believe me, but wait and see, Charisma." Gideon patted the magazine in front of me. It was a catalogue of new homes, advertisements for expensive new dwellings that had features like hardwood floors, pedestal sinks, wainscoting, and Juliet balconies. The model his fingers rested on had two acres surrounding it and a kitchen with a double wall oven.

"You're laughing now, but you'll see. Give me a few years, and I'll have these medical school loans under enough control to get you a house fancier than this one."

He leaned back in his seat and played around with the grilled chicken and baby carrots on his plate. Even in the dim lighting of the hospital cafeteria, he shined full of hope and promise. It was only our second date, if that was what it was called, but dreams and plans had already been dished out between us like the mounds of mashed potatoes and gravy filling our plates.

"What is so funny? Why do you keep laughing?"

I could not stop laughing. Imagine me, the wife of a doctor, an M.D., a psychiatrist. Wouldn't that be a funny story? Charisma, the girl from Sinclair Street, with the mother who had no college degree but had found her fortune doing hair, living large somewhere out in Bel Air, Maryland, or Reisterstown, or maybe even Greenspring Valley. My mother . . .

I suddenly stopped laughing. I'd forgotten where I was. Even though I wore a name badge that matched his (without all the extra letters of course) I'd forgotten where my mother was and the revolving door she kept entering on the third floor. The Howard G. Phillips Unit. The psych ward.

"Charisma." His voice was a whisper in the sharp chatter of the cafeteria, his hands warm and massaging, covering mine completely. "Your mother would want you to surpass the goals she created for herself. She's leaving you a legacy to leap over with large bounds and bigger shoes to fill."

I swallowed hard. Bigger shoes to fill. What did he know about my feet? How tired of walking they were? How worn, how ragged, and in my estimation, how small? Did anyone know how much of my mother's illness had fallen on my shoulders, and still I had to keep walking forward?

"Charisma." He said my name with such poetry, and his name badge was so prominent; I wanted to believe that he knew. I wanted to believe that he had answers. That's what I had come looking for at Baltimore Metropolitan Hospital – answers, not a job. But that's what I found, a job, and him, and it was a beginning. I felt it.

Dr. Gideon Joel. My Dr. Gideon Joel. It was time for me to shake off the darkness that pulled me back again and again to those green walls and metal doors on the Howard G. Phillips Unit. My mother was there. I could not control that. But I could control this, I figured. My future, my destiny. Dr. Gideon Joel.

That day, in the cafeteria at Baltimore Metropolitan Hospital, over plates of half-eaten chicken breasts and large mounds of mashed potatoes, I made a decision to be with this man, this doctor. Leave the questions, the darkness behind. I had more incredible feats, more impossible mountains to march over, greater things to do because of and with this man, Gideon.

It was settled, my destiny delivered. I sat back in the booth and finished my diet cola.

His picture was one of the ones on the invitation; not Gideon's, but his old friend and colleague, Dr. Miles Logan. They'd done their residencies together, and only two years his senior, Dr. Logan had returned to become chair of the psychiatric department at Baltimore Metropolitan Hospital upon Gideon's departure.

"Rise, shine, give God the glory, glory!" Sister Monique Leonard, the children's Sunday School devotion leader cut through Charisma's thoughts with her shouts and directions. The thirty-some children in front of them jumped from their folding chairs, maracas, tambourines, and rhythm sticks in hand. Charisma followed Monique's lead, bending down, hopping, raising her arms, and clapping. It was almost time to break out into their separate classes. Charisma winked at April, who was waving her arms in the front row.

"Rise, shine, give God the glory, glory!"

Glory. That's what Dr. Miles Logan carried with him. His research, his speaking skills, his charm all wrapped up together to create one of Baltimore Metropolitan Hospital's finest. Gideon and Miles had been friends, but competitors. They both knew the unspoken rule, the quota in place. The esteemed psychiatric department had room for only one African American showpiece, one spot for a prized psychiatrist of color.

They were friends, partners, back-scratchers, backstabbers.

"I'll call him," Charisma mumbled to herself as she collected the tambourines and put them back in a plastic crate. Dr. Logan had just returned to Baltimore to accept the vacant position at the hospital a few months ago. She'd spoken only once to him by accident since then when they bumped on an elevator during her night shift in the radiology department. Shame, butterflies, and heat rose inside of her for a moment when she recalled that last conversation. But she would still call. She had to respond to the invitation.

Dr. Logan did not know the story.

If he had known Charisma Joel was thinking about him, he probably would have handled his morning very differently. Dr. Miles Logan rolled over in the bed and searched the floor for his clothes. He hated Sunday mornings. The hangovers, the clingy women left over from the night before already dreaming up their fairy tale futures. The quick getaways. He looked over at the pillow next to him trying to remember this woman's name. Melody, Meisha, something with an M.

It worked every time, the fishing game that he played on the Saturday nights he wasn't on call. He didn't need a hook or a net to catch his prey. His degree was bait enough. Sistas—hungry for a brotha with a real job, high status, his own home, nice car, no kids, no drugs—would be all over him the moment they found out who he was and what he did. He was a good catch, an educated catch, a doctor. He knew it but was careful enough not to get caught. At least not for more than a night.

Miles grabbed his socks, the rest of his clothes from the floor, blinking to make sense of the décor that surrounded him. Diplomas and certificates hung in frames of different shapes and sizes throughout the small studio apartment. Each frame held various career degrees and certifications, making the cramped interior read like the catalogue of a career school brochure: real estate agent, cosmetologist, travel agent, massage therapist, medical billing and coding specialist, veterinary assistant, private investigator, interior designer, wedding consultant.

"This woman has been all of these?" He shook his head as he pulled his leather belt through the last loop, squinting his eyes to make out her name again in the calligraphy prints.

"What was that, sweetie?" M-girl was awake, her head propped up on an elbow resting on the pillow. A white sheet was pulled loosely to her neck.

"You have quite a . . . resume." He nodded his head to the walls with a questioning smile.

"I know. I was going to be a wedding consultant to plan my own wedding but I didn't even have a boyfriend, so I went back to get my veterinary assistant degree because you know having a good pet is better than having nobody at all. And I did the travel agent program at the same time because I figured one day I would get married and I'd need to plan my honeymoon. Actually, I ended up quitting two programs because I realized that they were not for me, and now I'm working on my paralegal degree so I could meet a nice lawyer, but you're a doctor so maybe I can become a medical transcriptionist. Do you have your own secretary?" M-girl spoke in one breath, her words toppling over one another like falling blocks.

Miles stood motionless, his hands frozen on his coat zipper. He didn't remember her talking that fast before, but he didn't remember a lot of what happened last night. She had a nice body though, curves in all the right places, straight teeth, a good girl to take out when he wanted to get wasted. Maybe he'd keep in touch. He smiled. "Where are you working now?"

"Work? Oh," she ran a gingersnap-colored hand through her limp, jet black hair, "I've never actually had a job, unless you want to count the three days I did at Burger King and the week I spent in Nashville and the day I worked in front of the White House, but that's a long story, and, you know, I really don't want to get into it." She was crawling out of the sheets now, no shame, no effort to hide her bare body as she went in the bathroom, leaving the door open under his gaze. Miles wondered if she was this casual with every man she'd known for less than twelve hours.

"My father died years ago and left me a huge trust fund, which my mother's trying to take away from me. She did something to it so I can only get a little bit of cash each month instead of the lump sum I want to use to buy a set of golden mechanical wings I saw online. I'm determined to fly one day. I truly believe that if we concentrate real hard and focus on our inner psyche, we'll tap into our superpowers. You're a doctor, what do you think?" She flushed the toilet as she spoke, then sprayed a blast of cherry-scented air freshener before turning away to wash her hands.

"I think I'll get back to you on that." Miles backed his way to the door. He decided to pass on adding her to his little black book. He did not need to be socializing with someone who could easily be one of his patients. A diagnosis was already forming in his mind. But he checked out her thighs, the fullness of her bosom one last time. She'd be good for a late night drink—real good—but the hangover would not be worth it. "Okay. Well, I'm going to go now. Early rounds at the hospital." Miles pulled on the gold knob.

"Oh, you don't have to rush. It's almost noon. I know enough about hospitals to know that rounds would have been made by now." She jumped and landed back on the mattress with a squeaky thud and patted the space next to her. "C'mon, stay for awhile. I'll cook you a nice brunch, and if you're still hungry, we can swing by my mother's house later. She's really big on having Sunday dinner when she gets home from church. She doesn't like me coming over, but I bet she would like you." M-girl studied the ceiling as she continued. "You have to meet my mother. She's crazy, the way she tries to order everything in her life, the people in it, especially me. She's always trying to control me. Even my father used to tell me . . ." Her face drew up in a dream, in pain. "You probably could help her, you being a psychiatrist and all. Do you like salt water taffy?"

"Thanks for the invite, Mu—, Mei—"

"Maya." The girl glared at him. "Maya Windemere."

"Yeah, Maya. You know I was just messing with you. I could never forget such a pretty name like yours."

She smiled, her lips a tight circle around her teeth.

"Anyway, thanks for the invite, but I really do need to go."

"No problem, Dr. Logan. I'll call you later today."

Miles sucked in a deep breath as he loosened the chain on her door. Had he really given this girl his phone number?

"Is it better for me to call you at home or on your cell? Or should I just page you?" She jumped up to walk him out.

"I'll call you. Maya." He shook a playful finger before swinging back around to face the door. He had to get out of there.

"Maya. That's my name. You know I was named kind of after my mother? Her name is Madelyn Windemere, and I'm Maya Windemere. Get it? I know, I'm so stupid, standing here talking about my name and all 'cause I don't want to see you go. You are so unlike the man I met Wednesday night. He was, like, this crazy magician or plumber or something, and you're, like, a doctor. No, I'm thinking of the man I met on Monday. He was the magician. Oh well, I'll call you in a few hours. Or you can call me first." Maya let out a loud laugh that sounded like something between a cat squeal and a stalling motor.

Miles left with her laughter in his ears. Even as he closed the door, he felt like it hadn't been shut all the way. He tried in vain to remember what other information he'd given the girl last night.

"Dr. Logan," she was standing in the doorway, a blanket with an Aztec design wrapped around her shoulders, nothing else. "You never did tell me. What do you find so charismatic about me?"

"Charismatic?" This girl was going to be hard to get rid of.

"Yeah. Remember? Charisma? You kept saying I looked like charisma last night." Maya suddenly looked embarrassed, running fingers through her limp hair. "I'm sorry, I'm sorry," she gushed. "You're trying to go get to your patients, and I'm holding you up talking about your little pet name for me. I'll just call you later and then we can talk. This is going to be special. I can feel it in my soul." She pressed her right hand over her heart with those words as she leaned against the door. "See you soon, Dr. Logan."

CHAPTER 5

"I will say of the Lord, He is my refuge and my fortress: my God; in Him will I trust." Charisma Joel stood on her feet with the rest of the congregation, trying to balance a Bible and a paper fan between her clapping hands. "Amen. Amen," she shouted along.

Last night had been the hardest of the week. She remembered the fight that started after she returned home. It started the moment he got in the bed, the first time in months. She wondered if he knew where she had just come from—or rather where she *almost* just came from. She wondered if he cared.

A part of her wanted to draw him close, find a way to make him feel better, find a way to feel better herself. But most of her was repulsed. Half-clothed, a heap, a pile of moodiness and agitation, he did not even bother to ask where she'd been, or even turn her way. Not that she really wanted him to turn to her, considering the way he looked, the way he smelled. But even still, it had been over a year since he last found a reason to turn her way in bed.

This time the fight was over mounting subscription bills for medical journals he wasn't reading. She could not remember how it started or ended, but she did recall him yelling, throwing, her sucking back cries, not wanting April to wake up. Charisma tried to hide so much from April, but she knew there was only so much a bedroom door less than two inches thick could hold back from an eleven-year-old trying to sleep in the next room. Thankfully, she'd managed to sweep up all the glass, more for his sake than April's. The way he eyed the sharp shards made her nervous. Gideon had his moments, but they were just that, she was sure: moments. He was too smart to carry out any of his threats, she believed. Even still, the moment he fell asleep she'd swept up the vase he threw from her dresser.

Charisma wondered what hate felt like, and if that was the name of the feeling that was growing inside of her. Not hatred of him, but hatred of *it*; the demon that seemed to be suffocating the life and everything good out of her husband. Holding a simple conversation with him had become impossible.

"I will say of the Lord, He is my refuge and my fortress: my God; in Him will I trust!"

"Amen. Amen!" Charisma shouted along.

All around her, people were standing, jumping, kneeling, clapping, praying, and crying. She felt numb in her shoes, wanting, waiting for the buzz she needed to begin her week, to get through her week. Some people called the buzz the Holy Spirit, the supernatural jolt that quickened willing hearts, the anointing, a filling. Charisma just wanted to feel refreshed. She wanted a long, slow sip of spring water for her dry soul.

"Say it again, church!" the pastor boomed from the pulpit, his voice a deep guttural cry. "Psalm 91:2, church! Say it again!" The microphone crackled as spit flew with his words.

"I will say of the Lord, He is my refuge and my fortress: my God; in Him will I trust." Charisma shouted to the tops of her lungs, waiting for the weight on her feet to let go. She wanted to jump along, soar. The organist joined in the sermon with a series of quick minor chords.

She had been saying things about the Lord all morning, stories about Him, songs about Him, even greeting her church family with facts about Him.

"God is good—"

"All the time—"

"And all the time—"

"God is good."

"Praise Him, sister. Bless Him, brother."

"Hey, church!" The pastor grabbed the microphone out of the stand. "Are you getting it? Are you hearing me? Are you saying it?"

"I will say of the Lord, He is my refuge and my fortress: my God; in Him will I trust."

Charisma had been saying things about Jesus all day, to the children in her class, to the women in her pew. She looked down at April who at the moment was playing with two paper plates made into a wheel that showed water turning into wine. It was the craft from this morning's Sunday School lesson, the first in the series of the miracles of Jesus. The first miracle, turning water into wine.

Yeah, that's what she needed right now, Charisma thought as fresh tears pricked her eyes. She wanted a long, slow sip of spring water; but oh, if that water could be turned into wine. She would get drunk. Real drunk, so drunk that she wouldn't have to remember anything that happened before today or think about what could happen tomorrow. She did not want to think about him and what he was doing to her life.

Drunk, girlfriend, I mean good, all-out, word-slurring, foot-stumbling drunk.

Isn't that what they all wanted, these people shouting and groaning in the pews of Greater Glory? Something to ease the pain just a little while longer, something to take the edge off and make laughter and giddiness the norm?

Turning water into wine. That was Jesus' first miracle. He knew that's what the people on this planet needed to see Him do first. They needed to know He could turn plain water into the best kind of wine.

Charisma sat back down in her seat, hunched over, her hands covering her face, shaking. She shook so hard, her high heels clattered on the hardwood floor beneath them.

"Mommy?"

April brought her back, thank God. Charisma straightened herself up, sat up, wiped the tears that almost fell down from her eyes. She could not have people looking at her like this. There would be too many questions, too many conclusions. There were some things they did not need to know, would not understand.

God, if I could only get some of that water turned wine.

"Here, sister."

Where had Pepperdine Waters come from? Charisma did not know, but there the woman was, sitting next to her, a cup of cool water in one hand. "Take this, baby. Drink." Charisma had not noticed her or the hand she was using to circle the small of her back.

"I'm okay." Charisma cleared her throat and quickly turned back to the service, nodding her head along with the rhythm of the sermon. She didn't want to have to explain. Not even to Sister Pepperdine.

"I know, but drink it anyway."

The water felt good going down her throat, like ice thrown on fire, a spring rain falling on smoldering ashes. Cold. Clean. Charisma closed her eyes and let the feeling wash through her. The sermon was ending and the benediction was nearing.

"You'll be at the meeting on Tuesday?" Sister Pepperdine stood to head back to her seat. "You had some good ideas for the women's retreat last time. We'd love to have some more of your input."

Charisma smiled, not trusting her voice to talk anymore. The retreat. That was at the end of April, a season away. It was still winter right now, late winter. Charisma had gone to the last planning meeting and given her two cents on possible topics and activities that could renew and refresh the women of Greater Glory. But that was before the invitation came forwarded in the mail. She could not think past the invitation.

"So, you think you'll be there Tuesday, Sister Joel? We loved your ideas. It always amazes me the gifts and talents we have hiding in the pews." Pepperdine smiled even as Charisma held back tears. Who knew what Tuesday held for her? She had to focus on getting her and her daughter home right now. She had to focus on making it through Sunday night and all day Monday. It was waiting for them, in the shadows, in the corners. He was home waiting for them. She could never shake the feeling.

"I'll see," she whispered just before the pastor gave the final prayer and benediction. She had survived another Sunday, no major outbursts, no meltdowns, no stares. No questions. Now she had to go home.

"Mommy, I like the story you told us in Sunday School this morning."

Charisma and April were walking down the church steps. The sun bore down in an unusual March showing. She adjusted the yellow hat on her head, letting the cloth brim shield her eyes from the slight glare. She liked the hat on her head. It did not just top her off, it completed her, wrapped Momma's arms all over her, the old Momma, the one who wore bright yellow hats with new suits from Macy's. Charisma felt bold in her shoes.

"Have a blessed day." She grabbed Sister Walker's hand on her way down the sidewalk. She needed to speak and greet to fit in. She felt bold in her shoes.

"Oh, that was *you*!" Sister Walker, the head of the deaconess's board, recoiled. "I spent all service trying to figure out where the smell of moth balls and cedar was coming from. It's that hat you're wearing. Girl, where did you get that thing from?"

Charisma took the hat off but never looked behind her. She grabbed April's hand and pulled her to their car. She had to get away before more questions came. Questions that tapped into stories she didn't want to get into. She was quiet as she drove, listening to April hum a song they had sung earlier in class.

It was the stories that kept Charisma quiet—not the stories that had been told to her and that she taught in Sunday School, but the stories that she knew.

CHAPTER 6

"Your mother is suffering from clinical depression." He didn't even blink when he told me. We were trying to be professional, him sitting behind the desk in the generic office, me waiting for the verdict in the plastic chair in front of him. He'd just finished rounds with the rest of the medical team on the Howard G. Phillips Unit. I'd watched the group of white coats circulate from room to room after I finished a double shift in the radiology department. This was during one of many extended stays on the unit for Caroline Jackson.

I remember shuffling in my seat, looking down at my fingernails, fumbling with my name badge, doing anything, everything to avoid having to ask the obvious. "What does this mean? What's wrong with her?"

"Charisma," the professionalism was gone as he reached over his desk and entwined his fingers with mine, "there's no shame in her condition, no reason to get embarrassed. It's most likely a chemical imbalance, that's all. Some people get diabetes. Some people have thyroid disease. Your mom has depression. It's part physiological in nature. That's why it's good that she's here to get treatment. In your mother's case, both intensive counseling and medication may help stabilize her mood. Right now, the wiring in her brain has got her feeling pretty low. We're going to fix that wiring so she can resume her normal functioning. She can't just snap out of it. It's good that she's here to get

help. We'll talk some more about what's next later." *Dr. Joel settled back in his seat, still holding onto my hands.*

"So that's it. It's that simple. Pop some pills and she'll be all better." I closed my eyes, an unexplainable knot tightening in my stomach. I had to loosen my hands from his grip just to take a breath and process his words.

"Nobody's saying it's simple, not for her. Not for you. But at least you have some answers now to explain her behavior—"

"The sleeping all day, the crying spells, the meals she won't eat, her stopping all the stuff she used to love to do? She acts like just getting dressed is impossible and she talks like there's no hope for anything. There's been plenty of times when I've felt blue myself, but I never—"

"She's not just feeling blue. From what you told me, this has lasted for more than two weeks. It's been a few months. She is clinically depressed. Without help, she's not just going to snap out of it." He paused, letting his words sink in. "Look, Charisma," suddenly he was coming from behind the desk, sitting in the seat next to mine, stroking a single lock of my shoulder-length hair, "I know the past few months have been overwhelming for you. I know you want to see your mother well, and things normal again, but you can't let this suffocate the life out of you too. You were right to bring her here. She won't be able to harm herself or anyone else. She has the help she needs. Now you need to accept the support that's offered to you as a family member. Will you reconsider sitting in one of your mother's psychotherapy sessions?"

I wanted to hide the shame that came with my next words, but there was no way around it. "I—To be honest with you, Gideon, it's hard being in the same room with her, talking to her, being around her. The darkness, the fog she's living in right now . . . It's like a living substance surrounding her, and when I get too close, I feel it. Dark arms, a black web tangling up everything, choking, blocking out light, reason. I don't like the way . . . I don't like that darkness, and I don't want to be anywhere around it. I don't know how you do it, Gideon. I don't know how you stand being around so much heaviness and darkness every day."

A dark glimmer washed through his eyes as he turned away from me. I should have realized it then, but I guess, as usual, I chose to ignore it.

"Why do you do it?" I continued to prod instead. "What made you want to be a psychiatrist and study all the disorders of the human mind and soul?" I smiled, wanting to feel lighter at that moment, wanting relief from the tension that seemed to have filled the cramped office.

"Depression can be part genetic, you know." He changed the subject as he reached for his suit jacket. "That's why I've got to take care of you and make sure you stay happy so nothing negative gets triggered in you." He winked as he opened the office door. "Let's go grab a quick breakfast from the cafeteria. I know you must be hungry after working so hard all night."

He was still sleeping on the couch when they came home. Charisma opened the screen door with a squeak, turned off the blaring radio, and slipped past him and the stacks of old newspapers, magazines, and medical textbooks. All were dusty, most were unread, but the stacks remained like fragile columns in the living room and throughout most of the house. As much as she wanted to get out a bucket, mop, and scouring powder; as much as she wanted to put on some dancing music and throw April a dust rag and cleaning sprays and move and scrub to the music; as much as she wanted to work together with her daughter to disinfect, purge, and reorganize, she knew that cleaning up would come with a complicated cost. This was Gideon's chaos and to correct it would set him off on a course beyond her control.

The mess was too massive to wrap her head around; so she sighed and used her feet to walk around it instead, bitterly accepting for the moment the ever-mounting price of peace. April jumped through the front door, a rare smile on her face. A melody passed through her lips as she made up words to go along with the song they learned in Sunday school.

"Mommy," she shouted, her eyes blinking to adjust to the darkness, "what do you think of my new verse?" She giggled as she continued her song, dancing her way past the sofa to the kitchen, where Charisma was arranging containers from a carry-out on a space she had cleared on the table.

"Sing, girl, sing," Charisma laughed along, grabbing the side of her skirt to do a quick two-step like Sister Beatrice at church. "Praise him, daughter." She jumped like fire was in her shoes and grabbed a paper plate to fan herself.

April laughed louder and spun around, adding a new chorus to the song "Deep and Wide." She spun and sung until she crashed into the figure standing unnoticed at the kitchen threshold.

Silence flooded the room. Charisma turned back to spooning creamed spinach and rotisserie chicken onto plastic plates.

"You don't have to stop singing." Gideon Joel wiped sleep from his eyes and offered a sheepish grin. "I'll sing with you if you want to. Come on, Charisma, do that dance you were just doing again." He grabbed his wife around the hips and lifted her a few inches off the floor as he stomped his foot on the linoleum floor.

Charisma swallowed hard, seeing only the globs of spinach splattering off her spoon, and the uncertainty in April's eyes.

"Gideon, please." Her plea was light, a laugh laced through it. Her eyes darted between the puddles of spinach under her feet and the tightness taking over April's face. "Put me down. We're making a mess."

"Dance, Charisma. Sing, April." He was still smiling, but Charisma could hear the change in his voice, the change in his mood.

"Gideon, let me fix your plate."

"Fix my plate?" Pain seared through his words, his face. He let go of her and she landed with a hard thud on the heels of her feet. "Fix my plate? I don't want you to fix anything for me. I can make my own plate. You think I can't make my own plate? You think I can't do anything? That's it, isn't it? You think I'm incapable of doing anything. I want you to dance! Dance, Charisma!"

In one movement, the tub of spinach was airborne. Charisma held back tears as green globs smeared across the opposite wall and streaked down to the floor. Gideon snatched the roll of paper towels she immediately reached for. He tore off piece after piece in a frenzied rage before slamming the remainder of the roll onto the floor.

"I'll clean it! You don't think I can clean it? You dance, Charisma. April, you sing! Sing! Sing!"

April stood frozen, her eyes wide. A monotone note, flat, forced, and low, moaned through her perched lips.

"Louder, louder! I want to hear you sing. You don't

want to sing for me? Are you against me too?" His voice roared unnaturally as his hand reached for something else to throw. The headless, garlic-roasted chicken suddenly took flight, and grease and gravy and shreds of white meat joined the dripping spinach on the wall. Paper plates and plastic forks and knives pelted the air next as Gideon threw everything he could reach from his corner of the small kitchen. Charisma ducked and darted through the shower of plastic utensils and found her way to April, shielding her, cradling the frozen girl.

"You don't want me here, do you? You wish I was dead sometimes, don't you?" Gideon trembled, his voice curling away into a hoarse whisper. "Say it, Charisma. You'd be better off if I wasn't here. You wish I was dead."

She swallowed hard, noting the way he stared at the last plastic knife in his hands. It was a look of desire. She watched as he ran fingers over the grooved edges, held the white plastic against the brown skin of his wrist. She squeezed her eyes shut and instinctively covered April's. The air was tight, stale in her lungs. But then she heard his whimper and she found breath again.

"I'm sorry." His voice was a long groan. "Look at this mess. I'm sorry, Charisma. God, I'm sorry. I don't know what's wrong with me, what got into me. I just need more faith, I guess. Healing, in the name of Jesus!" He knocked the unopened pill bottle to the floor. "You both seemed so happy coming home from church and I . . . I remembered how good going to church used to feel, but now . . . I can't—Look, I'll clean up. You don't have to dance. I was just trying—April, come here, give me a hug. God, I'm sorry . . . What's wrong with me?"

He looked from his wife to his daughter, his daughter to his wife. When nobody moved, he shut his eyes and stumbled blindly back to the couch. As radio static then music flooded the house once again, Charisma put on a large smile and darted across the kitchen to grab her purse and her car keys.

"April, I know what we can do," she spoke as if she had a juicy secret. "Let's go get some chicken nuggets from McDonald's." Charisma nearly tripped over her feet as she scrambled back over to April. She put a firm hand on the young girl's shoulder and led her through the back door. Going the back route meant a longer walk to her car, but there was no way she was going to go walk by that sofa to get to the front door right now. April had been traumatized enough, she reasoned. *And so have I.* It was not until they were both sitting in her car and the engine was humming that Charisma felt herself exhale.

They drove in silence the three blocks to the neighborhood golden arches. Charisma saw April safely to a booth with a combo meal and then went to the pay phone next to the restroom. She gave April a smile and a thumbs-up as she picked up the receiver.

The number. She'd torn it up the moment he wrote it down, but the seven digits remained seared in her memory. She could not forget how to reach him if she wanted to.

Dr. Miles Logan. Charisma had seen him only once since his return to Baltimore Metropolitan Hospital. She could tell from his greeting that nobody had told him the story. He was the same as ever—too confident, too cocky, too pretty for his own good. She'd been able to rein away his advances years ago when she was just Charisma Jackson and not Mrs. Gideon Joel. But the way he looked at her, smiled at her when they bumped in the elevator two months ago at the close of her night shift, opened enough of a window for her to see a way out.

"Jesus, what am I doing?" She dialed quickly before she could change her mind. She tried to convince her conscience that she was making the right step. *He's a psychiatrist*, she told herself, *an answer, help*. Of course there were other doctors, support groups, hotlines she could call, ones with no strings attached, no secondary motives; Gideon had lists leftover in his files from his former medical practice. *But I don't just want answers. I don't just want help*. She was honest with herself. *I want a new life*.

The daydreams were always the same. A man—the face changed constantly—would draw her close enough to let her feel his firmness, and she would pull him closer to her until they would both find a release in her fantasized escape. The daydreams, the stories she controlled, were the only stories she knew that let her feel pleasure, alive.

She was tired of daydreaming.

"Hello?" It was his voice, but irritation and impatience ruined it. Charisma slammed down the receiver without saying a word.

"Lord, forgive me," she mumbled as she hurried back to April's side, remembering the scar on her own foot, the story behind it.

God, I made a vow to you and to Gideon. Her prayer was silent as she split a side of fries with April. *For better or for worse, for richer or for poorer. In sickness and in health*. It was the last phrase, that vow, in sickness and in health, which had kept her in a house with him for the past year. *Lord, I've been keeping that vow, but what do I do now? How long do I have to keep waiting for a change?*

CHAPTER 7

He'd thought it was Maya Windemere calling again. Dr. Miles Logan pulled the phone cord out of the wall and stared down again at his cell phone. He couldn't turn that off. What if someone needed him at the hospital? Miles dropped his head in his hands.

His Owings Mills garage townhome had been the one place he could stretch out and relax. Alone, uninterrupted, no show to put on, no speeches to impress. He did not want to lose this one secret corner of his world, his privacy. He rarely even brought his weekend catches here, opting most of the time to take the women he met to extravagant penthouse suites overlooking the Inner Harbor in downtown Baltimore or equally impressive hotel rooms in nearby D.C.

"I will never drink again." He kicked himself as he lay back in the black leather chaise that completed his living room set, wanting to take back the entire weekend, especially the part when he convinced Maya to join him for a few drinks in a Fells Point bar. He threw back another shot of Cognac. This girl had him drinking hard on a Sunday afternoon, two hours before his next sixteen-hour shift at the hospital. She'd called in excess of twelve times since he'd left her Mount Vernon studio earlier that morning. The last conversation had consisted mainly of her hysterically crying in his ear because he refused to accompany her to her mother's Sunday dinner.

"I've got to nip this in the bud," he told himself once again. He checked the number on his cell phone's caller ID and quickly dialed. The phone rang awhile, but eventually someone answered, identifying herself as a manager of McDonald's. It was a payphone, Miles realized.

"I don't mean to trouble you, but can you find out if someone just called a Dr. Miles Logan. I'm a psychiatrist at Baltimore Metro, and one of my patients may be trying to contact me for an emergency." Miles shook his head as he spoke, ready to be rid of Maya for good. He was not prepared for who greeted him instead.

"Dr. Logan?" She was nervous, but it was her. He had never forgotten her voice.

"Charisma Jackson? Is that you?"

"Charisma Joel."

"Oh yeah, Mrs. Gideon Joel. So how are you and my friend faring these days? How is his research sabbatical going?"

A long pause ensued before she answered. "Listen, I can't talk right now. I'm at McDonald's with my daughter, but I was wondering if I can . . . talk to you later?"

"Does your husband know you're calling me?" Miles didn't have to close his eyes to remember Charisma's full-blossomed appearance. Charisma with the heavy chest and extra-padded hips, the deep black eyes and nervous smile.

"Yes—I mean, no. It's a . . . surprise I'm planning for him. Look, I need your help. I know you're busy at the hospital, but is there a time I can meet you there? Maybe off the unit?"

Miles didn't know whether to feel disappointed or hopeful. Charisma Joel was one of the few women he'd never been able to fully shake out of his mind, even after she accepted that gaudy ring from Gideon Joel.

What she had seen in the man, he could not figure out. True, women seemed to go for the tall, dark, handsome types, but Gideon had always struck him as having a darkness to him just under the surface. Gideon had a type of glimmering midnight mysteriousness running in his veins that reminded Miles of a blues guitarist he'd heard once at a café near the Harbor. Melancholy. Gut-wrenching, layered honesty that, like an undeveloped film negative, would wither and dry if exposed to too much light.

During their shared residencies, Dr. Joel approached his patients and research with the diligence of careful passion, but he stayed to himself and said little to anyone outside of his lunchtime rendezvous with Charisma, the x-ray technician from the radiology department. Joel had helped her get the job, from what Miles could remember, after the girl's mother became a regular on the Howard G. Phillips Unit. He'd tried even then to shake her out of Gideon's grip, but she saw through his advances. It was her deliberate dedication to the man that made Miles tremble under her gaze.

"Charisma, is everything okay?" He held his breath, not sure how he wanted her to answer. He'd had brief relationships with other men's wives before, but something told him this could cut too close to his heart.

"Yes," her words said one thing; the fact that they were whispered said another. Miles felt his heart skip a beat.

"Miles," she continued, "let me be honest with you. I need your professional opinion on a matter. That's all." Suddenly she sounded strong, certain. Miles almost felt relief, like a deadly fire had just been squelched at the root.

Almost.

"Well, I have a long day tonight and tomorrow, really the rest of the week; but if you want to catch up before you begin your night shift, we can talk on Tuesday evening."

"That's perfect. My daughter might be with me for dinner in the cafeteria, but after I get her settled for the night, we can meet and catch up."

"You bring your daughter to work with you?"

"Yeah, uh, we've been getting the house exterminated. Ants. She's been staying in, uh, one of the extra beds near the radiology wing." It sounded like Charisma was holding her breath.

"Well, okay," Miles smoothed down his suit and checked his eyes for redness in a nearby mirror. "I'll see you Tuesday."

"Yes, Tuesday." Charisma hung up the phone. April had finished her strawberry milkshake. It was time to go, but she wasn't ready to go back home. From the tense look on April's face, Charisma could tell her daughter wasn't ready either. She could go straight to work and hang out with April in the gift shop until her shift began. She had a small locker on the unit that was big enough to keep a change of clothes for both her and her daughter. The waiting area April slept in some nights was largely unnoticed and ignored by both staff and security. The one or two times someone inquired, she'd been quick about giving a reasonable response. Getting the house exterminated? That was a good one. Why hadn't she thought of that before?

It was not a nightly routine. April, for the most part, slept soundly in her metal twin bed at home. But the days when his moods were unusually unpredictable, the nights when his behavior was past explaining—or enduring—it was easier for Charisma to get her job done when she knew April was snoring safely under the fluorescent bulbs of Waiting Area J. And if she wasn't scheduled to work, or even just simply wanted to call out, she had the gift certificate she'd won in a raffle at April's school to use at the Solace Inn downtown.

Nobody would notice. Gideon usually added more hours to his near all-day sleep schedule after his "bad moments," as she named them for April. And Mrs. Windemere, for all her nosy nit-picking, was usually asleep, lights out, by the time Charisma left for her 11:00 P.M. to 7:00 A.M. shift. And it was Sunday evening now. Mrs. Windemere would be too busy playing dinner host to her four children, four grown sons, to look for Charisma and April to come home.

Just hold out until Tuesday. Tuesday evening. She would miss the meeting with Pepperdine Waters at church, but this was more important. Charisma wanted more than answers, more than help. She wanted more than stories—not the ones she taught, or the ones she imagined, but the ones she knew. She wanted more. She wanted out. *Jesus, I don't know what else to do.*

"Remember that talking doll we saw in the gift shop last Monday? Maybe we should just go ahead and buy it right now." Charisma kept her voice light and cheery, but she did not miss the weak smile April cut short as she turned to dump her trash.

"Baby, look at me." My mother's voice had been sharp and hissed as she grabbed my chin in her hands. "Don't nobody need to know all our business. Now stand up straight and take that scowl off your face."

I was twelve at the time and my mother and I were standing in the rain on the steps of New Zion Hill Fundamental Church. An usher was waiting to let us in to morning service. I could hear the organ piping out chords for the choir's march around the offering table.

A white veil and a large dip in the straw hat covered the bruise on Caroline Jackson's forehead. Two coats of eyeliner and the latest shade of gray-green from Fashion Fair cosmetics diminished the blackness around her eye.

"What happens at home stays at home. You say anything and people will start talking, especially church people. One day you will understand. Mr. Garrison didn't mean anything he did last night. I didn't even know you were up, baby girl." She planted an anxious kiss atop my head. The emerald-cut diamond ring sparkled on Momma's finger as she straightened up and readjusted her hat. I remember wondering even then if anyone at New Zion Hill ever suspected that my mother wasn't really married to the man who lived at home. Shacking up, living in sin, that's what the preacher called it. And when he screamed and hollered about damnation for fornification (as he said it), my mother, Caroline Jackson, would be the main saint running through the aisles and shouting amen.

"There are things you don't know about life, baby. Life ain't nothing but a string of stories. You learn which ones to share and which ones to keep secret." The rain was making the mascara bleed around her swollen eye.

"You're black, and one day you'll be a grown woman. Put those two together and you ain't got nothing but a tale that nobody else needs to know. Keep your mouth shut, girl, or you'll learn the hard way what happens when people know your business." The usher was opening the door and Caroline Jackson's sudden smile was as sure as her threat had been seconds before.

"Praise the Lord, Brother Williams." Her voice faded in the distance. I joined my mother's smile and tucked away another story.

CHAPTER 8

The night's meeting of the women's ministry leadership committee would be a short one, Pepperdine was sure, at least the official business part of it anyway. Most of the planning for the upcoming women's retreat, the main item that needed to be discussed, had already been done. Sister Pepperdine Waters laid a copy of the agenda on each of the empty metal chairs surrounding the rectangular table. It had been an unusually long Tuesday in the church office, and she was ready to go home, eat her cornbread and beef stew, and get in her bed.

The heat was working in the narrow basement for a change, so the arthritic pains in her ankles and knees were not bothering her too much. She hummed an old spiritual as she worked, finding a solace in the rich minor alto notes filling the church hall. In another half-hour or so, the place would be buzzing with all the latest news and gossip ten church ladies could carry with them.

Pepperdine usually let them chit-chat a few moments before officially commencing the meetings. She'd been heading up the women's ministry for over ten years now, long enough to know that women comfortable with and around one another were more likely to open up to one another about the issues that really needed to be addressed. The announcements and minutes and to-dos and planning to her were really secondary matters.

Ministry began where the agenda ended.

"Jesus, have your way," Pepperdine prayed aloud, stopping to put a drop of oil on each seat she passed. "Please be with each woman of Greater Glory Worship Center. Let us who are in charge of the women's ministry be in a right place with you so that we may lead everyone to the same destination."

She swallowed hard at her own spoken prayer, reflecting on the prayer requests and tears many had shared with her in confidence; past sins and shames, hurts and heartaches that had become a part of who she was as a church mother, mentor, and leader of everything female at Greater Glory. She wanted these women, regardless of where they were in life—wives, widows, new mothers, abused lovers, students, singles, former this, present that—to know their shoes had already been worn by many and broken in by a billion miles.

The Good Book says there's nothing new under the sun, she reasoned, and although generations that come and go may have different hairstyles and wear different clothes, the heart beats the same way it did when Eve first saw Adam; lungs exhale the same way they did when she groaned and pushed that first baby out of her womb; and tears fall with the same salty weight as when she mourned the first death, the murder of her second son, Abel, by the hands of her firstborn, Cain.

Men are men. Women are women. Life is life.

She wanted these women, her daughters of Greater Glory, to know things she could not speak. Where words failed her, service had succeeded.

"Is it enough, Lord? The time I give in service, the ears I give to listen? Are my gifts to them—to you—enough? " She prayed this prayer every day and waited with a heavy heart for an answer.

She prayed that prayer now, as the basement door swung open with the first attendees of the meeting, Sister Floretta Hines and Mother Black, the feuding co-queens of the church kitchen. Following close behind were Tarina Mitchell and her sister Bianca, Greater Glory's dynamic singing duo and praise team leaders. The next three women headed up several of the women's and children's Bible study groups and classes, Monique Leonard, Shakita Dawson, Rayna George. No sight of Charisma Joel. *I have to call that girl*, Pepperdine made a mental note.

She laughed and listened as the women sat down beside her. That Bianca was too funny with her wisecracks and jokes, and Shakita, as usual, was too quiet. Pepperdine straightened a stack of papers as she smiled and studied her church daughters and her church sisters. She then nodded at Mother Black. Each of these women had a calling and purpose and was using their gifts and talents to fulfill the needs of the church. Each of them served on so many boards and committees, and yet dedicated themselves to centralizing their offices and duties under her direction as the women's ministry leader.

"Good evening, Sister Waters. Hi, Pepperdine."

Pepperdine gave a curt nod as she was greeted by each. She let Monique finish a cute story about her son, Dontae, let them all share one last laugh, and then called the meeting to order.

"Sister Hines, we need to finalize the food budget for the retreat . . ." she began, but her mind was not at rest.

Is it enough, Lord?

CHAPTER 9

The first time Miles saw her was at a party. Several of the residents had decided it was time for a break from the stress and demands of hospital work and met at a resident's apartment on Centre Street for drinks, for laughs, and for fun.

She was one of three black girls there, the only one not a resident or an intern, and the only one standing awkwardly against the wall. He remembered the look on her face and the way she held her frosty glass of ginger ale away from her. Her eyes, black and glossy as a teardrop, darted around the dimly lit basement apartment that swarmed with sweaty white skin in halter tops and T-shirts. It was one of the old Victorian-style row homes famous in Baltimore's monument district that had been converted into a multi-dwelling living space. The place smelled of old wood and mildew, and ornate iron fixtures crawled over unused fireplaces and arched doorways. Dave Matthews Band blared from two speakers set over their heads, and giggles, hoots, and loud voices came from the dance floor, the futons, and the bar stools set around stacked milk crates.

She was alone when he approached her.

"Dr. Miles Logan." He'd extended a hand toward her, seeing for the first time the high cheek bones that spoke to a Native American ancestor somewhere in her gene pool, and the clear, smooth complexion of her medium-brown skin. She was not typical of the beauties he was usually attracted to, more round, fuller; but there was something in her eyes—the question, the pensiveness, the depth—that made him want to wrap his arms around her and push her head into his shoulder.

Vulnerability.

"I work on the Howard G. Phillips Unit." He smiled to break the ice, but she was quick to let go of his grip, he remembered. Her hands were still cold from her soda.

"I know who you are." It was the only time she looked at him that night, and both acceptance and accusation rang in her tone.

"Miles." Gideon came from behind and laid one hand on Miles's shoulder and grabbed her wrist with the other. "I see you've met my Charisma." He smiled and Miles realized then that he had never seen Gideon smile before. He had a surprisingly boyish smile; one that looked awkward on his sharply cut face.

"Gideon, it's good to see you outside of the hospital," he said because he could not think of anything else to say.

"Yeah, well, it's time that I have some balance in my life." Gideon's hands gripped tighter over Charisma's and both of them shared a twittering laugh. Miles stood back watching the unspoken dynamics between the two. He'd never felt jealousy before that moment. He'd never had a reason to.

The hospital cafeteria was about to close when Dr. Miles Logan and Charisma sat down at a table. April was within view at a booth two tables away, quietly enjoying a large apple pie-flavored ice cream sundae. Charisma, wearing lavender scrubs and white tennis shoes, was silent as Miles fielded off last-second calls and pages. *Jesus, what am I doing here? What do I say to this man?* Finally he smiled up at her.

"So, Mrs. Joel, what can I do for you tonight?"

She ignored the curl in his lips, the slight tilt of his head, as she sucked in a deep breath. She could feel her heart racing and wondered if he noticed. This was not the way she expected to feel, but being this close to him after so many years unlocked something she must have hidden from herself deep down inside her.

"Look," she kept her words pointed and even, "I can't talk for long right now, I just need your help with something."

"A surprise, right? You're planning something for your husband?"

His smile was too playful. Charisma began to feel annoyed. And guilty. This wasn't the right step. He was the wrong resource, she could feel it. She needed to find neutral territory. Gideon needed help and she wanted a new life, but maybe there was another way to handle this. Another idea came to mind.

"Yes." She took out a pen and a sheet of scrap paper from her purse. "Our fifteen-year wedding anniversary is coming in September, and I want to surprise Gideon with a party. I was hoping that you were still in contact with some of the doctors you two used to work with when you were both doing your residencies here."

"That's all you wanted? I can get a list of addresses ready for you by the weekend." Miles took a slow bite of his lemon cake, licking his lips, never letting his eyes leave Charisma's. "You know that I'll help you with anything you need." Even as he spoke he felt a tingling in his midsection that only strengthened with the fantasies he kept re-playing in his mind. Charisma had picked up a few pounds over the years but the weight was in all the right places. And Gideon Joel was the one enjoying the expansions. Miles felt his face darken. "We should meet again so I can go over all my contacts with you and help you fine-tune your plans."

Charisma fumbled with the paper and pen in her hand before suddenly standing and motioning for April to re-join her. "I have to go."

"How about Friday evening?"

"Huh?"

"Friday evening. We can meet here before your shift begins and talk some more, maybe even catch up on old memories."

"April, now." Charisma felt herself shaking. Miles Logan was not the type of doctor who wore a starched white lab jacket or scrubs. Dressed impeccably in a tailored olive suit and tan soft leather shoes, he looked like a poster child for *GQ:* trimmed curly black hair, fresh shave, clean nails, teasing smile.

It wasn't his appearance that was getting to her. It was the reminder of the life she had with Gideon. Broken promises. Disposed dreams. She felt ugly and exposed in Miles's presence.

"Charisma." She almost jumped when his hand touched hers, albeit a brief second. "How about it? Friday? Same place? Different meal hopefully."

His chuckle calmed Charisma. Maybe she was thinking too hard, taking this too seriously. Innocent enough, she figured. Here was a man, groomed, cleaned, functioning in his right mind, wanting to talk about party plans. Normal conversation. No harm done. She felt herself breathe.

"Okay, but I really need to go. C'mon, April." She shut her eyes as she squeezed past him. There was no real party to plan of course, but the idea of having conversation—normal, routine, boring, drama-free talk—appealed to the hoping side of her. *A new life.*

"Mommy, who was that?"

Charisma didn't feel like smiling, didn't feel like answering, didn't feel like explaining. So she didn't.

***

Miles watched as the mother and daughter scurried out of the cafeteria. Workers were closing down food stations. A man in a blue uniform splashed a dirty mop around the empty tables. It was almost eleven o'clock, another sixteen-hour shift coming to a close. No major episodes on the unit—a couple of discharges, one new admission, and the new nurse from the ER had finally given him her phone number. A good day.

Miles studied the seven digits scribbled down on the back of his prescription pad. As fine as the new girl was, he could not get his mind off Charisma. The legs, the full bosom, the extra cleavage.

"Charisma, Charisma," he mumbled with a smile. *Why should Gideon have all the fun?* The thought sickened him. He'd have to do something about it.

"Why are you calling that woman Charisma? I thought you gave that name to me."

The voice came from behind as well as the fingernails that suddenly dug into his shoulder blades.

"Maya? What are you doing here?" Miles spun around in his seat. Maya Windemere hunched over him wearing an almost sheer black mini dress and gobs of makeup on her face. He didn't miss the plastic hospital band around her wrist.

"I wanted to surprise you. I called the unit and they told me you got off at eleven. So here I am." She massaged his neck muscles and jumped in his lap before he jerked her off and jumped out of his seat.

"How did you—What—" He scanned the empty cafeteria quickly to make sure no one was watching.

"I came in through the emergency room. It was the only way I could get in here since visiting hours are over."

"Maya—"

"I told them I wanted to kill myself and they let me in." She giggled. "Before they could finish registering me, I sneaked out of there and went to your unit. Someone told me you were down here and now here I am." The smile suddenly disappeared. "So who was that woman and why were you calling *her* Charisma?"

"Maya, you have to go. Now."

"Just tell me who that woman was you were looking at so hard. Tell me or I'll find out myself." Her voice was getting louder. "Tell me now, Miles."

A security officer was approaching the table, a walkie-talkie in hand. "Ma'am, do you need an escort back to the ER. Sorry about this, doctor."

"I want you to tell me who that woman was or you'll be sorry, Miles!" She was screaming now. The security officer grabbed her wrists.

"Get off of me! I'm going to sue! Get your hands off of me!" Maya broke free from his grip and took off. She continued to yell profanities as she ran toward an exit. Just before she ran out the door, she looked back with a sudden smile. "Miles, I still love you." She blew him a kiss as the door slammed behind her.

"What in the world?" The security officer shook his head. "We see it all working in this place. I guess you especially." He pointed to Miles's badge.

Miles noticed for the first time that several cafeteria workers had been watching the scene from behind counters and food stands, pointing, mumbling, and laughing.

"Yes, she's a patient with multiple diagnoses—several severe mental disorders." He cleared his throat and smoothed down his suit jacket.

"I have a cousin on the Phillips unit, and he is nothing like her." The security guard was shaking his head, walking away.

"Yeah, well, she's a pretty extreme case."

"Is she dangerous?"

"Potentially. More so to herself, probably."

"Well, just the same, I'd keep her away from you, doctor. And away from your other girlfriend too." The officer winked.

CHAPTER 10

The cello concerto was a thick needle piercing under his skin. Sharp, digging downward, shrill pain in its bass chords. Gideon closed his eyes, finding a compressed pleasure in the dark tones of the overture despite its similarity to the screech of the crash last June. Just when he would sink under the memory, the chords would bring him back up. He could feel the bow, the strings, the tension, the fine line between melody and moan.

The house was quiet, not rare for a Tuesday night, except Charisma had taken April with her to work again, and the absence of the girl's soft sleeping sounds reminded him just how empty the house was.

Empty.

Where had he gone wrong? Gideon swung long, bare legs off the couch and stared at the set-in imprint of his body on the burgundy slipcover. He knew that the corded material Charisma had sewn together served the same purpose for their old sofa as much of his outward life had served him: covering holes, tears, ripped-up foam, bruises.

The people from his childhood town in Texas would be ashamed, sorrowful, if they saw him now. Gideon Joel, son of Marisa and Tate Joel; Central High's valedictorian and track star; winner of the governor's scholarship and top graduate of Tulane's biology department. When he crossed the stage that last time to shake the hand of the dean of Johns Hopkins Medical School, most of the families from his hometown in Texas were represented somewhere in the crowd. He remembered the colorful floppy hats speckling the auditorium from several of the good church mothers who'd made the journey. They'd saved up money to come to his medical school graduation and worn their best Sunday clothes. There was even a homemade sign, a banner with his name in bright crimson letters, glitter, pom-poms, stretched out across a rear row; "Our Dr. Gideon Joel," it read.

It had been a painstaking but quick rise to the top for him. When he became the youngest and the first African American to head the psychiatric department at Baltimore Metro, pride stretched and grew like the rubber celebratory balloons that decorated the party thrown for him on the ward. Those were the blue sky days, the years of his life when the clouds stayed quietly at the edges. He could control it then, the secret darkness that always threatened to overtake him, the darkness, the thoughts he'd spent much of his teen and young adult years warding off. He could control it then, by fighting his way through. Accomplishment after accomplishment. People thought he was just being an over-achiever. They didn't know that he was fighting for his life, his sanity, the blue skies to win. They didn't know. And Charisma had been the sun for him. In the light of her love, he had been certain the dark thoughts, the unexplainable weighty moods, wouldn't come back.

But they did. A little at first, and then the downpours.

Gideon looked back at the slipcover. What it had tried in desperation to hide was now showing up in its own tattered edges, frayed threads, spills, stains. He ran an ashy finger over a broken seam. He should surprise Charisma, get the last one hundred dollars left in his bank account and buy a new cover for the sofa.

Something pretty, with red in it, and flowery. A rose pattern. She liked roses.

He'd had that one hundred dollars in his account for months now. He had lost everything else. Everything. During the blue sky days, he had been quick to spend money and slow to save, determined to impress his wife and show the world that he had indeed "arrived." But the only destination to which he had arrived was at the doorsteps of debt. Deep debt. School loans, car loans, house loans. Loans, loans, and more loans.

Now, he did not have anything to show for his former six-figure income but that last one hundred dollars in a secondary savings account. Charisma did not know about it. She thought it was all gone. Every day he thought of something different to do with the money. But every day his ideas ended with the same thoughts. If he spent that money, the last of his once-hefty salary, then he really would have nothing left, nothing to show that he once was a great man, a renowned psychiatrist at Baltimore Metropolitan Hospital.

Was.

Besides, how would he be able to buy anything anyway? That would mean going outside, and it had been almost nine months since he last went beyond the front porch.

The last time he'd gone home to Texas, to bury his mother, he'd told them all of his travels to medical conventions and engagements in Switzerland, Munich, Venezuela, Cape Town, Tampa Bay.

There was nothing else left for him to see of the world.

He came to that conclusion almost a year ago, and that day locked himself in his office on the Howard G. Phillips Unit and did not come out for four days. The hospital directors were not sure what to do.

That was the beginning of the final downpour, the one he was in now. It had started and never stopped, only worsened beyond control. But there was one way to stop it, a better way, a more certain way than that last attempt. These thoughts, he had to stop thinking. Too much.

He reached for the radio to change the station. When the lively chorus of a gospel quartet filled the room he snapped it off. Silence enveloped him like a fog, and then there was a knock.

Bang. Bang. The front door shook like thunder was in its hinges and then suddenly sat so still that Gideon wondered if there had been a knock at all. From the dim light of a nearby streetlamp, he made out a jagged shadow on the dingy marble front steps. It was almost eleven o'clock at night and Charisma's Grand Am was not parked on the street. Whoever it was would go away if he waited long enough.

He was falling asleep and the memories began immediately replaying in his dreams. That perfect June day last year, blue sky; soft, scattered white clouds; the purr of his old Benz going sixty around a sharp bend on Cromwell Bridge Road. The decision, the moment he closed his eyes on purpose behind the wheel. He didn't see the other car.

Bang. Bang. Bang. This time the door rattled louder and Gideon shook himself awake. It's just a dream, the bad memory reliving itself, he concluded, but then he thought he heard a low moan, a whimpered cry. A voice. Was this some kind of sick trick? Was God playing games with him, getting him back for what he'd done? Gideon had heard a moan that cursed June day, had seen an outstretched hand. Blood.

"In the name of Jesus." Whispers rattled through him, shaking him. Sweat stung his eyes as he began to hyperventilate. “In the name of Jesus, I can fight this. I just need more faith. Jesus, Jesus.”

The banging at the door did not stop. It sounded like it was being slapped with open palms. Gideon stumbled to his feet. The fog lifted high enough for him to find his way to the door and open it.

“Oh my God, she won’t answer the door and I need to call her right now! I know she’s in there! Where’s your phone?” A woman pushed her way in, stomping, crying, and tripping over the books and stacks in the dark.

“Excuse me?” Gideon’s voice was a whisper from unuse. He stared at the young woman who’d flicked on the lights and was digging through telephone books, newspapers, and back-dated issues of *Ebony*. She was dressed skimpily for a chilly March night, a sleeveless, thigh-high black dress barely covering her shapely figure. Despite the bright pink and red makeup running off her face, her light brown skin was paled and her eyes were wide with anguish. Her hair was matted on one side, long and tousled on the other.

“Where is your phone?” she screamed and tossed an empty fish fillet wrapper aside before pointing an accusing finger at him.

“I’m sorry, who are you?” Gideon’s voice was dead. It was hard to care these days. Even now, with this strange woman rummaging through his living room, it was hard to care.

“My mother, I need to call my mother! I need to talk to her! She needs to talk to me!” The woman was back to her search, pulling, ripping, shrieking, crying. “Where is your phone?” At the kitchen doorway she shrunk into a tight, sobbing ball. “My mother, next door. She needs to talk to me!”

“Your mother lives next door?” The fog wanted to lift. A wave of brighter memories—textbooks, research papers, patient consultations—hit him. This young woman and her mother needed some kind of help. He was Dr. Gideon Joel, renowned psychiatrist.

Was.

Clinical notes, thoughts, conclusions flashed like a lit sparkler in a night sky, and then fizzled into blackness. The fog found its way back home and enwrapped his head, his heart. It hurt too much to think, to feel. Saying nothing, he stretched back onto the imprint on the sofa, turned the radio back on to the concerto and shut his eyes.

The woman's sobs lowered first to whimpers and finally to steady sniffles from the pile of her on the floor. He was almost asleep when the smell of apple-and-flower-laced perfume drifted him back to consciousness.

"You know, you're kind of sexy. You mind if I stay for awhile?" He opened his eyes to see her standing next to the sofa, her hair and face still disheveled, both arms bleeding from zigzagged scratches; but a teasing grin had erased any hint of sorrow or wrath.

"My name's Maya," she giggled. "What's yours?"

He studied her, seeing the cloud that controlled her in her eyes, in her smile. But he was too burrowed under his own fog to reach out and help. Or care. He turned back over on the couch and only listened as a series of curse words pelted him and a potted plant fell into jagged pieces on the floor next to him.

"You ain't all that anyway. I don't need you. I don't need any of y'all. My father used to tell me—" Fire breathed through her words. "Look, you can tell my mother I don't need her either." The door slammed.

Hours later, Gideon would still be staring at the broken ceramic pot on the floor, the jagged edges, the sharp points, beckoning to be embraced in his arms like a long-lost lover.

CHAPTER 11

Madelyn Windemere let the white lace curtain fall back into place and sat back down on the edge of her bed in the darkness of her room. She was still shaking. Nearly midnight and she had not had one wink of sleep, though she'd been wearing her floral velvet nightgown since exactly 8:45 P.M., and her pink hair rollers and black bonnet since 8:56 P.M.

She gave one last look out at the street below. Almost empty. No new lights had flicked on in the homes across the street. No curious onlookers. No crowd, no scene. Madelyn's breathing steadied as she lay back under the emerald jacquard comforter. She relaxed even more as voices and laughter rolled off a nearby bus stop. A young man shouted an obscene joke to another man down the street. More laughter.

Any other night, the talking, the laughter, the cursing would get to her, but tonight it was a comfort. With all the usual activity fluttering down an inner city street at a quarter to midnight, few people would have raised an eyebrow, or even noticed the commotion that just occurred at Madelyn's door. Commotion was common. At her front door it was not.

Maya! she wanted to scream. *Maya!* she wanted to shake her. Horror, embarrassment, shame, anger. The girl was beyond a nuisance. She was plumb crazy. Didn't she know by now that she was not welcome? It had been years since Madelyn let her youngest child into her home. Maya had left a disjointed message on the answering machine just that past Sunday, Madelyn recalled. She should have known then a major meltdown was coming.

The knocking, banging, and screaming had continued this time for ten minutes before moving on to the Joels' door. Charisma's Grand Am was gone, so she was at work, Madelyn figured; and the husband seemed to stay completely to himself so he would not have paid Maya's knocks any mind, Madelyn guessed. It had been quiet now for a while so Maya must have left, disappeared back into a world Madelyn wanted nothing to do with.

Now she was too awake to sleep, so it only made sense to make good use of the time. She had to bake three apple pies for the annual church Easter dinner three weeks away. She could bake them now and freeze them and have time to get something else done later, she reasoned. Madelyn was almost out of her bed and in her slippers when another thought occurred to her. If perchance a neighbor was up and had watched the prior scene from behind a darkened window, he or she would know that Madelyn was more than a random victim of Maya's pounding and screaming if she turned on a bedroom light now. She had to appear disassociated, unperturbed. Most people knew nothing of Maya, and those who did, well, they had not seen her in so long, they probably had forgotten.

The Egyptian cotton sheets felt cold on her skin as she cuddled back in the bed. It was nights like these that she missed Harold the most, his warmth, his stroke, his wisdom. He would have known how to handle it, how to handle her. Madelyn smiled at the thought of her late husband. With his firmly set mouth and unfaltering gaze, many people thought him stern and severe.

But Madelyn knew his smiles, his laughter. The day she gave birth to their fifth child and only daughter, Harold had carried the girl around on a satin pillow.

She blamed the girl's simpleness on his spoiling. *Harold, don't give her anything else, she's just going to break it.* Break was an inadequate word. When the fits began, Maya decimated anything she could get her hands on. The older she grew, the more varied the fits became. By the time Maya reached fourteen, she would be angry, loving, social, withdrawn, violent, hyper, imaginative, carefree, careless, depressed—all within a single hour. And whatever Maya felt, she felt and lived it extremely.

Harold would have known what to do. Madelyn winced at the still-fresh memory of Maya banging on the door just an hour earlier. Her sobs, her cries. She'd sounded like a wounded cat, animal, un-human.

Then again, Harold probably would have let her in, accepted her back, just like he wanted to do long after Madelyn kicked her out at age fifteen. As promiscuous and disrespectful as Maya had become, Madelyn could not have people thinking she was raising a whore. It was better for people not to know Maya existed than to second-guess Madelyn's mothering-skills.

"I'm a good mother. I'm a darn good mother." Madelyn blinked back hot tears in the darkness, surprised that she'd let such strong utterances come out of her mouth. "But I *am* a good mother. Look at my boys. I'm a better mother than that Charisma Joel will ever be." She took comfort in that thought, remembering Sunday when she saw Charisma going in her house with fast food takeout. What kind of Sunday dinner was that? Madelyn's sons always praised her for her home-cooked meals. That's what a good mother does. No quick fixes, lazy solutions. No takeout. Long, hard labor was necessary, Madelyn huffed.

It was Harold's fault. He'd spoiled Maya too much. And now even in death, he was giving the girl more than she deserved.

Money.

Why had he left so much for her? For Maya and not for her brothers. Sometimes Madelyn felt like Harold was trying to pay the girl back, redemption, pardon. But for what? Had he been intent on spoiling the girl even more to make up for spoiling her in the first place?

Money.

That's what Maya had been calling and screaming and crying about. She needed money to buy a new Explorer, although she did not have a driver's license. She needed money to go live in Morocco for two months. She needed money to buy a balsam model airplane kit. Money to start a $5,000 armor collection. Money to buy things she had no use for, no interest in, no ability to handle.

Madelyn was sick of the delivery trucks that came by her house several times a month with packages of copper plates or princess costumes or live animals or used books on mermaids; packages with Maya's name and Harold's estate for billing.

All this money and not a week's worth of work to show for it. Maya couldn't hold a job if it was tied to her hands. Responsibility, maturity, self-control—she knew nothing of them.

And now the girl wanted her entire inheritance in one lump sum. There was no telling what absurdity would come in a delivery truck if that ever happened.

A lawyer once told Madelyn there was a way to get complete control over Maya's share of Harold's money. With the right hospital ward and the right court, everything could change. But the idea of a written report that chronicled Maya's life and emotional capacities and promiscuity and financial irresponsibility typed up with a final conclusion stamped at the end . . . What would that say about Madelyn and her mothering abilities? Not to mention the horrific accusations Maya used to make about her dear old Harold. What kind of investigations and threats would surface if hospital officials got wind of Maya's sick lies?

After all Harold did for Maya, after all he gave that girl, and she still insisted on telling those awful lies, those horrendous stories about him? The thought of the shame and degradation that could come on the Windemere name because of Maya was unbearable, intolerable. Unacceptable.

Maya was thirteen when she first came to Madelyn with that evil, reprehensible report. And ever since that day, when Maya stood in their white carpeted living room, with the white upholstered sofa and the white drapes, and held up a pair of dirty panties for Madelyn to see, a part of her thoroughly hated the girl, her stories, and her lies.

A report, a story like that. Awful, terrible lies about what her husband Harold was doing to their daughter, Maya. What would people say? Madelyn had worked too hard to get labeled by her neighbors, church members, and friends as anything short of a virtuous wife and a good mother with a picture-perfect family.

"I *am* a good mother." Madelyn turned over in the bed just as the phone began a fresh deluge of rings. She immediately pulled the cord. "Look at my sons."

I was an only child, my mother's darling. I remember the nights in our home on North Avenue—the old North Avenue before the downward changes formed a chokehold on the endless blocks—when my mother would let me crawl up in her cherry poster queen-sized bed and let me sleep under the crisp sheets and the fuzzy velour blankets. The sheets, the blankets always smelled of Tide and Ivory. Momma would read me book after book from the Enoch Pratt Library. Stories of faraway castles, queens, princesses, knights in shining armor, lands of gold and gems, mysteries and adventures, diamonds and genies.

Indeed my own childhood bedroom was fit for a princess, a canopy bed with pink ruffles everywhere, a white dresser, and a mirrored vanity table with a matching wrought-iron stool. The first one hundred dollars Caroline Jackson made from her beauty shop was spent on my room, adding colorful borders, pale pink curtains. But as much as I loved my personal paradise, I looked forward most to the nights Momma was alone, between men, when I could get in the cherry poster bed and let the crisp, Ivory-scented sheets and velour blankets tickle my toes.

"It doesn't matter how you got here," Momma would murmur as my head lay in her lap, the smell of Royal Crown hair dressing wafting through the bedroom as she carefully parted, brushed, and braided my soft black coils, plastic beads clanking with every move. "God knew I needed you. God knew I needed a little princess to keep me smiling. That's what you are, Charisma, my dazzling princess darling." Momma would smile and dab another glob of hair oil on my scalp and I would believe her words. I was a princess. My mother was the queen.

And when my mother sharply descended her throne, I held my breath and waited for another person to take me back to happily ever after.

***

The labor on her knees was like the labor of childbirth–tears, moans, groans, sometimes understandable to nobody but God. There was the pressure, the pain, the push, and then the release, the breakthrough to something new—new hope, new life, new peace. For Pepperdine Waters, prayer was that moment, that fine line between life and death, birth and miscarriage. Laboring on her knees, Pepperdine prayed to Jesus Almighty and many a life had been reborn. *The effectual fervent prayer of a righteous man availeth much.* Pepperdine kept these sacred words from the Bible as a life mantra, quoting the verse from James when she could think of none other.

She was praying now, three o'clock in the morning, the room still and quiet except for the whispers that came out in fiery waves, ebbing in songs, rising in shouts of praise. Tears flowed down her cheeks and landed on the looseleaf papers in front of her.

Her prayer journal looked like a grocery list, names scribbled one under the other, some with dates next to them, most with scriptures, a couple circled in red. Next to the journal was an old Bible, leather-bound with thin, gold-edged pages falling out of it. Programs and bulletins from Greater Glory Worship Center were stuffed inside; a notepad was tucked in an outer pocket.

"Father," she groaned in earnest, "you know this women's retreat is needed. You know my sisters and daughters and mothers need to come away to be encouraged, need to hear a word from you. Lord, do a mighty work that weekend next month. Touch, move, transform. We need this time to come together, to be freed, to be revived."

Pepperdine grew quiet, reflecting on the planning meeting that had occurred at the church earlier that night. The menu was in place, the retreat center deposit paid, the speakers secured.

But something was missing. She felt it, couldn't put a finger on it. So she continued in prayer.

"Lord, what is it? What's missing? I feel it in the bowels of my soul that there's something that hasn't been touched, there's a mountain, a high hill, that needs to be shaken, that needs to be moved. I feel it, Lord, the highness of it, the impossibility of it, the looming darkness of it. Lord, *what* is it?" And then a thought. "Or should I be praying *who* is it? *Who* is missing? *Who* is wrestling with this mountain?"

She skimmed back through her lists, shuffled pages, some dog-eared, others brand new.

"Bring it to light, Lord. Bring that mountain to light."

And as she prayed again the phone rang, a loud, shrill ring that announces trouble in the late-night hour. She held her breath and picked it up. "Hello?"

No answer.

Pepperdine waited, listened, but only silence spoke and then whoever it was hung up.

"Jesus, I don't need a name to pray over. I've got *your* name, and that's more than enough. So whoever it is that's trying to fight a mountain, get them over victoriously, in Jesus' name."

She prayed and peace took over, but a thought still nagged her as she finally got in her bed and pulled up the covers. *Who is calling me?* It was the second time that week someone called and hung up.

She was almost asleep when the phone rang again. The jarring clang pierced the silent darkness, startling her from her rest and sending her heart thump-thumping wildly. Pepperdine fumbled blindly for the rotary phone before finally snapping on her table lamp. She reached for the bright red receiver wondering who was waiting for her on the other end.

"Hello?" Her voice was groggy, her orientation confused.

"Praise de Lawd, Sista Waters!"

"Father God, please." She was still hal
did not realize her plea was spoken out loud.

"Pepper, de Lawd done laid a song on my he
you in this midnight hour. Like He did for Paul
Silas in the jail cell, my God has put a song on my lip
and He told me that you needed to hear it."

"Deacon Caddaway—"

"Hallelujah, amen. My spirit is troubled about all the backsliders and sinners down at Greater Glory. I ain't trying to tell you what to do, but I think you got too many hypocrites in your women's ministry."

"Earnest—"

"Now take that Floretta Hines. She so busy cooking all them collard greens after service that she done forgot to repent for her murdering ways."

"Murder?"

"That's right! Hallelujah, amen! The Bible clearly states that 'Thou shalt not kill' and that 'out of the heart proceed evil thoughts and murder,' so I know that she was plotting to kill me when she put that fried chicken on my plate last Sunday. I done told her a million times that my bad heart can only take baked foods, and she still keeps right on putting them grease-dripping drumsticks in front of me to eat. Now, I know that you would never do anything like that to me, amen, hallelujah. You just like my holy Ethel, trying to stay on the straight-and-narrow path, hoping to make it in. There's just too many ungodly womenfolk down at Greater Glory and God wants you to separate yourself from them. You need to repent and join me on the right side of the war!"

"Now Earnest—"

"*I'm a soldier in the army of de Lawd.*" Deacon Caddaway's off-tune baritone voice drowned out Pepperdine's pleas as he broke out into a ten-minute rendition of his favorite song, a song he used to open every devotional, prayer, or Sunday morning service.

"Jesus, help my dear brother." Pepperdine wrote an extra note beside his name in one of her prayer journals after putting the phone receiver face-up on her nightstand. Earnest's shouts and moans continued to echo through the static. She could still hear his cries and yells of jubilation coming through the telephone line as she left the receiver on the stand, clicked off her lamp, and nestled back under her covers.

"Lord, please send that man a word, a wife, or something," she mumbled as sleep finally took over.

CHAPTER 12

Friday night came as easily as a breath of air, a quiet breath exhaling relief, hope, anxiety. For Charisma, all these things were one and the same, as lingering doubts and a troubled conscience loomed overhead.

She was meeting Dr. Logan again.

There was no doubting his intentions as he stood to greet her. Dressed flawlessly in a tailored black suit, he pulled out a chair for Charisma to sit.

"Charisma," he kissed both of her cheeks and squeezed her hands. Aftershave and spearmint gum lingered faintly in her nostrils as he pulled away.

"I'd forgotten how nice they kept this doctor's lounge." She was always amazed at the extravagant care and detail that went into the exclusive café for the MDs set on the top floor of the hospital. Like a penthouse suite, it had gracious views of the Baltimore skyline, which now, draped in darkness, looked like a constellation of twinkling streetlights and sparkling tall buildings. The plush velvet, carved metal, and heavy window treatments of the intimate dining area added to the feeling of importance. There was a brief time she'd felt at home in here.

"I'm glad you agreed to join me." Miles's gaze was long and deep, except for when the hostess, a tall blond with what looked like watermelons squeezed inside her blouse, skirted by their table. "It's so good to be able to catch up with you again. Your daughter's home?"

"Yes," Charisma fingered the multiple silver forks and spoons in front of her. The week had been quiet, relatively uneventful after Sunday's flying dinner. She felt comfortable letting April sleep in her own bed at home this time. She fought the urge to look into his hazel-brown eyes.

I shouldn't be here. I shouldn't do this. There's got to be another way to get Gideon help.

"The addresses." Miles patted down a couple of typewritten pages and placed them in front of Charisma. "I pulled together every name and address I could find."

"Addresses? Oh yeah, the addresses. Thanks, Miles." Charisma flipped through the stack wondering what else was left to talk about since he'd quickly gotten business out the way.

"You start your shift at eleven, right?" He was checking his watch.

"Yes."

"Then that leaves us slightly less than an hour. You don't look like you're that hungry. Are you?"

"No." Her words felt blank, pasted into the conversation.

"Good, because there's something I wanted to show you. C'mon."

They were on their way back down the elevator when Charisma realized where he was taking her. The doors opened, keys jingled, doors shut. More locks, more keys and keypads. Finally, they were on the unit, just outside of Dr. Logan's office. Gideon's old office. Charisma trembled as they stepped in.

"Look what I found." He looked proud, confident as he put a box down on the mahogany desk and stepped away for Charisma to see.

She took one look in and threw her hands to her face. "I have to go." She had not meant to whisper, but it was the only way to keep her words from coming out in a scream. “Thank you for the addresses, but I have to go.”

He reached out to grab her arms, but Charisma had already spun around and started down the corridor. Her purple scrubs swished forcefully as she walked as fast as she could without running.

“Charisma!”

God, please let there be an open elevator right now, she prayed and sighed with relief when a bell sounded around the corner. She nearly knocked over a cart as she pushed herself in and landed on the upholstered wall. The metal doors slammed shut.

“You really need to watch where you’re going.” A food service worker rolled his eyes at her and muttered something under his breath.

Charisma closed her eyes and exhaled. She was going to have to find another way to deal with Gideon.

Dr. Miles Logan did not know the story. She opened her eyes as the worker pushed the cart out on another floor.

She could not believe that box was still in the office. Miles did not know the story.

Now, she did not want him to ever find out.

We had a September wedding, early September, when the leaves are just beginning to brown on the edges and the heat of summer blows one last stifling breath of air. I had gone through great lengths to keep the ceremony small and intimate, no frilly extravagances. Twenty-five invitations, mostly great-aunts and second cousins from Virginia. A simple supper afterward in Pepperdine Waters’s apartment. A homemade cake, one bridesmaid (the pastor’s daughter), a gown with no train. A wedding plain, perfect, except that my mother was not there.

I allowed one indulgence: flowers. Red, orange, and bright yellow arrangements decorated the stairwell and scattered a bridal pathway through the Victorian mansion. I'd arranged for the vows to be said at the historic estate on the grounds of the Cylburn Arboretum. The trees and early autumn blossoms were a panoramic backdrop for the twenty-minute ceremony.

Gideon wore a black tux with satin trim and his eyes glittered with tears. I remember his smile quivering on one end as he repeated the words, the promises directed by the pastor. After we kissed, he took my hands and put them to his face. I can still feel the cool ruggedness of his cheeks, soft and full under my touch.

When it was all over and before we left for a resort in St. Lucia, he drove me to the hospital and took me to the top floor lounge. He left me sitting in one of the velvet couches and then reappeared with his hands behind his back.

"A box," he said. And then he gave it to me.

It was a simple cardboard box tied with jade ribbon and fresh flowers as a bow. I remember pulling the silk threads, holding my breath as I lifted up the flaps.

"This is what I'll be for you."

And he was.

At home. That's what she wanted to feel. But it was hard to feel that way in her own house. Home is not where strangers live, and Gideon had become one to her. Saturday morning, Charisma tried to make the day feel normal. Spending time with Dr. Logan, which she thought would accomplish that purpose, had left her feeling worse.

"Jesus, what do I do?" Time to get and follow direction from Him. Her plans had not helped her along. She thought of that box Gideon left in his old office—now Miles's—and shuddered.

"Jesus, what do I do?"

Gideon was downstairs so she lifted a window shade in their bedroom. The whirl of the plastic winding upward was followed by a rare blast of cleansing sunlight. It looked like a nice day to drive April to the playground—not the glass-littered, graffiti-covered one on their street, but a spacious plot of green grass and wood chips several neighborhoods over.

An hour and two McDonald's sausage biscuits later, April was sitting motionless on a swing. Charisma started to sit on the swing next to her, started to ask April what she was thinking about, but Charisma was not sure what that action, that question would accomplish. Instead, she found an empty park bench and laid out her supplies for the morning: workbooks, her Bible, a lesson plan and outline for the next day's Sunday School class.

The miracle to teach this week was Jesus healing a sick man by the pool of Bethesda. Children laughed and squealed under the late morning sun as Charisma read and re-read the first nine verses in the fifth chapter of John.

"April, do you want some ice cream?" She looked up for a moment as a crowd of young children ran toward a chiming truck. The weather was breaking. March's approaching exit had brought along an unusually warm day, and a prelude to warm spring days with it. But April did not budge from the flat plastic seat. Her eyes were on the ground. Her feet still, the swing dead.

"April?" Charisma shook her head and went back to her studies. She could understand April's apathy. It was hard to get excited about anything when most everything in life felt wrong. But what was she supposed to do? Charisma gave one last look back at the ancient Bible story and with a pang of guilt set it aside.

The invitation. She had it tucked inside her notebook. The Baltimore Metropolitan Hospital fundraising gala was a short three weeks away and the R.S.V.P. date was looming.

"I just won't answer," she mumbled, and wondered if the committee or the chairperson or whoever would notice that the response card from Dr. and Mrs. Gideon Joel was never returned. She thought of Miles and wondered what, if any, role he played in the function. The questions he might ask. The info he might be given.

She wanted to burn the box in his office, but all she had was the invitation in her hand. She crumpled it up and threw it. It landed on her open Bible.

"Why, Jesus?" Tears burned her eyes. "If you were so busy wanting to heal people back then, why can't you heal my husband's mind right now? Why won't you heal him?"

She closed her eyes to keep the tears from falling and in her mind she could see the pool of ancient Bethesda—people sick, invalid, broken, lying around the edges, desperate to get healed, waiting for an angel to move the water so they could get in and get their strength restored.

She saw the man Jesus chose. She imagined the man lying there, knees knobby, thin legs limp and twisted under him. Unshaven, unkempt, unclean. Sick, lying there, alone. Thirty-eight years of disability. And he still had hope. Thirty-eight years of sickness and solitude and infirmity, and he still held onto hope. He had stayed there at the pool. And Jesus saw him.

"Jesus, do you see my husband out of many? Do you hear my prayers out of many?"

She saw the man, the expression on his face when Jesus walked up to him—walked, something the man could not do—and asked him, "Do you want to be made well?"

What kind of question was that to ask a man who'd been alone and sick for almost four decades? Here, this Jesus who knows all things and can do all things, asking such a question. *Do you want to be made well?*

The man answered, his voice polite but pleading, *"Sir, I have no man to put me into the pool when the water is stirred up; but while I am coming, another steps down before me."*

Honest answer. Truthful answer. When he would go to get healed, others got in the way.

"Do you want to be made well?" Charisma thought on the words of Jesus. The man had to *want* to be healed; he knew what he needed and was honest enough to admit what was stopping him. Other people kept getting in the way.

Charisma picked up the invitation and smoothed down the wrinkled paper with its ribbon edges.

"Gideon, you have to want to be whole. *We* have to want to get help. And we need to know what's keeping our family from getting well and not let anything get in the way of your healing. Our healing. I can't let other people and what they might think or do get in the way."

Get help. Seemed like an easy answer. That's what she wanted, that's even what she'd been trying to do through Miles Logan. What was missing? She read through the passage again. Honesty. The man who had been sick for thirty-eight years was honest with Jesus, a stranger to him, about what had kept him ill for so long.

Openness. Honesty.

There's no shame in your mother's condition. Charisma could hear Gideon's voice from years ago, that day in his office when he put a name to her mother's depression. But putting a name to her mother's illness was different from putting a name to his. He was Dr. Gideon Joel. He was supposed to be the answer to her questions. *I came looking for* answers, *not a job, not him.* It was time to get answers now, a name to his condition.

There is a Name that is above all names and at the Name of Jesus, every knee should bow.

Get help. There's still hope. Whatever name is put on Gideon will not be above the Name of Jesus. And Jesus is the one who could spot a sick man among many.

Jesus said to him, "Rise, take up your bed and walk." And immediately the man was made well, took up his bed, and walked.

Get help. A decision had to be made. Immediately. Charisma closed all her workbooks, notes, her Bible, and put it all back into her tote bag. Only the invitation and her cell phone remained. She dialed slowly one number that came to mind, one number that had no strings attached, no ulterior motives, no pricks in her conscience.

"Hello." Pepperdine Waters answered the phone.

"Sister Waters, it's Charisma." She felt her heart beating faster.

"Charisma. How are you doing, baby? We missed you at the retreat planning meeting Tuesday night? Is everything okay?"

Charisma could hear what sounded like hot oil sizzling in the background. She imagined Pepperdine standing over her stove in a flowery housecoat with floured drumsticks in her hand.

"Is everything okay?" Pepperdine asked again.

Such a normal life, Charisma thought, frying chicken on a Saturday afternoon. Children playing in the park, eating ice cream, laughing. Mothers watching toddlers waddle around barefoot in the grass. Boys playing basketball on blacktop courts, slapping backs, high fives. Normal.

"Charisma?"

"Yes, Sister Pepperdine," she cleared her throat. Open. Honest. "I wanted your opinion." She fingered the invitation in her hand. Black-tie, it said. "I—my husband and I have been invited to an event at the hospital he used to work at, but I don't think they realize . . . I'm not sure how to respond—"

"Your husband, Gideon! He's a doctor, a psychiatrist, right? I haven't seen him in so long, I forgot!"

"Yes, I mean, he used to work at Baltimore Metro, but . . ." Charisma shut her eyes. *Do you want to be made well?* "But . . ."

"I heard he was a mighty big doctor down there at BMH. What's he in, private practice now?"

Open. Honest. The man told Jesus what was keeping him from his healing. But he was still there by the pool. He had hope. After thirty-eight years he was still there.

"Yes." She answered with such conviction, she wanted to believe it was true herself. "He's in private practice now. Between his patients and conferences I hardly even see him myself," Charisma forced out a laugh.

"Mm, mm, mm. A black man doing great things in this world. That's so wonderful! We should have him come speak sometime and encourage the young people. Better yet, Charisma, that's it! We could have him speak at the women's retreat. I think that's the missing piece in our plans. As a people, and especially in the church, we don't talk too much about mental illness."

"So you want Gideon to speak at the retreat? That's a thought." Charisma wanted to scream.

"I read somewhere that one out of every six adults in America has a mental disorder. I don't even know what the numbers are for our people who are less likely to get help or treatment. I'm sure there are mothers, daughters, sisters, and wives in our church who know the truth of those statistics firsthand."

"Probably . . ."

"It might be good to get both medical and spiritual insight from your husband in a retreat setting where women are more likely to be open and honest about such an issue. I know it's kind of last minute, but what's the best way to formally contact your husband?"

Open and honest.

Charisma shook, scrambling for a response. "He can't do it, I'm sorry. I just realized the fundraising gala is the same weekend as the retreat."

"That's right, the gala. I'm sorry, honey, that's why you called me in the first place. What opinion did you need, sweetheart?"

"I, uh, just wanted to know . . . if you think yellow is appropriate for a black-tie event."

"Yellow? Like you had on Sunday? Honey, I don't know all the rules and protocol on such matters, but if that's what you want to wear, and you feel beautiful in it, then don't let nothing hinder you."

Don't let nothing hinder you.

"Thank you, Sister Pepperdine. And I'm so sorry I'll be missing the retreat."

"I am too, but you do what you have to do to keep your husband shining. You shine, too, baby."

"Thank you." She was ready to go.

"Oh, Charisma, by any chance, did you call me earlier this week? I've gotten a couple of phone calls and the connection or something hasn't been good."

"No, I haven't called. That wasn't me."

"Alrighty then. See you tomorrow."

Charisma hung up the phone and threw it and the invitation in her bag next to her Bible. "April, time to go."

CHAPTER 13

She was waiting for him in the parking lot at his home. It was just getting dark. Miles pulled his red BMW convertible into his assigned space and never saw her coming. Today she wore a sweatshirt and sweatpants and her hair was gone. Cut down to a knotty half-inch all over her head. She fell to her knees as he opened the car door.

"Miles, I'm sorry. I love you and I don't want you to hate me. Please forgive me and tell me you still love me. I want to live." She clung to the cuffs on his pants.

"Maya, get up." He grabbed her wrists, noticing for the first time several scars on them. He pulled her up eye level with him.

"You are the best. I knew you would forgive me." She laid her head on his shoulder before he pushed her away.

"Maya, listen. You need help. There are some things going on with you, and I don't know who let it get this far without treatment, but today, you are going to get some help."

"Help?" She jerked her head back and the smoke began rising. "I don't need help. I don't know what you're talking about." She crossed her arms and waited. Miles did not miss the quick streak of fear, doubt, worry, shame that flashed in her eyes.

"Look, I think you might benefit from sitting down and talking with a doctor, a counselor, a therapist, somebody."

"I don't need another doctor. I have you." She tried to lock her fingers in his. "If you think something's wrong with me, then you be the one to help me. You're, like, the best doctor in the world. I'd love to be your patient. C'mon, Miles, let's go play doctor." She forced his fingers on her chest. He'd forgotten how good that chest felt, but he did not let his fingers linger.

"No, Maya. I can't be the one to help you. It wouldn't be . . . right."

"Oh, I see," Maya smiled a full smile and winked. "We can't let a professional relationship mingle with our personal one."

"Maya, we don't have a relationship. Now, here, take this card and call this number today to get some help." He thrust a business card into her hand, the number of a colleague who worked in a mental health clinic on the west side of town, ten miles from Baltimore Metropolitan Hospital. "Tell Rosa I sent you."

"What do you mean we don't have a relationship? You're everything to me and I'm supposed to be everything to you!" She tore up the card. "There's nothing wrong with me. You're the one with the problem if you can't see how good I am for you."

"Maya—"

"I hate you!"

Before another word could be said, Maya picked up a rock and threw it at the car door window. The glass had barely finished shattering at Miles's feet when Maya picked one particularly large shard and threw it at his cheek.

"I can pay for that," she spoke sweetly, as if she were talking about treating him to a meal and not replacing a window or fixing his face. "I have a lot of money, and I'm about to get the rest of what belongs to me. Don't worry. Just promise that you'll never leave me. Don't you think I'm worth it?" She pecked his cheek where blood was beginning to pool and then took off.

Miles stared at the glass scattered around his feet and on the beige leather inside his car. He wiped his face with the back of his hand and looked at the blood that covered it like wet paint. He took out his cell phone and dialed 911. Within minutes, a peace order had begun processing and a warrant was issued for Maya's arrest.

All of them saw it in the window, but I was the one who gasped. A glass sculpture with shades of blue, green, and turquoise, large as a man's hand, flowing, with no beginning or end.

An embrace.

The figurine in the window of the boutique in Southern France was the final masterpiece of a nineteenth century artist who died too soon, the small woman at the counter had explained in broken English. She wore a colorful kerchief around her head and a matching apron. Most of the wares and knick-knacks in her store were made of wood, straw, and earth—materials taken from the French countryside from which they were wrought.

It was three months before our wedding, Gideon's first international speaking engagement. Dr. Miles Logan was also a guest speaker at the conference in Nice. The three of us, along with a couple of women friends Miles talked into coming, stayed in a four-bedroom villa not too far from the French Riviera. I had my own bedroom with a terrace that offered views of rolling green, small villages, fields of flowers, vineyards.

That day, the last day of the extended weekend trip, the five of us toured museums, ate Salade Niçoise and fruit de mer at a quiet café and walked through a flower market. The boutique was on the way back to our rented car, a small window front tucked on an isolated residential street.

All of us saw it, but I was the one who gasped. The colored glass, centered and forefront in the window display, splintered light and attention away from the other charms around it. I stepped in first as a wind chime announced our entrance into the one-room shop.

"Enserrer." *The shopkeeper held the delicate glass to the light as she read the inscribed name off its bottom. "Surround, Hold, Hug Tightly" was the English equivalent she offered in broken speech.*

I remember taking the glass in my hands, using a finger to trace the exact smoothness of the embrace, a circle unbroken between two faceless figures, one above the other. "Beautiful," I breathed the words as a single ray of sunlight shone through it, making the greens and blues a sea of color; the brilliance, the sparkle of the French Riviera's turquoise water trapped in solid glass.

"How much?" Gideon asked with a calculating eye.

"7,500 euros."

"Are you kidding?" Miles's laugh shook the shop. "That's, what, around $10,000? For a glass paperweight?" His laugh rolled like waves, and the two women with him tittered lightly on either side.

"Thank you." Gideon grimaced as he took my hand. I shrugged my shoulders and shook my head.

"$10,000 for a glass paperweight. That's crazy." I tried to sound convincing and fought to keep my eyes off the small figurine as the woman nestled it back on

the window shelf. "Crazy," I muttered again as our car jumped into gear.

Three months later, after our wedding and before we left for a resort in St. Lucia, Gideon drove me to Baltimore Metropolitan Hospital and took me to the top floor lounge. He left me sitting in one of the velvet couches and then reappeared with his hands behind his back.

"A box," he said. And then he gave it to me.

It was a simple cardboard box tied with jade ribbon and fresh flowers as a bow. I pulled the silk threads, holding my breath as I lifted up the flaps.

"This is what I'll be for you."

Silent, I smiled as I held the glass out in front of me. In the dim candlelit room, the blue and green sparkled and shimmered like the city lights twinkling just beyond the curtains.

"Gideon" was all I could say.

I would eventually place the glass on the mantle in the living room of our home, the home he had built for me in Columbia, with four bedrooms and three full baths. Every day I looked at Enserrer *over the fireplace, brilliant over the flames. Every day I gazed at the embrace.*

And then there was the day Dr. Miles Logan came over.

Nighttime had already descended when Charisma pulled onto Marigold Street. The old Grand Am buckled to a stop right in front of their house.

"April, finish your cheeseburger before we go inside." Charisma closed her eyes and lay her head back on the seat, listening to the laughter, talking, and shouts of neighbors on doorsteps, stoops, and behind brick row home walls.

"We're going to get help," she whispered. Her eyes opened and fell on April, who looked back with a puzzled look on her face and mustard on her lips.

"It's going to be okay, baby girl." Charisma used a napkin to blot off the mustard. "Are you finished? We need to go inside and talk to Daddy."

April stopped chewing and Charisma could see her legs and arms stiffen. "Tell you what, why don't you go play jump rope with Shaneeda and them over there and I'll call you in for bed in a few minutes." She pointed to a group of girls perched under a streetlamp just down the street. Their voices were synchronized in a playful rhyme as a whirling rope kept the beat.

"Do I have to?" April's stiff arms and legs did not loosen any as she eyed the girls.Before Charisma could answer, a loud rap sounded on the glass window.

"Charisma, what are you doing in there? Do you plan on staying in your car all night?"

Madelyn Windemere had a broom in her hand and a frown on her face as the mother and daughter both got out of the car.

"Good evening, Mrs. Windemere. How have you been? I haven't spoken to you in a while." Charisma tried to keep her voice and smile even.

"That's right, we haven't spoken, and there are some things we need to talk about."

Charisma ushered April along as Madelyn followed them to their front door.

"Now, I'm tired of asking you to cut down that dried-up bush that's falling onto my steps. It's old and rotten and sending ants and dead caterpillars on my front walk and messing up my rose bushes. And that tree in your backyard keeps spilling bright red berries all over the place, and I'm tired of washing that juice up twice a day. When are you going to get rid of it?" She had one hand on her hip and used the other to balance the broom and clench her green housecoat tighter around her bosom.

"I'm sorry about the berries, Mrs. Windemere. I'm working on getting someone to get rid of it soon. Maybe April can help you sweep sometimes."

The girl was half-hidden behind Charisma, but nobody missed the rolling eyes.

"Are you going to do something about that?" Madelyn pointed an accusing finger at April before turning the finger back to Charisma.

"Look, this is the last time I'm going to say this, but you need to take better care of your property. You work nights, so you can do something about it during the day instead of disappearing with your daughter all the time. Where are you always running off to anyway? That's no way to act with a husband at home. What's he doing in there?" She moved her head and strained to see around Charisma through the slightly cracked door. "What is that smell? And why is that girl still out so late at night? She should have taken a bath and gone to bed hours ago."

Madelyn did not wait for an answer but instead jerked her broom back into action. "I tell you, you young mothers these days embarrass me. At least you keep pretty flowers on your porch."

"C'mon, April," Charisma finally nudged. She never knew how to deal with Madelyn's complaints and inquiries.

"That was a compliment I just gave you. You need to say thank you." Madelyn's words fell on Charisma's back. She turned around and gave a weak smile as Madelyn's barrage continued. "You ought to be glad I haven't called the police about all that music blasting from your house. You're going to make me and that little girl of yours go deaf before it's all over with.

Young mothers." Madelyn turned around with a huff and resumed sweeping down her walkway.

"Good night, Mrs. Windemere. Say goodnight, April."

April rolled her eyes again and stepped into the house. Charisma sighed, chose to let April slide, and followed her in, closing the door behind them. The house did have an odor. Stale, rotten, old, dirty. She flicked on the lights and just as quickly a figure on the couch jumped up and flicked the lights back off, but not before she saw the usual clutter, the piles, the stacks, the trash.

"I told you, leave the lights alone." The whisper was weak. The smell was strong.

Charisma did not feel like fighting.

Well after midnight, Maya still stayed hidden behind a cement block in an underground parking lot not too far from her Mount Vernon studio. She peeked back through a gate. The police car was still there.

Darnit. Why did Miles have to go there? Or maybe it was her mother who made the police come get her. She'd tried calling Madelyn after she left Miles bleeding in the parking lot, but the moment she'd said something to her mother about broken glass and blood, the woman hung up.

She was sick of it. Sick of them. Maybe it was time to go start a new life somewhere else. Yeah, that's what she would do. Catch a bus to New York or Dallas or San Diego or Boise and take on a new name and a new life. Somewhere far and exotic. She would become a real estate agent and wear black eyeglasses and carry a briefcase stacked with business cards and housing brochures. Or maybe she'd learn tap and ballet and open her own dance studio on a large tree-lined boulevard somewhere. Or better yet, she'd become a cop and carry a gun and come back and arrest the bastards trying to get her now.

Maya smiled at plan number three, imagining herself in a black uniform, her hair pulled back in a short ponytail under a shiny cap. Wait, she had no hair to pull back into a ponytail. A frown formed on her face when she remembered she spent the morning trying to see how she would look if she'd been a man. She'd used a pair of kitchen shears to cut off as much of her hair as she could, leaving behind an uneven teeny-weeny afro.

"Hello, my name is Myron Windemere." She made her voice deep and throaty, like her father's used to sound when he first woke up. "No, Mason Winona. My name is Mason." She put a Southern twang in her words and let out a loud laugh.

"Ma'am, are you okay?" A short, balding, toffee-colored man with thick glasses walked toward her. He was shining a flashlight and wearing an orange vest that glowed in the early morning darkness. "Turner's Parking" was sewn onto his jacket sleeve.

"I'm fine, good sir." Maya kept the deep voice but couldn't stop laughing. The man looked her up and down with no humor in his eyes.

"We're closed, miss. You can't stay down here."

"But *I* am not here. *I* am Mason Winona."

"Look, I don't care who you are, or what you are. All I know is that you need to get out of this here garage before I call the police for trespassing."

"Police?" Maya shrieked. "No, not you too. Oh God, I want to die. Everybody wants me to go to jail. I didn't do nothing, you hear? Nothing!"

She had to get out of there. She had to get away. She searched for breath to get out her next words.

"I'm leaving," she whispered deep in the man's ear.

"I'm leaving and I'm never coming back. You can tell them all I said that. I'm leaving, but not before I get my money. I'm getting all of what belongs to me. All of it."

Then she took off. She would have to leave everything she owned back in her studio. Start from scratch. But she was on a mission, like a spy, a superhero. Superheroes were like magic. They didn't need bags and clothes and suitcases. They had special powers to help them do what they had to do.

Maya ran out of a back entrance and looked to the right and then to the left. The downtown streets were nearly deserted except for a few cars waiting at a stoplight half a block down.

The subway station. That's where she would go. She had enough change in her pocket to ride the train back and forth for a while to give her time to finish her plans. The theme music from *Mission: Impossible* played in her head as she ran barefoot to the Lexington Market subway station several blocks away. She'd left her tennis shoes on the bus coming back from Miles's house. Too girly looking, the pink and white Nikes.

She was Mason Winona. Defender of all evil. Rectifier of all wrong. And the first mission on her agenda was getting the rest of her money from her mother. All of it, the entire $100,000 appreciating trust fund her father had left her at his death over ten years ago.

It was Sunday, 2:37 A.M., a lighted clock on a bank building read. She gave herself a day, exactly twenty-four hours, to be sitting on a bus, any motorcoach bus leaving the depot on Haines Street. Twenty-four hours to get what belonged to her. Twenty-four hours to set the record straight.

And, she decided, if her mother or Miles or anybody else for that matter tried to get in her way, she'd do something they would all regret.

Make them sorry. Make them pay for not loving her the way she deserved to be loved.

CHAPTER 14

Charisma drifted in and out of sleep. First a car door slam and laughter somewhere down the street jerked her consciousness for a brief second. Then the ping of a toaster oven next door. Finally a bird. In Charisma's sleeping mind, the bird had become part of a dream, soft chirps then louder, stronger squawks that tore at her eardrums until she realized it was not a bird waking her, but a voice.

"Mommy! Mommy!"

Charisma sat up instantly and grabbed the pair of hands that were reaching out to her. April crawled into the bed and snuggled her face into the warm scent of Charisma's cotton nightshirt.

"Another bad dream?" Charisma smoothed down the uncontrollable bangs that topped her daughter's face. April gave a deep nod, clutching a lumpy pillow.

"Everything's okay, sweetie." Charisma kissed the girl's forehead before collapsing back down on her own pillow. Loud snores from Gideon ascended from the living room sofa. "It's Sunday. Let's go get ready for church." She sat back up, stretched and extended a foot to the bare hardwood floor.

"I don't want to go."

"Excuse me?" Charisma jerked her head back. She'd never heard April's voice sound so defiant.

"Mommy," this time tears laced the plea, "please don't make me go today. I'm tired of Kayla and Antoinette asking me where my daddy is. Mommy, please can we stay home? Just this once?"

Charisma took her foot out of her slipper and took her daughter's head in her hands.

"I know it's been kind of bad these days with your father . . . acting so weird, but I promise you, everything is about to get better." Charisma fought back tears, wondering how much the eleven-year-old, twelve in a few weeks, understood Gideon's moodiness, how she interpreted his actions, how she felt herself.

"Tell you what, sweetie, we're going to stay home today, just this once, so Mommy can talk to Daddy. Everything is going to change now, I promise you." Charisma wiped the single tear rolling down April's face. "Stay right here. Go back to sleep. Mommy's going to go take care of everything."

Charisma watched as April disappeared under the heavy blue comforter. She grabbed her slippers, her bathrobe, and tightened the belt around her waist.

"Okay, Lord, this is it. I want us to be whole." She took a deep breath and turned toward downstairs.

Our first home—the one he built for me in Columbia—had large bay windows that offered views of the suburban neighborhood in all directions. Green, flowers, driveways. Gideon surprised me with the brand-new home the day after I told him I was pregnant. It was a spec home, nearly ready to move in, offered by an esteemed custom builder. All I had to do was pick the kitchen cabinetry colors, the powder room spigot, and the wall paint—a welcomed task after being crammed as newlyweds in our small apartment in a quiet section of northwest Baltimore.

A fairy tale, really, that home, those years of my life were. And like a fairy tale, it was a whimsical, almost fantasy-like experience. I felt awkward, out of place the entire time. Trying to entertain, be pretty, be witty for his constant flow of important guests. I survived by pretending that I was my mother before depression. I tried to live up to my name in her honor. Her charm, her grace was mine, except that I stayed just off-center, unnoticed in a way my mother never would have been. I imagined, I pretended, I acted, and I dressed my always quiet April in fancy clothes like my mother had dressed me, her always quiet child.

I'd done the house in sunny yellow and white, sewing curtains and painting picture frames, embellishing lamp shades, and hanging artwork from Brenda Joysmith and Charles Bibbs. Every day I polished the cherry wood furniture in my living room and dusted off the glass sculpture on the mantle. Enserrer.

We had been living there for less than a year the day Dr. Miles Logan knocked on my front door. Gideon was working late at the hospital in his quest to outdo Dr. Logan for the coveted permanent position on the Howard G. Phillips Unit. The current chair would be retiring in a couple of years, and Gideon and Miles both knew the esteemed psychiatric department only had room for one African American showpiece, one spot for a prized psychiatrist of color.

They were friends, partners, back-scratchers, backstabbers.

"Nice house," Miles nodded as he stood in the living room, hands locked behind his back. I held out a silver tray of butter cookies, the tray a hand-me-down from Momma, the old Momma. The Momma who used to love to entertain and put out fancy dishes and platters. Momma before depression. April slept quietly in her crib upstairs.

"Are these originals?" Miles fingered the framed paintings on the living room walls, gazing at them before gazing at me. I remember shifting under his stare. He noticed.

"No, not yet. One day we'll be able to afford the originals. I'm fine with what we have here already." My eyes drifted to the mantle. Enserrer.

"Ah, the glass paperweight. I forgot about that." With large fingers he picked up the delicate glass, turning it over and around in his hands like it was a plastic ball. I did not like the way he held it, but I did not move from my place.

"That's not a glass paperweight." I knew I sounded defensive. "That's a $10,000 French sculpture named Enserrer. *It is an embrace, a hug. See the figures, the one over the other, the closeness, the continuity. That is what Gideon said he would be to me." I said the last words with certainty, confidence, silver tray still in hand.*

"Will be what to you? Glass that breaks and shatters at the wrong move, that cuts and pierces when you get too close? Or will he be a weight that holds you down, traps you, buries you beneath him?" He was smiling when he spoke, a mocking smile, a teasing smile.

"It is not a glass paperweight." I turned away. He stepped closer.

"Charisma, don't be upset. I'm not trying to upset you," he still smiled. "I'm sorry. Have I ruined it for you? Did I mess up your memories? Here, let me give you a new memory to consider when you look at your glass paperweight."

And before I could make sense of his words, his lips were on mine. Large, heavy, forceful, and then soft, long, wet. I pushed him away.

"There. You have your new memory. Every time you look at your glass paperweight, you'll think of Gideon, and what he is to you. And then you'll remember me."

He didn't stay for the cookies. He left, and Gideon came home an hour later.

Those were the blue sky days, the years when the clouds stayed quietly at the edges. I often told April about how Gideon gave Enserrer *to me on our wedding day. I smiled when I told the story, as if the happy memories would somehow subtract the other ones. When the downpours began, Dr. Miles Logan was several states away at another hospital, the starring black psychiatrist on another unit. Gideon was the chairman on Howard G. Phillips.*

When the downpours began, I asked Gideon to keep the statue in his office on the unit.

"When you need a good thought, you'll have this to look at," I told him.

I did not want the thoughts. I did not want the memories. And as far as I was concerned, Dr. Logan would never know what Gideon had become to me.

CHAPTER 15

Pepperdine Waters tapped her foot along to the melody, sung a few notes, then settled back in her seat when the song was over and the pastor retook the podium. From her seat behind the first lady in the pews of Greater Glory, she could make out the usual flurry of activity on the choir stand—candy passing, fans flapping, whispering, giggles. The restlessness among the purple and white robes matched the unrest in her soul. Something was wrong. Very wrong.

Ever since she spoke with Sister Charisma Joel the day before, she'd had an uneasiness that would not go away. She tried to pray about it, read some Scripture on it, hoped the Sunday morning service would usher away the bad feeling. The fact that Charisma had called out on her Sunday School class and skipped the 11:00 A.M. service made her more uncomfortable.

"Church, I will be speaking to you today from the texts of Second Corinthians 12:7–10 and First Samuel one, verses one through twenty. Turn with me in your Bibles to those passages." The pastor stood contemplatively and took a quick sip of water as the sanctuary filled with the sound of many pages turning.

It was like putting two and two together, Pepperdine reasoned to herself as her own fingers spread down the pages of her Bible and served as bookmarks. Two and two should equal four. But something with Charisma wasn't adding up right. If her husband was doing so well as an internationally known doctor, why was she always so excited to receive another bag of hand-me-downs from the church's Helping Hands ministry? And why would she be living in a row home on one of the worst blocks of Marigold Street? Pepperdine had never been to her house, but as church secretary, she had access to all of the congregants' phone numbers and addresses. She'd mailed Charisma plenty of birthday, Christmas, and thinking-of-you cards and the like.

"For a topic, a theme, if you will, I'd like to use the title 'When God Says Yes and When God Says No.'" The pastor adjusted the microphone on the lectern.

Maybe she had been too forward yesterday. Pepperdine dated a piece of paper to take notes as she continued to speculate. Charisma had called her for a reason, and she'd been so eager to engage the young woman and show care and concern and support that she never really gave her a chance to talk. Maybe she should have just listened instead of jumping to so many conclusions and bombarding her with so many questions.

She wanted to kick herself for asking if Gideon could speak at the women's retreat. They usually have women speakers on such occasions anyway. Maybe Charisma was offended that Pepperdine asked to borrow him right after Charisma had clearly stated she hardly saw him herself. And then Pepperdine had gone on and on with all those statistics and numbers, trying to impress her, trying to let the wife of such an extraordinary psychiatrist know that she, with only a high school diploma to her name, knew a little something too. Pepperdine closed her eyes and swallowed her guilt as the unease continued to rise.

"We see two prayers in these texts, two people crying out to God in desperation, begging, pleading with God. In one case it's a prayer of addition. Hannah, barren and grieving, is asking God to give her a son. The other prayer is one of subtraction. The apostle Paul tells us he prayed in earnest for God to remove 'a thorn in the flesh,' some kind of undisclosed infirmity, a weakness, a pain, a hardship. Two people, two prayers, and two different answers."

What should she do, Pepperdine sighed. What prayer, what fast, what action should she take? Something wasn't right and the uneasiness wasn't bestowed on her without reason. She knew she had to do something. The preacher's gravelly voice spoke over her thoughts.

"Now I know that both of these prayers were pleas of desperation. Paul said he went to God *three* times and begged that the splinter would depart from him. And I guarantee you Hannah's prayer in First Samuel chapter one was not the first time she had gone to the Father in tears. She'd been barren for years, vexed and teased about her condition. I'm convinced she had some talks with Jesus at least a few times before then."

"Don't I know it!" A woman with a tall, feathery hat shouted from the front row. A few other yells and claps began to warm up the sanctuary.

"Let me pause here and give a word on desperation."

"Well," someone else cut through the pastor's words.

"Sometimes God will wait for that last, deep, desperate prayer before He answers. He'll wait until you have come to the end of yourself, reached your last leg, your wit's end, when you have nothing left but a mustard seed-sized faith and tears to eat, like Hannah, who the Bible says was 'in bitterness of soul and wept sore.' Those around her could not even understand why she was so sad, so desperate."

Pepperdine scanned the congregation one last time. Maybe Charisma had come in late. Nope. No sign of her or her daughter.

"I tell you, church," the pastor boomed, "I'm sure Hannah had prayed for a child many a time before, but that last prayer—that last one of final desperation—"

"Say it!" Shouts heated the sanctuary.

"—When she did not care how she looked in church—"

"Halleluiah!" another woman cried.

"—Crying and pleading before the Lord so desperately that the priest Eli dismissed her as a drunk. I tell you, church, it was that last prayer, when she poured out her soul before the Lord—"

"Jesus!" A man shouted from the balcony.

"That prayer of desperation, *that's* the one God answered! And then she bore a son and dedicated him to the Lord and His work. See, God hears prayers of desperation." The pastor mopped his head, cleared his throat, and waited for the congregation to settle.

"'But wait a minute,' I hear some of you saying. 'Wait a minute, Pastor. Did not Paul pray a prayer of desperation? Didn't he earnestly beg and plead for God to reverse his situation?' Didn't he pray, children? 'Why didn't God answer?' I hear some of you asking." The pastor chuckled. The woman on the front row fell to her knees with a loud sob.

"Oh, but He did answer, church. Paul says God gave Him an answer. The Lord told him, 'My grace is sufficient for you; for My strength and power are made perfect in weakness.' To which Paul responded, 'Therefore I will rather glory in my weaknesses and infirmities that the power of Christ may rest on me because,' say it with me church, 'when I am weak, *then* am I strong.' At the pinnacle of your perplexity, God is all-powerful. Jesus Himself is our Strength and our Redeemer. Say amen, church!"

Cries and moans thundered through the aisles and the balcony. Pepperdine wiped a tear from the corner of her eye as a rushing wind seemed to blow through the medium-sized congregation. The stained-glass windows of the gray-stoned building rattled under the worship. The pastor waited for a pause in the outcry.

"See, when you've prayed a prayer of desperation and God says yes, like He did to Hannah, there's glory. A seed of life is planted in the womb of your spirit and great things are birthed in and through you, and you are strong. Halleluiah!

"But when God says no, I'm not going to change your situation, like He said to Paul, there's a *greater* glory. Halleluiah! On this one, God says, 'You're going to have to depend on *Me*.' Where you are weak and infirmed that's where *He's* strong. Halleluiah! So if God says yes or if God says no, blessed be the name of the Lord! On the one hand, He gives a glory you can see; on the other, He gives a glory others can see on you!"

Fire breathed through the church and almost everybody was dancing in their seats and in the aisles. Even Pepperdine, with her arthritic knee, came to a stand and stomped a foot in unison with the shouts of praise around her.

"An answer," she felt it. "An answer, as usual, somewhere in those sacred words." She did not know exactly what, how, or why, but she knew the day's sermon was one CD she had to buy. After the benediction, she was one of the first in line at the church bookstore and media center.

"A CD please." She slammed a five-dollar bill on the counter. "No, make that two." She dug through her wallet.

"Hold on to the rest of your money. The second one's on me." The store clerk, an older man with gray whiskers and dark freckles on his face, put two CDs in Pepperdine's hands. "That word was so good today, I know somebody else out there needs to hear it."

"You're telling the truth, Brother Anderson." She grinned a large, wide smile, showing off several gold fillings. And in a quieter voice spoke, "And I know just who needs it." She tucked the CDs in her purse and headed for the church office. She wanted to call Charisma first to make sure she was home before she stopped by.

CHAPTER 16

They were sitting in the kitchen, the two of them, husband and wife. April sat quietly on the steps, nearly out of view, hands folded, watching, waiting, almost unnoticed in the living room. The smell of Ajax and Joy detergent wafted through the downstairs as the kitchen sink, empty and clean, reflected distorted images of Charisma and Gideon hunched over the small table.

The sink was shining; little else had changed. Charisma swatted at a fruit fly then re-clutched her husband's hand.

"So, are you going to call for an appointment? I can call for you if you like."

Gideon dug his head in his hands. "I'm embarrassed, Care."

Charisma swallowed hard at Gideon's old nickname for her. When was the last time she'd heard that? She could not remember.

Gideon pressed his hands deeper into his forehead as he continued to speak. "How can I go see another psychiatrist in this city, in this state, anywhere in this world without someone talking? I'm known in my field. I'm seen as an expert. A lot of people have respect for me. How do I explain where I am right now?"

"Where are you?" Her whisper was soft.

"Baby, I'm depressed. I've been depressed. I've been fighting depression for as long as I can remember, and now it's just too much. I can't stop feeling this way. Most of the time, I don't even want to live."

"Gideon, I—"

"No, listen, Charisma. You have no idea what this is like for me. Yes, you went through this with your mother, and I never meant to bring you down this road with me, but there's no doctor I can see, no unit for me to go where somebody hasn't heard of me. The medical community talks, Care, and if they find out how low I've gotten, I'll never be respected again. You see how nobody from Baltimore Metropolitan Hospital even talks to me anymore. They don't even talk about me, like I never existed. I'm a shame to them, a mark."

"Gideon, those are just wrong, evil thoughts that the enemy has you believing." She wondered if she should tell him about the invitation.

"Charisma, I don't know if it's Satan or just me. All I know is that my career is over, and I don't know why my life shouldn't be over as well. I'm down, baby, I'm down. I just need more faith, that's all I need. Jesus, Jesus. Healing in the name of Jesus." His hands covered his face. Charisma studied the faint glimmer of the gold wedding ring on his finger. "Things are rough right now. You're depressed, severely depressed, but like you told me with my mother, that's nothing to be ashamed of. It's something to get help for. And getting help is worth it because I need you as a husband, and April needs you as a father." She glanced back to the living room, where she could see only April's knees peeking from the steps, her hands a tight ball on her still lap.

"I understand," she continued. "You're embarrassed because you want to be seen as the helper, not the victim; the doctor, not the patient. Don't let that pride get in the way of our family getting whole. Nobody will look down on you for getting yourself better. We need you better, Gideon. Our house is a mess, and April and I are tired of walking on pins and needles around you.

We need to resume a normal, regular, functioning life. You can't get so upset when I want to clean up or bring food home. Why don't you find someone you can talk to? And what about those pills you've been keeping on the table?"

"No!" His shout made April jump in the other room. He quickly lowered his voice. "I mean, I'm sorry, Charisma." He shook and flinched at her touch. "It's just, if I take that medicine, it will mean I'm not trusting God for deliverance, right?"

"Gideon, you told me yourself that God can use science and medicine and counseling to get His healing through. Healing is right there. It ain't that He's holding it back from you. Sometimes, you just got to go get it. If you had a headache, you'd take Tylenol. If you had strep throat, you'd take an antibiotic. If you're as depressed as you say you are, it's okay to take medicine to feel better. You've told countless patients that. Why can't you receive that for yourself?"

"You don't understand. I need to do this my way. I promise, I'll get better. I promise. Just let me do this my way."

"They want you to speak." The words blurted out.

"Speak? Who? What are you talking about?"

"The invitation." Charisma closed her eyes and shook her head. "You got an invitation in the mail a few weeks ago for the hospital's one hundredth-year celebration gala and fundraiser. You and I are invited, and they want you to speak." The card was in her tote bag at the other end of the table. She took it out, smoothed the ribbons, traced the embossed letters, showed him. "See, you're still respected. You're depressed, Gideon, but you've never stopped being a great man."

Gideon's fingers trembled as he took the invitation. "I can't . . . Oh, God . . . What do I say . . ."

"Miles will be there too." His name felt sinful on her tongue. Gideon's eyes darkened.

"I forgot about him. I heard they gave him my position. Have you seen him at the hospital?"

Charisma did not know how to answer.

"Of all people . . ." Gideon shook his head, "He can't know . . . Charisma, I'm going to accept that invitation. I'm going to go down to the hospital tomorrow to accept the invitation personally. They put me on medical leave for undisclosed health reasons. The last time they saw me was when I locked myself in my office for four days. I have to go there in person so they can see there's nothing wrong with me. I have to accept the invitation. This is the only way for me to get out of this, to reclaim my sanity, Care. This is the only way I have a chance at getting back my career, getting back my income. I'm going to get you a nice house again, Charisma, a better life, I promise. Tomorrow, I have to show BMH that I'm fine. " There was finality in his words.

"Tomorrow?" Charisma studied her husband. Sitting at the table, unshaved, unclean, unkempt, a blue bathrobe hanging off his bare bones, hair dirty, knotty, bushy, uncombed. Ash, pallor. "Tomorrow?" she blinked. "Won't that mean leaving the house? You haven't done that in nine months."

She could see Gideon freeze, his arms and legs stiffen. She watched as he licked then bit a dry, cracked lip.

"Tomorrow," he whispered, the finality weakened.

"Gideon, don't you think you should first—"

"Let me do this my way!" Gideon slammed both fists on the table.

"I just think—"

"Charisma, please!" Panic filled his voice. "Let me do this or let me die!"

The phone was ringing. As Charisma left the kitchen to answer it, she gave April a thumbs up. The girl rolled her eyes.

"Hello . . . Sister Pepperdine?"

"The patient presented on emergency petition at approximately 2:00 A.M. with signs of acute severe psychosis including homicidal ideations and auditory and visual hallucinations. She was accompanied by her parents, sister, and a family friend. Upon admission she immediately required restraint and an injection of Haldol IM for de-escalation before being secluded on the unit. Diagnosis: schizophrenia. A treatment planning meeting will be scheduled by the unit social worker."

Miles clicked off the dictation recorder and set it on his desk.

"Man, what a day, and it's still not over." He opened a cola and leaned back in his leather seat. The unit was quiet now, but Miles knew another admission would be coming soon. The weekends seemed to bring on the worst cases sometimes. This Sunday night was no different.

He did not mind the challenge though. The pressure was his time to shine, to show the hospital chiefs they made the right decision to bring him aboard. He was good at what he did. And of course, when the shift was over, he'd find plenty of ways to unwind and release himself. The new nurse from the ER was still waiting for him to accept her invitation for a late night drink. Fine as she was, he had no intention of keeping her waiting much longer. If only he didn't have the big bandage on his cheek. Miles touched the gauze on his face and winced. Six stitches and almost a day later there was still no sign of Maya. Miles did not know whether to feel on guard or be relieved. Either way, there was no way he would let that girl come within two feet of him. Somebody needed to emergency petition *her*, get her escorted to the psych ward.

"Dr. Logan, call on line one." The unit secretary buzzed his intercom.

"Thanks, Katy. I'll take it." Hopefully it was good news.

"This is Dr. Logan. How may I help you?"

"Oh good, I've finally gotten through to you." The female voice had a sharp accent, a Spanish-speaker. "This is Martina Rodriguez. I'm in charge of planning the hospital's one hundredth anniversary and fund-raising gala scheduled in a few weeks."

"Yes, I know who you are." Miles rolled his eyes. He'd gotten several memos, letters, and phone messages requesting a response to an invitation to speak. As much as he liked working at BMH, he did not want to be there on the few weekends he was off. Saturdays, especially Saturday nights, were his time. But he knew the protocol, the expectation. Might as well accept the inevitable.

"Do you think that you will be able to fill in for the opening comments at Saturday's brunch?"

"Saturday, hmm. I thought you already had someone to do that." Miles didn't know what the woman had, but he needed to stall her as he checked and re-checked his calendar to see what other plans he could come up with for that weekend.

"We did, actually. Or rather, I had sent out an invitation to your predecessor, Dr. Gideon Joel, but I've met a lot of resistance here at the hospital."

"Resistance?" Miles slowly put the calendar back down. "Isn't Dr. Joel on leave to complete some research?"

"That's what I thought, but from what I hear, Dr. Joel was placed on medical leave."

"Is that so?" Miles tapped a pencil on the dictation tape recorder. In the three conversations he'd had with Charisma Joel over the last week, she'd made no mention of Gideon being ill. A slow smile spread across his face. *What is Charisma hiding from me? And* why? He licked his lips.

"Tell you what, Ms. Rodriguez, I'm going to help you with whatever you need. Gideon Joel is an old friend of mine, whom, unfortunately I've lost touch with over the years. I'll contact him tomorrow and see if maybe we can both play a role in the anniversary brunch. How's that?"

"Uh, if you think that would be okay. Like I said, I'm not sure what happened to Gideon Joel."

"Don't worry. I'll bring him out of hiding." *And maybe get his wife too,* he grinned as he hung up the receiver. It was too easy. He squeaked his chair around and found what he was looking for with no effort. The box. *Enserrer*. Charisma had practically run away from him when he unearthed it the other night, and he had not heard from her since.

Now he knew why.

Miles had never forgotten that conversation, that kiss by the mantle. And from the way Charisma had run out of his office, he was sure that she had not forgotten either.

It was time to pay his dear good friend a visit. Miles picked up the simple cardboard box and sifted through the packaging peanuts. Maybe he'd wrap it for them. A get-well present.

Sunday evening. Only a few hours remained until her self-imposed deadline.

"I need to get out of here." Maya whispered to herself as she sat alone in the bus terminal. She'd been sitting there for a while, checking schedules, ticket prices. She still needed a good plan to get her money. A fool-proof plan to make Madelyn sign over all at once the entire inheritance due her.

"Memphis," she drawled the word. The perfect place to match her new voice, her new identity. Far away enough, and in her mind, foreign enough, to start a new life, a new name. She checked the departure times and saw that the motorcoach bus was not scheduled to leave until Monday evening, way past her deadline, but possibly worth the change in plans. Her mother would be able to access the funds only during business hours, so the extra time was a good thing, she consoled herself.

"One-way ticket to Memphis." She slammed three credit cards on the counter. One of them was sure to work.

"Sorry, ma'am." A wiry woman with silver-streaked hair pulled back in a fake bun handed all three back after several attempted swipes. "Declined."

Maya rolled her eyes and dug through the paper and trash in her wallet for one of her other five credit cards. "Try these." She gave a quick smile. If none of those worked, then she'd have to get another one. It was easier to find a way to open a new account than it was to pay off a maxed-out one. Late fees, finance charges. Most of the time when she saw the bills, she tore them up and found a way to buy more off the account. It was like laughing in the creditors' faces.

"Sorry, ma'am," the woman shook her head again, "seems like you'd be better off paying in cash if you can. Next in line, please."

Paying in cash. Maya knew what she had to do. A plan was already forming. She was getting on that bus to Memphis. Madelyn would have no choice but to give her the money.

CHAPTER 17

"You want me to come over now?" Pepperdine was already stocking her purse with fresh tissues, peppermints, and a pocket-sized Bible. Ministry tools. Charisma cried softly on the other end of the phone.

"We need help. My family. My husband . . ."

"I can bring one of the deacons with me to talk to your husband, if you'd like." Pepperdine scanned the emptying corridor outside the church office door. It looked like only Deacon Caddaway was left. She groaned. He must have heard her words because he spun around on the heels of his brown shoes and started walking back her way.

"Praise de Lawd, Sista Waters! You need me to go out and help bring a lost sheep back into the fold? Who's the wayward soul that needs repentin'?" He immediately took the phone out of Pepperdine's hands. "Who is this?"

"Charisma Joel."

"Mmm hmm. We'll be there in fifteen minutes. C'mon, Pepper." Without another word, he hung up the phone and put his hat on his head. All Pepperdine could do was catch up with him at his Cadillac to drive the few miles to the Joel residence.

***

Charisma took one look at her living room, where Gideon now lay sleeping on the sofa, and knew that only a miracle equivalent to the parting of the Red Sea would get her home in the kind of condition acceptable for receiving visitors. Especially a visitor like Deacon Caddaway. *Jesus, what have I done?* She had moved only one stack of dusty books into a closet when the knock came.

"Hallelujah, amen. Today is the day of salvation. Where is the lost sheep? Pepperdine, go get my prayer cloth from the back seat." Deacon Caddaway pushed his way through the door. "What the devil is that smell? A rumbay, rumbay, rumbay, rumbay, rumbay." The deacon closed his eyes and spoke a few more words that sounded like tongues. "Mmm hmm, da Lawd done told me to tell you, Sista Joel, that you need to get your house in order if you want your husband to stop cheating."

"Cheating? He's—"

"Don't interrupt the Spirit of the Lawd!" Deacon Caddaway pushed out a hand. "I feel a spirit of rebellion in this house, a spirit of deep, dark wickedness the likes of Jezebel. And it's emanating from that corner over there. Pepper, go find some Crisco in that kitchen so we can bless it and use it to anoint that side table. I forgot my oil."

Pepperdine groaned. "Now, Earnest, we need to—"

"Oh, Jesus, the rebellion is spreading." Deacon Caddaway cut her off. "Quick, Lord, break the strongholds in this house."

"My husband is not cheating." Charisma's voice was weak, soft. Tired. "He is depressed."

"Depressed?" The deacon noticed for the first time the sleeping, half-clothed man lying on the couch. "Oh, that's an easy deliverance." He stomped over to Gideon and grabbed him by the wrists. "Wake up."

Pepperdine gave Charisma a reassuring smile and quickly followed the deacon to the sofa. As much as she wanted to shake the old deacon, she knew from past church meetings and pastoral interventions, little could be said or done to sway Deacon Calloway. She proceeded cautiously. "Earnest, we can pray together and ask Jesus to guide this family to the right help, the right services, and right medication if necessary."

"Medication?" Deacon Caddway looked offended. "All this boy needs to do is repent of his sin and walk in faith. And you too, wife." He shook a finger at Charisma. "That's it. Now, I said wake up." He shook Gideon harder now.

Gideon rubbed crust from the corners of his eyes and mouth and slowly rose to the side of the sofa. "Deacon Caddaway, Pepperdine," he acknowledged them while keeping his eyes to the floor. "Charisma, you didn't tell me we were having company."

She saw the shame of her husband and never remembered feeling so low. Forget the house. For anyone to see her husband like this was almost more than she could bear.

"Repent in the name of Jesus for your disobedience, for your lack of trust in Him." The deacon was standing with his Bible open, walking in a circle around the room. "It's your faith that is the problem. If you really believed God, if you really took Him at His word, you wouldn't be this filthy mess. You wouldn't be so down. You don't need no doctor. You don't need no prescriptions. You just need to repent and trust God." The deacon's voice roared through the room as Gideon's head slunk lower to his chest. April sat frozen on the steps.

"If you can't trust Him, don't blame nobody else for your condition. If you are depressed, it's because that's how you want to be!" His words howled and rumbled and seemed to shake the windows. Charisma was sure she'd hear something from Mrs. Windemere about "the noise over there" before the night was over.

"Earnest, do you think yelling at Brother Joel is the best way to get through to him?" Pepperdine was trying her best not to yell at the old deacon.

"He needs to hear the truth, Pepperdine. The Bible says it's the truth that sets you free. He ain't depressed, he's just backslidden. Now's the time for him to pull himself together and get free. Sweet talkin' and back rubbin' ain't gonna save him at this point. Show me one sample from the Bible when God was all gentle-like dealing with the disobedience of depression."

"Elijah." Pepperdine let the name settle in Deacon Caddaway's ears. "First Kings chapter nineteen says the prophet was so down he wanted nothing more to do than lay down under a tree and die. God gave him space, gave him time, and through an angel—outside help—gave him food and water—inside help—to keep on living. God recognized the hardness of the journey the man had to take, and only after he was finally of the right mind and strength to take it, God showed Elijah Himself. And the Lord wasn't in a wind, or an earthquake, or a fire. He was in a still, small voice.

"Sometimes, Earnest, restoration comes just like that. Before God could move Elijah on to the next great miracle, Elijah needed to rest and see Jesus in a new way. He needed an angel to intervene to give him physical nourishment for his body. Gideon might just need a doctor or somebody to intervene to give him counsel or even medicine for the same. Ain't nothing wrong with that. God gives us faith, Earnest, and He also gives us wisdom. Every resource we need is already here, and sometimes it's right in front of our faces."

"I've been in every prayer circle." Gideon's cry broke through the room. "I've touched and agreed with so many over the years. I've laid hands on the television while some preacher prayed and stretched out on the floor at countless revivals. And through it all, after all these years, it's only gotten worse. I can't even work anymore! I can't do anything!"

Charisma sat next to her husband and took his hand, unaccustomed to his tears. She knew his shouts, his anger, but she did not know his tears.

"You don't know this, Charisma, but I tried to kill myself last year. Remember my Benz? I told you it was stolen? It wasn't. I totaled it trying to drive off the road. I was feeling so down, I just wanted to die."

"Gideon," Charisma gasped. "Why didn't you tell me? Thank God He spared you. Thank God nobody got hurt."

Gideon fell quiet at her words. Then his face darkened. "Okay, Sister Pepperdine, Deacon Caddaway, thanks for your visit. I appreciate you stopping over, but my wife and I need to talk."

After Charisma closed the door behind the church mother and the deacon, she collapsed in her husband's arms. "Finally," she exhaled.

But he was turning away. With no other words, he collapsed back into the imprint on the sofa.

"Gideon?" Charisma could not get his name out louder than a whisper.

"You have to let me do this my way." He looked small, shriveled on the sofa, then got up and went to the kitchen. Charisma followed him and smiled as he took the unopened bottle of pills in hand and slowly opened it. Her smile quickly faded as one by one each pill went down the shining sink.

"If the other doctors at Baltimore Metropolitan Hospital found out I needed to take medication to perform my duties, they would never look at me the same. I can't have that, Charisma. Please understand." He turned to face her, a heavy darkness penetrating his eyes. "I'm going there tomorrow." He brushed past her on the way to the steps then quickly turned back around. "And for the record, don't ever embarrass me again in my own house by telling people that I need psychiatric help. I claim healing in the name of Jesus."

He stormed up the steps with Charisma close behind. A door slammed and shouts and yells ensued.

Charisma helped April to bed a few hours later. The girl had never left her post on the steps.

CHAPTER 18

My mother looked small in front of the congregation, the two hundred dollar suit somehow looked cheap, her hat not big enough to hide her shame. I was nineteen the Sunday my mother was made to stand in front of everyone at New Zion Hill Fundamental Church.

"This harlot has made a mockery of our church, praising the Lord on Sunday mornings, moaning and rolling around like a street dog in a strange bed on Saturday nights." The pastor leapt around her, his voice crackling like fire.

The church mothers shook their heads; some wept, most clicked their tongues. The men held their heads high and looked low.

"She is not worthy to stand in God's house with us this morning, and for the sake of these young girls sitting in the pews, we need to make an example of this whore and publicly denounce and dismiss her from our congregation."

Sitting in a front row with enough space on either side for five people to sit next to me, I could hear the chorus of whispers around me.

"It's about time she got put in her place, coming in here with them pretty suits looking like Delilah herself," one woman muttered behind a fan.

"Mmm hmmm." Another whisper joined in. "She thought she was all that. Look at her now. Ain't worthy of the shoes she's standing in."

"All her money and that uppity hairdressing shop don't mean a thing." The pastor's wife frowned up her face, murmuring the parishioners' sentiments. "There's others out there, but I'm glad she the one got called out today."

"The daughter's probably just as hot to trot as she is." This time a middle-aged man glared and stared. "Look at her sitting there all pretty and proper in them lace gloves."

Momma was walking down the aisle toward the exit, her face and eyes set in stone. I did not think to join her until I realized all remaining eyes were now on me. I grabbed a hymn book, thinking it was my Bible, and excused myself one by one past unmoving feet and knees. I was in my late teens and still fumbling around like a clumsy child. I had been sheltered for so long. Too long.

My mother, Caroline Jackson, was waiting outside at the bottom of the steps, her hat in one hand, a cigarette in the other.

"See, I told you. Church people."

"But Momma, you—"

A single slap cut off my words. The sting lasted the entire twenty-minute walk back to our home farther down North Avenue.

"I ain't repentin'," my mother huffed. "I ain't sayin' I'm right, but it ain't all my fault either. God kept giving me these menfolk who only wanted something from me and refused to marry me. Ain't my fault. You hear that?" She stared up at the blue sky as she shouted. "It wasn't my fault you gave me everything I wanted but a good man. I ain't repentin'!"

I felt at that moment nothing would be the same. A page was turning in the story, a new chapter beginning. The beginning of an end that had started years before.

"You still a virgin?" Momma's words caught me off guard. I remembered the quick kiss I'd let Eugene Parker, the young man who delivered hair supplies, give me in the back room of Queen Jackson's Hair Parlor. I swallowed hard, still feeling the guilt that came with his hands' brisk brush over all my body parts.

"Well, is you or ain't you?"

"Yes, ma'am."

"Good," Momma sighed as she opened the screen door. "Stay one. Don't ever give away what you can't get back. You might as well give away your life, your breath."

That was the day Caroline Jackson kicked Mr. Matthews out of the house, the man who had followed Mr. Garrison, Mr. Foster, Mr. Mike, and Mr. Wingate.

That was also the day Caroline Jackson started skipping meals, skipping phone calls, and by my estimation, skipping life.

She would leave the house at exactly 8:15 A.M. Go to the post office, the bank, the dry cleaners, stop at a nursery to see what new flower or plant she could add to her garden, and then stop for lunch at a deli in Northeast Market.

Maya knew Madelyn's Monday morning routine by heart. It had changed little in over two decades. Waiting in a bus stop shelter one block away, Maya could see Madelyn finish her sweeping, picking up any litter the derelicts and drug dealers had left on her property the night before. She watched and waited for Madelyn's Lincoln Continental to roar to life and pull away from the curb, go two blocks down Marigold Street, and make a right turn onto Chester Street.

"It's now or never." Maya scurried around some bushes, tip-toeing to the small row home, looking behind and around her the entire way. There should be a key tucked into the bottom tray of one of the small porch's cement planters, Maya reassured herself.

But she could not remember which one.

Slowly at first, and then in a fit of rage, she knocked over one, two, then the third planter, still unable to find the key.

"Forget it." She mumbled some curse words and picked up a metal spade that had been resting against an empty flowerpot. In one hard, quick throw, the bottom glass pane of the window nearest the porch shattered on the dark mulch below.

"Shoot," Maya nursed a small cut as she used the spade to push up what was left of the window. Better hurry, she thought, as adrenaline fed her imagination. She was a secret agent, a spy on a classified mission. She flipped through the window, landing on several picture frames set out on a table.

Pictures of her brothers.

One by one she let each drop to the floor, enjoying the noise and the danger of glass breaking. Better hurry, she thought again as she headed for her mother's old secretary's desk. The papers she needed were in there, she was sure. Her mother kept everything concerning money filed away alphabetically on a shelf in that desk.

"Here it is," she smiled at the official-looking document naming Madelyn Windemere as the benefactor of Harold Windemere's estate. The paragraph listing Maya's share of the inheritance was there, including the stipulation that Madelyn oversee the funds until Maya's twenty-first birthday. How her mother had managed to keep the bank believing that Maya was still under age, she didn't know. What she did know was that all of that was about to change. She was going to First Savings and Company that morning. And they would think she was Madelyn.

Maya tucked the paper into her sweatshirt and then ran up the steps to her mother's room. The right look, the right wig, the right makeup. She was sure she could pull it off.

"I'm here to sign this account over to my daughter in full." She practiced making her voice sound like Madelyn's as she went through her mother's wig collection. A wig with gray-streaked loose curls fit perfectly on her head. She tousled some of the spirals into her face to keep attention from her eyes, the one feature on her face people said looked nothing like her mother's. Then she rummaged through the closet and picked out a gray suit with white trim. Very business like. Now if only she could make it fit right, she considered. Padding! The linen closet in the bathroom was a great source of pillows, towels, and blankets. With one hand, Maya sent the extra perfume and lotion bottles her mother kept stashed in the closet crashing to the floor and used several linens for extra padding in her bosom, abdomen, and thighs. Perfect.

Well, not really, Maya thought as she studied herself in her mother's mirror. The lipstick was orange against her complexion, and in her haste it looked like she had colored her lips outside the lines. The blush on her cheeks looked like half-dollar-sized red polka-dots, and one of the pillows she tucked into the skirt made it look like her legs were pregnant.

But close enough. She went to the jewelry box where her mother routinely stashed fifty dollars in cash. Cab fare. And lunch. She placed a wool hat on her head and looked at her profile.

"Hello, my name is Madelyn Windemere."

She was about to go back down the steps when she saw her old bedroom.

The memories.

Her father.

"You lying heifer!" her mother had said. "You no-good, spoiled rotten, lying heifer! How can you say those awful things about the man who is keeping a roof over your head and food in your stomach? Lies! All lies!" Her mother's voice spoke to her and all she saw was white. Then black. Rage.

Maya found a pair of sewing scissors and went back in Madelyn's room first, and then the rest of the house. She cut, she tore, she threw, she stabbed until she remembered what time it was. A stickler to her routine, her mother was certain to be coming through the front door soon.

Out the back door, down the alley. Just because, Maya left the kitchen sink water running. Every good secret agent has a signature, she smiled.

"Well, I tried it your way, and ain't nothing got better. Now it's time for me to take some matters in my own hand."

It's not really what she would have said out loud to Jesus, but it is most certainly what she felt. Charisma remembered the enlightening lesson she thought she'd learned preparing for Sunday School the past Saturday. The story of the sick man, his healing, his wholeness. She had been sure that deliverance for Gideon and her family was on its way, and thought it was sealed and delivered when Pepperdine Waters agreed to come over the day before.

But nothing turned out the way she expected, and from what she could see, her husband was on the final brink of madness.

Early Monday morning she watched his chest rise then fall in steady rhythmic snores. In between getting April ready for school, she kept walking by the open bedroom door, peeking in at him, wondering what was next. In another hour the alarm would be going off. He set it for 9:00 A.M., determined to make this the day he would set his record straight at Baltimore Metropolitan Hospital.

What was he going to say? *What was he going to do?* The questions scared her as she thought of all the irrational actions his moods had dictated over the past year. She wanted to support him, wanted to believe that all of a sudden, as he seemed to believe, everything would just be all right. Back to normal. Pick up the pages like the chapter had never paused.

But she had a bad feeling about today.

She felt it when the sun first tried to peek through the window shades, blocked by the opaque plastic from entering the room in full morning glory. The threat strengthened as she waited for April's cherry toaster tarts to finish heating in the toaster, the red coils getting brighter and brighter, hotter and hotter until there was nothing else for the tarts to do but spring out with a loud ping. Done, burnt around the edges.

Even when she took April to school, Charisma only noticed the slow, heavy steps the girl made dragging out of the car, down the sidewalk, toward the metal doors of the middle school. Each move of her feet seemed exaggerated in Charisma's mind, a laborious march, the sound of it hard, crunching, moving forward in looming terror.

"Jesus, what is going to happen today?" she prayed as she made a U-turn on the narrow street, but she really didn't want an answer. For once, she did not want any answers.

CHAPTER 19

He could hear the electric buzz in his sleep; the single, high-pitched alarm that sounded like a scream jolted him awake. Gideon sat up in the bed, rubbing crust out of his eyes, stretching, then standing. This was it, the day he would prove to everyone, prove to himself, that he was okay, healed. Delivered. He was bigger than Depression.

He looked in his closet. His clothes looked foreign to him. Which suit? He went through the single row of dark blues, blacks, grays, remembering the day Charisma packed all of them so they could move from their house in Columbia to this dump in the middle of the city. Gideon pushed the suits and the dress shirts down the metal pole with a loud squeak. There, that one, a light blue shirt, black suit, yellow tie to bring it all together.

He ironed with deliberate strokes, the steam hissing methodically in the quiet darkness. Then he showered and shaved. Using some clippers he never opened from two Christmases ago, he cut hair both on top of his head and from off his face. Ten pounds seemed to free from him and fall to the floor. Finally, he dressed, sitting on the edge of the unmade bed, putting on the shirt, the suit, ending with a pair of black shoes that had not seen past the back of his closet for a year. He gave the shoes one last buff, cleaned off his old leather briefcase, and looked in the mirror. The suit nearly hung off of his shoulders—had he really lost that much weight?—but it would do.

He tried to smile but his heart was beating like thunder. The front door was in front of him. It took eight tries before he finally turned the knob and let the door swing open. He let his legs loose onto the porch, tried to stop shaking and took a deep breath. Swallowing hard, he started down the sidewalk to the bus stop to get to First Savings and Company. It was time to take out that last one hundred dollars he had left in his account. He needed the cash for cab fare to get to the hospital and, who knows, maybe he would just go on and buy something pretty for Charisma.

First Savings and Company was housed in the same building it opened in 1918. The original lion heads and gargoyles marked both the windows and either side of the entrance at the top of a tall flight of marble steps. Though worn from time, the exterior had never been neglected, unlike its neighboring buildings on Howard Street. Apart from the renovated and re-opened Hippodrome Theatre on nearby Eutaw Street, most of Downtown's Howard Street was a ghost land of vacant, dilapidated buildings boarded up with wood, and covered over and over again with posters of upcoming parties, concerts, and CD releases.

The light rail stopped right at the steps of First Savings and Company, and Maya Windemere had been one of the first to enter the building at 9:04 A.M. That's why she did not understand why she was still being made to wait in the lobby, a large room with long red Oriental carpets and maroon velvet couches with gold fringes and tassels.

The wig was hot on her head, and the sweat and the makeup combined with the fake curls and the wool hat were starting to make her itch. A little at first, and then uncontrollably. She could not stop scratching her face and neck.

"Excuse me." She dug her fingernails into her matted scalp, rubbed her palms back and forth over her temples as she walked up to the large maple desk where she had signed in as Madelyn Windemere.

"Yes, dear?" A woman with long brown hair and plastic glasses that hung on a chain around her neck sat behind the desk. She studied Maya up and down and pushed her chair back slightly as Maya re-adjusted the flannel blanket tucked down the front of her shirt. Part of the red-and-white plaid peeked out between her breasts.

"When am I going to be seen? I have urgent business today. I must sign over all of my funds to my daughter as soon as possible." Maya drummed her fingers on the finished wood surface, something she'd seen an actress do once in a movie to get whoever it was she was rushing to hurry up. It must be working, she smiled, because the receptionist re-dialed whatever number she'd been calling since Maya entered the building.

"Please have a seat. Mr. Sherman will be with you shortly."

"I've seen a lot of people who came after me get called before me. What's going on? Are you a racist, Miss"—she picked up the metal nameplate—"Avondale?"

"I assure you, we only want to provide the best service that we can give you, Mrs., uh, Windemere."

Maya leaned her head over the desk and put her face close to the woman's, another trick she learned from the movies.

"You better be." She let her breath roll out, hot and heavy against the woman's pale skin. Satisfied at the receptionist's startled expression, Maya straightened up.

"Thanks for your help," she said sweetly, then turned around and headed back to her seat.

Despite the crowded waiting area, she had an entire couch and the four chairs nearby to herself. Most of the bank's patrons were gathered in a cluster on the other side of the room.

"Hi," she waved to a man peeking at her from behind a newspaper. The paper rattled and the face disappeared.

She was just scratching her way down to her feet when the front rotating doors brought a face of color in—a black man dressed in a suit and tie. A briefcase swung at his side. He was dark as a ripe blackberry with skin that was clear and smooth.

"Ooh, hot chocolate," she giggled. She watched as he made his way past the receptionist's desk. Maya stood, scratching her arm pits, smoothing down the wig, and readjusting the pillows bulging out of her clothes. She approached him from behind.

"Ain't you a cutie?" She just couldn't help herself as she reached out and grabbed a chunk of the man's rear end.

"Ow! What? You again?" The man jumped back, dropping his briefcase and nearly falling over the desk. A plastic cup filled with paper clips and rubber bands fell over and landed in the receptionist's lap, which made her lose her grip on a stack of folders filled with loose papers.

"Security, *please!*" The receptionist re-dialed the number she'd been calling since Maya first approached.

"Have we met before?" Maya was oblivious to the confusion she was causing, blind to all the eyes around the lobby watching her every move.

"You're Madelyn Windemere's daughter, right?" The man was backing away, seeing that Maya was indeed beginning to recognize him, and that recognition for some reason was making her angry.

"I am not Maya Windemere, I am Madelyn herself." Her voice suddenly sounded two octaves higher and shook in vibrato as if she were a seventy-year-old woman testifying in church.

"Miss *Maya* Windemere, we're going to have to ask you to leave now." Two men in dark brown suits were approaching. Both looked ready to pick her up and fling her down all of the twenty-two marble steps.

"With all the extra padding she's stuffed in those clothes, she probably wouldn't get a single bruise if they tossed her out." Someone's snicker echoed in the lobby.

Maya did not hear the laughter or the snide comments. Her eyes rested only on Gideon as the two security officers escorted her away.

"I was this close to my money. This close." Her words hissed like steaming water. "You came in here and messed everything up. You'll pay for this, yes you will! Don't forget, I know where you live."

The man seemed deaf to her threats, hearing only the receptionist's cheery voice calling him for service.

"Dr. Gideon Joel?" The receptionist read the man's name off of the work ID badge displayed prominently on his breast pocket. "How may we help you this morning?"

The bad feeling would not go away. When Charisma unlocked the front door of her home, she knew Gideon was not there. Whether to feel happy or alarmed, she did not know.

"Maybe I should warn somebody," she mumbled to herself as she stepped back onto the porch to get out of the smell. She imagined Gideon in dirty jeans and a T-shirt stumbling into the chief administrator's office, crying or yelling. Or both.

And Miles might see him.

Be anxious for nothing, but in everything by prayer and supplication, with thanksgiving, let your requests be made known to God. The words from Philippians crossed her mind, but she blocked them out. This was not the time to pray, she decided; this was the time to act.

Her Grand Am roared back to life, and she was on her way to the hospital with no second thought. As slow as the bus ran from their street to Baltimore Metropolitan Hospital, she was sure she would beat Gideon there.

In thirteen minutes, she was hanging her parking permit on the rearview mirror and pulling back into a parking space. She cut off the engine and laid her head on the steering wheel for a second before jumping out the car.

"I need to talk to someone, but who?" she said to herself.

She flashed her hospital ID badge for the front desk and made her way past the main corridor. There was a chapel at the end of the hallway, on the right side of the main elevators. Hues of blues, greens, reds, oranges, and yellows sifted through stained-glass windows donated by some sisters of mercy group. Charisma peeked in, noting how hushed the mahogany-furnished room seemed in comparison to the outside hallway, which was coming to life in routine Monday-morning madness. Doctors, nurses, visitors, patients in blue gowns pushing IVs, workers in green uniforms pushing carts and carrying trays, all hustled by, nearly thrusting her the rest of the way through the chapel doors.

Be anxious for nothing, but in everything by prayer and supplication, with thanksgiving, let your requests be made known to God. The verse crossed her mind again, but she let the heavy oak chapel door close without her going in.

I can't go in there right now. I've got to do something. She panicked, afraid that Gideon would come running through the front door at any minute.

The elevator door opened with a soft ding, the arrow pointing up. With no thought of a plan, no clue of direction, she got on. It was empty and she enjoyed the moment, resting her head on the padded interior with her eyes closed. When it stopped and the doors opened again, her eyes were still closed, her mind still racing.

"Ah, we pick up where we left off. Weren't you running onto an elevator the last time I saw you?"

Miles Logan.

Charisma opened her eyes and forced a smile. She still had no game plan, and with him standing there, facing her, his back to the closing elevator doors, blocking the only way out, she waited for him to say "Checkmate." His smile, his laugh, was more confident than usual. He knew something. Was she too late? Had Gideon already come? Just play along.

"Dr. Logan—" she tried to sound even, kept her breathing steady—"sorry about last time. I think something I ate didn't agree with my stomach. I made it to the bathroom just in time, if you know what I mean." Had she really just said that? She wanted to kick herself for giving that man the opportunity to imagine her sitting on a toilet with bowel dysfunction.

"Oh, I didn't take it personally," he smiled. "I figured something was going on with you."

She did not like the smile that danced across his lips, like he was carrying a secret. Had she really been too late? There was only one way to find out.

"Yeah, I left so fast last time, I didn't take that box you found in your office with me. I'd been looking for it for awhile." She held her breath.

"Yes, the box," his voice disappeared for a second and his eyes drifted away. But only for a moment. "If you have a second, you can come get it from my office now." It was a dare, a challenge. A trap. She knew for sure.

The elevator doors were opening on the fifth floor, the Howard G. Phillips Unit. She stepped off in silence next to him.

"Dr. Logan."

"Hello, Miles."

"Hiya, doc."

A chorus of female hellos seemed to meet them at every corner, every hallway, as they went through doors, locked entrances. By the time they reached his office, Charisma felt sick to her stomach. All those women, and she was the one he was whisking into his office suite at that moment. The keys in his hand rattled as he drew the window shades down. Finally he turned to her.

"How are the party plans?" he inquired.

"Party? What are you— Oh, yeah, the anniversary party." Charisma turned away, fumbled with her purse. "Thanks for your help again. Gideon's really going to be surprised."

"Tell me the truth, Charisma." He was suddenly standing next to her, his voice tender. She could not look at him. She felt his fingers pulling at her hair and suddenly wished she had not cancelled her last touch-up appointment.

"Tell me what Gideon has become to you," he whispered in her ear as his other arm drew her closer. His fingertips brushed the side of her face, her chin. "Tell me if you are ready for what I can be for you."

***

He stared up at the large letters as the cab pulled away. Baltimore Metropolitan Hospital. Briefcase in sweaty hand, he walked up the steps feeling like his knees could give way at any moment. Leaving the house for the first time in nine months had felt like a dream at first, but now, with only a few steps and an elevator button between him and the executive offices, the dream had faded and reality was setting in.

"Get behind me Satan, in Jesus' name. I plead the blood of Jesus. I claim healing in the name of Jesus." He mumbled the prayers over and over to himself, first in whispers and then out loud. There were stares and giggles as he walked through the front door.

"Help me, Lord. I am healed in Jesus' name. Get behind me Satan." His hands shook as he walked slowly toward the staff elevator, trembled as he pressed the "up" button. More eyes, more giggles. When the elevator doors opened, he stepped on alone, despite the small crowd that had been waiting with him. At the next floor, an orderly rolled a stretcher onto the elevator. A woman lay on it, her arm stretched out, a loose, bloody bandage covering it.

The arm. The blood. The metal and glass. "Help me" had been the slight moan coming from the driver's seat of the other car. He'd driven away before any other cars, any witnesses could round the sharp corner to see the twisted carnage, the wrecked remains of the other automobile that had come from nowhere. He had only wanted to kill himself. With his eyes closed and his hands off the wheel, he never saw the other car coming.

"Sir, are you okay?"

"In the name of Jesus. Oh, God, oh God." Gideon's heart pounded through his skin and sweat poured out of every available pore. With deep, quick breaths, he leaned against the wall, feeling lightheaded, dizzy, sick to his stomach.

"Sir, are you okay?"

The elevator doors opened, and Gideon recognized the ornate oak doors that led to the executive offices. This was his floor.

"Oh, God, oh God." He could not stop shaking as he exited the elevator. The orderly called after him until the elevator doors slammed shut. Now he was alone, only one door left ahead of him.

"I claim healing in the name of Jesus. Get behind me Satan, behind." He sat his briefcase on the floor and then found himself sitting on the floor beside it. His forehead rested on his knees, one tight ball, rocking, heaving sighs shuddering through his body. "I can do this. In the name of Jesus. I am fine. I am healed. In the name of Jesus." Finally he stood. He remembered the security code and punched it into the door's keypad. He was in.

A man wearing an expensive suit and shiny black shoes sat at the front desk of the massive office suite. He looked up from a pile of papers he'd been marking with a pen and stared at Gideon a full twenty seconds before speaking. "Can I help you?"

"I . . . am here . . . to resume . . . my position as . . . as . . . chair of the Howard G. Phillips Unit." And with those words, he was done. Exhausted. Nothing. He shook under the weight of emptiness.

"I'm sorry, who are you?" The man was reaching for his phone.

"No, don't call security. No need. I am . . . I am . . ." Gideon knew it was pointless. He was failing. Even the secretary did not want to give him a chance. "I was."

He turned around before he had to explain anything. Back on the elevator. It was over. His career. He finally knew it. It had taken almost a year to stand back in that office and gather strength to say those few words. A year to get that much, or rather that little, out. And he had nothing else left to give, left to say.

"Give me a reason to live," he whispered to no one in particular as the elevator soared downward. The doors opened again. This time the Howard G. Phillips Unit greeted him. For some reason, he got off and started walking, remembering the codes to the locked doors like he had just made rounds yesterday.

"Hi, Katy." The same unit secretary was still there. He waved at her as if he was just returning from lunch. Phone in hand, her conversation stopped mid-sentence, eyes wide, mouth open. The shock did not alarm him.

His old office. The door was closed. Was Miles in there, sitting at his old desk, using his old computer, being what Gideon could no longer be? Gideon felt numb, out of body as he opened the door with no knock.

There. On his desk. His old friend. His wife. Together. A kiss. Hands.

"Gideon!" Her voice was a whisper, but a shriek. Charisma jumped to her feet, straightened her clothes. He saw the glass statue on the edge of the desk. *Enserrer*. He saw it as it fell toward the floor. Charisma had jumped too fast, too suddenly, and the glass was too fragile. It broke in one single shatter. But he did not see the pieces on the floor. He was already on the other side of the door, the slam as loud as the shatter.

"I was." He paused on the other side of the door, and then he turned away. "I will." He made a decision.

It had taken a year of avoidance and hesitancy, but he finally had a foolproof plan.

CHAPTER 20

She had splurged today, spent $48.99 on a single flower, a rare bud from an Asian country somewhere. Madelyn looked at the potted flower positioned securely in the backseat of her Lincoln Continental, along with the dry cleaning, a tray of pink begonias, and a pharmacy bag filled with pills and tonics meant to relieve her recent onslaught of migraine headaches.

"1:22 P.M.," she read the digital clock on her dashboard. "Perfect timing. I should be home by 1:30 P.M."

Her stomach was full from the Caesar salad, tomato soup, and grilled cheese sandwich she had for lunch, and sleep was pulling at her eyelids, but there was far too much for her to do to stop for a nap. Mr. Herbert, the owner of the nursery where she shopped every Monday, was adamant that the rare flower be planted in freshly mulched soil immediately, and then there were the living and dining room drapes she had to take down and prepare for the cleaners. Spring would be here soon and she planned to sew more curtains—maybe a pale green sheer to replace the weighty jacquard—but that meant oiling the sewing machine she'd been using for over twenty-five years and replacing the needle. And then she still needed to bake the three apple pies for her church's annual Easter dinner.

She was debating between Granny Smith and Golden Delicious when she reached the front of her home. Parallel parking had never been difficult for her, but she suddenly was uncertain whether to put her car in reverse, drive, or neutral.

"My house!" She froze in her seat, her car diagonal to the curb, unable to make sense of the damage before her. The windows facing the small porch front were broken. The screen door was broken. All of her ceramic flowerpots were broken. Brown earth and green leaves spilled down the steps, making the carefully scrubbed marble look like cheap cement.

"Who—" It was all she could say as she got out of her un-parked car to inspect the damage more closely. The front door was ajar, and she could see through the opening that the chaos continued in her living room and up the steps. The faucet was on at the kitchen sink, and water had soaked through the hardwood floors in her dining room, had saturated the braided rug in her foyer. The thought that someone could still be inside did not stop her from marching through the rest of her home. Her bedroom had been ransacked, dresser, drawers, shelves, all out of place, with clothes, wigs, toiletries, and toilet paper strewn about. Goose feathers sprinkled the room like fresh fallen snow, and sheets and blankets covered the hallway floors.

Madelyn picked up a nail file and set it back in its place, closed a squeezed-out bottle of lotion, hung up a wool sweater. But the disorder was too great to fathom to know where to begin.

"Somebody had to see or hear something," she decided, peering out a torn window shade at the street below. "This has to be the work of one of those junkies down on the corner, looking for money for their next fix." Madelyn never tried to be obvious about her money, but she was sure that many of the neighbors who'd replaced those who'd died or moved out knew she was a woman of substantial means.

"The neighborhood has changed over the years," she finally admitted to herself, certain that this assault would be the final straw in her sons' efforts to get her to move. "I should have accepted that fact the day the Joels moved in with that loud music and unkempt yard." True, there were other homes on the block that were in far worse condition, but to have that level of disorder *right next to her house* was far too close to home.

"That's it." She marched down the steps, unsure of what she was declaring. She stopped at the bottom of the stairwell and surveyed the broken living room one last time. The pictures. Her pictures of her sons. Everything broken.

Madelyn stepped back outside and headed next door. Though Charisma's car was gone, she was certain she would get an answer. Gideon Joel, from her observations, never left home. Maybe he could help. No music was blasting out the small row home, a good sign, a chance that he heard something.

She knocked and waited. Knocked again and waited longer. When there was no answer she tried the door and found it unlocked.

The smell, the sight was enough to make her gag. She covered her mouth and gasped. Her home had been ransacked, but this place was rancid.

"Only a *crazy* person could live in this . . . this trash hole." She was scared to move beyond the doorway, afraid now even to touch the door again. "Gideon!" She waited. "Gideon Joel!"

With no answer, she was convinced he was not home.

She was also convinced—certain—that she knew the culprit behind her home's attack. Anybody crazy enough to live in this condition, anybody crazy enough to never leave his home while it was in this condition, anybody who would suddenly be gone from their home the very day her house took on this condition was crazy enough to be committed to a psych ward or, better yet, she decided, thrown into a jail cell for destroying her precious property.

"Yes, I need an officer to come to my home right away." She was already back in her living room, spraying Lysol on her hands and the clothes she wore as she talked calmly into the phone. "A dangerous lunatic just severely vandalized my property. His name is Gideon Joel."

She stared at the pieces and thought of how each jagged one represented a part of her life.

Pieces, parts of a whole, each one sharp enough to prick, to pierce, to stab, to kill. How many stories had she known, stories gathered over the years, chapters strung together to form the whole of her life, had had the capacity to do the same? To prick her conscience, to pierce her heart, to stab her security, to kill her dreams.

Charisma stared at the glass on the floor of Miles's office. *Enserrer*. There was no semblance of the embrace it once captured, no likeness of a hug. Only broken shades of blue. She saw only the pieces, and she saw only the blues.

"God, I wanted more." She did not care that Miles was only steps from her, could hear every word. "This is not the life I wanted. Everything close to me has been broken and blue. My mother. My husband. And now I've only added to it." She closed her eyes, seeing anew in her mind the look on Gideon's face when he opened that office door and saw her in the arms of another, her lips entwined with a man he once called friend. It had been a brief moment, a quick second that she gave in to what she knew was an empty promise. Only a second, but long enough to reap lasting damage.

All the years, all the time she'd spent not understanding, questioning how her mother gave in to so many air-thin pledges of love and a better life, and now, just like that, she understood. She had officially been there, done that. One second, and the pain of her actions was already unbearable. No wonder her mother finally fell under. There'd been many seconds for her, many moments that like small weights had added one on top of the other. At some point her mother was bound to break. The load was too much to bear.

Come unto me, all ye that labour and are heavy laden, and I will give you rest. Take my yoke upon you, and learn of me; for I am meek and lowly in heart: and ye shall find rest unto your souls. For my yoke is easy, and my burden is light.

She shook off the words of Jesus written in the book of Matthew. Guilt, fear, exhaustion would not allow her to do otherwise.

"Gideon, I'm sorry. I haven't helped you," Charisma whispered.

"Aw, come here, Charisma." Miles's voice sounded distant although he was standing less than three feet away. "Don't worry about Gideon. From what you've been telling me today, it sounds like he went off the deep end a long time ago. What he just saw between me and you ain't going to push him any further than where he already is. There are medications that can help bring him back, but you don't have to be a part of that process. You deserve better. You deserve me."

She actually saw pride in his face, no shame in his smile. He even had the audacity to start walking toward her, to come into her space again. With both hands she pushed him away.

"You." She let the word hang, and it was enough to accuse, but Miles did not seem to care. He looked amused.

"Look, I can call the cleaning lady to come sweep up your little glass, if you like, and then if you hang around for a few minutes while I go check on a couple of patients, we can go catch a late lunch in the Doctor's Lounge. Shrimp scampi, I think, is the special today."

"Miles, I'm not having lunch with you. I'm not having anything with you. I need to help my husband. I need to go."

"Charisma, wait." He grabbed her arm just before she reached the door. "Okay, it's been a difficult day so far, but really, I just want to help. If all you want is help for Gideon, then that's what I'll do for you." He grabbed a pen, some paper. "Here, write down your phone number and address, and I'll talk to Gideon myself."

"No." Charisma nearly knocked the pen out of his hand. "You can't be involved in this, in our lives, anymore. That's it." She turned away and exhaled, began the long walk to the elevator. Thankfully, he did not follow her.

"What am I going to do?" Charisma felt numb as she entered and exited the elevator, walked through the long hospital corridors and made it to the garage.

Be anxious for nothing, but in everything by prayer and supplication, with thanksgiving, let your requests be made known to God.

But she still did not feel like praying. After what she had just done, she wondered what she could say to the Most High. There was only one person she could imagine talking to right then. She took out her cell phone, stared at it as she started her car, then turned it off.

"I can't keep bothering that woman. Sister Pepperdine don't need to be wrapped up in my mess." Besides, the deep guilt and shame she felt would have kept her from telling Pepperdine the whole story anyway. *How could anyone understand or forgive me?*

A long walk, a good cry, ice cream. The traditional ways she had handled stress and sorrow in her life, all three of which allowed her to daydream, to escape to safer stories. She opted for choice three and turned toward the nearest Baskin Robbins. She wasn't ready to face Gideon yet. What would she say to him? Over several scoops of rocky road-, mint chocolate chip-, and pistachio-flavored ice cream, she would figure out her next move. Ice cream may not be the best answer, she reasoned, but at least something would be good in her day.

She'd thought the whole thing in Miles's office was what her nerves had been preparing her for since the morning. But the bad feeling that she woke up with was only intensifying. She felt deep in her soul things were only about to get worse.

"Can you put caramel on that?" She smiled at the young girl on the other side of the counter. What else was there to do? It hurt too much rehashing the stories she knew.

Sitting comfortably in a booth with her ice cream, she reached in her purse and pulled out the flyer from Chocolate Heaven. A man named G, the feature for Ladies' Night, was pictured centerfold. The mocha brown chest, the built arms, solid legs, the look that called from his eyes, his pursed lips . . . Between the sweet chill on her taste buds and the heat rising from the night club leaflet, she tried to feel happier, tried to slip into a world of fantasy.

Living seemed easier when she could control the stories.

CHAPTER 21

The church office was quiet, even for a Monday. Pepperdine Waters looked at the spreadsheets before her, the files, the minutes from a meeting she needed to type. A lot of work needed to be done, and with the lack of interruptions, the day would have been the perfect time to play catch-up, but she felt further behind.

Pepperdine looked up at the dry-erase calendar over her desk. The women's retreat was less than two weeks away, and though every detail from the speakers to the menu had been thoroughly discussed and planned, she still felt something was missing, still felt something was wrong.

"Jesus, what is going on?" she murmured as her fingers ran smoothly over her computer keyboard. A mass choir CD played soft harmonies from a portable stereo perched on the windowsill. From her seat, Pepperdine had an easy view of a mural of Black Greats—Martin Luther King, Jr., Frederick Douglass, Harriet Tubman, Eli Whitney, among others—painted on a brick wall overlooking an empty, grass- and litter-filled lot across the street.

Greater Glory Worship Center was housed in a sanctuary that had been built in the 1920s. It stood like a sentry on a corner in the working-class urban neighborhood it called home. Despite its almost formidable worn stone exterior, the interior was newly renovated with purple carpet, white paint, and polished wooden pews. The stained-glass windows had been updated with a fresco of pastel colors, and two large chandeliers that dipped from the ceiling made the main floor feel like a favorite great-aunt's home—elegant, warm, inviting.

The church office, Pepperdine's work space for nearly twenty years since her retirement from the Social Security Administration, was small and slightly cramped. Still, she had managed to nurse a tender, cared-for quality about it with several potted plants placed skillfully throughout. Wooden file cabinets that displayed cards and plaques from parishioners and a few politicians also held artwork and cozy knickknacks. Scenes and figurines of cherubic children singing, preachers in long robes preaching, and women in fancy hats dancing and profiling were her constant company, scattered on the walls and bookshelves of the cozy church office.

"I might as well call it an early day," Pepperdine huffed as she shut down the computer. She eased her hips to the end of her chair and stood, listening to the series of pops and crackles that had been greeting her movements more and more as of late.

"I need to call Dr. Wilkes for a refill on my arthritis prescription." She shook her head as she tidied her desk and watered a small plant. "I need to call Charisma." She let herself say aloud the thought that had been running through her head all day. She was certain that Gideon Joel was ready to make steps toward healing after yesterday's visit from her and Deacon Caddaway. He had even smiled as he walked them to the door. But just the same, it wouldn't hurt to follow up.

Pepperdine scanned the office, looking for a reason to visit the Joel home unannounced. Her eyes fell on a cardboard box under a table filled with unclaimed church member offering envelopes.

"Here it is." She struggled back to a stand from her knees and re-adjusted the calf-length denim jumper she was wearing. "Number 392, Gideon Joel." She patted the small box and put a check mark next to his name on a sheet of paper. She rechecked the Joels' street address and headed for her car.

With rush hour still almost three hours away, the streets through Baltimore City's east side were still drivable. Pepperdine turned onto Marigold Street after only a ten-minute drive. She was three blocks from Charisma's house when she recognized a familiar face strolling down the street. She immediately pulled over and got out of her car.

"Gideon, is that you?" She wanted to enclose him in her arms, she was so happy. Standing there with a smile on his face, a fresh haircut and shave, a business suit, he looked like a different man from the shadow she'd just seen yesterday. "Look at you! You look good, Brother Joel. I can tell you're doing well today."

Gideon took both her hands in his and nodded. "Thank you, Sister Pepperdine. Thank you for everything." He let her hands drop and began walking away.

"Gideon, is everything okay?"

He turned to face her again. The smile was still there and an urgent certainty resided in his eyes. "Yes. Everything is how it should be. I know exactly what to do now. Thanks again, Ms. Waters."

Pepperdine watched his back a few seconds as she leaned on her open car door. "Well, Lord, I guess you are moving in some kind of way." She watched him strut away a few more seconds and then yelled out to him.

"Oh, Brother Joel, wait! I almost forgot." She huffed her way to him and handed him the small box she'd brought from the church office. "Church envelopes, for service on Sunday. I can't wait to see you there."

At first he said nothing, and then he opened the box and took out the envelope for the following Sunday. He fished some dollar bills and loose coins from his coat pocket.

"Seventy-eight dollars, three cents. It was a hundred, but I needed cab fare today." He placed the money in the envelope and licked it closed. "Can you take this for me?"

"You don't need any more cab fare or anything?" Pepperdine felt slightly uneasy, but could not put a finger on what was troubling her.

"No." His smile was strong, confident. "I don't need anything. Thank you again, Sister Pepperdine. For everything." He turned away a final time.

"Lord, I guess you're working," she mumbled again. She still felt uneasy, but chalked it up to her tendency to over worry at times. "He certainly seems fine. Just the same, I'll check on them later."

It was too easy, Gideon smiled to himself. Why had he not thought of this before? Finally, a fool-proof plan. Finally, a resolution to the pain, the suffering, his life. He would no longer be a burden to Charisma, who obviously wanted out of the marriage. She wanted Miles's arms, not his, and why blame her? April, well, she'd endured having a shell of a father for so long, what difference would it make if she had none at all? He did not deserve to be called "Daddy." He did not live up to the title of "Doctor." Now, he told himself as he stopped at a corner store to get one last bag of salt and vinegar potato chips—his favorite—he would no longer have to feel guilty about living or being. Death was due him. He was not worthy of breathing God's fresh air.

These things he mulled over as he walked the last two blocks to his house, rehearsing the details of what he would do, the final preparations. The car crash last June had been a bad idea, a last-minute, poorly thought-out alternative for suicide that ended up hurting someone else. Gideon swallowed hard at the memory, the guilt of leaving someone else, status unknown, in a broken car months ago.

But this time, he would not fail. This time, nobody else would be injured. It was too easy, he told himself as he skipped up the front steps. There was a police car parked next door and broken glass, ceramic, and dirt covered Madelyn Windemere's steps. He could not concern himself with such matters; he had his own mess to clean.

And clean he did. With newfound energy and peace, he found the broom, opened a box of trash bags, and filled a bucket with soapy hot water. The medical books, no need to keep them. The newspapers and old magazines, trashed. The refrigerator was emptied, scrubbed, disinfected. By the time the church bell from a cathedral up the street rang three times, the entire downstairs sparkled, smelled fresh, and looked catalogue perfect. Laundry was in its place, either in the hamper or in the closets, clean, dry, and folded.

Only one thing left to do. A letter. Gideon searched for paper, pen, sat down and began in long hand the closing statements of his life.

CHAPTER 22

"Thank you, Keisha." Miles read the name badge and winked at the young woman sweeping the blue glass off his office floor.

The woman, with thick makeup and a long hair weave, smiled back, a deep gap showing in her teeth. "Anytime, Dr. Logan. Let me know if there is anything else I can do for you." Her blue uniform was tight around her curvy hips, which he watched her sashay all the way out the door.

Yeah, there's plenty you can do for me, he wanted to say, but his mind was still on Charisma. That kiss. Man, he had been so close to getting her shirt buttons free, his pants unzipped.

And then Gideon Joel. Always Gideon Joel.

Miles slammed his fists on the desk. Everything in that office, everything he had worked so hard to get, somehow, someway, always seemed to have Gideon's mark on it.

At some point, there had to be a stop, an ending point, a period. Miles was tired of the commas, the question marks.

"Charisma, Charisma," he breathed out her name, shaking his head, wondering what she had been feeling when he touched her. The way she responded, the ease with which she held him, told him something heated was going on in that head of hers, regardless of what she was saying. Actions speak louder than words, the saying goes, and one can only act out what he or she's been thinking.

"It's time to get this settled, once and for all." Miles changed his voice mail to state he was gone for the day and reached for his coat. He only wanted to talk to her, maybe even talk to him. Getting an address was no problem.

One shard of blue glass, a particularly large, thick piece with a sharp, ragged edge, lay missed by Keisha, hidden partially under his desk. With slight irritation, he picked up his phone, about to page the housekeeping department once more. But then another idea came, and a smile spread across his face. Miles used delicate fingers to lift up the glass, which was slightly larger than his hand, then wrapped it in newspaper. A memento, he thought, to give to Charisma.

"*Enserrer*." He laughed with a fake French accent. He would never let her forget their embrace.

"What do you mean you can't arrest him? He destroyed my home!" Madelyn Windemere glared at the responding officer standing in her foyer. "First it takes you forever to come, and then when you get here you tell me there is nothing you can do? That is unacceptable!"

"Ma'am," the uniformed cop stood with his back to the damaged screen door, "I did not say that I wasn't going to do anything. I'm just saying that I can't go arrest your neighbor based on pure speculation. You have no proof that your neighbor was the person who ransacked your home." His voice was calm, low next to Madelyn's shouts. "Now, we can send out a team to take pictures, gather evidence, and then we'll move forward to arrest and charge the perpetrator of this crime."

"Look at my house!" Madelyn paced the floor, stopping in a puddle by her oak dining room table. She noticed for the first time water from the kitchen sink had spilled down the carpeted basement steps. Anger allowed no tears. "My house! Everything! Why would he do this to me? He needs to pay!"

"Mrs. Windemere," the officer had a pad in hand, "let's start from the beginning. Let's look at motive. Is your neighbor, or anyone else for that matter, holding anything against you? Do you have any enemies, or are you at odds with any friends or family members? You mentioned you had four children. Are any of them—"

"I did not raise any crazy children!" She slammed her hands on top of her antique secretary's desk hard enough to form a splintery crack. "My daughter—"

"I thought you said you only had four sons." The officer raised an eyebrow. "Does your daughter live here?"

Your daughter. The words themselves felt like an accusation. Mrs. Windemere felt lightheaded, nauseous. What had she been about to say about Maya? At that moment, she did not even know herself. What Mrs. Windemere did know was that she had to get the focus of the conversation back on the crazy man next door. She narrowed her eyes at the officer. "Are you going to go and arrest Gideon Joel?"

"Ma'am, I can't—"

"Then get out!" Madelyn gripped his arm with both hands and pushed him toward the door. Surprisingly, he did not fight against her or her continued yells. "Get out of my house right now! If you're not going to help me, there's nothing for you to do but leave. I did not raise any crazy children!"

On the porch, while carefully stepping over the shards, the dirt, the broken pots, he handed Madelyn a brochure. "If and when you're ready to resume the investigation, give us a call. In the meantime, you can always call this number."

Madelyn glared at the officer as he pulled away and then glared down at the pamphlet in her hands. *The Citywide Crisis Hotline, Emergency Mental Health Services for You or a Loved One*, it read. She imagined he kept a stack of them on hand, ready to pass out at any hint of crazy. She read the front cover and did something she always thought herself above doing.

With one flick of the hand she tossed the paper in the air and watched it join the rest of the litter on the sidewalk.

"I do not have any crazy children," she muttered before looking over at the Joel residence. The windows and shades were open for the first time she could remember, and the scent of Pine-Sol and Pledge wafted through them.

"I need to get those people away from me before the police come back here and think something is going on in *my* household. I need to get those people away from me. Today."

When Madelyn made up her mind about something, she counted it as good as done. She was just stepping back into her house when she heard someone yelling half a block away.

"Right now! I need my money right now! You are going to give it to me!"

The figure, the shouts were closer. Madelyn scooted into her house, but there was no lock on the door, no way to seal the windows. Everything was broken.

"Maya, please!" Madelyn groaned at what she saw, the pillows bulging underneath one of her favorite suits, the blankets trailing on the ground, an old wig falling off her daughter's head. People were sure to start looking. "Come in here quickly," she hissed and pulled the young woman in. She looked up and down the street before shutting the door. "What did you do?"

"I didn't do nothing. It was that man next door. I just wanted my money, and he had to come mess everything up."

"I knew it was him! Did he do something to you too? Why do you look like that?"

Maya was in tears, her voice hysterical. "I had to dress up like you; I had to. I had to look like you—"

"Oh my goodness! Did he attack you? And he wanted you to dress like me? That's enough. Let's go to the police station. You can tell them everything, and we'll get rid of that sick pervert once and for all!" Madelyn reached for her purse, her car keys, but Maya immediately grabbed her arm.

"No, wait! We can't go there! We can't go to the police station."

"What's wrong, Maya?"

"The other one—Miles! I can't go to the police! Not with what happened with Miles!"

"Miles? Who's Miles? Girl, what are you talking about? Gideon wasn't alone? Who else hurt you?"

"They all hurt me!" Maya pulled on her mother and both of them fell to the floor where her head landed in Madelyn's lap. "Miles, Miles! Why did you do this to me?"

"Maya, calm down." She shook her. "Calm down, Maya. It's okay. I'll take care of everything." She stood to her feet and looked out the window one last time, hoping, praying that nobody had seen or heard anything. She had Harold's memory and her dignity, among other things, to protect.

***

She pulled in front of April's school half an hour early and fought the urge to go get her daughter right then. Let the girl finish the school day, she decided. No need to rush April into the insanity that had become their lives.

Charisma shut off the motor and pushed her seat back, imagining April as a young woman. What lessons would she tell her daughter about love and marriage, men and life? Another daydream started and this time the man in it looked like Miles—except his eyes were a different color because it would be a sin to think directly about him. An imagined man, one with no real name or clear face—that was a different story. She could feel his lips on hers, his hands inching lower down her spine.

It was a rush that filled her, took her away. She was no longer Charisma Joel waiting outside Lombardy Middle School in an old Pontiac Grand Am about to face a husband who'd showered that morning for the first time in ages and was too depressed to stay awake longer than forty-five minutes. She had become someone else, an exotic beauty, wanted, desired by a man who could have anybody and still chose her. He was strong and sexy and spent most of his time wanting to please her—mind, body, and soul. She imagined flowers, jewelry, trips, chocolate. Of course he was well off and spent most of his fortune spoiling her. She put together the perfect body—maybe the stripper G's—under the face that looked like Miles's minus the eyes, and then imagined a veiled canopy bed somewhere by a private beach on an empty island. It was such a far-gone fantasy, but she was completely there.

"Mmm, mmm, mmm. Lord, why can't it be?" Charisma opened her eyes, immediately aware that the Lord had suddenly invaded her thoughts. Verses about crucifying the flesh, denying the self, renewing the mind, and putting off such things followed next until she told herself that her fantasies were just thoughts, not actions; just empty pictures about men who did not really exist, places she'd never go with them if they did; things she'd never do because she knew better.

As he thinketh in his heart, so is he. That's true, she considered the words from Proverbs, wondering what had been Gideon's thoughts that had helped turn him into the man he had become over the past year. *But that verse doesn't apply to me*, she argued, *because I've been nothing but a faithful wife, despite my situation, despite my thoughts.* Except today. With Miles. In his office. Charisma winced, feeling guilt anew at the kiss that had been heading for more if her husband had not opened the door. *No, I would have stopped.* She was certain. Well, almost certain. *As* she *thinketh in her heart, so is she*, Charisma swallowed.

"Mommy?" April looked just as surprised to see Charisma as Charisma did to see her.

"April, what are you doing out of school early? Did the bell ring?" Charisma saw hesitation before April opened the car door. "And where's your book bag?"

"No homework tonight." April sat down with a loud huff, barely looking at her mother.

Charisma raised an eyebrow. "What's in your hand?" Her daughter was fingering a folded piece of paper, the only thing on her besides a thin coat. "Let me see."

"It's just a bus ticket." April extended her hand for Charisma to see.

"A bus ticket? Why do you have that? You know I pick you up everyday."

"I'm sorry, Ma," April looked out the window, away from Charisma. "I bought it from someone at school. I wasn't sure if you were going to pick me up today. That's all."

"Not pick you up? Why would you think that? Since when have you caught a bus anywhere? Don't I always pick you up?"

"Yes. It's just, you know, with Daddy acting all . . . weird, especially yesterday when he was talking about going back to work and all. I didn't know what you were going to do today. I thought maybe you were going to go talk to that doctor friend of yours down at the hospital again."

"Dr. Logan?" Charisma blinked. Okay, that's enough of the fantasies. She shook her head to herself. She had to get rid of that brotha—physically, emotionally, and most important, mentally. *I can't let this girl get wrapped up in my confusion. She called him my friend. What else has she noticed?* "No, April. I'm not talking to Dr. Logan anymore. He was an old friend of your father's who I thought would be able to help him, but—" Charisma was not sure what else to say. "Anyway, that still does not explain why you left school early and where you were planning to go with that bus ticket." For some reason, she was not convinced that home had been April's intended destination.

"Mommy?" They were at a stoplight and April had turned completely around to face her. Charisma thought she saw something she recognized in her daughter's eyes and tried to name it, tried to answer it. But the light turned green and a car behind them was honking; the moment passed, and neither of them said anything else the rest of the way home.

When she pulled onto their block, four things Charisma saw did not make sense: open windows at her house, Miles Logan getting out of a red BMW, Madelyn Windemere banging on Charisma's front door, and a young woman with white feathers in her hair and a plaid blanket tucked around her body screaming and running toward all of them.

"April, stay in the car."

CHAPTER 23

I spent my twenty-first birthday in the waiting room of the ER at Johns Hopkins Hospital. I had come home to find my mother, Caroline Jackson, lying on the black and white tiled bathroom floor. Two different pill bottles, both empty, lay at her fingertips.

"Momma." I remembered getting on the floor next to her, between the toilet and the bathtub, shaking her shoulders, throwing cold water on her face. The note, placed on my bedroom pillow like a mint left by a hotel maid, was simple, short.

"You don't need me anymore. Happy Birthday, Love Momma."

When the doctors came out and told me Momma was fine, stable, I breathed for what felt like the first time in my life. The slap that welcomed me on the day of my birth did not compare to the sting that greeted my first day of legal adulthood.

"I was so angry at you. Angry, afraid, bewildered, relieved." I wrote in my journal that night, dated it. Another story, another record written down. I remember closing the journal, my mother's note tucked inside. I remember thinking that I would never write in that journal again. I was done penciling down the stories that I knew, the ones I could not control, the ones I wanted hidden.

But my journaling had only just begun.

***

The moment Charisma stepped out of her car, time flew, stopped, collapsed. Everything. All at once.

Miles Logan was running toward her, and so was the woman with feathers in her hair.

"Maya, wait!" She heard Madelyn Windemere calling, but strangely Charisma's only concern was finding out why the window shades were up in her house.

Gideon never opened windows. "I need the darkness," he routinely said.

By the time Charisma had reached her front door, the others were there too, except that Madelyn was turning away. "I'm calling the police," Madelyn yelled. Her words were the only ones Charisma heard above the shouts, the screams numbing her ears.

The woman named Maya had something in her hands; Charisma could sense it but could not see it.

Violence. Charisma felt it, but she wanted only to go inside, see Gideon, see why the window shades were open.

She went in and Gideon stood shaking in the middle of a spotless living room. She wanted to take a moment to make sense of the order, the clean, the scent of Mountain Berry Glade; the chaos, the pushes, the shoves around her; Miles, Maya, the feathers; but the only thing that drew her attention was the knife in Gideon's hands, the small knick at the side of his wrist, the trickle of blood on his fingers.

"Gideon!" Her first words.

"Dr. Logan." His only response.

And then whatever deaf ear Charisma had turned to the commotion, whatever pause button she had pressed when she left April in the car, whatever it was, it lifted.

"Get your hands off me!"

"I hate you! I hate you!"

"You're sick; you're crazy! Get off of me!"

The screams, the shouts, the curses of everyone all at once, the many hands swinging, fighting, were a firestorm, a funnel that vacuumed any sense of reason, that locked her in the middle of moving arms.

Anything was possible.

Charisma heard every word, but said none herself. She stared only at Gideon whose trembling had stopped. His eyes were locked. Not on her. On Miles.

A hard push, a tumble. Somebody fell, somebody pulled. She was in the middle and she felt the basement steps on her hips. She was falling. A hard hit on her bones, a bruise for sure. All of them were falling, down the steps, into the basement. And the basement, unlike the upstairs where the windows were open and sunlight poured in, was dark. Unfinished, windowless, broken light bulb. Pitch black. With her eyes closed, everything not only looked black, but felt black.

"Stop it!" Charisma found her voice again, but her voice sounded so small and the fight so big.

The knife.

On her knees, she felt the floor, felt for Gideon. Elbows, palms, fists, feet. She felt those too. In the distance she could hear a siren. Help was on the way. But it was distant and the violence too near.

"Gideon, give me the knife," she whispered. And then it was over, or rather, light flushed through the dark basement. Light and a scream.

Charisma did not want to open her eyes, so she waited. Waited until the sirens came closer. Waited until footsteps, heavy boots, ran overhead. Walkie-talkies. More yells. Madelyn Windmere shouted through the front door. When had she returned?

"Down the steps. They are down the steps! The basement!"

Charisma waited until someone grabbed her wrists, pulled her, dragged her. She did not want to stand. She did not want to open her eyes. But it was inevitable. She had to see what the light revealed.

One eye opened. Then the other. There was no missing it, mistaking it. He was lying there and he was not moving. Dead.

"Miles?! Miles, wake up!" Maya cowered in a corner, her hands shaking in front of her, eyes wide, dry. Blood everywhere. On all of them.

Gideon stood center in the room. Charisma never remembered seeing him so calm, so certain. The police had guns drawn, handcuffs. Charisma held her breath, waited. Handcuffs. She held her breath, waited, wondering which one they would pick to wear the metal bracelets. She held her breath and then exhaled. There would be no picking, no choosing. Gideon's arms were outstretched, ready for the metal, the clink of the lock.

Charisma closed her eyes again. *She could still feel the metal, cold on her hands as she grasped the wheelchair to roll Momma along, loud in her ears as the locks clinked open and closed with a thud. Her mother didn't belong here, she had wanted to scream.*

She opened her eyes again, only a blink. They were halfway up the steps, the police, Gideon. Halfway but blocked. Something was in the way. Charisma found her voice again.

"April, go back upstairs! Who let her in?" Charisma scrambled to her feet, grabbed the girl's thin shoulders, pushed her face away. Blood everywhere. On them all. Too much in that basement for an almost-twelve-year-old to see.

But even as she pushed, shoved her way up the steps with her daughter, she saw the officer, the first one who had come down the steps with the light. She saw his face, the questions. The doubt. He was studying Charisma.

"Ma'am, we'll see your daughter to safety. We need you to stay here at the scene to answer a few questions."

Charisma looked around the room, the eyes on her, Maya shivering in the corner, Miles lying dead on the floor. She eased her grip off of April's shoulder, blinked at the bloody handprint left behind, watched as a young female cop took her away.

"It's okay, Mrs. Joel." The officer seemed to look right through her. "We only need to get your side of the story."

PART 2:
A GREATER GLORY

Psalm 91:1 He that dwelleth in the secret place of the most High shall abide under the shadow of the Almighty.

CHAPTER 24

Twenty-four hours ago she had been a virtual unknown, a radiologic technologist working the night shift at the local hospital, the Sunday School teacher for the nine-to eleven-year-old girls' class at Greater Glory Worship Center.

Today, cameras surrounded her house. News vans mounted with antennas, reporters holding microphones camped in her front lawn and all along the narrow city street waiting to capture any words she said, any movements she made, ready to broadcast and translate her life to the entire world.

"When you open the door, don't hesitate. Walk straight to the car we have waiting for you. Don't worry, Mrs. Joel, we will handle all of your public statements right now." The man next to her patted her knee and offered a firm smile.

She hated what she saw in his eyes. Pity. She did not need that, not for herself, not today, and especially not for her little girl. Where was April anyway? Charisma Joel scanned the living room, sealed off from the rest of the world with the shades drawn tight, and the television muted. She could not believe what kept running across the screen. That was her face in the pictures, her life in the headlines. She had to find April. As if reading her mind, another suited man shouted over the frenzy in her living room. Were all these people really necessary?

"April's okay. We sent her to your next-door neighbor's house."

Next door. Charisma did not know whether to sigh in relief or cringe in horror. But she had no time to do either. They were already walking her to the door. It was time to face the cameras.

"Remember, let us do the talking." The man smoothed down his suit jacket and cleared his throat.

That was fine with her. She had nothing else left to say. Not a statement, not a story, not a prayer.

The door was swung open and the light actually blinded her. Not the sunlight, but the flash of a camera held by someone who ran as soon as the picture was taken.

"Quickly, Mrs. Joel."

She felt a strong hand on her elbow, pushing her forward. Faces, featureless faces, surrounded her. More flashes. Microphones.

"There's a small platform at the end of the sidewalk. It's ready for you, for us. You're not alone, Mrs. Joel." Charisma could see the platform, a large piece of plywood really, laid out in front of Madelyn Windemere's rose bushes. A nice backdrop. She looked to the left, to the right, at the suited men beside her, the attorneys, the spokespeople given immediately to her from the executives at Baltimore Metropolitan Hospital. This involved them too, their lives, their history, their stories at stake.

I wonder what the story will be, she heard herself think, questioning silently what the suited men would say in the microphones, into the cameras. It had been only sixteen hours since a dead man lay in her basement. A dead man. Her basement. Miles. The chief of the Howard G. Phillips Unit. The psych ward.

It had been sixteen hours. They still had not found the knife.

"We would like to issue a short statement on behalf of our clients." The tallest of the suited men spoke into a group of microphones: Herman Steinbridge--Charisma remembered his introduction from one of the hospital's executives. Many lives, livelihoods were on the line.

"Last evening the current chairman of the psychiatric department of Baltimore Metropolitan Hospital, Dr. Miles K. Logan, was found fatally stabbed in the residence of the former chairman, Dr. Gideon Paul Joel. Dr. Joel is currently in the custody of the Baltimore City Police Department for further questioning. Charges are pending." The speaker, Mr. Steinbridge, grabbed Charisma's elbow and began pushing her toward a waiting car.

"Is it true that Dr. Joel has been on leave from the hospital since last year after locking himself in his office for four days?" Charisma did not see where the reporter's microphone came from. She saw only Mr. Steinbridge's hand push it away. Two other microphones took its place. "Is your husband suffering from any mental or emotional disorders?" A different reporter chimed.

"Is it true that unbeknownst to responding officers, a wanted fugitive, Maya Windemere, was also on the premises at the time of Dr. Logan's death and is still wanted for questioning? Do you know how she got away? Did you see where she went? Do you know where Maya Windemere is?" The reporters clamored over each other.

"Mrs. Joel, what was your role in these events?"

It was the only question that made her freeze, stop breathing.

"Where were you at the time of Logan's death?" She lost her step, her way. The reporters, the cameras, the flashes, lights, microphones. Blinding.

"No further comment." Herman Steinbridge gave her one final tug and she was sitting on beige leather, the interior of a sleek black Audi. She smelled cigarettes, leather attaché cases, men's cologne.

"I need to see my husband." The first words she'd said all day. Her voice was a hoarse whisper, scratchy from disuse. She watched as bodies pressed on all sides of the vehicle, shouts, questions blocked by glass. She imagined a mute button had been engaged and the lights and crowds around them were simply a moving screen with no sound. She was watching her life, this moment, from the outside.

The car inched its way up Marigold Street, passing the corner stores and the neighbors who were standing, sitting on porch fronts, pointing, talking, straining for a view of the wife of an alleged high-profile murderer.

"Is your husband suffering from any mental or emotional disorders?"

"Mrs. Joel, what was your role in these events?"

"I need to see my husband," Charisma whispered again, zeroing her attention to the back of the driver's head. She could not see his face, only blond hair, slicked back with gel so fresh she could make out the comb trails. Herman sat on one side of her, another man in a black suit, name unremembered, sat on the other. The lead attorney for Gideon, a woman she disliked the moment she'd met her, sat up front in the passenger seat.

The attorney, Paige Dillery, turned around. "You'll be able to see Gideon soon, okay?" She smiled, a plastered smile. Her words, her tone spoke down.

Charisma recognized the type. In Gideon's old circle, there had been a few doctors like that, Charisma recalled, the kind of professionals who'd become so above the people they served that they treated patients, clients like playthings, pawns in the universes they controlled. Humoring them, smiling in their faces, but all the while never seeing the same cloak of human skin, human experience that put them *all* in the same finite category: human.

Before, Charisma would have had slight value in this woman's eyes. Before, she was the wife of an internationally esteemed doctor. Today, she was the wife of a murderer, another client, another case, another victory to add to the woman's resume.

Charisma watched as the attorney's shoulder-length red hair swung back into place over her plum wool suit jacket, listened as she chatted nonstop on a cell phone about files, dates, arguments, laws.

Why am I getting consumed with this woman? Charisma caught herself and immediately began trying to pry off the fingers of jealousy that were threatening to choke her. Jealous not over the woman's career, position, beautiful plum wool suit; but rather, jealous over the normalcy, the routine this woman had. At the end of the day, after meeting with judges, lawyers, Gideon, and whoever else might come her way, this woman, Paige Dillery, would go home, eat dinner, maybe read a book, crawl into a plush bed. Go to sleep.

Charisma noticed the wedding ring on the attorney's finger and had the sudden urge to ask her about her husband. Did he talk about politics, stocks and bonds over dinners of lamb chops and tarragon chicken? Did he play golf on the weekends, treat her to monthly massages, watch football games on TV, kiss her good morning every day?

Normalcy. Routine. Charisma felt—knew—she would never know such things again. But then, had she ever?

The obsessing, the daydreaming had been a successful distraction, Charisma realized as the car made a right turn into Primary Booking. Her husband was in there.

"Charisma?" Herman Steinbridge's large, hairy hand smothered hers. He was a tall, broad fifty-something-year-old with full, thick gray hair and brown wire glasses. "I understand that you're a Christian. This might be a good time to be praying." He patted her hand again.

She turned her head, looked out the window, concentrated on a fly circling around the car. *Pray? What am I supposed to say to Him? Jesus, you knew this was going to happen. You let this happen.* She swallowed the lump in her throat, remembering her face and Gideon's on television that morning. Her house, their backyard, front porch on the news. The comments, the questions, the speculations, the opinions all these people, all strangers, all experts, had to say about her life, their lives. She'd only been trying to keep her story private, and now the whole world was privy to her business and free to add chapters, take away sentences, and scariest of all, offer adjectives and descriptions.

One thing did not make sense. She searched for the wrinkle and sought to expose it. "Excuse me, but why are the television reports focusing on me as much as, if not more than, Gideon?"

Paige Dillery turned around one last time in her seat as an officer neared the car to open the doors.

"Well, it didn't help the case when several witnesses came forward to expose your affair with Dr. Miles Logan."

"Affair?"

"The late night dinners at the hospital cafeteria and in the Doctor's Lounge? Even your neighbor's daughter, Maya Windemere, reported before she disappeared that you were the woman who ended her relationship with Dr. Logan. And, the most damaging account, the unit secretary on the psych ward informed officials that Gideon walked into Dr. Logan's office and saw you with him only hours before the murder." The woman looked smug, satisfied that she had a category in which to peg Charisma.

"Damaging?" Charisma tried to make sense of the word, its meaning.

"Well, the fact that the killing happened hours after he saw you two and not right at that moment might suggest premeditation. It will be hard for Gideon to change his mind from pleading guilty to pleading insanity if the prosecutors can identify both premeditation *and* a clear motive." The smug look on her face deepened. "The affair definitely does not help."

The killing. The affair. More words Charisma could not wrap sense around. She closed her eyes just as they had been closed the moment *the killing* happened. How could anyone know for sure what happened, how it happened? It was dark in that basement, even darker behind closed eyes. In the scuffle, in the confusion, she'd asked Gideon for the knife. It all happened so fast, and in complete darkness. How could anyone know for sure? *She* was not even sure of what happened, of what *she* did, feeling disconnected, outside of that deadly moment. *What did I do? What didn't I do?* More questions would be coming, more answers demanded. Charisma shuddered at that reality,

"Pray." Herman Steinbridge walked behind her, all of their footsteps echoing in the dimly lit corridor. Concrete. Metal. Locks and bars.

I would never want to have to stay here. For the first time, Charisma felt afraid.

CHAPTER 25

Her house had been completely ransacked in yesterday's first assault—the assault that left her windows broken, her floors ruined, her fine things smashed. All had been touched, damaged, and destroyed—all except for one drawer. The drawer had been touched later, the last victim in the cursed day's crimes.

Madelyn held a bittersweet smile on her face as her fingers brushed over the red velvet of the drawer, now empty by her own doing. It was a small safe she touched, hidden in the wall behind her antique secretary's desk.

The police and detectives were still busy outside, next door, and along the narrow street. So busy in fact that none of them had noticed her calls, her trips over the past twenty-four hours.

That was fine with her. Madelyn slammed the safe shut, locked it, and repositioned her desk to cover the vault that blended into the wood-paneled wall. She went back to the vacuum cleaner, the furniture polish, and the sponges, rags, and trash bags waiting in the living room. There was still much cleaning to be done, she sighed, giving one last look at the desk and the secrets held behind it.

Tears stung the back of her eyelids, but she refused to let them fall. She had done what had to be done. It was necessary. Painful, but necessary. There had been no other options. She had tried calling her sons, all four of them—their home numbers, their work numbers, their cell phones. But, as usual, none of them were available. None of them answered. And Sunday, the only day any of them came over to eat dinner at her demand—not to talk, just to eat—was still five days away.

She'd had no choice. There was no other way to get the money, she reassured herself. She gave one last look back at the wall that held her bittersweet secrets and her safe in its belly. The jewels, the diamonds, the precious stones handed down to her from her mother, and her mother's mother, and the gold and silver given to her from Harold—all of which had called the safe home just twenty-four hours before—now lay enclosed in glass cases at a jewelry exchange store in Pikesville. Fine jewels for cash, the ad stated. She must have known this time was coming when she cut the ad out of a newspaper several years ago and placed it inside the safe next to the jewelry and stacks of hundred dollar bills.

She must have known then, but even still today it hurt. In the cover of darkness, the night before, while April was sleeping soundly in the guest bedroom (Madelyn had poured four teaspoons of Benadryl in April's dinnertime juice to ensure the girl slept well), Madelyn made that dreaded trip down Reisterstown Road. She'd given her precious emeralds, her rare rubies, the multicarat diamonds one last look, one last rub before laying them on the counter. The man on the other side of the counter had a thick accent that she barely understood, and thick hands that managed to move delicately like a woman's. A magnifying glass was strapped to his eye. Madelyn left her treasures there, the bitterness of the moment still raw in her memory. But she exited the store with her pocketbook filled with enough cash to make that last and final stop before she came back home.

That last stop was what made the sacrifice sweet.

There was only one thing left to do to finish turning her sorrow into joy. Madelyn grabbed an empty trash bag and headed for the staircase.

But April Joel was coming down the steps, a lazy stroll to her gait, a slight scowl on her lips. The girl was finally awake after sleeping most of the morning. Why the authorities had decided that Madelyn was the best babysitter for the child while they talked to Charisma and her crazy husband, Madelyn could not understand. But she would make do for now. More hands made less work, and there was much work that needed to be done to get her house back in order.

At the moment, however, Madelyn wanted the girl to stay downstairs. Madelyn had important work to do upstairs. She was determined to finish the project she had started last night.

"April, I need you to finish sweeping the plant soil off the floor and polish the water-stained silverware on the table. When you finish, I'll prepare your next meal."

This one time Madelyn ignored April's rolling eyes and sucking teeth. With the empty trash bag in her hand, and her empty safe in her wall, she started up the steps to complete the process that would finally gain her freedom.

CHAPTER 26

"I am directly responsible for Dr. Logan's death. I deserve to be here," Gideon repeated in a calm, steady voice. He looked the investigator in the eyes, keeping his hands folded in his lap. The investigator leaned closer to him, the coffee on his breath hounding Gideon's nose.

"Details, Dr. Joel. I just want you to give me specific details. Where were you standing? Were you standing? In which hand were you holding the knife?"

"I am directly responsible for Dr. Logan's death. That's all you need to know."

"Dr. Joel," the other detective emerged from his place in the corner, "you still have the right to an attorney. You have attorneys. Why don't we—"

"Look," Gideon slammed the table, "I've brought hurt, pain. Death. I *need* to be in here." And it was true, the way he saw it. He needed to be in a place that held him accountable for his sins, both known and unknown. Miles Logan, his old friend, his newest enemy, was dead. Who else was to blame for Miles's tragic departure? Was not the fate of the last falling domino the fault of the first flick?

And then there was the person he'd left on Cromwell Bridge Road last June. The victim of his first suicide attempt. If for no reason but for that life he left, bleeding, moaning for help, status unknown, Gideon knew he belonged behind bars. Jail was a satisfactory end to his life as he knew it. Any other attempt at finality would mean the destruction of another soul, he was certain. Every time he'd tried to kill himself, somebody else had ended up hurt.

Destruction. He'd done enough of it. In jail, he could do no more.

He looked around the room, the cold cement, the wooden starkness, the stale emptiness. Nodding his head he whispered, "Yes, that's all you need to know. I know this is where I belong."

The train screeched to a halt in the torrential rain. From her seat in the passenger car, Maya tried to catch a glimpse of the city that would be her new home, but the rain was falling too hard. Thunder loomed in the early afternoon sky as she grabbed the bag her mother packed for her the night before. She'd emptied it the moment she entered Penn Station back in Baltimore and refilled it with candy bars, magnets, snow globes, and magazines from a crowded newsstand. Essentials for the cross-country trip. Now, standing alone outside the Amtrak station, she emptied the bag once again. Time for another shopping spree. Time to buy the things she needed to begin a new life in a new place.

Alone.

She hated being alone. She needed to fit in, needed to find a way to fit in. She skimmed the street around her once more until she saw what would help. A gift shop. Taking five twenty-dollar bills from the thick wad of cash planted down her sweatshirt, she scurried to the store, darting through the rain. Twenty minutes later, she emerged from the souvenir store wearing orange leather cowboy boots, black leather pants, a multi-colored fringed vest, a red plaid shirt, and a cowgirl hat.

"Hello, Dallas." She smiled at the clearing sky. The bag on her shoulder carried new essentials: a map, a can of pork and beans, beef jerky, and a book on bison. Everything she needed, she believed, to begin life as a Texas cowgirl.

Only one thing was not in her bag. She'd kept it on her since the evening before, wrapped in newspaper and tied with a shoestring against her thigh. The police, the investigators never asked, never checked her. After they'd asked her a few initial questions, she slipped past the officers' attention, leaving that cursed basement to hide in her mother's attic, per Madelyn's instructions—and her promises of money. Lots of money! Maya giggled at her new fortune, but then somberly patted the hard lump on her thigh. Her mother had been too eager to give Maya her money and help her get out of town to even notice what Maya had tied to her leg.

Maya walked into a small café, laid a twenty on the counter and nodded at the waitress, an older black woman who approached her with an eyebrow raised. "Get me here a bowl of yer best chili," Maya slurred her words together.

As the waitress shook her head and turned toward the kitchen, Maya headed to the restroom. She pulled down her leather pants with care, a tricky feat made even trickier since she still had her sweatpants on underneath. Her mother had made her change from one pair of sweats to another, though Maya did not understand why. The sight of blood never bothered her like it did her mother. Indeed, it amazed her, excited her. How many times had she run a sharp nail or a pair of scissors over her own thin skin just to watch the red droplets form and trickle at the surface?

Maya shook her head, tempted by the thrill, but she had to concentrate, hurry. The chili would be hot only for so long. With quick fingers she undid the shoestring tied around her thigh, unwrapped the newspaper.

The knife.

Maya held the black base in her hands, ran a finger over the serrated edge, examined her reflection on the red-stained silver, her face awash in Miles's blood.

There were only two types of people in the world, Maya thought to herself as she wrapped the knife back up in the newspaper, adding a layer of toilet paper to the packaging before standing on the toilet, opening a window and dropping it into a metal dumpster on the other side. Only two types, Good and Evil. There was no in between, no middle ground. She'd spent a lifetime sorting out the people she knew—the people who loved her, hated her, lived to destroy her—into those two categories.

Miles—she loved him, but he didn't know a good thing when he had it. It would be hard, almost impossible, facing life without him; nonetheless, it was time to move on. She flushed the toilet in libation for his spirit.

The shoestring.

She looked at the white lace, stained red throughout, and wondered what to do with it. Her father, Harold Windemere, used to tie strings around his fingers when he wanted to remember an errand or a chore Madelyn requested of him. She remembered the nights he was in her room, in her bed, and she would focus on the strings tied around his fingers, strings that, she would imagine, could tie tight around her neck, so that her head would detach and float away like a balloon.

Remember. That's what she would do. Maya retied the bloodied shoestring around her thigh, a monument, a testimony to the power of love and hate, good and evil. She would never forget. Miles. She would never forget him. A loud wail threatened to break out of her throat as she walked out of the single-stall restroom, a place now deemed holy in her mind. A loud wail threatened, but then she saw a man sitting near her bowl of chili at the counter.

"Heya, sexy! My name's Carrie Mack." She eased onto the stool beside him, happy to have found a new friend.

Pepperdine rarely turned on the television, hardly ever watched the news. After working long, full, solitary days in the church office she usually went straight home to fix her dinner, soak her feet in Epsom salt, and go to bed. Most of the time, clicking on the dial to the evening news and adjusting the wire hanger attached to the old black and white set in her living room led right into all-night prayer sessions. Prayers for families left homeless from hurricanes or mudslides. Prayers for mothers rocking thin babies in lands of famine. Prayers for citizens of countless countries wailing the loss of husbands, brothers, sisters, children in costly wars.

But today, she'd called out sick, the arthritis pains in her fingers and hips too much to bear as she adjusted to a new prescription that cost less under her health plan. She settled in her off-white upholstered armchair, straightening the crocheted doilies on each arm, a steaming lunch of chicken and dumplings waiting for her on a nearby tray, the retreat planning papers and a pen resting in her lap.

"Come on down." She waited for the theme music for her favorite game show, *The Price Is Right*, to begin. Instead a news reporter from Channel 13 standing in front of the Baltimore City Jail filled the screen. The words "Breaking News" flashed at the bottom.

"Lord, I don't feel like hearing no bad news." She eased to a stand to turn the station, but then the photo of a brown-skinned woman with sad eyes and a pensive smile took over the screen. Charisma Joel.

"Oh my, what is going on?" Pepperdine immediately began to pray as she turned up the volume.

". . . Investigators are confirming reports that Dr. Joel's wife was indeed allegedly having an affair with the victim, thus giving a clear motive for the killing that has sent Baltimore Metropolitan Hospital officials on a major PR push . . ."

"Affair? Killing? Charisma?" Pepperdine reached for her glasses, pushing the plastic frames up the bridge of her nose. She leaned closer to the television, which now showed the Joel residence on Marigold Street swarming with police and sealed off with yellow tape. "Video from Yesterday" was typed in the top left-hand corner. The camera zoomed onto a black woman with graying hair standing in front of a rose bush.

"I knew the moment they moved next door that something wasn't right with that family. They kept that house filthy and loud, and they were too secretive. I had no idea Gideon Joel was a doctor. He never came outside before today. I guess he had it planned all along. I just feel sorry for the little girl." She shook her head before another reporter cut in.

"What happened?" Pepperdine's heart beat faster than her pacemaker could control it. She grabbed the phone, remembering that she had silenced it yesterday before one of her naps, and had forgotten to turn the ringer back on since then. Sure enough, the broken dial tone of her telephone let her know messages were waiting. *How many people from church have tried to call and tell me what was going on?* But she did not have time to listen to messages. She quickly dialed the phone number to the church office. Pastor usually met with the deacons and trustees in his office on Tuesday afternoons, so he should hear the phone ringing, she reasoned. She waited through five rings and was about to hang up when someone picked up and fumbled with the phone.

"Praise de Lawd," a scratchy voice finally answered.

"Deacon Caddaway?" Pepperdine tried to keep the urgency out of her voice. "Is Pastor there?"

"Mmm hmm. You callin' 'bout them Joels, ain't you?"

"Earnest, let me speak to Pastor."

"Mmm hmm. See, you shoulda let me finish 'buking them demons whilst I had the chance on Sunday night. I knew that boy just needed to hear a few good Bible verses to get the devil out of him. Now look what done happened."

"Earnest, you can't just throw a couple of scriptures around with no love and expect to change a man's heart. And for whatever state of mind Brother Joel was in, he sure didn't need somebody beating him over the head with a Bible. Even Jesus, at the hour of His greatest anguish, praying in the garden of Gethsemane, had an angel there strengthening Him. We need to be about the business of strengthening and encouraging a brother who's in despair, not beating him, and burying him under our words and knowledge."

"Well, all I know is that a man's dead, and—"

"—And maybe if we had listened, instead of talking . . ." Pepperdine shook her head. She didn't have time for all this. "Look, is Pastor there?"

"No." Deacon Caddaway sounded pleased that Pepperdine had given up challenging him. "He just left for the day. You might try and find him at—"

Pepperdine had already hung up. Her knees hurt, her fingers were stiff, but there was nothing else left to do but find Charisma.

CHAPTER 27

The air was stale, stagnant, cold in the small room. Gray walls, gray ceiling, gray floors. Charisma clicked her fingernails on the wood table before her, waiting. She watched as men and women in uniforms passed by the open door, talking, laughing, humming down the hall.

She sat alone, the lawyers, the officials long gone, having excused themselves to an empty room in another part of the building to eat a quick lunch.

Eating.

She could not imagine. Was this how Gideon had felt all these months, his stomach a burden to keep under wraps, a cavernous hole left unfilled?

She closed her eyes and imagined her life just a week ago, or even two days before. Gideon, lying on the sofa, the house a dark hole, a dungeon where their secrets were kept safe from the world, which at that moment was literally tearing apart, turning over every pillow, opening every drawer, ripping every seam she'd tried to keep hidden.

All things come to light. Wasn't there a verse or something that said that?

A knock at the door straightened her up. Herman Steinbridge. Charisma noticed for the first time the bags under his eyes, the slight sloop of his body underneath the black suit. She wondered if her burden of the past twenty-four hours was heavy enough to weigh down another, and took a small comfort in realizing she was not the only individual struggling against consumption. Albeit her reasons were personal, and Herman's were merely professional.

"You can see him now."

She felt herself following the older man, and a uniformed woman she had not seen, beyond the doorway. She'd been asking to see Gideon for the past two hours, and now that he was merely steps away, she realized she did not know what she was supposed to say to him. What does a woman say to an alleged murderer who is her husband? What does she say after horrific events that have ended months, years of hiding?

He sat on a wooden straight-backed chair at a circular table. There were windows on two walls that revealed the city skyline past barbed wires, the wires themselves a constant reminder of where they were. A man with a gun stood guard on the other side of the doorway.

She sat down opposite Gideon at the table, the metal at the bottom of the chair legs screeching against the floor as she pulled herself closer to him.

Complete silence. Charisma searched for something to say. "They've given us a nice room to talk in." She studied his face, seeing slight creases, wrinkles on his cheeks and chin that had been hidden under months of facial hair and grime. It was new, seeing her husband so clean-shaven, so clean.

"They don't think I did it, Care." The words didn't sting her, but the way his eyes bore into hers did, the questions in them.

She reached across the table, wanting to stroke the brown hands that once upon a time had brought her warmth, pleasure in their touch, but now sat hard and cold, folded tightly together on the wobbly table.

"Gideon—"

"—Charisma." The chair screeched as he pushed back, visibly cringing at her touch. "I know I belong here. My sins are many. I don't deserve to live, and it's too dangerous for everyone else for me to try to die. Do you understand?"

He spoke of guilt, but was that accusation in his tone? Charisma blinked and swallowed hard.

"Gideon, please listen to me." She wanted to find a way to tell him—to tell him the truth she knew, the truth she wanted to believe he knew. "We can get through this together. Together," she stressed the word, "we'll get through all of this. You do not have to go through this alone. You don't have to claim the blame by yourself." She wanted to tell him, only him, her questions, her doubt. *What did I do? What didn't I do? It was so dark in that basement. I don't know . . .*

There was the knife, in the darkness, her eyes closed. She'd asked for it. From him. She remembered the blade, the metal in her hands. Beyond that, beyond that moment, she did not remember, even wondered if her mind, her body had been there at all in that moment. The moment Miles's spirit violently left his broken frame and entered eternity's gates. She wondered how much of that moment Gideon remembered, saw, how much of him was there too.

"Let the investigators finish their job," he whispered, as if he was in her mind, reading her thoughts. "Let them finish their tasks, state their conclusions. But be assured, I know I belong in here so this is where I'm staying." He settled back in his seat, his face firm, head high.

Charisma studied this person, this man she had met and fallen in love with years ago. This was him, Dr. Gideon Joel, with the square jaw that clenched when he was determined to do something, finish something. Stubborn. The eyes, deep brown, impenetrable, that never were the first to break contact. The full lips, pursed as if about to speak or command or declare, but never fully parting, leaving one to wonder what great thought, what revelation had just been left unspoken.

"It took prison to free you."

"No." Gideon shook his head. "I started on medication last night. I know that it will take a couple of weeks to take real effect, but this is the clearest I've been able to think, to see in a long time. And they gave me a Bible to read in my cell." He turned his head toward the window. "It took surrendering to free me—surrendering to Christ, to what I needed to do, should have already done, taking the medicine, getting help . . ." A single sparrow flew off the perch. They both watched as it started up toward the heavens, then suddenly dove down and landed on a trash bin at a nearby gas station.

"Surrendering frees, Charisma, but I'm not completely there yet." He turned back to face her, his eyes a dark glimmer hiding secrets.

She thought of his words and wrestled against the bottom of her seat. *Surrendering frees*, she wanted to soak it in, find meaning in the statement for herself, her own life, her dreams, her own relationship to Christ. Her conscience. She reached for his hand, but he quickly pulled away.

"You don't have to pretend to enjoy being here with me." He stood, motioning for the guard.

The wall between them was back. When, she wondered, had the first brick been laid? Had she missed the mortar, the clay, brick by brick, stone by stone, that had wedged a fortress around him? Or was it around her? She looked to the gray walls, the gray floor, the gray ceiling, as if the answers to her questions were there.

"And for the record, Charisma," he faced her a final time as the guard led him down the hall, "I forgive you. The affair. Miles. I forgive you. But don't come here again. I may not have succeeded with my attempt, but consider me dead to you."

CHAPTER 28

Madelyn watched in disgust as the girl picked through the eggplant parmesan on the opposite side of the table. April stabbed a fork through the cheese-covered vegetable, scraping the fine china with the sterling silver fork tines.

"I'm sure your mother taught you better manners than that. I hope so." Madelyn sipped from a porcelain teacup and watched as April used her fingers to write her initials in the tomato and basil sauce. The table was set with a fresh flower centerpiece and four-course service for two: plates, saucers, and salad bowls in a blue and yellow checked pattern, cloth napkins. April licked some of the red sauce off her fingers and used a starched white napkin to wipe off the rest.

"Okay, that's enough." Madelyn reorganized the foccacia on the bread platter, determined to teach, to show civility to this child who obviously had none. "Now, you will help me with the dishes." Madelyn put on an apron and held out a dish towel for April to use.

April did not budge from her seat. Instead, she rolled her eyes and tapped her foot on the damp carpet. Apart from a mild mildew smell throughout the lower half of the house and the scattered nails missing pictures and frames dotting the living and dining room walls, little was present to hint at the chaos that had been present in Madelyn Windemere's home the day before.

"Young lady, I asked for your help in the kitchen." Madelyn frowned at the girl, wondering how any mother could let her child get so far gone. "Well?"

"That lady, the one with the feathers yesterday, she's your daughter?"

Madelyn froze, but only for a second. Without missing a beat she snatched a cooling apple pie from the counter. "Would you like a slice?" Her voice was sweet, her smile broad. "I baked it for my church's Easter dinner, but I can bake another one later. I have some ice cream to go with it. What do you think?"

She was already snatching bowls from the cabinet, reaching for a knife to cut the pie in perfect eighths. This was the third time that day April had hinted at Maya. *Who was she? Where did she go? Why had she been yelling and screaming at everyone?* Madelyn winced at the questions, wondered why April seemed so fixated on Maya, and, even more importantly, would anyone else start coming around demanding the same answers?

"Here you go." She set the bowl in front of April, watched as the eleven-year-old first shrugged her shoulders then gulped down the cinnamon-and-molasses-laced apple pie and French vanilla ice cream. "Good, help yourself to some more if you like. I'll be right back." Madelyn slipped off her white apron and headed for the steps.

April's questions, inquiries unnerved her. She could not take any chances. If a child could be so curious about her daughter, then who knows what the authorities could wonder, say, or do. Or unearth. It was enough sitting through the questions from the detectives and news reporters shortly after the tragic events at the Joel residence, and then holding her breath, hoping nobody would notice her leaving the house to turn her jewels into cash. After hiding Maya in the attic, Madelyn had made Maya go out the back door, walk through the alley, and get in her car several blocks over in the dark hours of the night. And April had slept through the whole thing!

Yes, Maya was her daughter. No, she did not live with her. She lived by herself like any normal twenty-nine-year-old. She was between jobs but lived well off her father's inheritance. Yes, Maya knew Miles in some capacity, though Madelyn was not sure what that was, only that Maya had accused Miles and Gideon of hurting her in some way, that Gideon had assaulted her during his assault on Madelyn's house. Yes, she was behaving bizarrely, but who would not after such a brutal assault and a failed heroic effort at stopping a homicide? Her daughter had probably run off somewhere to soothe shot nerves and re-gather her thoughts like any sane person would do after witnessing such a horrific crime. She'll be back when she's ready to talk, explain exactly what she had seen and heard.

That's how Madelyn explained Maya's role in the affair next door, as a hero, an intervener in a disastrous matter who was now too shaken to be found, too upset to talk to anybody. True, Madelyn had no real knowledge of what exactly her daughter had been doing in that dark basement, nor any real desire to find out. Making Maya hide in the attic was easy once Madelyn promised to give her the money she'd been wanting. It wasn't until after she'd seen Maya off at the Amtrak station that she found out from the police that Miles was her estranged boyfriend; that he'd recently had a peace order placed against her; that Charisma Joel was his new lover; that there was a warrant for Maya's arrest.

Only after did she know these things, and now she was even more certain she'd taken the appropriate steps. After all, Gideon Joel *had* confessed to the murder, so there was no need for Maya to avail herself as a suspect.

"The Windemere name does not need this kind of bad publicity." She peeked behind her shoulder before entering the bedroom that used to be Maya's. She'd turned it into a guest room after kicking Maya out as a teen, leaving only a few mementos, a couple of artifacts that attested to its former resident. The contents of one drawer, the bottom drawer of the single dresser, were all that remained of Maya's possessions. Madelyn took out a trash bag she had tucked into her housecoat and began finishing what she had started late last night and continued that morning. She pulled out the remaining contents one by one.

Her hand reached for the first thing, the satin pillow given to her as a present the day of Maya's birth. Maya's name and birth date were on the front, Bible verses inscribed on the back. *Lo, children are an heritage of the LORD: and the fruit of the womb is his reward. As arrows are in the hand of a mighty man; so are children of the youth. Psalm 127:3–4.*

Arrows. Weapons for warfare that pierce, that stab. Why would God refer to a child so violently, as one who could hurt, as one who could kill? Maybe it depended on the nature of the war, Madelyn considered, to find the value in a weapon. Maybe what mattered was who the target was in this war, where the arrow was aimed. Then the question, she realized, became who was doing the aiming and what was the warrior's intent.

As arrows in the hand of a mighty man. Surely her Harold was a mighty man; she'd never doubted it. It was not his fault one of his arrows had gone astray and missed the bull's-eye, God rest his soul. Even a skilled marksman occasionally misses his target.

Madelyn ran a finger over the inscribed pillow. She did not know why she had held onto it after all these years. Her only memories of it were ones of Harold carrying an infant Maya on it. She could still see the way he used to look at their newborn baby girl, the way he solemnly stroked her chubby cheeks. Maya was the child of her late age, a beautiful girl out of her middle-life womb, a body that had already birthed four—and looked it. She remembered hating the attention he gave to their daughter, the way he always pointed out the beauty of her youth.

Madelyn stuffed the satin pillow into the plastic trash bag and grabbed the next stack of memories. School papers, home assignments. First the ones she did for Maya to keep her grades up, then the ones she did with Maya after she started homeschooling her in eighth grade. Too many intrusive questions from teachers and administrators left her no choice but to keep Maya as close to home as possible. She had her husband's—and her own—reputation to consider.

Finally, the other papers. Pages of scribbled writing filled with short stories, dark poems, diary entries that Madelyn had found scattered in Maya's room and closet over the years. She'd kept the papers together in a folder as she found them and hid the folder under her night stand, reading them only on the nights when Harold wasn't home, which was often, since he traveled greatly for business, usually calling her at the last minute, after she'd just taken a roast chicken out of the oven, to tell her he would be back in two or three days.

Only on the loneliest of nights, Madelyn willed herself to read her daughter's run-on thoughts, chilled by the rantings, the disconnected sentences, disgusted by the claims. She flipped through some of the pages now, shocked again by the crude words, the evil, almost-cartoonish illustrations. What kind of sick mind, ill imagination could come up with such perversions?

"Fiction, all of it. Filthy, disgusting fiction." Anger welled within her, and she tore the pages up before thrusting them deep inside the trash bag. A teardrop landed with a quiet plunk on the papery pile, followed by another. She would have found more tears to release had a loud shout not cut through her thoughts.

"Mrs. Windemere, somebody's knocking at your door! You want me to open it?"

She hated the way the girl shouted through the house. Did not her mother teach her anything?

"Wait, I'll be right there." Madelyn stuffed the last of the papers into the bag, sealed it closed, and hid it for the moment in the closet. She wiped the small trace of wetness from her eyes and face before grabbing her slippers and tightening her housecoat around her waist.

The March evening air tickled her nose as she opened the door to face the next intruder.

"I'm sorry to disturb you. I'm a friend of the Joel family. I go to their church, really, and I was wondering if you knew by any chance where Charisma and April were?"

"Sister Pepperdine!"

Both women turned to face April who was running toward them. The girl swept by Madelyn and landed in the newcomer's arms, burying her face and half her body in the woman's bosom.

"April, please. You will knock our guest over." Madelyn studied the woman's heavy but feeble arms and legs and figured her to be at least ten, maybe fifteen years older than herself. But the feebleness stopped there.

What strength lacked in her frame was more than made up for in her smile, her voice, her warm eyes.

"I'm sorry, Sister Pepperdine. I don't mean to knock you over." April stepped back, looking up at the older woman with a full grin. Madelyn could not help but wonder from where this new April, this smiling, laughing, polite, happy April, emerged.

"Again, I don't mean to disturb you. I—"

"—Can I go with you, Sister Pepperdine? Please?" April begged.

"April, that is hardly appropriate, inviting yourself over someone's house. Please, young lady, let us invite her in first."

Pepperdine, still smiling, waved a warm hand. "No, it's okay. I don't mind taking her with me. I'm sure this tragedy has been trying to you as well, violence and despair so close to home." There was friendliness, care in her tone, and Madelyn suddenly imagined it was a different day, a different time, different circumstances, and Pepperdine was sitting with her at her dining room table, drinking tea, eating lemon pound cake, talking, laughing, listening, understanding. A friend. She'd never felt such instantaneous compassion before.

Nonetheless, this woman Pepperdine was from Charisma's church, so there could not be that much depth in a person who spent her Sundays whooping and hollering under some sweaty preacher hopping across a pulpit.

"If you want to take April, that's fine with me. I have no idea where Charisma is or when she's coming back, and I do have a lot of work I need to get done. Tomorrow is my laundry day, and I did not get my errands for today done yet." She kept her lips tight, firm.

"It's no problem, Ms . . ."

"Mrs. Windemere. Madelyn Windmere." She pulled her housecoat tighter against the growing draft. *You can call me Mattie*, she longed to say.

"Nice to meet you." Pepperdine smiled again at Madelyn before turning her attention to April. "C'mon, little girl." April was already halfway down the steps. Pepperdine nodded at Madelyn. "If you hear from Charisma, just let her know I have April for however long she needs."

"I will."

"And you have a blessed evening. I hope all of this hasn't been too hard on you."

Madelyn closed the door, but not before hearing April shout out, "You know my birthday's in two weeks! I'll be twelve years old."

"Oh you will, won't you?" Pepperdine's voice rose with a loud laugh over a car door slam. "What do you want for your birthday?"

Silence.

Madelyn peeked through the window, seeing April standing at the curb. A full thirty seconds passed before she got in Pepperdine's car, still not speaking, her face in a distinct scowl. The old April had returned.

"Good luck." Madelyn shut her blinds. She had business to tend to. First on her agenda was the trash bag she'd left in Maya's old closet. Thank goodness it would be another cool night, Madelyn sighed. The furnace was going to be extra hot again. Like the bloodstained sweatpants she'd taken off of Maya the night before, the pillow, the papers, the other odds and ends from Maya's old drawer would also meet a fiery fate.

An hour later, Madelyn watched as the last scrap of paper became one with the blue flames in her furnace. She closed her eyes, wiped her damp brow with a tissue, refastened the grate and headed upstairs.

Back in rhythm, back in stride, Madelyn turned the kitchen sink on and off, humming as she washed then dried her china, her silver. No word from Maya, who she instructed not to contact her under any condition with threat of arrest. Madelyn had told her to buy a ticket to any place she wanted to with the cash she had given her at the Amtrak station. Madelyn did not want to know where. The equivalent of the entire inheritance fund was now in Maya's possession, and she could do whatever she wanted to with it.

"I'll give you every penny of what your father left you, but only on one condition." Madelyn had whispered to Maya before the drive to Penn station. "I never want to see or hear from you again. Ever."

"Fine with me" had been Maya's cheery reply.

To avoid a suspicious paper trail, Madelyn had collected her most expensive antique and heirloom jewels, exchanged them for cash, and together with the rest of the money that had been stored in her safe, she gave Maya an amount equal to what was deemed for her in Harold's estate fund.

Without even a good-bye or a honk, she left Maya in front of the train station with a duffel bag, a clean change of clothes, and over $130,000 in cash.

The heat fuming out of the air vents was almost unbearable. Madelyn stripped off her housecoat and lay across her bed. It was Fourth of July hot in her bedroom, but Madelyn was enjoying every moment. With every fresh bead of sweat on her forehead, neck, and back came the realization anew that her house, her life was purged of Maya for good.

CHAPTER 29

Charisma made a left turn onto the tree-lined street. Somehow, even the early darkness of the evening seemed to anticipate her last-minute decision to get on I-695 and travel west because the moon cast just enough light on the car to keep her from blending quietly into the background.

At least that's the way she felt as her car roared down the empty suburban streets. Because she knew her destination, she felt like all eyes were on her, knowing as well. She hated coming this way, to this address. She was glad April was safe with Sister Pepperdine, as she had just learned from a phone call to Madelyn. Charisma had made a vow to herself never to bring her daughter to this place.

She made the last right turn at a stop sign and pulled into a parking space five houses away. It wasn't too late to turn around, she considered, as the engine rattled to a stop. She wasn't even sure why she had come.

The street, as usual, was quiet, except for a bass beat from a car stereo farther down the block. A townhome complex built in the early seventies, it was just beginning to show its age, the cracks, the chipping obvious in the cement façade. But the character, the dignity of the middle-class African American Randallstown neighborhood in Baltimore County remained. After debating a few more minutes, she finally got out of the car.

"1610 Redgrain Court." She stared at the house down the street, wondering how many of its neighbors knew its purpose, its residents. There was no sign posted to make it obvious, the passenger van parked in front had no name painted on the side. Charisma figured the only clue the neighborhood had about the people inside of 1610 Redgrain Court was the shift workers who entered and exited every eight hours around the clock.

She made her way to the front of the house, stopping at the beginning of the walkway, where two large evergreen bushes kept her hidden from view. The front door was open, and through the screen door she could tell dinner was just coming to a close in the three-bedroom, one-and-a-half bath townhouse with a generous kitchen, cramped dining room, living room, and steps that led to the plainly furnished upstairs.

Charisma could see two women sitting at the table, quiet, motionless, over half-empty dinner plates. One was fifty or sixty, maybe, with a scowl pulled tight on her lips, which she kept rubbing with the back of her hand. The other looked no older than twenty-two, her hair in a fancy upsweep decked by jumbo silver hoop earrings on either side. She held a fork in her hand and was smiling, looking off to an area Charisma could not see. Perhaps a television sat on the opposite wall. Charisma could not remember the exact layout of the house. It had been a long time since she'd been here.

Another woman came bounding down the steps. Charisma saw the bounce, the certainty in her steps, the quickness of her eyes scanning the others at the table, the laugh she gave into the telephone perched on her ear as she plopped onto a sofa. The residential assistant. Charisma identified her immediately. There was a different one every time.

Finally, she saw *her*, standing in a corner in the back of the kitchen, perhaps over the sink. It must be her night to wash dishes, Charisma assumed. She could see the chore chart posted in the living room, the names and duties too small to make out.

Look at her, still beautiful. Charisma peered through the green bushes, fighting a sudden longing to go and embrace the woman from behind, laying her head on her back, like she often did as a child.

"Momma." The word was stuck in Charisma's throat even as the woman in the kitchen turned around, a platter of chocolate cake in her hands. She walked into the dining room and said something that made the other three women grin as she placed the dish on the table. From her hiding place in the shadows, Charisma could see her mother's face aglow in the soft light of the chandelier.

Even here, Momma's face was flawless in its makeup. Foundation, lipstick and liner, eye shadow and blush, all natural tones that did nothing but punctuate her mother's striking beauty. Charisma remembered being nine years old, looking in the bathroom mirror, using Q-tips and cotton balls to wipe imaginary creams, oils, and powders on her face, imitating the pursed lips and sideways glances of her mother staring at herself in the mirror next to her.

And that hair! Momma said it was the Indian blood in her that made her hair long and straight enough to be the envy of not a few women on their street. Charisma remembered wanting her own hair to be that long and silky, but it was Momma who told her that the kinks and knots that crowned Charisma's head were her birthright from a thousand generations who celebrated the texture, the rhythm of their manes. *"Baby, there's power in that hair of yours. Don't be shamed of your crown."*

Crown. That was the word Momma used, and Charisma remembered the regal looks on the faces of customers leaving Queen Jackson's Hair Parlor. They were all queens, and when they left, their crowns were perfect.

Queen Jackson. Charisma studied the woman standing in the living room in 1610 Redgrain Court, her face perfectly made, smiling; her long, silky tresses shimmering with countless strands of silver amid jet black, much like the nighttime sky that glittered overhead. Black seas of diamonds, mysteries, stories untold, they both were, Momma and the nighttime sky.

Charisma stood in the darkness, wondering at the smile, the gentle moves of her mother serving cake to her two housemates and the woman paid to watch them. She looked happy, Charisma could not deny, at peace even. It was her, the old Momma. No, a better Momma.

You don't belong in there! Charisma wanted to shout, to scream in the blackness that surrounded her. Her mother's smile under the chandelier was real, genuine, so unlike the years before when her mother repeatedly tried to take her own life. Why was she in there? Why was she choosing to stay? Why live in a place so familiar with her history?

The Residential Assistant was coming to close the door. Charisma knew that if she was going to go talk to her mother, this would be the moment. It was one thing looking through the screen door and choosing to go inside. It was another thing knocking on a wood door and waiting for someone to hear, waiting for a door to open.

The door closed with a slam. Charisma blinked to adjust to the sudden onslaught of darkness, realizing for the first time how bright that house had been inside, how much of its light had been lighting the way for her to see. To see her mother. To see her mother to talk about Gideon. To talk period.

She headed back to her car, her steps quick across the pavement. A light rain was beginning to fall. She was embarrassed again. Embarrassed that anyone had seen her looking in at 1610 Redgrain Court. Embarrassed that her mother lived there. She turned on the wipers and left them on high as she backed out of the parking space. The car bucked under the accelerator. She had to get out of there. Quick.

The rain, which had been a tickle, a tease, when she left her mother's house, began to match the speed of her wipers, gradually at first, and then with fury. She ran through two stop signs and zigzagged her way back to the main thoroughfare, Liberty Road. The flash of red and white brake lights; red and green and yellow traffic lights, store signs, yield signs, stop signs, gas stations, water streaming down her windshield, was too much. Dizzying. She wanted to get out of there, out of Randallstown, out of Baltimore, out of Maryland, out of everywhere.

She pressed her foot down on the accelerator, hearing the engine of her old Grand Am rev up, as if for one last ride of glory. Speed, that was what that car was made for, what it was destined to do. She felt herself part of the engine, imagined that she was running with wheels and wings through rain, through wind. She rolled down the windows and let the rain come in. Almost immediately her face and hands were soaked, her hair a tangled mass.

The stretch of road before her was surprisingly empty, and her heart pounded with fear, pain, exhaustion, grief, and emotions she'd never felt, emotions she could not identify. She held her breath, wanting to breathe; exhaled, wanting to cry. But she only pushed down further, harder on the accelerator, knowing no limits, feeling no limits.

Blue lights, red lights shined through her car. The police. Charisma sucked in her breath and realized where she was, what she was doing. She slammed down on the brakes, feeling the tires grasp for stability on a wet and oily road. She pulled to the side, waited, both hands gripped to the wheel, the wipers ferocious on the windshield, waited for the knock on her door, the flash of the badge at the window.

It did not come. The blue and red lights sped past her. The sirens were for another transgressor. Charisma put the gear back in drive, slowed down the wipers, turned off Liberty Road into a parking lot, then cut off the engine. An abandoned grocery store faced her, the façade battered and bruised, the windows and doors boarded shut with wooden panels.

She sat in the car, in the rain, a long time. Gideon. Miles. Momma. Momma. Miles. Gideon. Thoughts ran over and under each other, building up, toppling over, rotating, cutting.

"Jesus, what am I going to do now?" The question was quiet in the wet darkness, muffled by the quiet pitter-patter of the rain.

"Jesus, what am I supposed to do now?" This time her voice carried weight, and the weight was something that she wanted off her.

"Jesus, just what am I supposed to do now? Help me! Help me please!" She rammed her fists on the steering wheel. A wail broke out from her belly, found breath in her vocal chords, found an exit through her mouth.

No more words, just screams.

"There are two ways to get yourself out of a jam, babygirl, just two ways." Caroline Jackson stood shaking a

smoking straightening comb in one hand, readjusting the flame on the gas stove with the other. I was twenty years old at the time, too old to be babied, but unwilling to leave the safety of Queen Jackson's castle. I sat waiting, head down, bracing myself for the heat wave coming near the nape of my neck.

Most people were starting to get relaxers by then, but I still found comfort in the hot comb ritual I'd shared with my mother nearly all my life. Like I was still trying to hold onto an era that both of us knew was over. The smell of smoke, burnt hair, and grease filled our small kitchen.

"You remember this: Either you can wait for someone to come save your behind, or you can get your behind up and save yourself. Now I know you hear them church folks talk about waitin' on Jesus, but there's some business you got to take care of yourself."

I remember shifting around in my seat, forgetting that the hot comb was already in my hair, right next to my left ear. "Ouch, Momma, that hurt!"

"Shoulda kept your head still while I'm straightening your hair. Why you movin' around so much anyway?" Caroline jerked my head still and ran the hot metal through again.

"You talkin' bout not waiting on Jesus, but I remember that's exactly what Sister Wilson said we should do years ago when I was in her class. She said Shadrach, Meshach, and Abednego had to trust God to save them out of the fiery furnace back in the Bible days. They had to wait until they got all the way in the fire before He showed up. Course, they were in that fire for holy reasons . . ." I gave my mother a sideways glance, a gesture I'd only recently struck the nerve to make. I was just beginning to get grown. Late bloomer.

"Girl, don't be trying to teach me no old Sunday School lessons. I'm a grown woman, and you still two months away from turning twenty-one. Now keep your head still. Why you movin' around so much?"

I took a deep breath and forced out the next words. "Momma, are you pregnant again?"

"Girl, hush your mouth!" Caroline raised her hand to slap me but instead blew on the hot comb, sending the smoke up in wispy swirls. "Since when you get so grown to talk to me like that? I don't care how old you are. I'm still your mother."

"Momma, you pregnant by that married man who used to hang around the shop, aren't you?"

It wasn't the first time Caroline Jackson carried a married man's child.

"Girl, don't you worry about my business. That's not your place."

"Momma, you talkin' bout taking care of it, *ain't you? The baby. You're not gonna have this one either, are you?"*

When her mother didn't respond, Charisma shifted again in her seat. "Momma, Sister Wilson said that if them Hebrew boys hadn't been trusting God to save them out of the fiery furnace, they would have surely burned."

"Girl, I'm too old to be havin' a baby and—"

"Momma, you're only thirty-nine. You said yourself you weren't getting your tubes tied until you turned forty-two. You've been saying for years that with the right man, you were going to get married and have one more baby. Your time is almost up. Why not just go on and have this one?"

"Look, I ain't got time to be waiting for another woman's husband to decide to help me raise his child. It ain't worth the trouble. Like I said, there's some

things you wait on Jesus for, and there's other things you take care of yourself."

I was quiet for a second before looking my mother square in the eyes. "I ain't worth the trouble?"

"Charisma, what are you—"

"Momma, you don't have to pretend like I don't know where I come from. I ain't a child no more. I done figured out that my father was a man married to another woman when you had me. But you told me a long time ago that you found Jesus while waiting for me to be born. You told me that I was your best gift from Him, that I helped bring you to the Light. Look at me, Momma, and tell me how waiting on Jesus don't get you out of any trouble. Momma?"

"Girl, don't you talk to me like that! I been through enough to know when to wait on Him and when to—Ouch!! Oh, shoot!!" The hot comb fell from Caroline's fingers and burned her forearm before landing with a sizzle on my bare foot. "Get me some ice, Charisma! Quick, girl! For both of us."

I grimaced and hopped to the freezer. I wrapped some cubes in a dishtowel and placed it where a large red mark was forming on Caroline's arm. I grabbed another ice cube and placed it on the raw blister forming on my own foot. When nothing was left but silence, a cold comb, and a half-straightened head of hair, I looked back at my mother.

"Momma, I'm not trying to be disrespectful. I just don't want both of us to get burned 'cause you don't want to wait on Jesus. At least pray about it. What you decide to do affects me, too. I know that because I'm here. Last time you waited for Him to help you, I got to be born. I got to be your daughter."

Charisma looked at the clock on her dashboard. 11:52 P.M. She did not realize how long she'd been sitting in that parking lot. Sleep pulled at her eyelids.

She kicked off her shoes, pulled off her wet socks, and wrapped her coat around her shoulders. The scar on her right foot, the one seared in her skin and in her mother's soul almost seventeen years ago, was faint but there.

The day after the hot comb burned both of them, her mother went to a clinic, wanting to leave behind her pregnancy. Two complications, one hospitalization, and three days later, she left behind her uterus.

"I was about to miscarry and didn't know it when I went to get rid of the baby. That missed knowledge cost me my womb because of all the complications. I wasn't ready to be rid of my uterus. I wanted one more baby one day. I wanted to have a chance to have a normal family with a good man. I don't feel like a woman no more." Charisma remembered sitting at the edge of her mother's hospital bed, listening to her mother's cries, loud and intense despite the painkillers.

And then came Charisma's twenty-first birthday, and the note left on her pillow, and the empty bottles of Percocet and Demerol, and her mother unconscious on the bathroom floor. After the first of many trips to the emergency room came the revolving door at the Howard G. Phillips Unit, the psychiatrists, the prescriptions, the therapists, more drugs.

"I was left with a Momma I didn't know and introduced to a Gideon I thought I did. That's what I was left with," Charisma said to herself.

She looked at her foot, flexed it in the washed-out moonlight, remembering a million different memories and close calls, but forcing herself to block out each one.

"It's so unfair. With all that everyone else does, it seems like I'm the one who ends up getting burned." Even Momma, after years of promiscuity, playing church, living in psych wards and group homes, looked happier tonight than Charisma could ever remember feeling. And Gideon, sitting in a jail cell, was talking about feeling free, and she was the one who had to walk outside and face the onslaught of cameras and criticism. Nothing made sense anymore.

"They all think I had an affair. They all are blaming me." Even as she spoke, her words were paving direction, a twisted path in the maze of her understanding.

"Jesus, I'm tired of waiting." She had reached her last scream, her last tear, but she did not want to wait to hear an answer, wait for a change. It was too dark, too stormy for that. For the first time that she could remember, she was ready to take her mother's advice. The advice that had left them both scarred. *"You remember this: Either you can wait for someone to come save your behind, or you can get your behind up and save yourself. Now I know you hear them church folks talk about waitin' on Jesus, but there's some business you got to take care of yourself."* Charisma reached into her handbag, pulled out her shimmering lip gloss, reached under the driver's seat and slipped on her sequined shoes.

"I just wanted a new life. I was waiting for a new life. Jesus, you didn't give it to me, so I'm going to make one for myself. That's all." She felt the rebellion in her words and did not care. She thought about April. Sure, she should consider her daughter in the decision she was about to make, but then when had anyone considered her?

It was done. From now on, she would write her own stories and let them end how they may. She looked back down at the scar on her foot and willed herself to look away.

CHAPTER 30

Pepperdine Waters struggled to sit up in her bed. At nearly seventy-nine years old, most of her body kept up with her mind and plans. Only her vision and the sharp arthritis pains in her hands and limbs continually reminded her that time and age were no longer distant acquaintances but close friends. Tonight, time seemed especially intimate, as she listened to each tick of the hallway clock. It was after midnight now, and she had not had one wink of sleep.

"What is it, Jesus?" She spoke aloud to another dear Friend. She grunted as she stood, waiting, wondering why sleep evaded her. She slipped on her robe and stepped into the kitchenette of her apartment, then set a pan of milk over a low flame.

The top floor of an old row home had been her private sanctuary for nearly twenty years, but she did not mind sharing it with a woman or child in need. In her younger years, she was known to take in a foster child or two at a last-minute's notice. Tonight, she felt transported back to that time, though the child sleeping on the sofa bed was not an orphan.

"You got good parents," she whispered to April, who collapsed on the sofa in a deep sleep the moment Pepperdine unlocked her front door. "Things will get better in due season."

Pepperdine shuffled back into her bedroom and lifted a shade. In early months of the year, when the tree near her window was bare of leaves, she had a good view of the streets surrounding her. Keeping the light off, she sat with her mug of warm milk next to the open window in her bedroom and studied the abandoned, boarded-up row homes across the street; the corner stores on every block she could see; the many steeples and crosses that dotted the city landscape; the tall buildings of nearby downtown; the derelicts, the junkies, the castaways struggling to survive another endless night.

"What is it, Jesus?" she prayed again, and this time she took notice of what was immediately in her view, the bare arms of the tree outside her window, limbs pointing upward, stripped of green life, planted in dry, rocky, litter-filled ground. There, on the branch closest to her, was a single bud, a single green leaf, struggling to grow alone in the chill of the late March night air.

"Season's changing." She nodded, satisfied. She finished the milk, slammed the window shut, never noticing the sudden chilly wind that ripped the leaf from the tree and sent the small bud fluttering away.

CHAPTER 31

She had been touring the streets of her new city for most of the day and now night was creeping up on Dallas. She needed a room, she decided, a place to stay—not so much for sleeping purposes, but rather for storage. Maya's arms were weighed down with shopping bags, boxes, and groceries. She'd spent the day exploring the large city, catching rides with strangers, meeting new friends, eating, partying, shopping.

Earlier that evening, she shared a joint and quick romp in a park with a man named Will. When he asked her if she was a movie star visiting from L.A., she immediately said yes then bought large pink sunglasses and a fur stole to confirm her status. She gave him cash to buy them more marijuana and to purchase a car from a Toyota dealer, then she offered to pay him three hundred dollars a day to be her chauffeur and gave him a week's pay up front. He took the money and never returned.

"So much for the weed, Will, and wheels." She tossed her head back in a loud laugh, staring up at the hotel in front of her, her elated mood unbroken. The visitor's guide she swiped from the train station said she was standing in front of the best hotel that side of town. She entered the lobby, marveled at the marble and glass, and immediately agreed.

"Bellhop, come help me with my bags." She dropped everything along with two fifties on the floor and then approached the front desk. "I need a penthouse suite. Top floor with my own elevator. Just like in this brochure."

She grabbed a wad of money first from her bra and then out of her pants leg. Half an hour later she was soaking in bubbles and champagne in a three-bedroom suite that overlooked the Dallas skyline. A man she met on the way to the elevator splashed alongside her and shared in the four-course meal from room service.

"What movie did you say you were in, Charmaine?" His name was Devron, and he could not keep his eyes off the clothes brimming with dollar bills Maya had strewn all over the marble bathroom floor the minute they reached her suite.

"Charmaine? Oh, yeah. My name is Charmaine Deveux, but you might have seen the name "Char" in the credits when I starred opposite Will Smith and Denzel Washington. My agent says I might even win an Oscar this year."

Maya closed her eyes and laid her head back, letting the rainbow bubbles moisten her choppy hair and the warm tingle from the champagne add to her high. For once her life was perfect.

She opened her eyes just in time to see Devron grab a twenty that had landed near the bidet.

"What are you doing?" She grabbed him by the neck and jumped onto his chest. His head went underwater for a split second until they both fought and splashed their way out of the tub, spinning and slipping on the wet marble. She grabbed a towel and tried to wrap it around his neck. "I will kill you if you touch my money again!"

The man, Devron, slapped her away and laughed. "You are good and crazy, you know that?" He slipped his clothes back on and laughed all the way out the door. "Good and crazy!"

Maya fumed for a minute before grabbing the terry cloth robe. She put it on and tied the belt around her, then got on her knees to recollect her money.

"I hope that bastard didn't take any of my money." She started counting. She could not afford to have anybody stealing from her. She was already down to less than half of her inheritance money, and a full day of shopping still remained in front of her.

"Forget tomorrow." Maya picked up the phone, dialed zero, and then waited for the front desk to pick up. "Yes, I changed my mind. I do want Internet access in my room."

A few minutes later, Maya trembled with joy as her favorite online auction Web site loaded onto the desktop screen in her room. She clicked through a few pages of the site until she got to the one thing she'd been wanting the most.

"Good, it's still there." She smiled and pressed the "buy now" option with great glee.

CHAPTER 32

The lead investigator raised an eyebrow, staring at the coroner over the typed pages of the autopsy report. "And you are sure about these results?"

The gray-haired medical examiner nodded, his eyes bleak and tired. He hated the rush and scrutiny that came with high-profile cases. Ever since the body of the black doctor from Baltimore Metropolitan Hospital was rolled into his care, his office had become a circus. Reporters from CNN, Fox News, and other local and national affiliates camped out and kept his phone ringing. Even now, six in the morning, there was no rest in the hallways.

"These findings aren't consistent with the suspect's story." The investigator slid the papers across a desk in the closed room, sighing, rubbing his temples.

"I just do the exams and record the findings."

"The officials over at the hospital are pushing for this to be an open-and-shut case. They don't need this kind of publicity, and you know how big they are in this city, how much weight they pull. Are you sure these findings are accurate? Nobody involved is going to like a long, drawn-out investigation."

"Look." The gray-haired examiner shook his head. "You have a suspect in custody who has already admitted to committing the crime. With an admission, there won't be a court case." He pointed to the file in his hand. "If you want to keep this investigation sweet and simple, you really don't need this report."

The investigator stood, sighed again, and tapped his fingers on the back of a desk chair. "I guess you raise a valid point. We don't really need to introduce your findings. As long as the suspect's assertions don't change, that is. Who knows about this autopsy report?"

The other man gave a slight shake of his head. "Just us."

"Hmmm." The investigator walked to the window and glossed over the waiting reporters, television vans, and poised microphones, then suddenly whizzed around to face the coroner one last time. "What do we do about the media? They are going to want to know all the details about the autopsy."

"Let me handle the media."

"You have my confidence."

Gideon watched the sunrise between the bars of his cell window. Pinks, oranges, and purples colored the heavens like a haze, giving the impression of warmth when it was in reality another cool March day. He watched the sunrise and found pleasure in the pureness of the moment. Though in prison, he'd been treated respectfully, impressively, given the best in care and accommodations such a place could offer. Despite the filed charges, nobody seemed to believe he was guilty. Nobody seemed to believe he should be there, even though he continually asserted that this was where he belonged. Nobody knew the true scope of his crimes, he reminded himself.

"Thank you, God, for another day of life. Thank you for letting me wake up in a place where I can't hurt anybody else." He prayed a prayer of thanksgiving, even as a surge of unsettledness grew within him. "Take care of my wife and daughter as I no longer can."

He trembled at the word "wife," wondering if love, and the feelings and emotions that came with it, was something one could simply package away, box up, ship to another destination, away from one's heart. What do you do with love when the one you've given it to hurts you?

"Charisma cheated on me."

That was one of only two thoughts that seemed left in his mind to think. The other was the fate of the stranger he had left bleeding on Cromwell Bridge Road a year ago. Should he tell? Who should he tell?

"Dr. Joel, your medicine."

He took in silence the small pill that had become part of his sanity. The other part, a Bible, was tucked neatly under his cot.

Thou wilt keep him in perfect peace, whose mind is stayed on thee: because he trusteth in thee.

He'd spent the night reading and re-reading Isaiah 26:3, the words themselves a sedative to his soul.

"I've got to keep my mind on you to stay in peace. On you, Lord, not on anything else." Gideon talked to himself, encouraging himself like he'd heard a preacher once say do. "I want your peace, Lord. I want to keep my mind on you, but how do I get these other thoughts out?"

By getting them out. The answer suddenly seemed so simple.

"I've got to talk to somebody to get these thoughts out. I need to clear my mind from what's disturbing my peace so I can keep it free to think on Jesus. I guess having a therapist really can make a difference." Gideon had been the doctor. It was okay, biblical even, he figured, for him to be the patient. Fear, in part, had kept him from taking that role—fear of being looked down on, talked about, belittled. *God hath not given us the spirit of fear; but of power, and of love, and of a sound mind.* The words in 2 Timothy spoke to Gideon in that moment like they had never done before. . . . *A sound mind . . .*

A sound mind.

He had to talk. He had to tell. Everything.

"Excuse me," he flagged down an officer passing by his cell. "I'm ready for an attorney, somebody, anybody I can talk to." It felt good to know that the medicine was helping him. It felt even better to know that the Word of God could go places the medicine couldn't, offering healing at the root, at the source of his depression.

"Ready to get out, huh?" The officer smiled at the clean-faced gentleman.

"No, just ready to be free."

CHAPTER 33

Freedom is what she wanted. Freedom from the hiding, the embarrassment that plagued her life, from the people she loved being mentally ill. Their shackles had chained her, debilitated her, as well. She wanted to be free from the fears of discovery, vulnerability, insecurity that had kept her feet blistered on a rocky path. Shame, questions, confusion, guilt. She wanted to be finished with it, with them, but on her own terms.

She wanted freedom, but she wanted to define it in her own terms.

After spending the night in her car, she had picked up April from Pepperdine's house at exactly 6:30 A.M., loud honks announcing her arrival. She did not knock on Pepperdine's door. She did not want her to see her. She was afraid of what Pepperdine might see, what Pepperdine might say.

She had rushed April to the Solace Inn room she'd booked with the help of an old gift certificate. Her home was still cordoned off. She hurried April into a clean school uniform and then dropped her off at the entrance of Lombardy Middle School.

"Mommy, I don't want to go back to school. Do you know what they all are probably saying about me?" Her daughter had shouted through the open window, her backpack slung over one shoulder.

"We have to get back into our normal routine. Bye, April." Charisma groaned inside as she spoke. She had been hoping a quick peck on the cheek would have sufficed for a good-bye. She did not want a long conversation.

"Mommy, my father is a murderer. His face has been on every channel, every T.V. station. How do you expect me to go in there? You haven't even gone back to work yourself."

"April, today is a new day. We both are going to have to start over. I've got to go now. See you at three." She shifted the gear to drive.

"Mommy, can you pray with me? We haven't had our morning devotions in months. Mommy?"

Charisma had pulled away with no answer, refusing to let guilt wash her anew. She had no answers for April right now. "It's a different day." She murmured under her breath.

Now, a few minutes before eight o'clock, she still had two hours before the places she wanted to go opened. She sped back down Orleans Street, weaving her way through the early East Baltimore traffic before turning onto Broadway and then making a left onto North Avenue.

Her West Baltimore roots were driving her back home.

Her mind was numb as she crept through the morning rush, cars and SUVs heading toward downtown. She watched as drivers sipped coffee cups, read newspapers, smoked, talked on cell phones, yelled out of windows.

Normal people having normal lives. Charisma closed her eyes at a traffic light and threw her head back on the seat. "Lord, why didn't you give me a normal life, no drama?" A honk behind her jolted her back. The light was green. *I forgot, I'm not trying to pray right now anyway. What's the point?* She pressed down on the accelerator, zoomed past Charles Street, sinking back in the familiarity of West Baltimore.

North Avenue had changed over the years; she shook her head as she passed Pennsylvania and Fulton avenues. Brick row homes, many with marble steps and four levels, showed signs of age, despair, neglect. She passed entire blocks of boarded-up homes and vacant businesses. The wood panels nailed over doors and windows were covered with graffiti and posters. Some of the plywood had been torn back, and empty bottles and cans peeked through. There were hordes of men on every corner: drug dealers, derelicts, grown men, young men, old men.

Her mother had loved almost every kind of man, Charisma remembered. She loved them, but she did her best to keep Charisma away from them.

"Don't be bringing no trash up in my house." Charisma heard those words every day after she turned thirteen.

Another light was red. Charisma sat there waiting, her hands gripped on the steering wheel, determined to keep her eyes straight. New Zion Hill Fundamental Church, the church of her childhood—the church that had kicked out her mother—was right beside her. The gray bricks and glass doors were dull and forlorn, much like the corner store and homes surrounding it, swallowing it.

"Why do you keep going to that church?" her mother had asked her every Sunday, rolling her eyes, sucking her teeth, even as she ironed new suits and gloves she'd bought for Charisma to wear to the congregation.

"I accepted Christ there, Mommy." Charisma remembered the long walk she'd made down the red carpeted aisle at her mother's insistence once she turned thirteen. "I accepted Christ there, and I got baptized there. I haven't done anything to anybody, so they can't run me out. Besides, you're the one that told me any respectable person is a churched person. You made me go in the first place." Charisma wanted her mother to be angry, jealous, though she did not know why she felt that way. She kept going to the church every Sunday well into her early twenties, though she never told her mother that she sat alone and talked to nobody, or rather, nobody talked to her.

After she met and married Gideon and eventually moved out to the suburbs, she joined another church, Greater Glory Worship Center. It felt like a new start, a new season, her marriage to Gideon, and she wanted no ties to her childhood, to her mother. Greater Glory was still in the city, still in the heart of a ghetto, the only part of her life still tied there, the only part not attached to green lawns and garage doors. It kept her connected to what she knew, gave her a sense of memorial, identity, safety.

And now she was back, in the city, that is. They'd had to sell their house in Columbia to keep up with the bills, the medical school loans, the unending calls from collection agencies. Charisma's little row home in East Baltimore was in a neighborhood not different from the decay she was driving through now. From one side to another, a perfect circle that left her at the same point from which she started. She'd been a good, churched, Christian girl, but still left in ruins. She'd done all that had been proper, kept her family secrets, prayed and went to church, but she was still tied to devastating mental illness, by both blood and by marriage.

And now there was more blood, Miles's. Where was Jesus after all she'd done to keep Him happy? Why didn't He intervene before it was too late? Where was He now, after all she'd done right? Because of the sins of her mother, and the secrets of her husband, she had been left a victim. A misunderstood, despised, and judged victim. Gideon and her mother looked at peace despite their current addresses—happy even—and what was she? Charisma felt the anger rising again. Unlike her mother, unlike Gideon, there was no blood on her hands, and yet she seemed the most miserable out of the three at the moment. There seemed to be blood everywhere.

"And where are you now, Jesus? Are you waiting for more bloodshed before you come rescue me?"

I shed My own blood. By My stripes you are healed.

The thought caught her off guard. She was not looking for Jesus to answer. She had not even meant to ask, but the words from Isaiah 53 played repeatedly in her mind.

He is despised and rejected of men; a man of sorrows, and acquainted with grief: and we hid as it were our faces from him; he was despised, and we esteemed him not. Surely he hath borne our griefs, and carried our sorrows: yet we did esteem him stricken, smitten of God and afflicted. But he was wounded for our transgressions, he was bruised for our iniquities: the chastisement of our peace was upon him; and with his stripes we are healed.

Sister Wilson, her old Sunday School teacher at New Zion Hill, had made her memorize those verses for a church Easter play. She remembered saying them over and over again for days. Even after all these years, the words broke through her mind and thoughts easily, freely.

"*Wounded for our transgressions* means gashed for our sins. *Bruised for our iniquities* were blows with no breaks, injuries under the surface, for our wicked acts. He died for our inside and our outside sins, and the pains and sorrows that come with them. He bore it all, from the inside on out." Charisma could still see Sister Wilson standing in front of them, teaching, her eyes lifted up to the ceiling, her hands sometimes extended in praise.

The light turned green. She pressed hard on the accelerator and sped away from the memories only to be faced with more.

There was a funeral home on North Avenue between Ruxton Avenue and Brandberry Street. Charisma could close her eyes and remember as if it was yesterday the one time she went into that roughhouse turned viewing parlor.

She had followed her mother from afar one Thursday night, watched her enter then exit the ornate French doors. Charisma was twenty-five at the time, grown and married, fourteen weeks pregnant with April, and had been on her way to tell her mother about her coming grandchild. Caroline was between hospital stays, and this was before she elected to live in a group home.

As she had neared her mother's home on North Avenue, Charisma saw Caroline entering the funeral parlor. Unsure of what else to do, Charisma had parked nearby and cut the motor just in time to see her mother coming back out of the fancy canopied exit, a distant look on her face. Caroline had not seen her and continued walking up the street to her residence. Out of curiosity, Charisma decided to see what—or who—was on the other side of the parlor's doors.

Charisma could still smell the musty odor that had filled her nostrils when she entered the dark oak foyer of Norman and Sons Funeral Home. She did not recall her mother mentioning the death of an old-time friend or neighbor. Maybe it was someone her mother knew from the shop, or even from the Howard G. Phillips

Unit, Charisma considered. Caroline had probably come to view someone Charisma never even knew, but something had kept her walking down the dimly lit corridor anyway, peeking into each of the viewing rooms, waiting for some familiarity.

The dankness, the smell of carnations had begun to wear on her nose, and she was turning to leave when the face in the last viewing room caught her eye. It was not so much the face but the profile of the man in the casket that compelled her to enter the corner room. Charisma had never seen so many flowers in one place before. Dozens of roses, all red, were laid out from one end of the mahogany coffin to the other. A businessman, she surmised, a man of means, wealth, prestige, respect.

Nobody else was in the room at the time, and she did not bother to read the nameplate. Instead she focused on the man himself. A darkness beyond death shrouded his sleeping face, and the solemnity extended into the black suit he wore, the black tie, and matching handkerchief. His hands were clasped around a Bible, and a gold pocket watch was chained to his clothes.

He was a handsome man, she acknowledged as she studied the high cheekbones set in skin the color of fine cherrywood. The deep wrinkles on his forehead and at the corner of his eyes that meant to give his age gave instead a distinguished appearance. She studied his lips and nose, full of beauty and severity all at once. She wondered at the discrepancy and decided at last the answer to the duplicity must have been in his eyes. *The eyes are the window to the soul.* She studied his closed eyes, imagining what stories had been held in them. She bent down closer, taking in one last look at his profile. That is when she froze. There was a mirror opposite her on the wall.

His profile was hers.

Same high cheek bones, same lips, same nose.

Charisma jumped back and immediately felt sick. She remembered pushing past a crowd of mourners who was just entering the room, fighting her way back through the dark hall, not breathing again until she was standing outside on the scrubbed and polished marble steps underneath the flapping royal blue cloth canopy. She'd taken two deep breaths and felt the baby, April, give a weak flutter inside of her.

"Yeah, that was family. Your grandfather. I'm sure of it." She'd rubbed her belly and never spoke of the man in the mahogany coffin again. She did not make it to her mother's house that day. Instead, she got back in her car and drove back to her new house in Columbia. The first house, the one with four bedrooms and two-and-a-half baths.

Her mother never talked about that man, Charisma's father, and apart from the day both Charisma and her mother were burned from the hot comb, Charisma made no mention of the man or the circumstances surrounding her conception and birth.

Charisma glanced down at her foot right then, shook her head, trying to shake off the memories. It hurt to dwell there, the place where the memories, the recollections rolled through her head like living snapshots, stories threaded together to form the whole of her existence. She wanted to shake off the people, the places, the things that had only played roles of pain or heartache or absence in her life.

So why had she stopped at last at the brick row home on West North Avenue where the stories began? She did not have an answer for herself, only quiet bewilderment as she sat in her parked car, staring up at the rotting flight of stairs, the ragged evergreen bushes, the boarded-up front door. She stared at the house that had been her mother's until nearly ten years ago when Caroline sold it to an investor who was supposed to turn it into rental units.

Charisma watched as a drunken man stumbled out of one of the broken windows; one hand still clutched a bottle, the other grabbed crumbling bricks for balance. He could have been somebody's grandfather, still was somebody's son. His eyes, a shade of red reserved usually for blood, told stories of tragedies unspeakable, memories washing away one brain cell at a time. She watched as he took another deep swig of the alcohol, his head swinging so far back he fell over with a loud belch. She wondered if it had been enough to wash the stories away.

She would get drunk. Real drunk. So drunk that she wouldn't have to remember anything that happened before today or think about what could happen tomorrow. She did not want to think about him and what he was doing to her life.

Drunk, girlfriend, I mean good, all-out, word-slurring, foot-stumbling drunk.

Isn't that what they all wanted, shouting and groaning in the pews of Greater Glory? Something to ease the pain just a little while longer, something to take the edge off and make laughter and giddiness the norm?

Turning water into wine. That was Jesus' first miracle. He knew that's what the people on this planet needed to see Him do first. They needed to know He could turn plain water into the best kind of wine.

It was almost ten o'clock. The stores in Mondawmin Mall were about to open their doors. She squeezed out the thoughts, the Sunday School lessons, the Bible verses, looked away from her scarred foot, and started another chapter.

CHAPTER 34

Bang. Bang

"Ms. Deveux?"

Bang. Bang. Bang.

"Ms. Charmaine Deveux?"

The door rattled a few more times from the heavy knocks as the telephone rang nonstop. Maya Windemere squeezed the pillow tighter over her head and pulled the plush comforter up to her chin. "Why can't these fools leave me alone?"

"Ms. Deveux?"

She wanted only to sleep. For the first time in three days, she was tired, exhausted, but the moment her head hit the pillow, the knocks and the ringing began. When fifteen minutes had gone by and the commotion had not stopped, she pulled a sheet around her and plodded to the door. It was almost one o'clock in the afternoon, and she had spent the last sixteen hours on a shopping spree with new friends she'd met on the streets of Dallas. She had not even been in the deluxe hotel suite in all that time, so what was the problem? She was ready to tell somebody off when she opened the door; but when she saw the six-foot-one, solidly built young man standing in the doorway, she had an instant change of plans.

"*Hola, señor.* How can I help you?" She loosened the sheet around her bare body just enough to let the outline of her curvy frame spark his imagination. But his demeanor was all business.

"Ms. Deveux? I'm sorry to disturb you, but as you know, we expect payment up front for our Ultra Grande Penthouse Suites. You only paid for one night—which was Tuesday, two nights ago. We need immediate payment for tonight, as well as for last night."

"I gave y'all $1,000 in cash the first day I was here." Maya crossed her arms. She was starting not to like this man, the way he did not crack a smile or notice her advances.

"Yes, you did."

"So what's the problem?" she snapped.

"The problem we have right now, Ms. Deveux, is that $1,000 only covered one night. If you expect to continue experiencing our service you must immediately give us $2,000. Might I suggest you submit a credit card to the front desk at this time for billing, so we can avoid this inconvenience in the future?"

"Credit card?" They were all maxed out, she was sure without them even checking. And besides, her mother told her to make herself scarce, leave no paper trails, start a new life. Plus, "Charmaine Deveux" was not one of the names she used on her credit cards. She'd been clever enough to remember all that the day before when she made her dream online purchase, clever enough to use a forgotten bank account that had a fake name, clever enough to use an obscure mailing address.

But there was no way to get around this guy. She needed plain, hard, cold cash. "Carlos Lopez" was printed on the gold name badge.

"Wait right here, Mr. Lopez," she mumbled, closing the door in his face. She reached for her jeans and found a five-dollar bill. Her leather vest pocket hid three ones and a quarter. She found her duffel bag under the bed. Five twenties, two dollars, and six pennies.

"I may not have been an 'A' student in math, but I know that none of this equals $2,000." She looked around the rest of the rooms, the bathroom, the sitting areas. Apart from a few stray twenties and one fifty, nothing. The banging on the front door resumed.

"Ms. Deveux?"

"Oh my goodness, what did I do with all my money?" She had come to Dallas with over $130,000. Now she counted only $220.31. "What did I do with all my money?" She wanted to stab herself.

"Ms. Deveux?"

Maya looked back at the door, now shaking on its hinges. She heard a jingle of keys and Carlos calling someone down the corridor.

"What am I going to do?" Panic struck her and she quickly grabbed a few clothes, threw some on, and stuffed the rest into her duffel bag before wrapping a few more items around her neck and arms. She slid the balcony door open and looked from left to right. She was on the top floor of a ten-story building. Despite its modern, chic interior, the hotel building itself was an old one. A fire escape began only inches from her balcony.

She quietly slid the balcony door shut behind her and threw her bag over her shoulder. She was almost halfway down when she heard shouts above her head. Carlos and two other men were on the balcony. They were pointing, and one of the men talked into a handset. A crowd of spectators was forming below. She could see one little girl with red curls and a red ribbon in her hair pointing up at her. Maya knew she had to move faster if she was going to get out of this with no trouble. She freed the clothes from her neck and arms and watched them float away in the wind. A pair of jeans, a T-shirt, her sweatpants flapped away.

It was only a quick glance, but she saw it fly away too. The shoestring. The shoestring stained with his blood that she had held onto after disposing of the knife. The shoestring she had held onto as a memorial.

"Miles! No, wait! Miles! Please, no!" She jumped off the last step and shoved her way through the growing crowd of onlookers.

"Hey, watch it, miss!" A woman pushed Maya. Maya pushed back harder, her eyes looking only for the shoestring. She saw the tip of it hanging out of a street gutter.

"God, please!" She reached the curb just as a cement truck sped by, sending a gust of air that pushed the lace the rest of the way down the grate for it to begin its journey through Dallas's underground sewer system.

"No!" Maya threw her hands to her head. She felt faint. The rush that had sustained her for days, weeks without end, was leaving her. In its place was an emptiness, a sorrow beyond words. She looked back at the hotel. Carlos and an entourage of hotel workers, bystanders, would-be heroes were rushing toward her.

"Miles, why did you leave me?" She started to sit down right there on the curb next to the gutter. What else was there for her to do? But then she saw the little girl with the red curls and the red ribbon in her hair.

"Mommy, what's wrong with that lady?" The girl looked up at her mother, afraid, alarmed, before staring back at Maya. "What's wrong with you?" The sweetness of the girl's voice did not match the accusation of her words.

A rush of red, a rush of memories jolted through Maya. She grabbed the girl's arm, yanked the red ribbon out of her hair, pushed her back to her frozen mother, and then ran.

What's wrong with you? What's wrong with you?

The question would not leave. Not as she pushed her way through the crowded sidewalk. Not as she ran across the busy boulevard, leaving screeching car brakes, horns, yells in her wake. The question followed her as she cut through side streets, alleyways, blind, lost, crying. She did not stop running until she realized she was surrounded by green. Green grass, trees, shrubbery. A city park.

She found some low bushes and collapsed behind them, opening her hand only then to examine the thin, satin strip of red she'd pulled from the little girl's hair several blocks back.

"Daddy gave me ribbons," she whispered, squeezing her hand shut again. She pulled her knees up to her chin and rocked back and forth in a tight ball. And then it all came, as it did sometimes—the questions, the memories, the doubts, the darkness. Her father, the ribbons he gave her, the bed in which he raped her, her mother's scorn. The things she bought, the money she lost, the things she did, the men she met, the people she hated, the strangers she loved. The thoughts, the feelings, though disconnected in form and in logic, became a united substance—one tumbleweed, one mass of disorder, a single ball of chaos, that, like a ball of yarn, zigzagged, looped around itself and easily unraveled.

She felt unwanted, unloved, unworthy, unnecessary. Undone.

Whimpers tore through her and she remembered the other moments she'd felt like this. The razor blade scratches and scars on her thin arms were constant testimonies of those troubled times. It always happened for her like this—days, weeks, sometimes months when she felt on top of the world; the queen, the superstar, untouchable. And then in one quick second, one quick pull of the red carpet from under her feet, the world fell on top of her. She could not see, she could barely breathe, she did not want to feel. It hurt too much.

CHAPTER 35

"So that's your story?" Herman Steinbridge, the counsel from Baltimore Metropolitan Hospital, tapped a pen on the table before collapsing back into his seat. Gideon sat solemn-faced on the other side of the table. His hands were folded in his lap, his focus on the two attorneys in front of him as he clenched his jaw.

"That's a very different story than what you first offered." Herman sighed, a look of reserved compassion filling his face as he tore out a new sheet of paper from his legal pad.

"Yes, very different." Paige Dillery, Gideon's lead attorney, looked bored. She shook her head then frowned. "Look, Dr. Joel, let me be frank with you. All of the evidence, circumstantial and otherwise, points to you. There is a clear motive, from the prosecutor's standpoint. And you already confessed. I—There's no way we can all of sudden change your story and have a judge or jury believe what you are now saying."

"But Paige, you know that might not necessarily be true." Herman interrupted. "You heard the detectives themselves expressing doubt at Gideon's admission. And the weapon still has not been located. Now if we—"

"The state's attorney has already offered a plea bargain. In all honesty, I think we need to seriously consider his offer at this point instead of trying to fabricate an entirely new and different defense. If we come back to the state with the story you're giving now, not only will they probably take back the offer, but they will probably push for a heavier charge carrying a longer sentence." Paige shook her head and rolled her eyes. "I know the prosecuting attorney. I'm surprised he even offered a deal."

"Fabricate a new defense?" Gideon had stopped hearing her after she had used those words. "You don't believe what I'm telling you, do you?"

Paige glanced at Herman before answering. "It's not a question of belief, just a statement of fact. Your new story will not hold. We have nothing to sustain it."

"The knife is still missing." Herman interjected without looking up from the notes he was writing.

Paige was silent for a moment before speaking. "Well, I guess we just have to wait for the coroner's report to see if it will help us." The two attorneys were checking watches, closing briefcases, readying to leave. Just before they did, Gideon said one last thing.

"Tell Charisma I'm sorry. I can't—I need to be free. Completely. I'm not trying to hurt her. I just need to be free."

"Don't worry," Herman smiled, studying the anguish on Gideon's face. "Everything's going to be taken care of. And we'll also look into that accident from last year you just told us about."

Gideon was quiet as he was escorted back to his cell. Last moments kept running through his mind. The last moments before he closed his eyes and ran into the other car last June. The last moments he spent in his old office at Baltimore Metro Hospital, finding his wife wrapped in the arms of another man. The last moments of Miles's life, the last words he heard before the light, the screams.

"Gideon, give me the knife."

He'd felt hands overtaking his at that last moment. Soft hands, delicate hands. And then it was all over.

"I'm sorry, Charisma. I'm not trying to hurt you. I just need to be free," he whispered again.

CHAPTER 36

"Thanks again, Sister Pepperdine." Charisma eased the phone back into the cradle, grateful that Pepperdine had agreed to pick April up from school and keep her for the rest of the evening. It had been an easy argument. The Joels' home was still sealed off with yellow tape, and with all the drama and trauma of the week, it was better for April to have a house to come home to instead of the run of the rack at the Solace Inn.

"Sister Joel, you know that you are more than welcome to come stay with me also. Please come; there's no reason for you to be out there by yourself right now." Concern had reverberated in Pepperdine's voice.

"I know, and thanks, but I really just want some time alone right now, to read my Bible and pray." Charisma had held her breath and then exhaled when Pepperdine let her go with no further inquiries.

Charisma had plans for the night.

She studied herself in the hotel room mirror, trying to recognize the image that stared back at her, glad that she saw no recognition. It was a new look, a new start, a new day. She ran fingers through what was left of her hair. She'd left ten inches of her tresses behind in a trashcan at a beauty shop she'd walked into on Liberty Heights. Now her hair was a quarter of an inch short and dyed platinum blond. Thick eyeliner surrounded her eyes, making her look, she felt, like a cat. She did not mind the feline effect, finding a certain satisfaction in the smoky silver mystique created on her face by a store makeup artist. She studied the clothes she had laid out on the plush comforter before slowly putting them on.

The manager of a boutique at Mondawmin Mall had handpicked Charisma's outfit. Charisma had enjoyed the thick accent that accompanied the words he used to describe the full curves of her body under the tight leather dress.

"This one." He nodded, chin in hand, motioning for her to twirl around in the triple mirrors before directing her to matching thigh-high boots. She charged several more outfits from him, all a size or two smaller than her usual size fourteen, sporting colors, cuts, and cleavage she'd never dared before.

And now the sun was beginning to set. The first part of her plan was complete. It was time for step two of her transformation.

Charisma waited for the clock to tick to 9:00 P.M., munching on a chicken box and sipping a half and half as she sat and stared. She'd gotten the chicken wings, battered and fried potato wedges, and mixture of lemonade and iced tea from a nearby corner store. She had been nervous the entire time at the store, afraid that someone would recognize her face from the news. Thankfully, nobody had even looked her way. The phone was quiet, as she had been careful to advise the hotel manager to keep her whereabouts hushed. She was tired of the reporters, and having used the Solace Inn gift certificate on a couple of other occasions, the manager knew her and sympathized.

She looked in the mirror one last time and left her hotel room before she could let her conscience change her mind. The elevator door opened with a quiet ping, and she headed for the rental car she'd parked in the underground garage for the occasion. Leather seats, sunroof, six-disc CD changer—all features in the rented Altima that did not come standard with her ancient car.

With each passing stoplight, her heart pounded louder, stronger. Finally, she pulled into her destination. The parking lot was already filled to capacity. *Ladies' Night With G.* She read the words on the billboard of Chocolate Heaven. Charisma parked on a nearby street, re-counted the one-dollar bills in her little black bag, re-glossed her lips, and got out. The door to the nightclub was propped open. She paused for a quick second at the entrance, but then went in.

The darkness was suffocating, the flashing lights confusing. Charisma held tight to her purse as shadows danced around her. She felt overdressed. She wondered where to sit. As if reading her mind, a voice called out to her, hands grabbed hers and led her to a padded booth. The music was so loud, the dark and lights so jarring, it took her a minute to make sense of the voice and hands directing her.

"Excuse me?" she leaned over to the darkened face, a mustache and baldhead all she could make out. They were not alone, she realized, seeing flashes of legs, arms, painted lips, sitting across from her. Shot glasses, ash trays, smoke, foreign smells swam around her. The man next to her placed his arm around her shoulders, his breath close to her ear, one hand on her knee. She still could not make out his words. He was drunk.

The room went dark, pitch black. Then a voice on a loudspeaker, a spotlight, a drum roll, a stage, a royal blue silk robe. She held her breath and waited for the show to begin.

One bicep, then another. A leg, a thigh, chest, six-pack. The music got louder, and a crescendo filled the stuffy air as limb by limb, rippling muscle by muscle, the man named G exposed his firm flesh to the whistling, screaming mob. Soon there was nothing left but a diamond-studded blue G-string. Charisma trembled in her seat, a feeling beyond guilt wrestling with the fantasy she was trying to make real. She swallowed hard, keeping one hand in her purse where the dollar bills lay ready. She grabbed a handful and brought it to the top of the table.

"Girl, you better give that man his money. His rent might be due. You know you want to help a brotha out." A woman sitting across from Charisma laughed as another woman howled beside her.

"C'mon!" Both women grabbed Charisma by the hands, pushed her through the throng, then shoved her to the platform where the lights were centered. "You better give that man his money!"

Charisma blinked in the blinding light, trying to make sense of the music, the screams, the gyrating man in the G-string just inches away. Up close, he looked all of eighteen, somebody's baby, a single pimple on his cheek giving his youth away. She was close enough to feel the heat radiating off his body, smell the sweat dripping from his oily skin. The sweat, the heat, carried an odor, and not a pleasant one either, but nobody seemed to mind. She had to steady herself in the swarm to keep from being trampled.

Charisma tried to reconcile this reality with her longtime daydreams. She waited for the buzz, the rush she had expected to feel.

The liberation.

Instead she felt the man's stinky sweat sprinkle all over her as he grabbed her waist and pulled. Before she could protest, she was on the stage with him, his wet body sliding all over her new leather mini-dress.

"Yeah, baby," he grunted as he grinded into her side, his breath smelling like cheese crackers and mint. "Tell me what you want me to do."

She wanted him to get his hands off of her, to let her go, to leave her be, but the music, the screams were too deafening, the flashing lights too blinding, the smell, the sweat too sickening for her to even figure out what to say. She felt lost, she felt nauseated, and even worse, she felt like a piece of toilet paper the man was using to wipe himself. He pressed harder into her side.

"Don't be scared," he muttered in her ear. "Your husband's behind bars. He can't kill me like he did your other man. Just tell me what you need."

Charisma had never felt as much strength in her body as she did at that second. Before the strobe lights circled the stage again, she had detached G from her body, jumped from the stage, pushed through the dollar-bill-slinging crowd, and spotted the exit.

"Wait. Slow down, baby." The baldheaded man who had helped her to her seat when she first came in draped himself around her shoulders in a drunken embrace. "He's just a boy. I know you came in here looking for a man."

Charisma shoved him off too and darted out a side door where someone was throwing up in the dry dirt and a fight between two men and a woman was brewing.

By the time she reached the rented Altima, her breathing was tight, congested. She was having an asthma attack, the first time in years. She coughed, gagged, struggled to find breath, to find her keys, the lock to the door, the old inhaler she kept in her purse at all times. She swung the car door open and sat down hard in the seats, realizing too late that the window had been smashed and glass covered her seat and the floor. The CD player was missing, and she saw other wires sticking out all over the front panel. She stumbled back out of the car, calming down long enough to take a breath from the inhaler she finally fished out of her purse. She wiped glass and bright blood off her hands and legs.

And where are you now, Jesus? Are you waiting for more bloodshed to come rescue me? She remembered her words from earlier that day as she wrapped a tissue around her palm.

Charisma slammed the car door shut, stood alone on the pavement and beckoned for a cab. She looked back up at the sign. *Chocolate Heaven. Ladies' Night With G.*

The rescue this time was simple. She just had to leave. It was a decision *she* had to make, and it was an easy one. There was no freedom here. She wanted only to be free, and it was not here.

"It took surrendering to free me—surrendering to Christ, to what I needed to do, should have already done." She remembered Gideon's words from the jail cell as she sat in the back of a cab, lights, movement all around her on the nighttime city streets. What did she need to do? What should she have already done? *He bore it all, from the inside on out*, Sister Wilson, her Sunday School teacher, had taught.

From the inside on out. Charisma could see herself in the taxi's rearview mirror, a face she had tried to distort, change, with new makeup, new hair; a face that had still been recognized, even with her hair gone, bleached.

From the inside on out. Her freedom would have to come from the inside, she now knew. Whatever that meant, whatever it was to be, *her* freedom would have to come from the inside and work its way out.

Surrendering to Him, to what she needed to do—should have already done—meant looking inside.

"How can I look inside, Lord?" she wanted to whisper as a single tear spilled down her cheek. The taxi bumped along in the darkness, stopped and moved at traffic lights. *"How can I look inside? There's too much hurt and pain, too many stories to have to pick through. I don't even want to know all that's inside of me. Why do I have to look there for freedom? Do you know what's inside of me?"*

She scanned the streets, now a blur of neon and streetlights through her tears; police cars, corner stores, hordes of people a whir whizzing by the windows on her way back to the Solace Inn. *"Do you know what's inside of me?"* She wiped her eyes, clearing out the pool of water in them long enough to see a church sign with a long Bible verse printed on it. She did not see the entire verse, or even make out the scripture reference. She saw only seven words: ". . . Christ in you, the hope of glory . . ."

CHAPTER 37

Madelyn gave the hardwood floor one last good sweep. She was upstairs, and apart from the slight mildew smell, and her damaged bedroom closet, complete order had been restored to her entire home. Now with April gone, and every single trace of Maya burnt to ashes, she felt like she could relax. She'd saved her closet for last, meaning to go through the clothes, shoes, and boxes. It was the one project she'd put off for ages. Now she had a ready excuse to pick through her old belongings.

She started on what had been Harold's side of their shared closet. After his funeral over twelve years ago, she'd given away most of his things, keeping only his favorite blue suit—the one he had been wearing when he took his last breath—a pair of leather slippers, and a yellow tie she'd bought him. She looked at these things now, sitting idly in the closet. She ran her fingers over the breast of the suit, pushed the cloth fibers to her nose and inhaled. Nothing. There was nothing to smell.

Madelyn shook her head and slid the heavy suit jacket off its wooden hanger. The day he died, she'd hung it up in the closet and had not moved it since. Now she held it fully in her arms, clutched it to her bosom. At last she put it on, the long arms falling past her thin wrists. She felt lost in its bigness.

She sat down on an upholstered chair next to her bed, wrapped the suit around her more tightly, the silk lining smooth against her skin. She closed her eyes, readjusting herself in the seat, in his suit. Something sharp poked against her chest, something in the inside pocket, she realized. She opened up the blue jacket and saw a white envelope peeking back at her. An old bill, a mortgage note, she concluded after reading the return address. *Mr. Harold Fitzgerald Windemere* was written in the center. She smiled at the name, smiled even more when she saw that Harold had written on the back of the envelope. A note, one of his last notes to himself, she surmised. He was always writing notes, tying strings around his fingers to remember his next errand.

"Poor Harold," she sniffled, "I wonder if you remembered to make this phone call." She shook her head at the name and number scribbled at the bottom of the envelope. She recognized neither, assumed it was related to the mortgage payment. The word "CALL" was printed and underlined three times beneath the seven digits. "Looked important." She wondered if he'd had the chance to make this phone call before the heart attack that killed him in an instant. He'd collapsed in a phone booth near his accounting business in Park Heights. She wondered if this person, this phone call, had actually been his last conversation.

She looked at the face of the envelope one last time. *Mr. Harold Fitzgerald Windemere, 319 Marigold Street, Baltimore, MD 21213*. The address was wrong. 319 was next door. The Windemeres lived at 321. He must have been calling to fix the mistake, she concluded. She wondered even more if he ever made the call, the daydream fanciful, a new memory to imagine.

She tucked the envelope back into the jacket pocket, draped the suit over her like a blanket. As she drifted off to sleep in the upholstered chair, the name, the phone number, floated in and out of her consciousness. A dream. She would call, Madelyn decided. She would call the number to hear the voice of the last person her husband may have spoken to. The number was probably out of service, she knew, but the small possibility of reconnecting, the thought that she could maybe even finish an overdue errand, brought a sweet excitement.

CHAPTER 38

"My father is crazy." April kicked at the butcher-block table. Though it was only six o'clock in the morning, she was very much awake. "He is a murderer. I am the child of a crazy murderer." She streaked her fingers through the scrambled eggs on her plate before looking up at Pepperdine, who was frying bacon at the tiny stove. The elder woman picked the hot slices out of a black skillet and set them on a waiting paper towel to soak up some of the grease. She turned to face April.

"Honey, I can't even begin to imagine how you are feeling right now, but I don't want you to think you had anything to do with it, or that what happened defines who you are, or what you can do or become. God created greatness in you. Christ calls you His own. There's nothing no human—even a mother or a father—can do to change who *you* are." She smiled at the girl and patted the thick bangs on her forehead. "Everybody has a story, a history, and we can't always determine the time, the place, the setting, and the characters who surround us. What we do have some control over is how the story ends. We have to make good decisions based on God's Word to get us to a peaceful ending."

"You mean happy? A happy ending?" April blinked hard, fast.

Pepperdine put down her dishtowel and walked toward her. "God says in the Book of Jeremiah that He knows the thoughts He thinks toward us, thoughts of peace and not of evil, to give us an expected end, or as one Bible I read said, 'to give us a future and a hope.'" Pepperdine pulled the seated girl against her side, hugging her thin shoulders. "We never know what the ending will be, but we can know that it will be peaceful and full of hope. And peace is joy that can't be explained—the ultimate happiness. There are no bad endings in God's book for God's people." She patted the girl's head once again and went to get some orange juice out of the refrigerator.

"Sister Waters, can I tell you something?" April's voice was barely a whisper, and her eyes were glued to the table.

"What is it?" Pepperdine left the carton of orange juice on the shelf and immediately sat down next to April.

"That man, the one my father killed, I thought he was going to save us."

"Save you? What do you mean?"

"My mother really liked him. She took me with her to meet him last week. He seemed real nice. I thought we were going to be with him. I thought he was going to save us. I even tried to leave school early on Monday to go talk to him myself, to tell him how crazy my father was and that he had to get my mother and me out of that house. But it was too late. My mother was waiting for me outside of school, and my father was waiting for him at home. My father killed that man before any of us had a chance to have a better future. Was that the expected end God had for me and my mother?" April looked up, hopeful.

Pepperdine was quiet for a moment, a rare frown pulling on her lips. "Baby, the story ain't over yet. Eyes have not seen, nor have ears heard the things God has prepared for those that love Him. What you got to remember is that it is *God's* love, *God's* salvation that gets us to *His* end. A mere man can never save you. I think your mother will even tell you that." Pepperdine shook her head. "Salvation is in Jesus alone."

April scraped her fork against the plate, her lower lip trembling. "Do I have to go to school today?"

"Well, I'm not your parent to make that decision, though I fully understand why you wouldn't feel like going. We'll talk to your mother to see what she says."

"Yeah, my mother." April rolled her eyes.

It was a closed-door meeting first thing in the morning. The media, the press, virtually nobody knew about it. The lead investigator and the prosecutor pored over a single folder, the report inside.

"We were going to try to get around it, what the autopsy showed, the cause of death. We really thought it was an insignificant detail, especially since the suspect in custody already confessed to the crime."

"Yeah, but now his story's changed." The prosecutor slammed the file shut. "It's no longer an open-and-shut case. And based on this report, we probably are holding the wrong person."

"That's what Dr. Joel is saying." The investigator shook his head. "And that's what the evidence says too." He looked back down at the autopsy photos, the puncture wounds, the small sealed plastic bag that held the main evidence in question. "We need to find out where this came from, what it is." He held up the bag, squinted at its contents, trying to make sense of the obvious. "Something very different than what we've been thinking happened in that basement on Monday. We need to talk to the other people who were present."

"Starting with the wife." The prosecutor flipped through some more papers in front of him. "And we need to find that other woman, the ex-girlfriend. Somebody's hiding the truth."

Maya wanted to go back home, go somewhere, go away. She crawled out of the bushes that had been her bed the past night, wiping leaves and grass off her clothes, out of her hair. The city park was filling with joggers, dog walkers, others who found a reason to rise with the sun. She wished she had a mirror, but using the back of her hand and her fingers, she could tell her shortened hair was a wreck. Her face was puffy and swollen from a night of crying, her clothes torn and ruined from yesterday's escape.

She did not care.

Even as passers-by stared at her, backed away, or scooted past, she wanted only to find a place to call home, where she was wanted, loved, cared about. Or, at the least, she wanted to find a place where she could have no feeling at all. Numbness was more desirable than the indescribable heaviness that blanketed her now.

She felt worthless, and based on the reactions of those in the park who looked the other way and rushed by, she knew that her feelings were justified. It was true, she had no meaning; she did not exist.

"I do not exist. I do not exist," she muttered repeatedly to herself, still wiping crushed leaves and berries off her hair and clothes. Nobody was even coming close to her.

Only one thought kept her from slashing her wrists, ending it all right then.

Her delivery.

The golden mechanical wings she'd purchased online would be arriving today. Here was her hope. She would concentrate all her energy into those wings, find flight, and wherever she landed, that would be her new home.

Maya closed her eyes and inhaled, the elated mood of the days and weeks before was returning to her, sending her afloat in the morning breeze. Today, she was going to be free. Today, she was going to fly.

She began the walk back to the corner café where she had eaten her first meal in Dallas. It was this address she had used for the delivery. The wings would be coming at any time that day. She had to be there at the door to sign for it, to get it.

She had waited an entire lifetime for this moment, waited for the money that was her due.

Today, she was going to find home. Today, she was going to be free. Today, Maya was going to fly.

CHAPTER 39

The orange and blue flowers on the worn comforter reminded her of someplace tropical. Charisma closed her eyes and stretched out on the double bed, imagining warm sun, cool breezes, swaying palm trees. Crystal clear blue water lapped up on her toes, and white—or better yet—pink sand surrounded her.

Daydreaming.

How much of her life had she spent writing and rewriting her own stories, living in her own created worlds? Charisma sat up and opened her eyes. She was not in the Bahamas or Bermuda. She was at the Solace Inn on Baltimore Street. There because her house was cordoned off for a homicide investigation. A homicide that came after years of daydreaming, years of fantasizing, years of ignoring, hiding, wishing, denying.

Enough was enough.

After the adventures of last night, she knew it was time to wake up, start living in reality. Face the truth head on like the grown woman she was, the grown woman who was still a child of God. Christ was in her, the hope of glory, the promise of a better day to come.

She was ready now.

She was ready to sift through the questions, the fears, the hurts; sift through the rubble to get to the riches. She was ready now to sit down and study the stories that had patched her life together like a random-made quilt—study the squares and rip off the ragged ones whose threads could not warm and served no positive purpose, cut off the patches that weren't designed by the Master. Take off the old, put on the new. It was time for the stories to form a new garment, a new covering, a cloak fit for a queen.

"Christ in me, the hope of glory. Because of Him, and despite everything else, I am royalty, the daughter of a King. Forgive me, Lord, for acting everything but that." For what seemed like the first time in her life, she got on her knees and prayed.

It was a prayer that involved few words because she did not know what to say or what to ask. She only believed—believed, as it was written in the Bible she read, that He was able to do exceedingly abundantly above all that she could ask or think, according to the power that worked in her. Christ would have to go beyond her petitions, beyond her imaginations. There was nothing concrete in her life at that moment, so faith would have to be her concrete, her substance. Faith had to be the living, moving, touchable thing on which she knelt and prayed and waited and listened and hoped and expected.

Out of desperation—because of desperation—she prayed.

She was still on her knees when the knock came at the door. In retrospect, she realized she should have expected it. Praying that intensely can only bring intense results. Even still, she stood speechless when she finally swung the door open.

Her mother, Caroline Jackson, filled the doorway with a smile, a newspaper, and a piece of chocolate cake.

***

"I don't know why she's not answering." Pepperdine pressed her lips together, sending up a quick prayer for wisdom. "She must have the ringer off, or maybe she told the front desk people that she did not want to take any calls. I could understand that. Even still . . . I don't know how to reach your mother." Pepperdine turned around to face April, who was leaning against a wall, arms crossed, fully dressed, a book bag slung over one shoulder.

"I'm not going to school. I am not going." April looked taller than her eleven-turning-twelve-in-two-weeks self. Her twisted ponytails were unraveling at the ends, a childish contradiction against the too-grown scowl on her face. "I'm not going, and you can't make me."

Pepperdine was not fazed. She hung up the phone and reached for her shoes, taking off her slippers. She took her coat off the hook on the back of her closet door. "April, I never said that you were going to school. I think it would be good for you to have some time off, considering the circumstances. We just need to talk to your mother and see what she wants for you right now. She's not picking up the phone, so let's go find her." She didn't say anything else. Instead she grabbed her keys, opened her apartment door, and stepped out into the hallway. April was still frowning, but she followed.

The building was an old three-story row house that had been converted into three separate apartments. Pepperdine lived on the top floor, a feat she took pride in, although her bones and joints were starting to complain. In a silence interrupted only by an occasional grunt from Pepperdine, the two descended the wooden stairs. They were sitting in Pepperdine's car when the elder lady realized she'd left Charisma's hotel room number on the writing pad next to her telephone. Or was it on her nightstand? Or posted on the refrigerator?

"Stay here, baby, I'll be right back." With two more grunts and a loud groan, Pepperdine began the long trek back up to her quarters. After digging through several papers and a notepad, she found the torn sheet from a spiral-bound notebook with the room number scribbled on it in the freezer underneath a bag of frozen broccoli.

"225." She adjusted her bifocals and squinted to make out Charisma's tiny handwriting. "Or is it 229?" She shrugged, deciding just to check both rooms when they got there. For now, she had to pick up the pace if she wanted to drive across town through the beginning morning rush hour and make it back in time for April's school day, if Charisma still wanted her to go.

"Lord, please don't let that girl have to go to school today." Pepperdine prayed as she eased back down the steps, her wide denim jumper ruffling against her legs. She sat back down in her car seat with a solid thud.

"Whew, that was my exercise for the day," she chuckled. "Now when we get to—April?" The seat next to her was empty. On the floor was Pepperdine's pocketbook, open with a few stray dollar bills scattered about.

"Oh dear Lord, where has this child done gone?"

CHAPTER 40

"I need to get this 'p' key fixed," Madelyn mumbled as she jabbed at her twenty-five-year-old typewriter. She was sitting at the desk she kept in the third bedroom upstairs—her home office, complete with file cabinets, three bookcases, and a computer still in its unopened box, a present from one of her sons four Christmases ago. The bookcases were lined with folders and boxes, all in a coordinating green and white ivy pattern, labeled with black marker, and in alphabetical order.

"Today is Thursday." She peeked over her glasses for the fifth time to check the date on the wall calendar. "Library and sewing club day." Grabbing a clean sheet of typing paper from one of the desk drawers, she began her daily task of typing out the day's to-do list.

"Thursday." She checked her calendar one last time before pecking out the day and date at the top and center of the paper. "Thursday? I forgot the 's.'" She reached for one of the bottles of Wite-Out lined up at the side of the desk. Then, changing her mind, she ripped out the page, tore it into two equal halves, fed it to the shredder, and started with a clean sheet in the typewriter. The stress, the thoughts of the last few days must have been getting to her, she reasoned.

A half-hour later, she was spell-checking the four typed pages in front of her. The first page was an outline of the places she needed to go, listed by order and given a time slot: the library at 10:00 A.M. the fabric store at noon, the sewing club at her church's community center from 1:30 P.M. to 4:00 P.M., and a visit to the produce stand at Northeast Market at 4:25 P.M. She would be back home at precisely 5:00 P.M., leaving enough time to roast some chicken legs, bake a potato, and boil green beans for dinner at 6:30 P.M.

The second page listed the books she needed to return and ones she wanted to check out, mostly cookbooks this week. The third page was a shopping list for the fabric store. She was in charge of keeping all the supplies stocked for her sewing club. She had noticed the last time she was there that the bobbins were running low. She had listed all the colors she thought she and the five other women in the club used the most, making a mental note to buy twice as much black thread.

The last page was a shopping list for the market. Topping the list was apples. Giving April some of her homemade apple pie the other night had thrown her off schedule for the church's Easter dinner. Though two of the three pies were still intact, she knew she would have to start all over. Madelyn liked consistency. All three pies should come from the same bag of apples. She was actually glad for the setback, deciding that it would be better to cook the pies the morning they were due instead of freezing them for close to two weeks. What was she thinking? Frozen pies?

Madelyn checked her wristwatch. 8:42 A.M. She was making good time; already dressed and fed, she still had over forty-five minutes to spare before she had to leave for the Enoch Pratt Library. She searched for something else to do, skimming the rows of neat, labeled boxes on the shelves and bookcases for a folder to fix, a book to straighten. No, everything was in order. She took off her glasses, heaved herself up, and headed back to her bedroom.

She'd finished reorganizing her closet before breakfast. Only Harold's blue suit jacket was out of place, draped like a blanket across the upholstered chair by her poster bed. She remembered the envelope in the inside pocket, the name, the number, his last note to himself scribbled on it.

"It's silly for me to call that number after all these years," she smiled, shaking her head, but she put her glasses back on anyway. Her heart stirred in fond remembrance of the man she had loved as she gently removed the envelope from its hiding place. She held the thick white paper in her hands for a moment before going downstairs and sitting at the antique secretary's desk in her foyer. Her telephone was tucked inside. She rolled back the cover, looked at the name, dialed the number, and held her breath. The phone picked up on the first ring.

"Union Mortgage. This is Judy speaking. How may I help you?"

"Union Mortgage?" Madelyn suddenly felt uncertain, unprepared. Why was she calling? What was she supposed to say? What would these people think? Sweat broke over her brow as she stammered through her next words. "I'm sorry. I thought I was calling First Home and Mortgage Company. Forgive me." She flipped over the envelope, studied the return address, then took out the fading statement inside.

"Ma'am? Don't hang up. You called the right place. We used to be First Home and Mortgage, but Union Mortgage bought us out a few years ago. How can I help you today?"

"Uh," Madelyn felt even more lost. "I—Is there an M. Miller there?" She read the name Harold had written down on the back.

"M. Miller? Oh, you must be talking about Mario. He hasn't worked here in years, but I would be more than happy to assist you. How can I help you, ma'am?"

"Oh, well," Madelyn cleared her throat. "This probably sounds a little silly. It's just that, uh, my husband, Harold Windemere, died several years ago, and I was just going through some of his things. I found one of his last correspondences, the mortgage bill, and it looked like there was an error on it. I think he had been planning, or maybe he did call already, to fix it. Our house is already paid in full, for many years now, but I thought it worth checking because the wrong address was given on the statement."

"Well, Mrs. . . . Windemere? That is your name, right?"

"Yes, it is."

"Okay. I'm sure everything is fine, but you can go ahead and give me the account number, if you'd like."

"Uh, okay." Madelyn cleared her throat again and adjusted her glasses. She felt like kicking herself for wasting so much precious time on nonsense. But she had started the task. She had to complete it. "Alright, the account number on this statement is 552YL."

Madelyn could hear Judy typing into a keyboard. There was a long pause before she resumed speaking. "Okay, Mrs. Windemere, I am showing this account. You are right; it has been paid in full. The address I am showing is 319 Marigold Street, Baltimore, Maryland 21213."

"319? That is not the correct address. We live at 321, next door."

"I'm sure it's just an old typo. At any rate, it doesn't really matter. Your house is paid for and has been for quite some time. Everything's fine."

"I just don't like that it's wrong." Madelyn could feel heat rising to her scalp. She hated incompetence, no matter how minor or outdated. Somebody had made a typo on official paperwork that involved her. How could she let that rest? "Surely there's something you can do to fix it? Or should I speak to your supervisor?"

There was a long sigh on the other end. "If it makes you feel any better, I'll go ahead and fix it, and I'll send you something in the mail with the correct address. How does that sound?"

"That would be the right thing to do." Madelyn sniffed and relaxed.

"Hold on for one second please, Mrs. Windemere." There was a loud click followed by classical music.

"*Arabesque Number One* by Claude Debussy," she mumbled, closing her eyes, humming along to the piano notes. It had been a while since she'd heard any music, with the Joels gone now from next door. She'd heard classical pieces come through their walls and windows a few times, but much too loud to be appreciated. It was good to have some silence to think, to listen. Silence was good for the soul, she surmised. It was good to have them gone, although Madelyn was not sure for how long or what would be next.

She peered out her door as the music continued in her ear. The yellow tape still touched the boundaries of her house and extended to the other side of the Joels'. But much to her chagrin, there was more than yellow tape. The investigators were back.

"How many times do they have to keep coming here? What are they looking for? What more do they need? They already have Gideon behind bars." Her heart's pounding now filled her ears more than the piano chords as she thought anew of Maya. Would they come back to ask her more questions? Would they want to talk to Maya again? Another police car pulled to the curb. More detectives piled out. The looks on their faces, the briskness in their gaits. . . . Something was wrong. Had something new come out in the news?

Madelyn jumped back from the doorway and shut the door. She had to get out of there before they started knocking with more questions. She did not think she could last another round of inquiries. It was awful, tragic, intrusive, the things that happened in the Joels' basement on Monday. She did not want to be revisited with any of the events. She wanted no part of it. Anything that had to do with Maya was ash in her furnace. The thought calmed her.

The music changed, another classical piece, this one by Sir Edward Elgar. What was taking so long on the phone? She had to get out of there. She had to leave the typo alone. But she could not hang up.

"Mrs. Windemere?" Judy cut in her thoughts just then. "Sorry that took so long. I was trying to fix the error, but then I saw some other information that did not make sense, and I had to check it out first."

"Look, I need to go." Madelyn was peering out of a window shade. A couple of the investigators standing on the sidewalk were looking up at her house, talking, mumbling, dissecting.

"I apologize for taking up so much of your time, but you need to know that your husband had two accounts with us, both your house at 321 Marigold Street and the house next door at 319."

"Two accounts? That doesn't make sense." Madelyn held her breath as she clutched the lace curtain. One of the investigators had turned onto the walkway leading to her front door. She exhaled when another man called to him and he turned back to the Joels' residence.

"Well, just so you know," Judy continued, "although the house is paid off, my understanding is that another name is also on that account."

"My maiden name is Madelyn Burroughs. Harold used that name for some of our joint holdings for a reason I never quite understood. I'm sure—"

"I've been told it's a different name, Mrs. Windemere, and because your husband is deceased and you are not associated with this account, I'm afraid I'm not able to offer any other information at this time. However, you can—"

"I need to go." Madelyn felt breathless as she slammed the phone down. At that moment, all of the investigators had disappeared inside Charisma and Gideon's home. If she was going to slip away unnoticed, this was the time. She did not have anything else to say to the authorities. She wanted no part of the investigation. She grabbed her list, her tote bag, slipped on her wool overcoat, grabbed her keys, and hurried to her Lincoln Continental.

It was not until she had dropped three quarters into a parking meter in front of the Enoch Pratt Library on Cathedral Street that she tried to make any sense of the information just told to her by Judy of Union Mortgage. Why would Harold be associated with 319 Marigold Street, and who was the other person on that account? She knew it wasn't Charisma or Gideon. They were renting the residence; she remembered Charisma saying that when they moved in.

At any rate, Harold had been dead and buried for years. Unearthing his old business relationships was not an efficient use of time. He'd had many associates throughout the thirty-six years they were married. Many partners, a lot of real estate, deals she had no part of. He'd probably bought 319 and maybe even a number of other houses on their street in an effort to stop the neighborhood decline Madelyn had often complained about, she decided.

She would have to deal with that matter later. Madelyn looked at her to-do list for the day. There was a slight time gap between her dinner and bath later that night. She would revisit the issue then. For now, it was time to check out the next round of cookbooks at the library before getting ready for her sewing club later that afternoon.

CHAPTER 41

They'd sat there talking about nothing in particular for a while now, Charisma and her mother, Caroline Jackson. It had been a little over a year since Charisma had last spoken to her. Their last conversation had centered on the logistics of the Joels' move from the suburbs of Columbia to the heart of East Baltimore. There had been little else to talk about since then. The newspaper Caroline had brought with her lay neatly folded in her lap. A large color photo of Miles in full doctor gear smiled up from the front page.

His widely publicized funeral was later that morning.

Charisma tiptoed around safe topics: the Baltimore Ravens, the chilly March weather, April's Easter clothes. She was never sure what to talk about with her mother, feeling awkward, afraid that she would say something touchy, something that would propel Caroline back into the darkness. When a moment of silence lasted a telling second too long, Caroline was the one who broke it.

"So are we going to talk about this or not?" Caroline flung the newspaper onto the table that separated their two chairs. The pages rustled and settled as she stared at Charisma.

Look at him. Charisma fingered Miles's picture, the chiseled features, the teasing smile, the cocky stance. In all that had happened that week, she had never given herself a moment to think about him, a chance to grieve. Only at this second, with her mother sitting across from her, a slice of chocolate cake covered with plastic wrap between them, Miles smiling at her from beneath a harrowing headline, did it seem real.

Miles was dead.

Charisma sucked in a gulp of air, pushed the paper from her, then looked away. She did not want to sob in front of anyone, especially her mother. Her crying—she knew what people thought, wondered what her mother thought—could be taken as confirmation of an alleged love affair gone bad. She could not cry, could not grieve his loss, regardless of what he had or had not meant to her.

He was a respected doctor of color, full of promise, a man of greatness who had not even reached the highest pinnacle of an already acclaimed career. That loss—the one for the community, for his patients, for his family—was worthy of her grief. Anything else she felt—the dead end to possibility, the memories that stung her conscience, the guilt—was just salt in the tears, salt in the wound. She did not want her mother to see her this way, both for her own protection and for what she believed was her mother's fragile shell. Anybody who'd spent as much time in a psych ward as her mother had probably could not handle a deep display of emotions. Charisma justified her stoicism to herself.

"You should go to the funeral." Caroline's eyes were a deep shade of dark brown, almost black, intense, surrounded by equally dark, thick lashes. "Closure."

"Momma, I don't know what—"

"You don't have to explain anything to me. I know who you are. You are my daughter. You don't have to explain what happened between you and that Dr. Logan, or you and Gideon. I already know." Caroline was folding the paper as she spoke, putting it into a large purse Charisma just noticed was there. “You are my child. Here, have some cake. I baked it myself.”

“Cake? I’m not hungry. And even if I was, cake doesn’t seem appropriate right now.”

“Cake is always appropriate for celebrations, even difficult ones.”

“Celebrations? I don’t think there’s anything to celebrate right now.”

“Of course there is.” Caroline peeled back the plastic, stuck a pinky into a mass of chocolate icing on the side of the paper plate. “Closure.” Caroline licked the chocolate off her finger and started digging in her purse. She pulled out a fork and held it up for inspection as she continued speaking. “A new day. Now, do you want to eat the cake before the funeral or after?”

“Are you serious? I can’t go to the funeral! What will people think? What will they say?”

“You’re always worried about what others will think. That’s half the reason why things got to this point. You weren’t like that before. I remember you kept going to New Zion Hill, even after they kicked me out. What happened? What changed you? Was it me? Was it Gideon? You should never let someone else’s mental state bind *you*. Mental illness is nothing to be ashamed of. Stop hiding. Let people think what they think. You need to go to this funeral for your own well-being. Closure.”

Charisma slid her chair out, jumped to a stand, started straightening the clothes and junk strewn about the small hotel room. The shopping bags from Mondawmin Mall, the hair magazines she’d picked up at a drugstore, the sequined shoes, and the black bag filled with dollar bills from last night. *Chocolate Heaven. Ladies’ Night With G.* She kicked the shoebox under the bed.

“Closure? What are you talking about? What do you think I need closure from?”

"Everything. Whatever was going on between you and Gideon, you and that doctor"—she paused for a slight moment—"you and me, it's time to let it go, move on. You're at a good starting point." She nodded her head at the open Bible on the hotel room's nightstand.

"You and me? What does anything that's going on now have to do with us?"

Caroline shrugged, sighed. "I saw you the other night. Standing next to the evergreen bushes at my house. I wish you had come in. We could have talked then. There's a lot going on, but like I said, you're at a good starting point."

Charisma followed her mother's eyes to the open Bible. Saint John, the chapter on Jesus' first miracle, turning water into wine, was the last scripture she had turned to.

"That's a good starting point. A beginning. But don't stop there." Caroline was quiet for a second, as if lost in another time, another place. "You still teaching Sunday School at your church?"

Charisma nodded, her eyes filling with tears anew, though she could not place why.

"Don't just teach those Sunday School lessons. Live them."

Charisma turned her back to her mother, readjusted a blouse on a closet rack hanger. A sudden surge of anger roared within her as one by one, pictures of her mother with men at their house on North Avenue, with men at Queen Jackson's Hair Parlor, with men at restaurants, standing on the corners, lying naked in her bed, came rolling through her mind; memories, images she was sure Caroline never knew she saw, all the while walking with her, sending her to Sunday morning service at New Zion Hill. When Charisma turned back to face her mother, her finger was pointed at Caroline, and she no longer withheld her tears.

"What do you know about living those lessons? You? You—" Her finger still pointed, her mouth was still open, but no other words could come out.

"More than you realize." It was the first time Caroline looked down, looked away. But only for a second. "Closure, baby girl. That's what I had to come to understand when I began to see what it meant to *really* know Jesus. My past, my mistakes, the things I did, the things others did to me, the darkness—those stories are over. Jesus closed the book and sealed it, started a new one, a fresh page.

"I don't hold on to guilt or depression," Caroline continued. "I don't live in darkness anymore. It was a long, hard road, one I tried to die on. But He did not let me. He kept me alive long enough to deliver me. And He *has* delivered me." She leaned forward, closer, as if Charisma was sitting next to her and not standing across the room. "Closure only came when I knew Him and believed Him for real, when He stopped just being something good to read about or go to church to shout about. I wish I could explain to you the day I realized that, the moment I believed Him for real. I wish you could have seen Him in that moment the way I did, sitting alone in my room one Sunday night. He became my Way, my Truth. My Life. He and His Word are that real to me." She sat back in her seat, breathing hard, out of breath. "That real to me," she whispered.

"Now I know that in spite of what you've been through," Caroline shook her head, "what me, Gideon, that doctor, and whoever else have taken you through, I know that you are a child of God. You trusted Jesus as your Savior from sin a long time ago. Now trust Him as your Savior from everything else and let His Holy Spirit fill you, free you. Let Him make you drunk with His wine so you can be free to dance, sing, move, laugh, whatever. Free to live. Let Him be who He says He is; let Him be that for you."

"Why do you stay at that house if *you're* so free?" Charisma blinked hard, trying to drink in all that had just been poured from her mother's heart.

"I'm there to help. I know my calling, and I know He's using me."

"But you don't have to live there for Him to use you. Go back and visit if you want. They already have a residential assistant. I saw her in there with my own eyes. Why can't you just let that woman do her job and you come back to live in a normal, functioning environment?" Charisma paused, squeezed her eyes shut to get the next words out. "It's embarrassing to say my mother lives in a group home. Why would you choose to stay there if you don't need to?"

Caroline stood, zipped up her purse, left out the fork, stretched, then finally smiled. "Charisma, baby, I don't know who *you* were looking at, but *I* am the residential assistant at that house, full-time, living in. If you had just come to see me, talk to me, know me, you would have known. Things aren't always what they appear to be. You, of all people, should know that." She beckoned to Miles's picture on the newspaper sticking out of her purse. "Everybody thinks you had something going on with that man. You may be my child, but you were never that type. It ain't in you to cheat or lie. Or kill."

She glanced up with an unspoken question at Charisma, who quickly looked away. She wasn't ready for the question. Caroline let out a loud sigh. "Girl, what am I going to do with you? Come on, we got to go to this funeral today so you can bury everything that's dead in your life, once and for all. Ceremonies, they're good for the soul. Here, eat your cake."

Charisma shook her head, smiling reluctantly. "Don't you usually wait until the end of a thing before you start eating cake?"

"Faith celebrates the end before it gets here. That piece of cake? That's your faith, baby, right there. Eat it now, girl. We're trusting God for your freedom. You need to be free to deal with whatever is coming next."

Charisma sighed, rubbed her hands together, and studied her fingernails. Finally, "You can take the cake with us, but let me choose when to eat it. We have to leave now if we want to get to the funeral on time."

Caroline reached out a hand, touched her daughter's short golden hair, rubbed a tear off her cheek, and grabbed her in a tight hug. "I'm sorry for everything." They barely let each other go as they put on coats, grabbed keys and purses.

"We'll take my car." Caroline walked out the door in front of Charisma who slammed it shut.

Neither of them heard the phone ringing inside.

Gideon looked up at the blue sky, his unbuttoned coat flapping in the wind. He stood on the corner outside Baltimore Primary Booking, wanting to take one last look at the crisp scenery around him before he had to get into the taxicab with Herman Steinbridge, who was waiting inside. He looked up at the Jones Falls Expressway overpass on the other side of the street where cars zoomed overhead; a number thirty-six bus roared nearby on Fallsway, leaving a thick plume of black smoke in its wake. He watched a bicyclist wearing a reflecting vest speed by, cutting off an SUV in the process. Gideon swallowed hard as the driver of the large, black sports utility vehicle honked his horn and shouted something out the window.

Normal scenes of traffic on a late Thursday morning. How long had it been since he'd watched traffic go by without feeling his heart pound in his ears, feel heat rising in his blood enough to make sweat beads form on his forehead and palms? Gideon swallowed hard again, wondering what Herman would tell him about the hit-and-run accident he'd had last June. He was free, out on bail, hopefully a good sign. He let himself enjoy the moment, his heart staying at a manageable pitter-patter. Peace must be a side effect of truth and transparency, he gathered. Then he stepped into the yellow cab, warmed both by the heat blasting through the air ducts, and Herman Steinbridge's smile and outstretched hand.

"Good to see you, Dr. Joel." Herman's greeting was short but reassuring as he gave Gideon a quick, firm handshake and resettled back in his seat. "We have a room waiting for you at the Noble Baltimore Hotel downtown. We wanted you to have something comfortable while the investigators sort everything out. Your release was kept quiet, though it will be only a matter of minutes before the media gets wind and starts speculating on what's going on. With the funeral being today, things are bound to get worse before they get better. I'm sure you know that, Dr. Joel, but don't worry. Nobody knows where we're keeping you, so you should not be disturbed."

Herman's words rushed through Gideon's ears like the downtown buildings that blurred around him. He did not know how to phrase his question even after the cab had stopped in front of the canopied entrance of the hotel across from the Charles Center Metro Station. With the click-click of the taxi's hazard lights sounding in his ears, Gideon struggled to gather his words but was determined to get one last weight off his conscience and freed from his thoughts and memory.

"The accident? Have you . . ."

"Yes, I was getting to that." Herman cleared his throat, looked over some papers on top of his briefcase before motioning for Gideon to get out of the car with him and walk toward the entrance. "The victim you hit last year was a drunk driver who actually ran into you and suffered only a broken arm and a scratched forehead. If you had stayed at the scene, you would have been cleared of any wrongdoing. But since you left, the state can charge you with leaving the scene of an accident. However, the prosecutor is working on a deal that would drop all charges if you agree to testify on their behalf."

"Testify for them?"

"Yes. By law, you cannot be forced to testify directly against your wife. They only want you to give an account of your exact actions the minutes just before and just after Miles's death."

"Testify against my wife?" Gideon swallowed hard, wondering what that would mean for him. And her.

"They are considering the role of the other person there also, Maya Windemere, but right now the investigators are deeply concerned about what your wife may or may not have done. They only want you to testify about your specific actions. That's all."

"My wife? I don't know who she is anymore. I don't even know if she is still my wife, if I even still want her to be." Gideon grimaced, betrayal's pain piercing him anew. He closed his eyes, remembering in exact detail the kiss, the embrace he'd seen between Charisma and Miles just hours before Miles's death. "I want to be with her, but I don't know who she is anymore. All I know is that she doesn't want me. But I guess I am willing to do whatever truth requires. You can tell the prosecutors I said that."

The door shutting out Baltimore Street's traffic was closing behind them. Herman adjusted his voice to the sudden onslaught of quiet in the hotel's luxurious lobby. "Don't give up on Charisma just yet, Dr. Joel. Remember, the investigators still want to talk to Maya Windemere again. Look at the car accident you thought you caused last June. All this time, you've been walking around with that immense guilt on your shoulders, and you were not even the cause. Alcohol was the culprit. It's always that one piece of evidence, that one truth that can change an entire story."

They were alone on an elevator, quiet, going up, when Gideon suddenly turned toward Herman. "That one piece of evidence, that one truth that can change an entire story? What is it in this case? With Miles's death? There's something else. They would not have let me go so easily otherwise. What is it?"

Herman looked down at his watch. "You'll be on the fifth floor. Stay there. Call me—only me—if you need anything. We're just trying to keep you from getting any unnecessary attention. I'll be checking in on you often, keeping you up to date."

"There is something you're not telling me. What is it? I need to know. Herman?" The elevator door opened. A man and woman got on as Herman and Gideon got off. Herman was still silent.

"What is it? Tell me!" Gideon demanded as Herman unlocked and opened a room door. Gideon slammed it shut in both of their faces before either could enter. "Herman, I need to know."

Herman sighed. "I'm really not supposed to talk about this yet." He pressed the key into Gideon's hand and turned away.

"Herman, I need to know."

The older man slowly turned back around and sighed. "I'm not even supposed to know."

"Please." Gideon pleaded once more. "What is that one piece of evidence that changes everything?"

"Glass." Herman shook his head as Gideon cocked his head to one side, trying to understand. "The autopsy found glass in the single wound that killed Miles; a tiny shard that looked like it was the tip, or on the tip, of whatever was used to stab him. The coroner found it lodged in his aortic vessel. It was so small, he almost missed it, and from what I understand he didn't even want to include it in his report, afraid it would complicate what was believed to be an open-and-shut case. But after you said what you did about not having anything in your hand at the time of Miles's death, the investigators knew they had to find out for sure where this glass came from. That one sliver might make all the difference in this case. I'll be in touch, Gideon."

Gideon leaned against the door, watching as Herman disappeared back into the elevator.

Glass.

Gideon could think of only one thing. He had to talk to Charisma. He had to know for sure what she did in that basement. He had to hear the truth from her. And he had a strong feeling that he knew exactly where to find her.

He waited until the lighted numbers above the elevator showed that Herman had made it to the first floor then pressed the down arrow himself. When another elevator finally came, a middle-aged woman stood alone in a corner, a newspaper in one of her hands. She stared down at a photo on the front page of the paper, and then stared at him, mouth agape. When he stepped on and the elevator doors began to close, she forced them back open with both hands and ran off. Gideon could see her brunette hair bouncing as she dashed to a hotel worker in the hallway, pointing at him. He did not care.

He would be out of the hotel before anyone else noticed him, realized who he was. And even if they did, it would not stop him.

He had to talk to Charisma, hear the truth—the whole truth—from her mouth. He had to hear her side of the story.

CHAPTER 42

It was not as high as she had dreamed, but it would work. The package was heavier than she expected, making just the thought of finding another location exhausting. Besides, the excitement welling within her had reached its peak; she had to do it. She had to test her wings.

It was time to fly.

Maya peered over the side of an overpass that looked down on the Central Expressway. Using her fingernails, she began tearing through the heavy tape that sealed her package, her destiny. She'd been born for this moment. She was determined to concentrate her twenty-nine years of living into one energy, one focus to help her new mechanical wings give her flight. It was an ambitious goal, she knew, but a goal she believed was fully possible. Not just possible: definite. She was invincible, a trait given only to a select few worthy of its responsibility. This attribute was not something she chose for herself; rather, this gift of flight, this endowment of power, was bequeathed to her from the universe, given to her because she believed.

Maybe she should wait until nighttime, when the constellations would be clear and the stars would be her guide. No, she knew this was the moment. No more putting off her destiny. She had to do this now.

Getting the express delivery had been a cinch. She'd been there to meet the delivery truck driver in front of the corner diner she'd used as her address, and the uniformed man did not even bother to request an ID or ask any questions. Little did he know the power possessed in the brown, unassuming package he wheeled out to her, she smiled to herself.

It had been a laborious task—pushing and shoving the four-foot-tall box through the streets of Dallas—but she had embraced the voyage, the weight of the package forcing her to free herself of all other burdens. It meant tossing off the remaining mementos of her mortal life along the way; her last change of clothes, the last three dollar bills in her pocket, a postcard she'd stolen from a hotel gift shop. She had watched in quiet reverence as the red ribbon that had symbolized her past went fluttering away in the wind.

She had even considered freeing herself of the clothes she was wearing, but decided at the last minute the jeans and sweater she wore were a type of spiritual covering, a veil to shield onlookers' eyes from the supernatural powers she held within, powers that would surely flash in a bright, blinding light when she began her ascent. Her hair had already been freed when she'd used scissors earlier in the week to release her tresses from her head. Maya ran her fingers through the short, stubby strands, relishing this last moment before her complete evolution.

Maya sat the package back on its side and flexed into a yoga position she'd seen once on cable television. She centered her thoughts and every ounce of her being onto flight. Then she looked down at the expressway, wondering which lucky drivers would be the ones to see her hovering over their car tops. She studied the downtown Dallas skyline, picking one of the tallest buildings as her landing place.

It was time.

With ceremonial gravity, she lifted the heavy, metal angel-wing-shaped contraption out of the box. The polished gold glinted in the sun, reflected off passing windshields. A sheet of paper with directions and a warning typed in bold font fell out of the box. Without a quick read or a second thought, she released this too into the wind. Where she was going was unchartered territory; what mere mortal could offer guidance, advice? How could superpowers be contained in step-by-step instructions?

She fastened the nylon straps around her, clicking the belts together. There was a string. She pulled it and a small motor whirred. Fan blades clinked on metal and vibrations rippled down her back. She gave one last sweeping look at the expressway below, the downtown Dallas skyline ahead. With an uneven step—the motor running gave the wings added weight—she placed one foot on the concrete barrier, the last obstacle on the path toward her destiny. She stood in this position a half-second, emboldened by the act, thrilled by the rush of adrenaline. She stretched out her arms, closed her eyes, and prepared to lift her other foot to the threshold of her immortality. It was time for her existence to come full circle. Freedom.

"Get both of them in here." The lead detective rubbed his balding head with both hands. "We need to speak to both of those women to find out what really happened in that basement." There was silence around the cramped office, men and women flipped through folders, comparing notes. A small plastic bag with a label and a tiny shard of glass sat untouched on a conference table.

"The neighbor's daughter, Maya, she would have had access to glass." A female cop with black, blunt-cut hair spoke over square frames. "Remember how her mother's house looked? There was plenty of broken glass inside of there. Did we ever figure out who tore up that woman's house?"

"Something's just not adding up here." The lead detective murmured. Heads nodded in silent agreement, but the silence did not last for long. A door swung open and a uniformed man rushed in, followed by a breathless Pepperdine Waters.

"We can't find the girl," the new officer stated.

"She ran away! I don't know where she done run off to! Oh, Jesus! God, help!" Pepperdine rarely looked frantic, rarely panicked, but at this moment, sheer anxiety made her look all of her seventy-nine years and then some. Her knees looked frail as they shook under her weight. She held onto the officer standing next to her for balance, as if merely speaking about the events of that morning would topple her over. "I don't know where the girl went!"

"Mrs. Windemere?" The lead investigator raised an eyebrow, searching Pepperdine's face for recognition, thinking that she was Madelyn. He had talked briefly to Madelyn Windemere the day of the murder, but did not recall Maya's mother looking this old or heavyset. "Don't worry." He rubbed his bald head again as he studied Pepperdine. "We'll do our best to find Maya. We were just thinking we wanted to talk to her again anyway. Please have a seat. Maybe you can answer some questions for us while we look for your daughter."

"Maya? My daughter? Who?" Pepperdine's limbs shook even more. A chair was slid over to her but she slid it back across the floor. "I'm talking about April, Charisma and Gideon's little girl! My name is Pepperdine Waters, and I go to the Joels' church. Charisma asked me to watch April for her, and this morning when I came back to my car after getting something out my house, April was gone. And now I don't even know where Charisma is either! I don't know—I can't—Look, I—Jesus—" Her words turned into torrents of prayer that nobody in the room understood. Somebody offered her a cup of water, tried to help her into a seat, but Pepperdine threw her hands in the air, weeping.

The lead investigator was momentarily mesmerized by the elderly woman who had suddenly transformed into a strong, robust praying machine, but then snapped back to attention with the realization of what she had just said. "Where's Charisma?" He shuffled through papers, then picked up a telephone.

The officer who came in with Pepperdine had a quick reply. "We don't know. The manager at the hotel where she was staying saw her leave with an unidentified woman in an unidentified car a couple of hours ago. Charisma's car is still parked in the Solace Inn garage, but a Nissan Altima she rented yesterday was found this morning broken into and vandalized outside of a nightclub in East Baltimore. We spoke with some of the people there who confirmed she was there last night, on stage dancing with a stripper. And—this you might find interesting—she has greatly altered her appearance; cut and dyed her hair, changed her style of clothes. We're working with the camera staff there to get a still shot of her."

"Really? That *is* interesting. I wonder what she is up to. Get in touch with Gideon." The lead investigator was scurrying to a dry erase board, picking up a marker to make notes.

"I just tried to, sir." The black-haired female cop twisted a phone cord between her neat nails. "One of his attorneys, Herman Steinbridge, just told me that they can't find him either. Apparently he left the place they were hiding him in as soon as he was alone."

"They assured us he wasn't a flight risk. We only agreed to let him go on the condition that he would be available for more questioning. Call our sources at the FBI. I want information about every checking, savings, credit account he has, past, present, and future. I want that still shot of Charisma ASAP. Check out all her accounts too, anything, everything. Find out who her family is, where they are. Get information on every recent financial action made from them within the last three days. While you're at it, look up Madelyn Windemere's accounts also. And find Maya!" The investigator paused for a moment, looking down at some notes scribbled on a sheet of loose-leaf paper before continuing.

"We already know Gideon's originally from Texas. Get on the phone with somebody down there to see if he has any family or friends who have heard from him recently. As far as April's concerned, send out an Amber Alert. We don't know what's happened to her. She could have run away; she could have been taken. She's had a rough week herself. She's probably scared, lonely, God knows what else. I want every available officer on this case." The lead detective's eyes swept over the entire room of motionless officers, and then he frowned. "Why are you still sitting here?" he barked.

With those words, the office scrambled to life, uniformed officers, men and women in plainclothes and badges scampered off in different directions. The lead investigator sighed and looked down at Pepperdine, who had finally settled in one of the comfortable lounge chairs that bordered the large office suite. She was silent, but her lips still moved in prayer.

"So, how long have you known the Joels?" The man grabbed a folding chair and pulled it close to Pepperdine before sitting down next to her. He noted her wringing hands, her heavy sighs. "Ms. Waters, are you feeling okay? Do you want me to get you some coffee?"

Pepperdine squeezed her eyes shut as tears pricked through them. "I only want all of them to be okay. That's all. The Joels really are good people. You should know that before you start thinking something bad about them."

The man inched forward in his seat. He held his breath and stopped himself from taking out a pen to jot down more notes. He wanted the old woman to relax and not feel like he was questioning her. "So you have known them for quite some time, huh?"

Pepperdine's lips pursed into a faint smile. "I've been praying for them for a while now. I'd been getting a sense that something was wrong. For one, I'd started getting these phone calls late at night, somebody calling without speaking and then hanging up."

"We'll check your telephone records." The detective felt importance in that disclosure.

"Plus, just this past Sunday, Deacon Caddaway and I were at their house and—"

"Phone call!" The office door burst open with an officer holding out a cell phone. Seeing the agitation on the investigator's face as he looked between Pepperdine and the outstretched phone, the officer quickly added, "Sir, you want to take this call. It's from Texas!"

Madelyn walked down the fabric-filled rows for the fourth time. She ran her fingers over heavy flannel, then over a spool of a colorful calico print. She walked to the metal cabinets in the center of the store where countless sewing patterns were tucked inside. She picked out a couple of patterns for suits, one for an elegant, calf-length dress, perfect for the upcoming Easter dinner. She looked, she picked, she felt, but she still could not rest.

She'd been at the fabric store for over thirty minutes—entirely too long—and still had not made it to the bobbin section. This was not like her. She could not concentrate, causing her to be inefficient with her time. This was not good, and she did not like it.

"Mrs. Windemere, are you finding what you need today?" A sales clerk approached her cautiously, her breath held as she kept her hands clasped together. "Please let me know if I can help you find anything. We did place the order for the mint green lace, as you requested last week. Sorry that it is not here yet, but like I told you when you last called, it should definitely be here by tomorrow. Is there something else I can help you find?" She held her breath again.

Madelyn shook her head, then flicked her hand to motion the young woman away. She was drawing too much attention to herself. Madelyn could feel the heat rising again. She had to concentrate. Her nerves were giving her away.

But why would Harold own the house next door? And who *owned it with him?*

The questions would not leave her. And those were the easy ones to answer. No matter how much she tried to shake them off, the questions simmered and swirled in the pit of her stomach. She was getting nauseous from not having the answers. She needed to know, and if she was going to have a productive day, she needed to know right now. She'd wasted too much time already wondering the whos and whys, knocking over books, bumping into shelves during her trip to the library earlier. She could not afford to waste another second, especially now that she was getting the attention of those who knew her, knew her routine and efficiency.

"Hold these for me." Madelyn's voice was forced and strained as she dropped a handful of black bobbins on the sales counter, a plastic smile plastered on her face. The young sales clerk, a longtime store employee familiar with Mrs. Windemere's regular visits and demands, quickly acquiesced to Madelyn's wishes, pushing the bobbins into a small white bag.

"Th-they'll be here whenever you're ready, Mrs. Windemere." The clerk stammered, then exhaled as Madelyn scooted out of the store.

Madelyn had to talk to Judy of Union Mortgage again. She should have never hung up without getting those questions answered, but it was a move that was necessary at the time. She could not afford to be hassled by those investigators again. She had to hang up and leave her house before they came knocking on her front door. Maya was out of her life. She did not want to talk about her or anything related to her. Maya and her lies. Sick Maya. Crazy Maya. She did not want to talk about that basement. Madelyn's stomach churned again, but she was comforted in knowing that she was doing something about it.

Sitting in the plush interior of her Lincoln Continental, she headed toward Belair Road where the mortgage company was located. She remembered the return address on the envelope in Harold's suit pocket, the street numbers now a secret code that would return order, balance to her senses.

CHAPTER 43

The podium was filled with great men and women, respected doctors, researchers, movers and shakers in the medical field. Charisma tightened the black knit scarf around her head and readjusted her sunglasses as a soft, chilly wind blew. She watched as each speaker stood in turn and took over the microphone. It seemed everyone had a speech to give, an anecdote, a memory to share about Dr. Miles Logan, both at the chapel—which had been filled beyond capacity by family, friends, associates, and the curious who'd been following the drama on CNN—and here now at the gravesite, which had been transformed into an outdoor auditorium around a grand fountain, with plenteous seating in front of a platform decorated with a wreath of exotic flowers.

The memorial service had been a lengthy, extravagant affair; the pomp, the grandeur a match to the man being remembered—flowers from every continent, mourners from every corner of the globe. Charisma never realized the spell Miles had cast on so many people. She never knew the height or depth of his outstanding research and too-short career. Even now, as the last speaker rose from her padded folding chair and took her place behind the lecturn, Charisma wondered why and how a man of such obvious greatness had become part of her world. She was not a believer in coincidence; she was certain that everyone who crossed her path did so for a reason.

She glanced over at her mother, who was completely absorbed in the last speaker's speech, a faint smile intense on her face.

What was the reason for Miles? Charisma watched the wind ruffle through the tall tree branches bordering the quiet cemetery. Had she filled whatever calling or purpose was meant by her life touching his? Had he been a better man for knowing her, for talking to her? She thought of their last encounter—a moment of seduction, yearning, a subconscious fantasy fulfilled. It was a selfish moment for both of them. If Christ had been at the center of her yearnings, how different would have been the outcome?

What was the reason for Miles? At this moment commemorating his death, she vowed to live a new life, a life that made the people who knew her better for knowing her. Perhaps if she had denied herself, taken up her cross, and followed Jesus at that moment—as He taught—a life besides her own may have been saved. Charisma squeezed her eyes shut as other Bible verses came to mind. *Reckon ye also yourselves to be dead indeed unto sin, but alive unto God through Jesus Christ our Lord* and *Set your affection on things above, not on things on the earth. For ye are dead, and your life is hid with Christ in God.*

Miles was dead, literally, his life gone. But maybe—she blinked back more tears as she pondered—there was a death that brought life, a dying to the self that gave rise to life not only to an individual but to everyone around him or her, much like a seed that had to be considered dead and buried in the ground before anything blossomed and grew from it. *For whosoever will save his life shall lose it: and whosoever will lose his life for my sake shall find it. For what is a man profited, if he shall gain the whole world, and lose his own soul? Or what shall a man give in exchange for his soul?* They were Bible verses, memory verses, from Sunday school lessons past, lessons taught, but had she ever really learned them, lived them?

"Ashes to ashes, dust to dust." A heavily robed minister sprinkled dirt over the ornate coffin, watching in solemnity as the graveyard caretakers began lowering the casket into the ground, a life now being buried. Charisma watched as the crowd began to slowly thin away. She watched the doctors, the dignitaries file out; the patients, the admirers, the curious quietly leave; the women, the many, many women whose sobs and tears told the other side of Miles's story—the escapades, the one-night stands, the heartbreak, the lust—leave with sullen frowns, downcast eyes. Miles Logan, the doctor, the man, the legacy.

For what is a man profited, if he shall gain the whole world, and lose his own soul? Or what shall a man give in exchange for his soul?

"I pray for your soul." Charisma whispered between cold breezes, the scarf and sunglasses a cloak. "I should have been praying for your soul." She picked out a single yellow carnation from a lavish flower arrangement and tossed it into the black void where his coffin rested below.

She was turning to leave with her mother when something caught her eye.

Gideon kept his distance from the crowd, recognizing many of his former colleagues and friends among the faces, wanting only to talk to Charisma by herself. Partially hidden behind a marble mausoleum about fifty yards from the last row of seats, he scanned the murmuring masses as they exited the memorial park.

Within minutes of the last speaker's remarks and the lowering of the casket, the crowd had thinned out enough for him to study more closely the few remaining females. He was sure Charisma was among them.

His suspicions turned into confirmations as he watched a woman drop a yellow flower into the unearthed ground. She was shielded by a full-length black coat, her head covered with a knit scarf, her eyes hidden underneath sunglasses. Just the same, there was something in her movements that seemed familiar, something recognizable in the self-conscious slouch of her gait, the slightly bowed head. This woman, this hidden woman, he felt he knew her, but in his heart he wondered how much.

This woman, this hidden woman, was she really his wife, the woman he'd married years ago? Was she just a stranger in black, or was she the person who'd shared many days and nights with him. Light and darkness had been their bed of intimacy, and now Gideon felt like he'd just awoken to see who the stranger was who had been lying beside him.

But this was no stranger, Gideon knew. This woman, this was his wife, the one person who had stayed with him during both the blue sky days and the years of black fog. Light and darkness. She'd been there to hold his hand, to hold his head, to hold him.

That is, until recently.

Gideon looked back at the green tent where only flowers rested where a casket once laid. He did not see the yellow, the red, the purple, the white blossoms. He saw only his desk, his old desk at Baltimore Metropolitan Hospital, where a man who'd once claimed to be his friend held in his arms a woman who had now become to Gideon a stranger, a woman cloaked, a woman hidden.

He did not know her.

It was a mistake to come, Gideon realized as a single tear struggled to break free. He did not know this woman. What was he supposed to say to a stranger? What questions was he supposed to ask? What truth did he really want to hear from her lips? Gideon turned away as the tear won its fight and streaked down his brown face. He rested the side of his head against the cold marble next to him; grief, heartbreak, betrayal the only feelings in his limbs.

Even as he tried to shut out the images of the past week, other images came to mind. Memories of their wedding day, their wedding night; their honeymoon and the house he gave her—the first one in Columbia, not the second. He had kept his promise of building her a fine home, he remembered, as memories of their first talks in the hospital cafeteria flooded his mind. Memories of the early days, the first few years, the birth of their only child, the trip to France—

Enserrer.

Gideon dried of all tears and straightened to a taut stand. He had come to this place for a reason, a conversation he needed to have, words he needed to hear. He needed to know the truth, the truth about Monday, about what happened at the hospital and in his basement. No matter how much it would hurt, he needed to hear it, and he needed to hear it from her.

He stepped from behind the mausoleum, standing in full view of whoever was left. He looked again for the woman, his wife, and saw her frozen by the green tent. Caroline Jackson, his mother-in-law and former patient, stood beside her. But it was not the sight of Caroline that stopped Gideon in his tracks. He saw what had Charisma's attention. He saw the look on her face. He knew that the next few moments would be unbearable to watch. He stepped back behind the mausoleum, wanting, waiting for it all to be over.

The police were there, and Charisma could tell from their stance, their stares, they were there for her. It was the gleam of a badge peeking out of a pocket that had caught her eye. Out of respect for the ceremony they had waited until the end, she realized, and was both appreciative and appalled at the gesture. She had assumed this moment would come, although she did not know why. She looked to her mother in silence for help.

"It's necessary. Closure." Her mother smiled, but had to step away because a man had come between them.

"Mrs. Joel, we can keep this clean and quiet. No handcuffs, nothing to alert the press or these people of anything that's going on right now. The black car, the last one at the end, that's where I need you to walk to, to get in. Take my hand. We'll walk together."

"I didn't do it." Charisma's voice was weak and raspy. She squeezed her eyes shut as she walked with the man, remembering in fuzzy detail the blackness in her basement Monday afternoon. The voices, the shouts, the pleas, the fighting. "I didn't do it," she whispered again, although the moment of Miles's death still seemed fuzzy to her, remote, distant. She was not sure exactly what happened in that dark second. She remembered only the darkness.

"Let's just get to the station," the man muttered, and then noticed for the first time the woman standing next to Charisma. He raised an eyebrow as the woman stayed by Charisma's side, but did not question her as she got into the car with her. Caroline nodded and politely smiled as the man shut the door behind her.

"We might as well get Gideon too." The detective pointed to the mausoleum yards away, and another plainclothes officer began walking toward it. Before he got there, Gideon stepped into plain view and headed toward them. His gaze, his gait were woven with certainty, confidence. Not until he reached the car door, inches away from Charisma, did a quick question shoot across his face, his eyes.

They were sitting in the back seat, the three of them, Caroline, Charisma, and Gideon. Charisma sat squeezed in the middle, her hands folded around Miles's obituary program. Gideon sat to the right of her, his attention focused on something outside his window, and Caroline was next to the other window, fumbling around with her open pocketbook, the slice of chocolate cake peeking out. They rode in silence as the black car turned out of the cemetery and sped toward a ramp for I-695 and then the Jones Fall Expressway. They were going to the main precinct.

Charisma squeezed her eyes shut, reminding herself to breathe, feeling numb, detached, desperate. She would have let the feelings swallow her, but a verse, words of Jesus, kept whispering gently in her mind. *And, lo, I am with you always, even unto the end of the world.* Even unto the end. The end.

This might be the end to the world as she knew it, but she remembered something else, another verse, words of Jesus in Revelation, the book in the Bible that talked about the end of times: "*I am Alpha and Omega, the beginning and the ending, saith the Lord, which is, and which was, and which is to come, the Almighty.*"

The beginning and the ending. The phrase rolled over and over in Charisma's mind.

If there was an end, it only meant another beginning was starting, and both the ending and the beginning were found in Him—are Him.

Charisma felt a wave of relief, no longer afraid of the stories that made up her life, the stories that were and the stories that were to come. She knew the Author of her life, and now she was choosing to submit to His outline, submit to His text.

I am with you always. Christ's words, Charisma's thoughts.

Charisma looked over at her mother's purse, reached for the cake, and smiled.

"Closure," her mother mouthed as chocolate crumbs piled in Charisma's lap.

The beginning and the ending, Charisma reflected. She finished the slice, licked her fingers, and nestled back into her seat for the rest of the ride to the precinct.

Gideon looked over at his wife, and sensing her peace, rested his head on the back of his seat. For once, they were in the same place, going the same direction, waiting together for an end, a beginning, whatever that would be.

CHAPTER 44

Madelyn popped another aspirin into her mouth and followed it with a large gulp of water she'd gotten from the water cooler at the office of Union Mortgage. She carefully placed the small white paper cup in a trash receptacle and then sat back down in the padded chair Judy had offered her during the wait.

The wait had completely thrown off her day's schedule. The wait was killing her nerves. She contemplated taking one more aspirin in an attempt to lessen the throbbing headache that had grabbed her temples but knew she had already exceeded the recommended dose. A trip to the emergency room would further disrupt her schedule.

She searched the small office for something to do while Judy and her boss were in another room, behind closed doors, discussing something or other about the house on Marigold Street that Harold owned but did not live in, the house next door to Madelyn. She needed a clue, an explanation, something, anything to bring order back to her day. Right now, everything, the wait, was driving her helter-skelter. She saw a few dying plants sitting on windowsills scattered throughout the mostly single-room office, and promptly grabbed a new paper cup and filled it with water to begin watering them. At least she would be doing something productive and not wasting time as the wait lengthened. Finally, the boss's door swung open.

"Mrs. Windemere? Hi, I'm Greg. I apologize for the long wait. Judy told me about your situation, and since this account had not been looked at in over a decade, it took awhile to get some background information on it. Please, come into my office, have a seat."

Madelyn cleared her throat, clutched her purse, and followed the young man into a plainly furnished office. Judy was on the telephone, but she smiled and nodded at Madelyn's entrance.

"Please, Mrs. Windemere, have a seat." Greg motioned to a chair in front of his desk. Madelyn did not budge from the doorway. "Look, I have a lot I need to get done today, and this time has already interfered tremendously with my scheduled activities. I only wanted to get the name of the other person on the mortgage that my husband paid for. That's all."

"I'm sorry for the long wait. Judy is actually still on the phone with the title company. It appears that the situation is more complicated than we thought. Not only did he have a co-owner with the house, but apparently, according to a lawyer we found associated with the account, your husband had a second will somewhere that left the house to a completely different person, among other things, including some savings accounts, stocks, and bonds that were not listed in his first will."

"Among other things? Second will? What on earth are you talking about? Harold left very specific directions concerning his estate. What other accounts did he have?" Madelyn was growing more impatient and confused by the minute. She checked her watch. Her sewing circle was probably cleaning up by now. She imagined one of the ladies sweeping up scraps of material and loose threads from the floor of the church's community center. How could she explain her absence to them? She glanced at Judy on the phone, knowing a phone call to her sewing friends was inevitable.

"Again, I apologize for all the confusion," Greg continued. "The people who handled this account years ago no longer work here, and we are getting information for the first time just like you. Because your name was not associated with the house, there were some legal hoops we had to jump through just to get you the little bit of info we have so far. Trust me, I know you want some peace and answers, and we—both Judy and I—have devoted our entire afternoon to giving you just that. The attorney was not able to divulge any names, so we're just waiting now for Judy to get through to the title company. A representative from there should be able to tell us to whom the house was left."

Maya. The house was left to Maya. Madelyn was almost certain. She slunk into the chair Greg had offered and blew out a loud sigh. It had to be Maya, she reasoned, although she could not think of one single explanation as to why Harold would do such a thing and, even more importantly, why he would not tell Madelyn. Maybe, she began to conclude, he'd left Maya the house because Madelyn had kicked her out as a teen, and that was his way of ensuring Maya had a roof over her head once he was gone. He probably had not told Madelyn, knowing that she would not have gone along with having Maya as a permanent neighbor.

Even still, that did not explain why someone other than Maya was also associated with the house, a co-owner who existed before Harold's second will was penned.

"Yes, I'm here." Judy suddenly sprung to life on the telephone, her voice breaking the brief silence. "Okay . . . okay. I see. Thank you." She scribbled something on a notepad before hanging up the phone and smiling back up at Madelyn. "Mrs. Windemere, I know Greg filled you in with everything so far, and I'm not sure how much this will help, but I did get an address associated with the second owner of 319. In the meantime, someone at the title company is helping to locate Harold's second will so we can find out to whom the house was left. I'm not sure how long it will take to hear back from them, and I know you have other things to do today. If you have a cell phone number, I'll call you as soon as I hear something."

Madelyn considered the suggestion and decided it would work. If she left now, she might still be able to catch her sewing circle, and she could just say she was detained at the fabric store, waiting for a shipment of bobbins that was being unloaded. If she got there now, she would not have to offer another explanation later. Madelyn fished in her handbag, looking for the prepaid wireless phone one of her sons had given her for emergencies. She rarely used it, except to add new minutes before old ones expired. She turned the phone on and looked at the screen. She had four minutes left.

"Yes, I'll leave you this number and you call me when you find out a name." Madelyn took out a pen and wrote the number on a legal pad Greg handed to her.

"Here's the address for the co-owner of the residence at 319 Marigold." Judy extended a piece of paper. Madelyn froze in her tracks, forgetting that Judy did say that she had an address to give her. Madelyn took the paper slowly from her, read it, tried to place it, tried to remember why it sounded familiar.

She was still trying to conjure up a memory, a place, as she started her car. The address sounded too familiar. She was almost at Christ Cathedral when she looked back down at the address written in Judy's neat cursive. The ladies from the sewing circle were emerging from a side door at the church, bags and fabric in their hands. None of them could see Madelyn waiting at a traffic light two blocks away. She watched as they laughed, hugged, and began to part ways.

It was not too late to go up to them and offer a reasonable explanation for her absence. It was not too late to pretend that this wrinkle in her day, in her life, in her world, did not exist, had not suddenly sprung up for no reason, with no reason.

The light turned green. Madelyn's hands trembled on the steering wheel as she pushed her foot down on the accelerator. One block away. The sewing circle ladies were already going their separate ways, some walking, others closing car doors. Madelyn realized she was holding her breath. Her heart pounded rapidly as another light turned red. She was on the other side of the street from the church. The ladies were walking away, were pulling away. By the time the light turned green, they were all gone.

Her day was done, her schedule completely demolished. There was nothing to do but keep driving, to go to the address that was evading her. She gripped both hands tighter around the steering wheel and continued forward. As she drove, she looked down at her cell phone waiting face up in the passenger seat. It was still on, still quiet. She wondered if and when Judy would call, and then wondered how that call, the information in it, would change her life.

For a brief second, Maya flashed across her thoughts. Where was she? What was she doing? But Madelyn quickly extinguished that line of questioning, reminding herself that her life was better off, her nerves better off, not knowing the answers. She had done what she had to do to get rid of the girl once and for all. She shuddered at the thought of Maya with all that money.

She could only imagine what the girl had bought by now, grateful that no new delivery trucks had stopped in front of her house. What was Maya up to?

"I'm better for not knowing." Madelyn spoke aloud to reassure herself despite a thick knot forming in the center of her chest, a sensation like rubber bands stretching, ready to pop. The pain sharpened as she realized she was only blocks away from the address Judy had given her. She looked back down at the paper, though the numbers were already seared in her memory, both now and from a time she could not put her finger on.

The scenery in this part of town did little to ease her nerves. Abandonment, dilapidation, litter, decay surrounded her on all sides. Madelyn said a quick prayer for safety as she parallel parked her car on a block that looked too familiar.

"I know I've been here before." She wanted to kick herself, scream, something, anything that would help her figure out why this address was overshadowed with recognition. She stood on the sidewalk, examining the desolate block—boarded-up buildings, broken row homes, broken lives all around. Despite the ruin, everything looked familiar, everything, that is, except the actual building at the address she'd been given.

She looked up at the glass storefront. A music and electronics shop stared back at her. Signs for new and used CDs, video games, and DVDs were posted in the windows, along with posters advertising hip-hop concerts, nightclubs, DJ and promotion services. She walked in and blinked her eyes to adjust to the sudden shift to darkness, the smell of marijuana, the shadowy figures talking softly behind a cash register at the back of the store.

"Can I help you?" The question, though friendly in word, held a bite, a sneer in it. Madelyn's heart almost stopped for fear as one of the shadows approached. "You need something?"

"No," she breathed out and nearly ran out of the door. She smoothed down her white wool coat, got quickly back into her car and started it up again. "Ungodly heathens," she muttered as she dug through her purse for the small can of Lysol she kept inside. She sprayed her clothes and the interior of the car as she drove away.

Her library books—the cookbooks—still sat on the backseat next to her typed to-do list for the day. She started to reach for it, to see what she could salvage of the remainder of her schedule, but her throbbing head and pounding heart needed a break. As much as she hated to do so, she would have to come up with another plan for the evening. She headed home.

As soon as she turned on her block, she immediately knew the decision to return home had been a mistake. A police cruiser was waiting outside her house, a uniformed man outside her door. She would have pressed down on the accelerator and continued straight ahead had not the man waved her down.

"Mrs. Windemere?" He motioned for her to roll down the window.

"Yes?"

Maya Windemere's mother?"

This could not be good news. Madelyn braced herself, feeling something inside her sink at the mere mention of that girl's name. She clutched the steering wheel even tighter, her heart thump-thumping like a Pimlico racehorse.

"We need you to come down to the station."

"Right now?" She tried to sound cheery, plastered on a smile.

"Right now." The officer was serious in tone, sober in demeanor. She wondered how long he had been waiting, if he had been in front of her house all day. *What were the neighbors thinking?*

She wanted to freshen up, maybe change her clothes, spritz on a fresh coat of body spray—floral-scented was her favorite. She started to ask the officer if she could run in her house to do those things but already knew the answer would be no.

Madelyn sat down with a heavy thud in the backseat of the cruiser, cleared her throat and dug through her purse for her mirror and lipstick. She would have to make do with what she had to make herself presentable, she decided as she pushed her glasses up the bridge of her nose and pursed her lips in the mirror.

At once obsessed with her appearance, she ran her fingers through her wig, wishing that all of her favorite hair pieces had not been damaged in Monday's assault on her home. She ran her fingers through the fake hair, patting down one side, picking through the other. It had been years since she'd gone out in public without a wig, her natural hair a victim of hereditary hair loss.

She was almost finished fixing the wig, adjusting the nape when it came to her. The address. The block that was so familiar, the building that had evaded her memories. The music and electronics store was new, but the address was the same.

It used to be a hair salon, that building, that address, a popular beauty shop on a once-thriving block of North Avenue. She'd gone there herself a couple of times many, many years ago. She waited for another revelation, a face, a name to come to mind, but none surfaced.

CHAPTER 45

Pepperdine Waters kept her Bible open in her lap as she sat in an empty room at the main police precinct. She read through her favorite Psalms, looking for comfort and peace in the prayers and songs of David, a man who faced dangers and disasters on an almost-constant basis, it seemed. She flipped to the next book, Proverbs, to glean wisdom and advice, stopping at the sixteenth chapter, the twentieth verse: "He that handleth a matter wisely shall find good: and whoso trusteth in the Lord, happy is he." She closed her eyes to pray, her voice a whisper echoing in the quiet room.

"Lord, all of us—Gideon, Charisma, that young doctor, Deacon Caddaway, the police officers—all of us have had a part to play in the events that led up to this disaster. Please let me handle my part in this matter wisely. You know that I have sought you and your wisdom on every turn, reading your Word, talking to and waiting to hear back from you. Please, Jesus, let there be a happy ending in all this. I trust you. Amen."

She kept her eyes closed, reflecting on her breakfast with April only hours earlier. The girl had been asking about happy endings. At this point, all Pepperdine could do was cling to the last verse she had just read, the promise in it. W*hoso trusteth in the Lord, happy is he.*

She was still rocking in her seat, quietly meditating when the door to the room was flung open. Gideon, Charisma, and Caroline were being escorted in.

"Ooh, Charisma, look at you!" Pepperdine smiled as Charisma's knit scarf came off, revealing her new micro-short, platinum blond haircut. "Baby, you look good no matter what—as long as that's you, and not you hiding behind someone pretending to be you." Pepperdine started to say something else but Charisma cut her off.

"Where's April?" Panic colored her voice and face. "They just told us that she's missing. Oh, God, help! Have you heard anything?" Charisma's words came out in one breath as she practically ran across the room and collapsed into Pepperdine's lap. But before Pepperdine could stroke a hand on Charisma's back in consolation, Gideon was next to her. He got down on his knees beside Charisma and wrapped his arms around his wife.

"April's okay." Gideon's words came out in a whisper.

"But where is she?" Charisma trembled as she spoke.

"I don't know, but she's okay." He wanted to believe April was safe. He needed Charisma to believe it too. He wrapped his arms more tightly around her.

Charisma wiggled out of his embrace, shook her head, then covered her mouth. "How can you be so calm right now? Our baby is missing and you—"

"I know, I know." Gideon gave in to the urge to stroke his wife's cheek, hold her closer. "We've been through a lot. Together. We've learned a lot. It's time to let those lessons help us keep our peace, keep our faith, and not panic."

Charisma looked to her mother who stood sober-faced behind Gideon. *Don't just teach those Sunday School lessons, live them,* she could hear her mother saying.

"God knew April would go missing, and it hasn't thrown Him for a loop." Gideon's eyes were watery although his voice was strong. "She's missing to us, but not to Him. None of His children ever go missing, even when they are lost to us. There's nothing we can do but trust Him, right now, right here. We've got to trust Him on this one."

Charisma inhaled, closing her eyes. *Don't just teach those Sunday School lessons. Live them.* The stories she was used to falling back on in times of panic—the stories, the fantasies she could control—they could not help her here. *Don't just teach those Sunday School lessons. Live them.* But this was hard, unbearable. Questions she could not phrase raged in her mind, but she had no other choice. She searched inside for a story that would bring peace for the moment. That's what she needed: peace for that exact minute. She'd deal with the next minute once she got through this one. *A story, a lesson. I need a story, a lesson.* It was a simple prayer that repeated over and over inside of her until the story, the lesson came: the miracle of Jesus healing the sick man by the pool of Bethesda.

She saw the man Jesus chose. She imagined him lying there, knees knobby, thin legs limp and twisted under him. Unshaven, unkempt, unclean. Sick, lying there, alone. He was there among many. And Jesus saw him. He saw him out of many, went up to him, made him whole.

What struck her at that minute was that there were many, and Jesus saw *him.*

April was out there among many. Charisma decided to trust that Jesus was seeing her daughter and knew her whereabouts. At that moment, at that decision to trust, she felt peace. With her next breath, the next moment, she trusted Him anew. More peace. She'd have to do this moment by moment, take it one second at a time.

It did not make sense. She did not understand the peace she felt, but another lesson, another verse learned confirmed what she thought she already knew, but now knew for sure: "The peace of God, which passeth all understanding, shall keep your hearts and minds through Christ Jesus."

"She's okay," Charisma whispered, slowly getting off of one knee. Gideon stepped back to give her room to stand, still holding on to her. "April's in good hands. Thanks for letting me be in yours, Gideon."

Gideon suddenly looked down at their entwined fingers, repulsed, as if seeing them for the first time. "For our daughter's sake, I'm here for you. For our daughter's sake alone." He drew back his fingers, his hand, turned his back, walked to the other side of the room.

"Gideon, you've got to believe me. Nothing happened—" Charisma started to follow him, but Caroline held her back, sitting her down between herself and Pepperdine.

"Not yet. He needs time, space." Her mother whispered softly. "He's just beginning, just like you."

Charisma watched her husband take his place by a window, his back to the rest of the room. He stood there silently for a moment before digging in his pants pocket. She watched as he unearthed both a small Bible and a large pill. He popped the pill in his mouth with no water, and then turned a metal folding chair toward the window. He sat down in it, away from all of them, ruffling the pages of his Bible.

After a few moments passed, he stopped ruffling the thin pages, and then slowly turned the chair halfway, slightly toward them. Instead of a full view of his back, Charisma now had a full view of his side. He glanced over at her, bit his lip, and then disappeared back into his Bible. She watched him, noticing the slight quiver in his sharply chiseled chin; noticing the way his fingers gently massaged the five o'clock shadow forming on his coffee brown skin; noticing the slight rise and fall of his broad shoulders that came with his every breath. Noticing, admiring. Wanting.

But for what seemed to be the first time, she knew for sure what she had to do, where she had to go. There, in the room with two other people, in a building bustling with officers, officials, and others she did not know, she closed herself off, withdrew—not into another fantasy or another daydream. She searched for a verse and remembered a sermon scripture.

"I will say of the Lord, He is my refuge and my fortress: my God; in Him will I trust." She thought on the words, considered the words, wrapped herself over and over in them until she felt the presence of God surrounding her, keeping her mind, her heart, her sanity, her hope. With each breath, with each second, she had to stay right there, with those sacred words—in God's secret place of safety and wholeness and not the dark secret places where she had been hiding and dwelling. Inhale. Exhale. She had to trust Jesus anew with each moment—not only for the safekeeping of her daughter, but also for the saving of her marriage.

CHAPTER 46

The investigative team was two doors down in another closed-door meeting. This time, the focus was not on a person, but on the one thing that had changed everything.

Glass.

Still packaged safely away in a small clear bag, the sliver sat center on the table. All eyes stared; all ears listened.

"We need more answers." The lead detective drummed his fingers. "Bring the cast and crew from down the hallway. I want both Charisma and Gideon with us to explain exactly what each of them was doing when it happened. Where's Madelyn Windemere?"

"On her way here now." Someone looked up from a folder.

"Good." The detective nodded. "Does she know about Maya?" When there was no answer, he looked back down at a sheet of paper in front of him—notes he scribbled during a phone call from Texas earlier in the day.

"Go get everyone. It's time to go back to the basement." Chairs screeched on the floor as everyone came to a stand.

They were almost finished emptying the room when a loud shriek pierced the hallway.

Madelyn Windemere had never had a public outburst like the one she'd just had in the hallway of the police precinct. She could not believe how loud she'd screamed, but there was no time to apologize, take it back, or explain. At the moment, not only did she want to scream again, but she also wanted to strangle the neck of the little rat-looking officer glaring in her face.

"Ma'am, you need to calm down." The officer continued to glare, no humor in his stance despite Madelyn's puffing cheeks, shaking shoulders, and twitching eyes. "Now if you can take a seat so we can finish talking about your—"

"Maya is not my daughter! I may have given birth to her, but she is not mine! Nothing like, like *that* could come from my lineage, my genes!" Madelyn bellowed again. The nerve of this man, asking her about Maya and whether there was a history of mental illness in her family. He had actually used those words—"Maya," "mental illness" and "the Windemere family"—in the same sentence. That is what had set her screaming. Enough was enough.

Madelyn sucked in a deep gulp of air, clutched her purse tighter to her body and brought her voice down to a sharp whisper, her face close to his. "You don't know who I am. I have nothing to do with that crazy girl. She does not belong to me. There is nothing else for us to discuss. Now if you don't mind, I am leaving, and I would appreciate it if you and your fellow coworkers would leave me alone." She turned to storm away, but the lead investigator, who had heard the commotion down the hallway, had come to intervene.

"Not so fast, Mrs. Windemere. We are not finished. It's obvious that you have taken no responsibility for your daughter, but that doesn't mean that you can't be held accountable for knowingly hiding information about her actions."

"I've already told you. Maya had nothing to do with that murder. Why are you even bringing her up? That crazy man next door already confessed to it. I don't see any reason for me to stay here. Good-bye." She turned to leave again but was held back by a firm arm.

"We're not talking about the murder, although I find it interesting that you've mentioned it. Mrs. Windemere, your daughter was found early this morning about to take a leap off of a Dallas highway overpass wearing $70,000 golden mechanical wings. A bystander tackled her to the ground just before she jumped. Now, can you tell us how she ended up with that much money and what she was doing in Texas?"

Madelyn opened her mouth to say something but was rendered speechless. The detective continued.

"Before you say you know nothing about her whereabouts, let me advise you that we have camera footage from a street corner near Penn Station of Maya getting out of your car with a duffel bag late Monday night. Thank the mayor's new camera program. Now, again, can you tell us how she ended up with that much money and what she was doing in Texas?"

With her mouth agape, Madelyn looked from one officer to another, her shoulders slowly drooping, the grasp on her purse weakening. "Wings?" she finally whispered, blinking hard. Her eyes darted around the room but then her lips tightened again. "I have nothing to do with her. As far as I'm concerned she should have just gone on ahead and jumped. It would have made my life a whole lot easier."

"What kind of mother are you?" The detective did not hide his disgust.

Madelyn narrowed her eyes. "I'm a good mother. Just ask my boys." A tear slid down her cheek. She quickly wiped it away. "I do not want to be put in some category because of . . . of her. I've worked too hard being a good wife, a good mother, and a good person to have 'crazy' associated with my name."

"Having a child with a mental illness does not make you a bad mother. How you *address* your child's illness is much more revealing of your character. You keep talking about your sons. Where are they? Why aren't they here with you now?"

Madelyn froze, blinking hard, stunned silent.

The detective eyed her for many seconds before speaking again. "The only thing crazy here is that you let your daughter get this far gone without getting her any help. She can't help but be who she is. You as the sane one—you as the parent—could have gotten her treatment before it came down to this. Things did not have to get this bad."

Madelyn quivered with anger. "You don't understand. You don't know what my life has been because of her. You're talking about what she needed, but what about me?" Her voice broke into choking sobs. "Maya is not what I had in mind when I gave birth to a perfectly formed baby girl with ten little fingers and ten little toes. She is not what I had in mind when I nursed her at my breast and placed her on waiting lists for the best nursery schools before she even turned one.

"She is not the daughter I thought I had. She is not the daughter I wanted. You don't know what my life has been like because of her, so don't stand there and tell me things did not have to get this bad. They have been this bad ever since the first time Harold—" Madelyn threw a hand over her mouth. "Oh my God!" She gasped, reaching behind her for a chair, settling instead to lean against a wall.

"Where are you going?" Madelyn wanted to scream at her husband. It was one o'clock in the morning, and

she listened in silence as he gently got out of their bed. She could hear him fumbling for his slippers in the dark. He left so many times in the middle of the night, and each time she pretended to be asleep. He would leave the house and return one or two hours later smelling like perfume, different perfumes, usually of the cheap variety. He would then get back in their bed, frequently patting her bottom—which she despised—as he pulled up the comforter, and be snored within seconds of his head hitting the pillow.

But that night, three weeks after Maya's thirteenth birthday, Madelyn did not hear him grab his car keys after getting out of their bed. She did not hear his heavy footsteps struggle to tiptoe down the steps. She did not hear the front door creak open or his car engine roar to life. What she did hear were his muffled steps pressing gently on the upstairs carpet.

Stopping at the bathroom.

Stopping at Maya's room.

Stopping back at the bathroom.

Coming back to his and Madelyn's bed.

This pattern repeated the next night, and then the next night. Weeks. Months. Years. Her sons were grown then, either away at college or having moved on to the next part of their lives.

The first time Maya came to Madelyn about her father's nighttime visits, Madelyn slapped her. Right across the mouth. Hard. The girl needed to be slapped. Profane, vulgar, the things Maya said. Harold was a good man, a righteous man. Sure, he had had his prior indiscretions with loose women, but he was a man, right? And men are weak and powerless against the vultures who want to pick on them, right? There are vultures in the world who wear cheap dresses and cheap perfume, who want to pick, pick, pick on mar-

ried men with deep pockets and handsome smiles. Her poor Harold. He struggled to fight against those vile women creatures, but those sins were of an entirely different nature from the transgressions Maya asserted. As weak and vulnerable as her Harold had been to the vultures, Madelyn was one hundred percent certain that he was not capable of committing such gross acts with his own daughter. Harold was too good of a man, Madelyn assured herself.

*And Madelyn was a good Christian woman, she told herself daily. The Good Book says it is a shame to even speak of those things which are done of them in secret; so she never spoke about it, any of it: the vultures outside of their home or Maya's horrible lies. Madelyn was a good Christian woman who quietly forgave. And why shouldn't she? Harold stopped leaving their house at night the year Maya turned thirteen. Never again did she hear him grab his car keys and drive off to secret rendezvous in the midnight hour to be devoured by vultures. He only went down the hall. And if—*if*—he was going into Maya's room, Madelyn told herself every night, it was only so that he could tuck Maya in, making sure she was sleeping comfortably. That is what good fathers do, right?*

Harold was a good father, a good husband, a good man. Madelyn was a good mother and a virtuous wife. Maya was just a dirty girl with a dirty mind who grew up to be plumb crazy. But then again, Maya's craziness was obvious even before Harold began tucking her in at night when she was thirteen. Perhaps her Harold had just been trying to calm Maya's wild and turbulent nature during his nightly visits to her room. He was tucking her in, maybe adjusting her pillows, rubbing her forehead goodnight, smiling down at his little girl. But her poor misguided husband did not re-

alize that his tender efforts would only make Maya's craziness worse, spoiling the girl with his fatherly love like that! Poor Harold. Sick Maya! Her lies, her lies, her lies! Dirty, sick, crazy Maya!

"Mrs. Windemere?" The detective was shaking Madelyn's arm.

Had he been calling her long? Madelyn wondered as she shook off both her thoughts and his grasp. "I have nothing else to say to you," she hissed at the uniformed man.

The detective shook his head and sighed. "Look, your daughter was put on a plane shortly after she was found. She should be here in a few moments. We're going to wait for her so we can go back to the basement at 319 Marigold Street and resolve everything once and for all. You need help, Mrs. Windermere. Not just for Maya, but for you too."

Madelyn cleared her throat, straightened her coat, stood tall. "Hmphff." She turned up her nose, looked away from them all.

"In the meantime," the detective continued as he shook his head, "you can wait with the others in the room down the hall." He pointed to a closed door and then took her arm and escorted her to it. When he opened the door and Madelyn saw Charisma and Gideon, she turned back to the detective to protest, but someone else caught her eye. When the door was shut behind her and she was alone in the room with the Joels and two other women, she narrowed her eyes and tightened her coat belt.

"Queen Jackson." Madelyn gave Caroline a once over before pulling out the address Judy had written down earlier that day. She looked down at the numbers, remembered the block, the hair shop, the woman with the long black hair who used to run it and who was standing before her at that moment.

Queen Jackson, as Caroline Jackson had been called, was the beautician to go to back in the day. Her hairstyles were legendary, her personal attention and care superb. Madelyn had ventured a couple of times to Queen Jackson's Hair Parlor on the west side of town a decade or two ago. Madelyn liked the way Jackson did her hair back then, but did not particularly like the mix of clients Caroline Jackson allowed in her shop. It did not seem proper to Madelyn to have a professional working woman under the dryer on one side of her and a street "working" woman on the other. The shop had closed long ago, though Madelyn never knew why. All she knew was that the regal-looking brown-skinned beauty was the original owner of the property that sat at the address given to Madelyn by the mortgage company. The mortgage company had assured Mrs. Windemere that the person tied to that address was the person who also owned property with Madelyn's dear deceased Harold.

"Tell me," Madelyn pressed her lips together and crossed her arms, "tell me why the house next door to me, 319 Marigold Street, has both my husband's and your name on it." Madelyn glared over at Charisma who looked just as shocked as Caroline.

CHAPTER 47

Charisma looked at her mother, trying to make sense of Madelyn's question. When her mother made no attempt at movement or speech, Charisma jumped to her aid, her fingers clutched tightly around a photograph of April.

"What are you talking about, Madelyn?" Charisma demanded. "You know that *Gideon and I* live in the house next door to you, and we've never even met your husband. Forgive me, but hasn't he been deceased for what, over ten years?" Charisma glared at Madelyn then threw a questioning glance at her mother. Caroline still stood frozen, quiet.

"And just who are you paying your mortgage to? I found out today that the house is completely paid for." Madelyn's lower lip quivered with rage.

"We're not paying a mortgage. We are renting the house." It seemed that Charisma and Madelyn were the only two in the room. Pepperdine sat wide-eyed and frowning from her seat on a bench by a back wall. Gideon never turned from the window.

"And who are you paying rent to?" Madelyn raised an eyebrow.

"A college fund." Caroline finally whispered. "For April."

All eyes turned to her, but she only looked back at Charisma, her eyes pleading for forgiveness. "I referred you to the house, remember? When you and Gideon sold your home in Columbia last year, I told you to check into 319 Marigold Street. I mentioned it to you, gave you a phone number. You did the rest."

"Momma, you said you found the house in a classified ad. You gave me a number to a landlord who I called and made arrangements with." This time anger tinged Charisma's voice. Madelyn looked shell-shocked. "I spoke to the landlord and he—"

"You spoke to your dead father's lawyer." Caroline's voice was flat.

There was a quick gasp and then the room deadened with silence.

"It was a college fund you were paying into, for April." Caroline inhaled, looked out the same window as Gideon. "The house was a gift to me from him, many years ago, but I wanted nothing to do with it—with him. His attorney had been renting out the house for me for years, taking over when I wasn't able to, and putting the money aside for April. But when you told me that you and Gideon had to leave your house out in Columbia, getting him to rent the house to you seemed like the best option. He left it to you." She turned away from the window, looking Madelyn square in the eyes. "I never knew the house was right next door to Harold and his family. Mrs. Windemere, I remember you coming to my salon a couple of times. I'm sorry. I was a different woman back then. Now I am—"

"*You*—you shut up!" Madelyn's entire body trembled. "Lies! You are telling terrible, terrible lies! Don't talk to me like you know me! Don't talk like you know who I am or who my husband was! You are a liar! These things you are saying make no sense. There is no reason Harold would buy you a house and want you or your bastard child to live next door. Even if Charisma is his child, considering the circumstances—which you are so cruelly lying about—it would make no sense for Harold to want his illegitimate child to live so close. He did not need another daughter near him. He already had one inside his home."

As if on cue, the door to the room opened, ushering in a team of detectives and officers. And then came in a young woman with her hair chopped short and uneven around her head.

"Maya." Madelyn's whisper was filled with contempt, her mouth contorting into a deeper frown.

Maya did not seem to notice her mother standing there, or anyone else in the room for that matter. She was mumbling broken words to herself, her head shaking back and forth slowly to a rhythm and beat she alone knew. She rocked, she shook, focused on nobody in particular. Her eyes were vacant, as if the world did not exist around her, or rather, she did not exist in the world. And then her eyes glued onto Charisma, who stood gaping and shocked, her own hands picking at her own shortened hair, bleached blond, but not able to disguise the truth.

Charisma recognized this woman, not for being the other person in the basement the day Miles was killed, not for being the strange female whose screams and feathers had added to the surrealism of that afternoon. Rather, Charisma recognized the rounded nose; the full, pursed lips; the slightly slanted eyes. They were Maya's and they were her own: the same profile of the man who had been in the coffin years ago in the funeral home on North Avenue. With both of their hairs cut short, the similarities in their facial features were undeniable. This woman—this stranger who had suddenly stopped her mumbling and was staring at Charisma with the same intensity she was giving her—this woman, Maya, was her sister.

The room was quiet as it seemed everyone present was seeing the truth for the first time, all eyes switching back and forth between Charisma and Maya.

"He said I looked like Charisma. Miles said it." Maya suddenly blurted and then began to laugh. She laughed so hysterically, one of the officers had to hold her up to keep her from doubling over. With each shriek and snicker, Madelyn appeared more disgusted. Her hands trembled, her jaw shook.

"I have nothing to do with this." Madelyn turned to leave. Pepperdine rose for the first time, grabbed Madelyn's hands and attempted to embrace her. Madelyn shut her eyes, initially pulled away, but then conceded both her hands to Pepperdine's—but only for a second. As Maya's cackles turned to sobs, Madelyn broke free, heading toward the door.

"I have nothing to do with this," she said again. Several of the officers and Pepperdine rushed to catch her, but the lead detective waved a hand.

"Let her go." He shook his head. "There's nothing else for her to add."

The officer who was holding up Maya looked uncomfortable with his assignment, his eyes darting around the room for help. He slowly eased his grip from around Maya's arms and she began to fall. Charisma rushed to her side and took over the officer's duty.

"I've got you. I can help you now." Tears filled Charisma's eyes as she glanced over at her own mother who was nodding.

"I'm sorry," Caroline mouthed, a tear gracing her own cheek. She looked like she wanted to say something more, but Charisma shook her head, pointing a finger first up to heaven, then resting it over her heart. . . . *Christ in me, the hope of glory*, she thought silently to herself. *He has been preparing me for this moment. All along He has been preparing me to forgive, to love, to be strong, to begin.*

She shut her eyes as Maya's cries began to lessen, slowing down to an occasional sniffle as she leaned heavily against Charisma's arm. Charisma felt the full weight of the young woman's burden on her own shoulders, but she refused to let herself feel alone. She'd been through too much to even think she was alone. She was surrounded. She opened her eyes to see her mother, Pepperdine. She opened her eyes to see Gideon move for the first time away from the window. He walked up to her, stood beside her. He did not look at Charisma even though he spoke to her.

"I know where she can get some help." His tone was all business as he studied Maya with the eye of an expert. Charisma searched his face for a sign, hope for the two of them, but there was no emotion in his timbre, no attachment in his stance. There was only his voice next to her, and it still held questions. There was only his voice next to her, but for the moment, it was enough. Charisma felt a smile forming on her cheeks, cut short only by the photograph she still clutched in her hands.

April.

"Don't worry. We are going to find your daughter." The detective seemed to be reading Charisma's mind. "An entire team is working on that right now. But as for all of us, we need to take a drive down to Marigold Street. I think all the answers we need are in that basement."

As everyone filed out of the room, Charisma saw Herman Steinbridge and Paige Dillery flying down the corridor toward them.

"What is going on?" Paige was livid, her cheeks as red as her hair. "You have no right—"

"It's okay." The detective held up a hand. "You can come with us too."

CHAPTER 48

The police cruisers formed a long chain of cars leaving the precinct. Despite keeping them all in the same room moments before, Charisma, Gideon, and Maya were each put in separate vehicles for the journey back to Marigold Street.

Charisma felt like it was the longest drive of her life, and yet not long enough. No part of her wanted to go back to that place of darkness, the basement. But she knew from the events and revelations of the past few days, she was indeed strong enough to go back.

She was equipped to face both the past and the present, no matter what either held.

Nonetheless, she was still taken aback at the truth the basement held for all of them. When the motorcade pulled up to the house, dusk was already flirting with the daylight. A single streetlamp shone overhead, and Charisma could see numerous eyes and faces watching them from behind curtains, window shades, and doors. Madelyn Windemere's face was not among them.

They filed into the house in silence, the officers and detectives, Charisma and those she loved. Herman Steinbridge and Paige Dillery were close behind.

"You do not have to say anything. Don't say a word," Paige shouted at Gideon. She was inflamed, ranting about how the investigation was being handled illegally and the state's case against her client was beyond repair. Charisma knew things were not proceeding the way Paige had planned, possibly causing a ruffle in her near-perfect legal resume. Charisma also sensed that the lead detective would not be allowing things to proceed the way they were if he didn't know what was going on. She held her breath, waited. They were all directed to the basement where an officer walked ahead of them with a flashlight.

"Miles, Miles." Maya began trembling and mumbling again.

"She can stay up here for the time being." The detective motioned for someone to watch her. The rest of them proceeded cautiously down the wooden steps, the flashlight leading and lighting the way.

When they had almost reached the bottom, and the entire cavernous room was exposed by the single flashlight, Charisma's heart paused. Her foot froze in mid-air.

The detective only nodded. "That's exactly what I expected to find down here," he mumbled to nobody in particular.

More flashlights were turned on and the revelation could not be more vivid.

April.

She sat cowered in a corner, her knees up to her chin. One hand shielded her eyes, the other clutched a large shard of blue glass. Dried blood caked on one end.

Charisma's heart jumped back to life times ten. Could it be? She shut her eyes, feeling faint, nauseous, wondering what she missed, how she missed; remembering only that April had been standing on the steps when the light came on that day in the basement and had been quickly ushered away before any questions or observations could arise.

"How did you know?" Pepperdine was the first to speak.

"Your phone records, Ms. Waters. Our investigators discovered that those late-night calls you were getting came from the waiting area at the hospital where Charisma let her daughter sleep sometimes. That was you, right April?" The detective offered a sympathetic smile.

April looked down. "Sister Pepperdine was the only person at church who seemed like she cared. I thought she could help us, but I didn't know what to say to her, so I didn't say anything," she mumbled

"Where'd you get the glass, honey?" The detective stepped slowly to the young girl, held out his hand.

April struggled to raise her head, a single large tear dripping from one eye. She looked from parent to parent and then held out the glass with a limp hand. "That lady with the feathers on her head grabbed it from Dr. Miles's front seat, but then she dropped it in the living room when everybody was fighting. I only wanted to show Mommy and Daddy. I remembered *Enserrer*. Mommy used to talk about it a long time ago, and I thought Mommy and Daddy would be happy again if they just saw it, even a piece of it. I just wanted them to be happy."

"What happened?" The detective's voice was a soft whisper as he took the single shard and carefully placed it in a clear plastic bag. Charisma's hands were on her mouth, her husband's hand tight on her shoulder.

April's voice was even softer as her eyes dropped to the ground. "I don't know. It was dark. I only wanted everyone to see what I had found, so I went down the basement after everybody, but I could not see where I was going, or even what was going on. I just held the glass and I did not let go. I never let it go. I'm sorry. I could not see anyone. And nobody could see me. I just wanted it all to stop, to end. I just wanted a happy ending, but nobody could see me."

"An accident." Paige Dillery blurted as nods and exhales joined along in unison. "A tragic accident. The knife had nothing to do with it." The police officers and detectives suddenly bustled back to business, and the basement filled with voices, notepads, gloves, legs walking, fingers pointing, heads shaking. Business. Everyone found something to do except for Charisma, who was still standing on the same step as she was when her heart froze just seconds earlier.

Her baby. Charisma trembled. Her April showers that bring May flowers, as she used to call her daughter when she held her close and rocked her back during the blue sky days, the days before Gideon went into the fog. Took them *all* into the fog, Charisma realized with pain. She swallowed hard, feeling herself fall limp against the wall. She could feel the air leaving her lungs, breath leaving her body.

With slow steps, small steps, she walked toward April, who still sat alone in the corner, alone and still as everyone moved about her, around her, over her. Charisma found her breath again, found her baby, knelt down beside her, wrapped her arms around her, rocked her.

"I see you," she whispered into her daughter's ear. "I see you, and I promise to never not see you again." And Charisma knew it was a promise she would keep—had to keep—no matter how thick the fog. The truth held in that dark basement was the last wake-up call she needed to face head-on whatever shade of blue waited in the future. She was strong enough now, or rather, Christ was strong in her. She knew the place she needed to go to get strength for a lifetime.

Charisma closed her eyes once more in the basement, seeing only darkness, but feeling only the warmth of her daughter's small arms tight around her, the hands of her mother on both of them, the embrace of her husband surrounding them all. She opened her eyes to push away the darkness. Light was all around her, and she felt love.

CHAPTER 49

Funny how time can change everything once you are aware that Jesus is holding the clock. He holds everything: time, lives, and seasons are in His hands.

Just over a year after Miles's death, Gideon and I have already been to over ten conferences together. The husband and wife who thought there was nothing left to salvage of their lives, their marriage, have built up a sought-after ministry addressing mental health. We are a team, a dynamic duo, speaking together all over the country, all over the world. And like a curse, a generational curse that has been broken, all that has been taken or destroyed in our hands and lives has been returned tenfold. The end truly did become the beginning.

The international media exposure that once had been a shameful embarrassment has actually catapulted our cause. Together we speak, giving practical information, encouragement, prayers; sharing scriptures at workshops, seminars, symposiums, and retreats. The annual women's retreat at Greater Grace Worship Center has become my personal favorite, where I can retell my testimony, my story, to my sisters as Pepperdine prayerfully and joyfully looks on. Gideon instituted a men's retreat through the church, where his testimony and the Bible verses he'd turned to for life have also become part of the tradition. At some conferences, my mother joins us, if her work schedule permits. We continue, the three of us, to move forward, only looking back to remember when it helps another family get through.

And April—you should see how big and grown and beautiful and happy my girl is getting to be. She has a gentle laugh, like a spring rain shower that brings with it a rainbow.

Gideon continues taking his prescription medications. He's turned down several job offers at esteemed hospitals and universities, opting to open a private practice that complements his speaking schedule. I run his office and book our engagements.

Momma continues clinging to her Bible, studying scriptures on healing, forgiveness, wholeness, and abundant life. Eventually she began leading a Bible study group at the new group home she opened for adult women with severe mental illnesses, some of whom were survivors of sexual abuse. She uses my old Sunday school materials and notes to form lesson plans. Maya Windemere was the first resident. The inheritance fund from her father—my father—provides the means for her to receive the best care.

There is a "for sale" sign in front of the house at 321 Marigold Street, Madelyn Windemere's old home. It has been there for several months now and will probably continue to be, as the rose bushes, grass, and weeds grow unchecked and unattended. We have not seen or heard from Madelyn since the day she abandoned Maya last year at the police station.

But Maya's big sister is here for her. Always. I am strong enough.

Things have not turned out exactly the way we all had anticipated, but God made provisions. For the prayers that have been answered, we praise Him. For the prayers that have not been answered the way we had hoped, we've found that His grace brings a greater glory, like an old sermon on CD once said, and Christ shines through our shortcomings. I still play the CD Pepperdine gave me back during the thick of the storm. I smile every time I listen to it, thanking God for His love, His grace, His promises, and the people He's put in my life to help bring me to an expected end. It may not be a "Happily Ever After" in the way fairy tales mean, but it is an ending that is perfect for the story of my life. With Jesus, an ending always means a beginning to something better. What greater happiness is that?

Charisma recapped her pen and closed the flowery pink notebook in her lap. It was a fairly new notebook, the eleventh one in her collection, the first one that wasn't all-black.

"Writing in your journal again?" Gideon chuckled from the seat beside her. "Someone would think you were writing a story instead of recording your thoughts."

Charisma only smiled as both of them swayed along with the curvy road. The limo they were in played soft gospel music, a calming presence as they neared their next destination. They were coming from the airport, having just left another conference, this one in Los Angeles. Their next stop was one Charisma had been anticipating for months. But even as they turned into the massive metal gates, she swallowed hard over a lump forming in her throat, remembering in vivid detail the day all of them—Gideon, Pepperdine, Caroline, Charisma, Maya, the investigators, and detectives—returned for the final time to the basement at 319 Marigold Street. The memories, the stories were hard to forget.

"It's okay, Care." Gideon squeezed her knee. Charisma grabbed his hand, grateful for the way he frequently seemed to know her thoughts these days and said what she needed to hear. She was even more grateful that she had found a place inside her spirit where she could slip away at any time, anywhere, and commune with Christ who always knew what she needed to hear.

Charisma held her breath as the gates closed with a loud clink behind them and the limo started down the long, tree-shaded driveway. Gideon squeezed her hand again. They were in this together. She thought it had been hard to see her mother in a psych ward, but the trip they'd taken last year was ten times more difficult. She shook her head before slipping on her black sequined shoes. They were almost there.

"Do you think Sister Floretta Hines really knows what she is getting into, marrying Deacon Caddaway?" Charisma chuckled.

"Well, it's too late now," Gideon shook his head. "We already booked this resort for their ceremony. That $5,000 deposit was nonrefundable." Gideon shook his head in awe at the natural beauty of the exclusive Caribbean oceanside resort they had reserved for the occasion. "I'm just glad Deacon Caddaway gave in to having the ceremony here."

"You got that right." Charisma reflected on how the deacon had at first been insistent that the wedding take place inside a church, but when it came out that seventy-three-year-old Floretta Hines had been dreaming of a seaside wedding for over fifty years, he grudgingly agreed. Everybody at Greater Glory Worship Center was so relieved that Deacon Caddaway was finally getting married, the Joels did not mind helping with the effort.

"I just hope the catering staff is prepared," Charisma chuckled. "Pepperdine told me that all but one of Sister Floretta's suitcases was filled with baked chicken legs. Imagine that scene at the airport."

Charisma and Gideon shared another hearty laugh before Gideon commented. "You know how Floretta Hines is about running the church kitchen. You can't expect anything less for her wedding reception. She's been waiting a long time for this moment."

"That's true." Charisma chuckled and then looked to her left. "And Mother Hines is not the only person who's been looking forward to this day. Wake up, April." She stroked her daughter's face as the limo slowed to a stop in front of a large fountain. Crystal water cascaded into a shallow pool on a lawn so green it looked painted.

"We're here already?" The baby fat that used to line the young girl's face had disappeared over the past year. Charisma could not help but wonder where the time had gone, grateful that the tragic events of a year ago had been ruled an accident and no charges had been filed. Gideon and Charisma had funded a memorial wall in Miles's honor on the Howard G. Phillips Unit at Baltimore Metropolitan Hospital and used a part of April's college fund to start a scholarship foundation in his name to help with the education of minorities pursuing careers in mental health.

"Yes, we are here. Happy birthday, April. You're thirteen, officially a teenager. Now let's get through this wedding and then we can go celebrate.

"That's right, happy birthday, young lady. The party is on." Gideon winked at his daughter who smiled back at him and then threw her arms around her father's neck.

It was a long ceremony and an even longer reception, drawn out by several lengthy speeches by Deacon

Caddaway, praising "de Lawd" for the wedding party, the resort staff, the cloudless sky, his new tux, the clean dishes, the baked chicken; and reminding those present not to turn the event into a "heathenish affair" by laughing too loud or smiling too much. "This is a solemn occasion, hallelujah. Amen!" He grumbled on end.

"Ain't he learned nothing yet?" Pepperdine shook her head as Charisma giggled in the linen-covered seat beside her. "I don't know what Bible he's reading, but mine says that in His presence is fullness of joy and at His right hand are pleasures forevermore. God's got a lot of laughing and smiling in His secret place. Ain't that right, Charisma? Charisma?"

Charisma was looking on at the early hints of sunset. A day about to end, another one soon to begin. The reception was over and April was beginning her own party. Charisma watched her daughter fling off her orange flowered flip-flops and run down a stone path that dotted the brightest green grass Charisma had ever seen. In the distance, at the end of the path, was a private beach with white sand and perfect palm trees. Aqua-blue water flowed seamlessly into turquoise skies broken only by a few scattered masses of dark-green seaweed and an occasional free-flowing white cloud.

"Go on, celebrate." Pepperdine nodded. Gideon took Charisma's hand and together they followed after April.

Charisma studied the man next to her, remembering a fantasy she'd had only a year ago, of being alone with the man of her dreams on an island away from everything and everyone else.

So the fantasy did not come to pass exactly as she imagined, and there were still many days when Gideon's old moods, though tempered by a combination of medicine, counseling, and Bible study, glimmered just under his eyes or whispered piercingly through his words. But she was living with a greater glory, a strength, a perfection, the likes of which can be bred only by fire, by storm, and that shines with enough brightness that she could be a light, a single flame of power, love, and soundness, even if everything else was darkness. In the midst of it all, she'd found her Strength.

Like she had told countless conference attendees and retreat participants, she was not just giving them facts and statistics she had read about; she was telling them what she knew. As she and Gideon walked to the water's edge, she meditated on her own words from the speech she'd given at their last conference in L.A.:

"We must take our past, our personal demons, our problems, and march right over them in the name of Jesus. Don't hide, don't be embarrassed or ashamed or stay in ignorance about something you don't understand or even want to understand, even something as hushed and hidden as mental illness. Come out of darkness, cast on the light, and claim your victory—victory for your loved ones, victory for yourself. Those stories we learned about in Sunday school as children, those Old and New Testament miracles, are not just stories or tales to make us feel good. They are accounts that prove we can overcome in the name of the Lord.

"But you're saying, Sister Joel, you don't know how bad it is. You don't know what I am going through. You don't know my family history. You have not seen my family tree. You don't know my roots or how bitter the fruit is. You might be saying all that, and you know what? You're absolutely right. I am not in your shoes. I only know my own. But there is Someone who knows exactly what shoe size you wear, what brand name you own, what holes may be in your soles.

"See, in His miracles, Jesus always spoke to the emotion or the need or the fear or the reality of the situation. He empathized, recognized, and never downplayed or belittled what was going on in the mind and thoughts of the person or people needing His services. He would identify the need, and then He would tell the person to get up, do something.

"That something was faith, and then the healing happened. A faith that leads to action is the key to your deliverance. Those servants at the wedding party had to fill the pitchers with water before it was turned to wine. The sick man had to take up his bed before he could start walking. Jesus does the miracle, but we need the faith for it to happen. We need to follow the directions He gives us, even if it's something as simple as using the resources He's already put in our lives—a pitcher, a rod, a bed. A doctor, medication, a counselor, a friend.

"Our God is a real God who still does miracles. Not always in the way we expect, so we have to keep our eyes open and our ears tuned in. And if the healing doesn't come the way you want it to, when you want it to, how you want it to, remember there's a greater glory that comes with Him being our strength right at the point of our infirmities and weaknesses. Follow Him, and you will always find a reason to praise Him."

Charisma smiled as she and Gideon stopped where the sand gave way to small ripples of water. The wet ground was soft, warm, molded to their bare feet. They stood side by side with quiet smiles, until a look on April's face brought concern. She was lying face up on the sand near them, her arms under her head, her eyes glued to the sky, a slight frown tugging at her lips.

"What is it, April?" Charisma was learning not to panic at every sad look. Even still, she rushed to her daughter's side.

"That blue thing, *Enserrer*, broke into pieces. It can never be glued back together." April lifted her head up, looked like she had more to say, but stopped short of saying it. Charisma and Gideon gave each other a quick glance.

"I love you." Charisma sat down beside her. Gideon sat on the other side. "And I will always love you. You too, Gideon." Charisma fingered his earlobe. "I don't need a statue to tell me what you are to me. In fact, I will be that, I am that to you, because it takes two to hug, two to embrace. At least two." Charisma held her daughter close and reached out for Gideon. "We were broken for awhile just like that statue, weren't we? But unlike *Enserrer*, we can be—and have been—glued back together by a lot of love, a lot of time, a lot of help, and a lot of Jesus. He has wrapped Himself around us. He's the ultimate embrace. And I will always keep my arms wrapped around both of you."

Her words were a whisper, gentle enough to float a smile back onto April's face, gentle enough to send Gideon looking off to a distant place beyond the setting sun, gentle enough to be carried away with the breeze and the waves, and find freedom in unending blue.

Like Gideon in the Bible – a man from a lowly background who wrestled with fear, doubt, and feelings of inadequacy but still believed God enough to lead a supernatural victory using only weapons of light and noise – this book is offered with the same intention: To bring light and noise to an issue that has sat in darkness and silence for too long.

For the millions out there who are suffering under a cloud of taboo, and the family and friends who are equally enveloped; for everyone who is trapped in a fog of any nature, this book is for you. For the weapons of our warfare are not carnal, but mighty through God to the pulling down of strong holds; Casting down imaginations, and every high thing that exalteth itself against the knowledge of God, and bringing into captivity every thought to the obedience of Christ (2 Corinthians 10: 4–5 KJV).

Readers Group Guide Questions

1. Charisma contemplates going to a night club rather than confront the challenges that await at home. Have there been times when it was difficult for you to return home? Where did you seek refuge? Was the place you visited helpful or harmful?

2. Many families have stories or memories passed down from generation to generation. What stories were handed down to you? What defining moments in your life would you share with your children? Are these stories meant to be shared outside of the family? Why or why not?

3. Madelyn feels strongly that worship should be a private and quiet affair. Clearly she does not approve of the worship service Charisma attends. Where do you worship? At church, at home, some other place? Are you open to different styles of worship services? Do you feel God is pleased with one style over another?

4. Charisma kept the invitation from her husband for what she considered a good reason. Is there ever a time when a spouse should keep a secret from his or her significant other? Explain.

5. Pepperdine hears an inspiring message about prayers of desperation. Reflect on the scriptures from that sermon: 2 Corinthians 12:7-10 and 1 Samuel 1:1-20. Have you ever had a desperate petition to present before God? How did He answer? What did you learn from that experience? How did that experience affect your relationship with Him?

6. Gideon describes his severe depression as a dark fog. Have there ever been times in your life that you felt like you were maneuvering through a fog? Describe. What was the nature of the issue with which you wrestled? How did you address it? Did you seek help? Why or why not?

7. Both Charisma and Madelyn struggle with the stigma surrounding mental illness when addressing the problems of their respective family members. Are their observations and feelings justified? Why do stigmas exist? What roles and/or responsibilities do family members have when a loved one is mentally ill? How does mental illness affect the entire family and household?

8. Deacon Earnest Caddaway is of the mindset that healing depression is an "easy deliverance" that comes through repenting and having more faith. Why does he feel this way? Do you agree with his perspective? Why or why not? What role, if any, do you believe the church has in addressing mental illness? Is taking medication a sign of weakened faith? Explain.

9. What is Madelyn's response to her late husband's infidelity and Maya's claims? What are her un-

derlying beliefs on these matters? Why does Madelyn react in the way that she does? What, if anything, can be done to address her feelings?

10. Miles Logan is a respected medical doctor who earns a high title and many accolades. He is also a relentless womanizer. Is his life a success? Why or why not? How do you define success? What attributes, achievements, and actions of a person are most important in defining who he or she is? Elaborate.

11. Charisma continually escapes to daydreaming in her effort to avoid dealing with the illness of her husband. What role do her fantasies play? What need(s) do they fulfill? Are her thoughts a safe place? Can you relate to her efforts of escape? How do thought patterns and musings affect our situations, if at all? Consider 2 Corinthians 10:4-5; Matthew 15:18-19, Philippians 4:8, and Isaiah 26:3 in your reflections.

Author Bio

Leslie J. Sherrod resides in Baltimore, Maryland, with her husband and three children. She is a social worker and the author of *Like Sheep Gone Astray*. She is also a contributor to the *A Cup of Comfort* devotional series and the writer for Paintbrush Poetry Original Art & Gifts.

Notes

Notes

ORDER FORM
URBAN BOOKS, LLC
78 E. Industry Ct
Deer Park, NY 11729

Name: (please print): ______________________________

Address: ______________________________

City/State: ______________________________

Zip: ______________________________

QTY	TITLES	PRICE
	A Man's Worth	$14.95
	Abundant Rain	$14.95
	Battle Of Jericho	$14.95
	By The Grace Of God	$14.95
	Dance Into Destiny	$14.95
	Divorcing The Devil	$14.95
	Forsaken	$14.95
	Grace And Mercy	$14.95
	Guilty Of Love	$14.95
	His Woman, His Wife, His Widow	$14.95
	Illusions	$14.95
	The LoveChild	$14.95

Shipping and handling-add $3.50 for 1st book, then $1.75 for each additional book.
Please send a check payable to:

Urban Books, LLC

Please allow 4-6 weeks for delivery

ORDER FORM
URBAN BOOKS, LLC
78 E. Industry Ct
Deer Park, NY 11729

Name: (please print):____________________________________

Address: _______________________________________

City/State: _______________________________________

Zip: _______________________________________

QTY	TITLES	PRICE
	16 ½ On The Block	$14.95
	16 On The Block	$14.95
	Betrayal	$14.95
	Both Sides Of The Fence	$14.95
	Cheesecake And Teardrops	$14.95
	Denim Diaries	$14.95
	Happily Ever Now	$14.95
	Hell Has No Fury	$14.95
	If It Isn't love	$14.95
	Last Breath	$14.95
	Loving Dasia	$14.95
	Say It Ain't So	$14.95

Shipping and handling - add $3.50 for 1st book, then $1.75 for each additional book.
Please send a check payable to:

Urban Books, LLC

Please allow 4 - 6 weeks for delivery

ORDER FORM
URBAN BOOKS, LLC
78 E. Industry Ct
Deer Park, NY 11729

Name: (please print): ___________________________

Address: ___________________________

City/State: ___________________________

Zip: ___________________________

QTY	TITLES	PRICE
	The Cartel	$14.95
	The Cartel#2	$14.95
	The Dopeman's Wife	$14.95
	The Prada Plan	$14.95
	Gunz And Roses	$14.95
	Snow White	$14.95
	A Pimp's Life	$14.95
	Hush	$14.95
	Little Black Girl Lost 1	$14.95
	Little Black Girl Lost 2	$14.95
	Little Black Girl Lost 3	$14.95
	Little Black Girl Lost 4	$14.95

Shipping and handling - add $3.50 for 1st book, then $1.75 for each additional book.

Please send a check payable to:

Urban Books, LLC

Please allow 4 - 6 weeks for delivery

ORDER FORM
URBAN BOOKS, LLC
78 E. Industry Ct
Deer Park, NY 11729

Name: (please print): ____________________

Address: ____________________

City/State: ____________________

Zip: ____________________

QTY	TITLES	PRICE

Shipping and handling - add \$3.50 for 1st book, then \$1.75 for each additional book.
Please send a check payable to:
Urban Books, LLC
Please allow 4 - 6 weeks for delivery